WALKING

INTO

THE

RIVER

A Novel

LORIAN HEMINGWAY

Simon & Schuster
New York   London   Toronto
Sydney   Tokyo   Singapore

SIMON & SCHUSTER
SIMON & SCHUSTER BUILDING
ROCKEFELLER CENTER
1230 AVENUE OF THE AMERICAS
NEW YORK, NEW YORK 10020

DESIGNED BY PEI LOI KOAY
MANUFACTURED IN THE UNITED STATES OF AMERICA

1   3   5   7   9   10   8   6   4   2

LIBRARY OF CONGRESS CATALOGING IN PUBLICATION DATA

HEMINGWAY, LORIAN, DATE
WALKING INTO THE RIVER: A NOVEL / LORIAN HEMINGWAY.
P.   CM.
ISBN 0-671-74642-1
I. TITLE.
PS3558.E479127W3 1992
813'.54--DC20   92-20043
CIP

Permission to quote from Norman Maclean's *A River Runs Through It*, © 1976, was
graciously granted by the University of Chicago Press.

A C K N O W L E D G M E N T S

I thank Dr. James Plath, editor, writer, and good buddy, for gracefully lifting a line from this novel to provide the title, and for always being there, even though I no longer call at two in the morning.

My deepest thanks to Susan Crawford, an agent created in heaven, who believed in me beyond all human capacity, and whose friendship I cherish.

My gratitude to Christopher Keane for his invaluable criticisms of the book in its first and final stages, and for being a comrade in serenity, courage, and wisdom.

My appreciation to Michael Daviduke, poet, who let me steal two of his best lines, willingly and with good humor.

Special regards to Dave Kasiwagi for giving me a rent-free computer, and to Michael Whalton in Key West for sending me anything I needed on short notice, even work.

My appreciation to Mitch Hale, a fine writer, for being so pleased by the publication of this book.

For my Miami family, Hilary Hemingway Freundlich, Doris Hemingway, Jeff Freundlich, Hannah Hemingway Freundlich, Anne Hemingway Feuer, Bill, Sarah, and Rachel Feuer, and Dr. and Mrs. Howard Engle, my thanks for being such *great* relatives.

My thanks to Kathaleen Elliott for carrying on Freda's tradition with wisdom and grace, and for telling me such swell stories.

For my late aunt Freda, who would be either pleased or wildly agitated by the liberty I have taken with her name in this novel, my dearest, most magical memories.

Profound thanks to Jeff Ward-Fischer, my dear sweet husband, who has been unfailingly cheerful during the writing of this book, and for his help in the final stages.

Most of all, my deepest gratitude and respect for Marie Arana-

Ward, whose remarkably keen editorial eye has sharpened my work, yet kept it whole in heart, and whose belief in this book has blessed me.

And thank you to Bill W. and Carl Jung, wherever you are.

This book is dedicated to

Jeff Ward-Fischer for his love and support,

Julie Woo for saving my life,

Susan Crawford for believing in me,

and Cristen H. Jaynes for

twenty years of surprises

And in loving memory of Mr. Cheese,

my son, my heart, my life,

the one and only Dee Dee Fischer,

Les Hemingway, the greatest uncle ever,

and Freda, my inspiration

Eventually, all things merge into one,

and a river runs through it.

The river was cut by the world's great flood

and runs over rocks from the basement of time. . . .

I am haunted by waters.

—NORMAN MACLEAN
A RIVER RUNS THROUGH IT

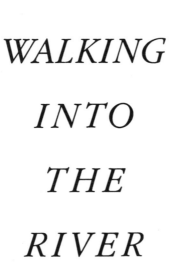

WALKING

INTO

THE

RIVER

O N E

In October things settled down. People burrowed in, thought about their families more, regretted the summer passions the way they regretted the twisters that drove spines of hay into the sides of barns as if the hay were made of steel. And they made amends to those they'd hurt. It was a month of reckoning with sins past.

The heavy greens of the southern summer were replaced by a bright, loose wash of color. Leaves from oak, poplar, and maple filled the yards on the rural outskirts of Yazoo City, Mississippi, moving in waves, hugging the earth. Each October *The Wizard of Oz* was replayed on television. Dorothy stood abandoned on a Kansas plain, kicking at the cellar door while the black spout of a twister moved closer, tearing light from the sky and sucking up everything in its path. I would watch in fascination, imagining what Dorothy felt, thinking this would be the time she wouldn't make it to the house, the one time the tornado would bear down on her and leave nothing behind but a pile of sticks. My palms would be damp from anticipation, and I would move to the big picture window, look out and feel safe. There were no tornadoes in October.

Summer was never safe. The humidity and heat brought out the recklessness and chaos, the old pain. My mother was most suicidal then, in summer, when bootleg liquor ran as freely as the rivers at flood stage. Even in the fifties you couldn't buy it legally in Mississippi.

Old boys made it in the woods in stills like kettledrums and sold it when the good black-market brands ran dry. It was hard to say who were the drinkers in Mississippi, those bad seeds among the crop of God-fearing men and women. It was all done under cover of darkness, when backs were turned and church lights dimmed.

We would go in the company car after dark, my mother, her husband, John Earl, and I, to an old shack outside Yazoo City where, from a lighted broken window, a hand would reach out with a couple of bottles wrapped in brown paper sacks, and my stepfather would reach back through the thick air and push some money through the window, always careful of the jagged edges, his hands never shaking as my mother's did.

"Yessir," I would hear the man inside the shack say. "That should do you for tonight."

And then he'd smile, as if he knew what the night would bring.

I could see the glossy pictures of naked women stuck with cracked cellophane tape to the unpainted tar paper inside the window, and occasionally the face of the bootlegger. It was a puckered, withered apple face made simple by years of inbreeding and moonshine. His teeth were black and his mouth brown as the tobacco juice he spit through the cracked window. In the dim, sulphurous halo of that light the big-breasted women with fat, red lips made me feel a little too clean. But the bootlegger's stare into the back seat of the car where I sat, my arms folded high on my chest, dressed me down and let me know that a few years away I might be tacked on that wall like a prize. I had seen pictures of these same women—they always looked the same—in the bottom of my stepfather's underwear drawer where he kept a silver flask of whiskey to get him ready for the morning. The sight of the things that helped him drink—a flask, ice cubes, tonic water, limes, cocktail napkins—gave me a floating feeling inside, as if I were high on a crest and about to drop. My mother kept her liquor in the freezer in a tall, frosted glass she would drain throughout the day and refill when she thought I wasn't looking. At night, when it was all gone, we would get in the car and take the dirt roads back into the heart of Yazoo County and search out the bootleg shack, each of us silent, each pretending I didn't mind at all.

I hated the Fourth of July, the one sign that told me summer had truly taken hold. I despised the make-believe patriotism fueled by whiskey, and turned red with shame at the sight of my mother and stepfather, drunk, at parties that included other children with drunken parents, but none so drunk as mine. It was worst of all that day, the drinking, and later the fighting, and later still, the moans. The funny talk. My mother screaming as if she wasn't hurt, but in some good kind of pain, crying out, "Oh OH OH, that's so good, baby, that's so good." I wondered what was so good she had to scream, and I couldn't stand to listen. I'd cover my head with a pillow or hum loud inside my head, then open the window wide to hear the cicadas buzz like high-voltage wires. It was instinct that told me she didn't need my help when she cried out like that.

I stood on my bed those nights, staring through the window at constellations that etched the dark, rural sky. I could name any star in the visible universe by the time I was twelve. Altair, Deneb, Vega, Antares. These were not human sounds but the throbbing dialect of a secret world. I would watch the form of the silver-leafed maple I had planted two summers before. In the soft, galactic light its leaves and branches moved and cast random patterns on the flat beige of the bedroom wall.

Mine was a room filled with treasures I had gathered on walks through the thick woods that ringed our neighborhood: an oak branch with acorns, dried wild onions, the entire shed skin of a king snake, a bluejay's egg, the clean red feather of a cardinal. I would watch the silhouette of the tree against my wall, smell the hot dampness of the summer night, the biting scent of wild onions, and wonder how I could disguise myself cleverly enough to run away. I had tried once, powdering my black hair dull white with talc, putting on a box-pleated wool skirt and a pair of my mother's heels stuffed with tissue. I believed I looked like an old lady, just ten years old at the time, with no wrinkles to show, but an expression on my face dead-serious. I'd wanted to take a train to be with my aunt Freda in Arkansas, but I had no money. A day would come when I would leave, much angrier than I had ever been during those Mississippi summers. And I would neglect to say good-bye.

Outside my bedroom door was the real world. My stepfather thrusting his hands knuckle-deep into my mother's hair, slamming her head against the door of the new dishwasher, my mother groping helplessly for something heavy enough to defend herself with. I'd tried to help once by running and tackling my stepfather's leg from behind, biting at it, but I ended up with a backhand slap that split the skin around my right eye. The next day the white was red as the cardinal's feather. After that I stayed in my bedroom and peed into a cup I kept in the closet, too impressed by my stepfather's rage to run across the hall to the bathroom.

Some nights my mother would take out the broken pieces of a revolver she had had in Africa and try to reassemble it with shaking hands. She never succeeded and would stagger through the house looking for a bottle of sleeping pills or a razor blade, shouting as she stumbled into the walls and across furniture, "I want to die, John Earl. You hear me. I want to die."

I would leave sometimes by the front door, going past the big picture window, out into the clouds of hot air that magnified the sound of the cicadas. Down the curved street lit by a single street-lamp, I would head for the ravine where frogs wallowed in muddy potholes and lay clusters of eggs that looked like black tapioca.

Those nights it was like breathing underwater, the water in the air hanging, pulsing, moving in great wet clots. I liked the wetness and walked slowly into it, breathing deeply, feeling the texture of it in my lungs, letting it soak my skin. The hard-packed red clay of the ravine bottom grew cool beneath my feet as I climbed down the bank.

There were nights when I could see by the bright disk of the moon, and when the moon was new I could feel the smooth, half-foot-deep potholes dug out by spring floods that sucked at the floor of the ravine as the water pushed with blind force toward another channel. The ravine was a tributary of the Pearl River, and in spring its tide carried whole trunks of trees uprooted by tornadoes, tangled fists of rusted bobwire, tires, and, once, the body of a young girl. I saw her thin blond hair matted with twigs and brown foam churning in the wake of the surge as she slid down the chute, far from where she'd started out, far from whatever safety she had known. Her eyes were wide open like two cat's-eye marbles, and the skin around her mouth was as blue and transparent as oiled paper. I used to think a lot about that girl, imagine where she'd lived, what she'd been like, why she'd ended up as a broken, dirty doll flying past my safe perch on the lip of the ravine. I told myself she had wanted to swim in the waist-high flood that spring, be carried, flying, by the current into some new, magical place she'd yet to see. Every kid wanted to ride the floods but few were allowed. She was the one who had dared to do it, ignoring her mother's warnings. She'd swum into a whirlpool and couldn't get out. A tree branch had clobbered her, or an old car part. She'd been knocked unconscious, then drowned. I dreamt about her for a while, and in my dreams she'd always come to life just as she bobbed past, raise her head up out of the mercury-colored water, and call to me, "It's okay, Eva. You can swim, too."

When I woke I would always wonder how she had known my name.

I thought of her a year or so after the dreams stopped. It was in Watson Chapel, Arkansas, at my aunt Leta's wrecking yard. The tow truck had brought in a mangled car, released it in a heap, and I'd stood with Leta asking questions about the accident. She told me a young girl had died in the crash, riding with her daddy out on the state highway. I peered in the smashed back window of the car and saw the seat torn loose and stained brown with old blood, the sharp edges of chrome embedded in the floorboard. Halfway beneath the seat lay a limp baby doll with blond hair, her print dress torn. My aunt saw the doll, too, retrieved it, and pushed it at me, saying, "I guess she needs someone to take care of her."

I remember looking at the glass eyes and thinking of the girl. After Leta went back to the office, I buried the doll in the wrecking yard, under a peach tree near the car. When Leta asked about the doll, I told her that it was too dirty—that I had thrown it away.

When rain filled the potholes of the ravine, frogs would lay their eggs in clusters along the sides. I would watch them by night with a flashlight. Their change had grace and definition; the eggs slimy black one day, a bit more transparent the next, and then what looked like a big eye would form. Next the sharp bud of a thin tail. In less than a week frogs were thick as eels in the potholes. I would slide my hand into their dark colony, feeling them move as smoothly as oiled ball bearings against my hand, crowding between my fingers, nestling in the cup of my palm.

I loved frogs and did not hold them in superstition. I never had a wart to show for having held one, or hundreds.

Frogs cry out like humans when they're hurt. I watched a playmate torture one once, with stones, the frog tied by its back legs to the handle of a tin bucket, a dangling target against the metal. Again and again the frog cried out with a sharp voice so tuned with fear and anguish that mothers threw open the doors of their houses and called to their children.

When the tadpoles became young frogs, sprouting legs and rounding out their narrow forms, I would catch them with the beam of a flashlight, blinding them so they stood still as green rocks, mesmerized. I'd hold them close against my chest and watch them blink. I remember the cool feel of their flesh against my own warm skin, how light and full of air they felt. Sometimes I would keep them in jars overnight, then set them free into the morning and the thick wet grass.

I had my escape routes, some more intricate than others, all well worn and familiar. I could follow the bed of the ravine to a catfish pond deep in the woods, or set out for the cotton fields that started up two miles out on the county line. But I could not stay home, day or night, summer or winter, watching my mother's eyes turn glassy, her hair fall into her face, her arms and legs go heavy. I fled into a world I understood, where touch and response were real.

I spent my anger on kids my age or older, always looking for a fight. When a kid would cry and plead at the hands of a bully, I'd come to the rescue, tearing at the boy's arms until his skin looked as if it had been slashed by a wild animal. I had a reputation then. Someone in the neighborhood called me murderous. I liked the way it sounded.

I had a thing about oppression although I did not yet understand the word. The weak needed a guardian angel, and that was what I set out to be when I was ten years old. An avenging angel. Murderous, if I chose to be. When my friend tortured and killed the frog, I planned his punishment. Every night for a week I followed him home, kicking rocks up as I went, stopping when he stopped, making hoot-owl sounds when he started up again, dying frog sounds the closer he got to home. In the dim light of the streetlamp I could see him turn quickly to look back over his shoulder, the sound of his sneakers growing thicker on the warm blacktop. When he was right outside the gate to his house, in the shadow of an oak tree, I called his name, low, deep, the way I could, and he scrambled over the fence yelling for his mama, catching his pant leg on the gate bolt and breaking his leg. I went to visit him the next week and signed his cast.

Some nights I would search for stones in the dark of the ravine. Often they were at the bottom of the potholes, or in the thick clumps of crabgrass that shot up after a rain. It was a trick to tell a stone's color at night, a game that had its own peculiar science. The black stones were colder than others and smelled cleaner. Red stones had the scent of iron, a deep metallic odor that made my mouth water. Gray stones smelled dry, like dust. Bent over the potholes, my summer nightshirt drinking up the water like a wick, I felt the weight of the stones in my palm and thought of David and Goliath, how one stone, placed right, could fell a giant.

I found a perfect oval of obsidian once, the size of a robin's egg. I used to hold it in the pocket of my jeans and rub it whenever my stepfather left town on a business trip. I imagined that by rubbing it constantly some evil would find him. He'd be killed before he made it home. There'd be a car crash on the interstate, or a knife in the throat out by the bootleg shack. Poison in his whiskey. I would do this in secret, with the stone safe in my pocket, a talisman to guard me. I wished him dead so often that I feared the evil would come back to me, like a bad stick thrown into the path of a tornado. It would be caught in the turning wind and drive free, straight through my heart.

The worst that ever happened on one of his trips was he got food poisoning from a bowl of truck-stop chili. I determined to rub the rock even harder the next time he left, wondering what incantation, what magic word, it would take to do him in.

T W O

Africa is my first memory, before Mississippi.

The trip was a gift from my father's father, a man I was told I had met once when I was very young; a man I would never meet again, except in the form of an obituary that my mother clipped from the newspaper and laid on the kitchen table sometime during my tenth year. He'd told my father to take us to Tanganyika to learn. He was the sort of man, I was told, who believed experience built character.

That year in Africa our family was my mother, my father, and a boozy nurse named Greta who had raised my father and wasn't getting any better with age. By the time she got to me she was an old woman, fat in a soft way. On her day off she would buy a bottle of gin and shave her toenails with a double-edged razor blade. Once, blind drunk, she split the soft pad of her big toe with the blade, and when it healed it looked like the cleaved meat of a purple Italian plum. Her fingers were fat and stumpy, her face the color of animal intestine with beige eyes punched into the flesh. I've never met anyone with beige eyes since Greta; she was the ugliest woman I'd ever seen. I didn't know it was the drinking that had done it to her.

We lived in a permanent camp, where canvas walls were reinforced with plywood, and each bed was shrouded by a mosquito net. We'd come from California where my mother had fled the South to go to school at Berkeley. It was there she met my father, while walking across campus with her sister, Freda, who had come to visit.

"He's cute," my mother had told Freda, pointing to an eighteen-year-old boy sitting on the grass.

From pictures I have seen of my father at that age, cute is all he was. His face is full of defeat, and there is nothing in his eyes I want to know. It is that way with pictures, not very often, but often enough. Something is captured on the developing paper, and as long as that image lives it is a testimonial to some trait the person tried desperately to hide all his life. It happens with murderers. "Something about his eyes" people will say, as they stare at the picture. With my father it was a heritage of fear, funneled up from generations past, something that spread in him like a virus.

Now, six years after my mother sighted him on the grass, we were heading onto the African plains in a jeep at dusk so my father could shoot birds. Dusk was more of a challenge, he said. It tested the vision. I rode in the back of the jeep, silent, knowing the birds would be tossed back with me. My father was a good shot, not quite as good as my mother, whose hands were steady then, but accurate on a moving target. I never got out of the jeep but waited for the birds to land in a soft heap beside me. I would watch their claws contract and their necks arc in a tired fight against suffocation. They looked like vultures with bald, scabrous heads and red eyes that, in the fading light, sometimes tricked me into thinking they were still alive even after they had stiffened up. Their claws would scratch on the bare metal of the jeep bed, and I would reach out carefully with one finger to stroke their feathers. I knew this was death and it impressed me. When they were dead I plucked their feathers and stuck them behind my ears, imagining I had wings for hair.

Back at the camp the natives waited, stirring a huge pot of boiling water kept alive with burning white branches shaved clean of bark. Into the pot the dressed birds would go, and soon there would be the smell of fat rising to the surface and catching on the wind, carried to the wild animals outside our camp. Lions would smell the game miles down the channel of wind, and when hungry enough they would prowl the edge of the camp.

At night we slept under nets of fine, meshed gauze the texture of cocoons. I would imagine I was buried deep inside a soft casing, unable to move except into another fold of darkness. At dawn we turned our boots upside down and pounded on the heels until the renegade scorpions or spiders fell to the hard-packed dirt of the floor. Scorpions made a nice crunch when I jumped up and down on them. I didn't weigh enough to crush them with the tip of my boot as my father did. I would watch him catch the stinger of the evil creature under his boot and hold it there until the body curled back on itself. The stinger would stay curled even after he'd lifted his foot, and it pulsed with an ugly yellow poison deadly enough to kill a grown man.

My mother and I bathed in the river with Greta while the natives stood guard in the brush along the bank, their dark bodies blending with the greens and browns of the land. I don't remember the name of the river but I do remember its deep brown color and the way it moved thickly, as if weighted down by sheer size. Above us, draped on the branches of the acacia trees, were long, fat snakes that bunched up as they slid from branch to branch, then stretched out thin as ribbons. I had no fear of snakes and liked the bright patterns on their backs, brilliant in the hot sun.

I would walk naked into the river, feeling the sun on my back and the water creeping up as warm as bathwater. I'd dip my head beneath its opaque surface, tasting earth and the bitterness of tannin leeched from the roots of trees along the bank. When I came up for a breath I'd turn to see the snakes lazy in the trees, my mother with her long, perfect dancer's body watching them cautiously, gesturing to the natives to keep their eyes up in case one dropped.

"Eva," she'd say. "Hurry up. I'm nervous here."

All my life I had collected snakes from the wild, even a baby coral snake that would sleep curled in my lap at night; bright lime-green grass snakes that would not keep still; and a fat, heavy king snake whose weight in my arms was reassuring. I slit the belly of a dead king snake once and found a boneless bird, half digested, the feathers still intact.

But I was allowed no snakes in Africa, placed under constant guard by Greta or one of the natives. My mother said it was abnormal to like snakes. I knew she did not want them coiled under her pillow, like the gift of poison ivy I brought her thinking it was just an interesting plant. I left it on her pillow wrapped in colored paper, disappointed that she was angry and that the ivy gave her hives.

So I made concessions to her fears, keeping giant African beetles in a cigar box. I didn't care for them, but they were what I was allowed as pets. They were huge and harmless and had no curiosity, just a blind urge to crawl and burrow, never stopping to regard me.

I shooed the dumb creatures in Greta's direction when she would not do as I pleased. She walked with a cane one of the natives had carved for her and moved just slowly enough to be terrified by the army of beetles at her feet. I didn't laugh when I set them loose on her, waiting instead to see the height of her reaction. I liked re-actions, particularly those I caused. Greta's was usually a pitiful look at me, an acquiescent nod at my cruelty, wondering, no doubt, what child from hell my father, whom she hated, had spawned. She had never been able to make my father behave when he was growing up, nor could she manage me. After I tortured her with the beetles, rounding them up and letting them loose five or six times in an afternoon, Greta would let me be for the rest of the day, or she'd cater to me, giving loving affirmations—how pretty I was, how smart. How unique. I liked that word. It reminded me of a little French girl, Monique, whom I'd seen in Paris on our way to Africa. Monique, with her round eyes and black hair, was unique. Pretty. And probably smart, although she never opened her mouth. I just liked to think of her that way. It was her mother who spoke her name while we rode on the train, over and over she said it, trying to put her child to sleep with the repetition of one sound. Monique. Monique. Monique. She spoke it as a chant, something sacred, in a French accent that sounded sweet for once. Unique. Unique. So Greta said, and even if she was saying it to be mean, I still remembered the word as good.

I had the natives carve a little cane for me so I could mimic Greta's walk, the way she rolled on the balls of her feet to keep the dirt out of the razor cuts on her toes. I didn't dislike Greta. I just saw a weakness in her that invited needling. I remember her standing with me in the lowland at the base of Mount Kilimanjaro, holding my hand, sweeping her fat arm up in an arc and saying, "You'll know someday what this means."

Greta was fond of telling me I'd know someday what things meant, as if my fuses weren't screwed in tight enough yet. But that mountain had a meaning for me even then, rising out of the dead heat of the

plains, its patchwork of blue snow absorbing light rather than reflecting it. It reminded me of death. Standing in the river I felt
alive. In the shadow of the mountain I knew fear. I imagined that
all the birds who didn't make it to the boiling pot were up there.
Still, in the Ozarks near where I live now I feel it—some ancient
genetic fear bound tightly in the chromosomes, speaking through
the centuries.

I never want to go to Alaska to see an iceberg mountain in a
black sea. I have seen pictures. It is enough. In Africa, Kilimanjaro
spoke to me of death to come. I stood defiantly, in silence, as Greta
made her grand gestures, knowing that later it would all come to
be bad.

I saw only one lion up close when we lived there. I was sitting
on a swing rigged by my father to the low branch of a tree fifty feet
from the door of the tent. It is what I remember my father doing
best—tying knots in the thick rope so securely I could never fall.
Each day I would swing at sunset if we weren't going in the jeep
for birds, facing north so the sun wouldn't blind me. At dusk the
air was yellow, so close to the color of the land itself it was as if I
swung high into an air made of flames. At first I could see only his
silhouette, the great cowl of a mane shaggy in the heat, the tip of
his tail switching wildly through the air. As I made out his full
shape I slowed the swing, thinking of what I had been told to do
if I ever saw a lion near camp. I watched him stand there, a mirage
of water gathering around him, then evaporating. My heart was
beating thin and fast, but I saw no threat in his posture. He moved
closer—a friendly walk, slow but not tense—and looked directly at
me. He ambled loosely as if he could come to nuzzle me, tug at my
shirttail, push me gently with paws that looked, even from a distance, to be the size of bowls.

I watched him steadily, holding my breath, as he returned my
gaze. For that one moment I knew him as he was, tired, hungry,
his fear of humans tempered by a need. His coat was mangy, his
eyes clogged half shut with some infection. He bled from a forepaw,
a claw had torn loose from its sheath. I wanted to pet and hold him
close, as I would a kitten.

His response came from the warmth of my scent and the hunger in his belly. He ran now, ready to spring, his shoulder muscles tense. His huge head took up the scope of my vision, and he was rushing at me like a locomotive. I cried out, "Simba!" thinking myself a traitor, and a Swahili girl snatched me from the swing, ran with me into the tent, then banged the door shut and held it tight with her body. I knew he would not come for us inside. A kill had to be wide open and helpless.

The natives tracked and wounded him, I was told, as if this would please me. I don't know who told me. Perhaps my mother, believing my fear to be as great as hers. Years later I learned what wounded cats do. They draw a circle with their own dripping blood, then lie in its center to wait for other predators to catch the scent and finish them off. Had I known this, I tell myself now, I would have honored him. I remember a picture of myself taken on a lion skin before we left the country, my eyes black as my aunt Freda's, unsmiling.

I do not recall much about my parents in Africa. There was my father's hand in the back of the jeep, letting the birds drop. The willow branch of my mother's body bending near the river, reaching out a hand to pull me free. Greta's arm sweeping toward Mount Kilimanjaro. The bare, black feet of the natives on the hard-packed dirt around the camp. There were body parts and Greta's fleshy face and cut-up toes.

I remember most clearly the golden air that moved out across a land so vast there was no horizon, just air swallowed in land, land meeting with the air. The birds in the boiling pot, snakes in the trees, and the lion cast gold in the sun before I saw his face and understood for the first time how when a need is great enough only killing can stop it.

My stepfather, John Earl, was a smart man, and mean. Mean in the way people who grow up poor and pretend they are better than you because of it are mean. Mean because he wanted to think he was better but really didn't believe it. Mean because in the tiny Alabama town where he grew up he had to wear shoes with holes in them or no shoes at all. And because he snuck down alleys to get home so no one would see the shack where he lived, not even as good as the cardboard and tar paper–reinforced hovels of the black field workers. Once, when I heard him tell about his life, I almost cried. He went to college, something no one in his family had done, and after he learned a few things from books, he became sarcastic. Bitter. Book learning did him no good; it never erased his hatred for what he was. He was insecure and showed it with his tongue, his fists, and the way his eyes would narrow in derision when he thought you were trying to show him up. It's hard to remember what he looked like—my impression is of a thickly built, dark man, short and powerful—but I remember well the shape of his fist, square, with big, flat knuckles. I hated him, probably more than I ever hated anyone. He felt the same about me, said I was spoiled, wild, stubborn, smart-mouthed. I was the child of another man and he hated me for that.

When my mother left my father somewhere in Africa, we came back to the States, home, to the South. There was John Earl on the front porch of my aunt Freda's house in Watson Chapel, swinging slowly on the big porch swing, sniffing for some taste of my mother. He reminded me of one of those rangy street dogs that ran in packs and veered off alone when they caught the scent of a female in heat. My mother was the one in heat, cursed with what Freda called "the sex thing." It ran in the family like a fault line through the equator, stirring up heat, trouble, deep rumblings. And ran and ran. Freda said it had nicked us all.

My mother's choice in men was sorry. Every one she'd had was a drinker except the one she'd married when she was seventeen so he'd take her to New York to become a model. She spent two years modeling Chanel suits and furs, her twenty-inch waist swimming in fabric, her hair fiery red. I've seen pictures of her then, outside the wrought-iron barred door of her New York apartment. She's wrapped in a long suede trench coat, her lips are painted black, and her long fingernails, also black, are pushed back through that short crimson hair. When she came home she found her husband had annulled the marriage and left her the car, which she drove to California. Freda told me later it was never my mother's intention to go to school, but to find another ripe and willing boy on that bright coast. My father.

After we'd left my father, I kept thinking he'd find us and push me high on the rope swing hung from Freda's pecan tree. I dreamt about him, seeing the smooth back of his neck as we headed out in the jeep to hunt, but never his face. I did not know at the time that he was a pathological liar who, in shame and secrecy, dressed in women's brassieres, girdles, sling-back heels, and wore nail polish, the brightest, cleanest red, and sometimes forgot to take it off. He'd been arrested once in a restaurant in Anaheim when he went into the ladies' room in drag. Before I knew his secrets, he was a hero to me. After I knew, I wanted to study his face to see what had gone wrong.

We stayed with Freda when we got back from Africa because it was what my mother, Rita, knew to do. Freda had looked out for Rita from the time Rita was a kid. They were eleven years apart, born in May on the same day. Rita was strawberry-haired and blue-eyed. Freda's hair was blacker than any storm sky I have ever seen, her eyes the same shiny tint as the obsidian I kept in my pocket. She looked like Vivien Leigh, small and sensual, and had the habit of tossing her head back and loosening her shoulders when she laughed. She laughed a lot, high and crazy and free, and it was hard to tell sometimes what was so funny. People often asked, looking at my black eyes, if I was Freda's child, and I said yes. As it happened, she was the one I would sit with years later when we both were dying.

She lived with her husband and adopted son in a house built back in the mid-1800s—a white frame home with red trim and twenty-foot-high ceilings, leaded-glass doors, each room filled with heavy mahogany furniture, crucifixes, candles, and antique glassware. Her son, Michael Paul, and husband, Owen, were a good bit like the furniture in that house; silent, unobtrusive, each given to the habit of being scarce whenever anything exciting was going on.

When I was young I believed ghosts lived in the steep-sided attic. At night I could hear them brush up against the eaves. One day I crawled through the opening at the top of the swing-down stairs, and scores of small black bats flew in a panic out a side window into a hot August sun. I could feel the scraping of their bony wings against my face as they beat past me. I liked the sensation, as if I were being touched all over by fluttering hands, and the deep, rich smell of their makeshift cave.

Freda hung her paintings on the walls. They were gray, black, red spirit faces, filling the frames like Edvard Munch's howling man. Years later she would finish a painting of the Manson family and hang it next to a gilt-framed portrait of Jesus, one in which he is decidedly Caucasian, with long, limp brown hair and eyes misty and forgiving. But in the portrait Jesus looked more menacing than Manson's wide-eyed teenagers huddled under a low rock, their arms around each other.

I remember a night at Freda's when we were back from Africa, the time she tried to shoot John Earl. My father, James, was there, run off by the black coffee-plantation owner in Africa he'd told my mother he loved. It was then he was experimenting with an interest in men. He had returned to try to talk Rita into coming back to him, saying he had made the greatest mistake of his life when he had told her to leave. She said it was good he could make the greatest something, but it was too late now, and then she turned to kiss John Earl. My father started to cry. I turned my head when he did this.

They'd had a lot to drink that night, even Freda, who would later swear off liquor when she saw it take her father, brother, and sister. Freda was strong that way. She learned from other people's mistakes. I trusted her instincts, the way she watched people and seemed to know what their next move would be. I could read these things in her face. That night she looked mean, as mean as John Earl, but it didn't scare me.

I had been Freda's from the very beginning. It made no difference that I was her sister's kid. We even looked alike and had the same mole in the same place, low on the right side of the back. Freda always said it made us closer than having the same birthday.

I dreamt things that came true: how we would come back from Africa on my sixth birthday and there'd be no presents because we'd left in a hurry, grabbing our clothes, my mother yelling out the door of the camp, "You lying, whoring son of a bitch." And how the stewardess on the airplane would give me a cigar band for a ring, and flight wings, and lean down to kiss me on the cheek, saying, "Happy Birthday." It all happened after I dreamt it under the mosquito nets in Tanganyika. Freda's dreams would come true, too. She said it was a gift, the Indian in us, taken straight from the bloodline of our Choctaw chief grandfather, Sequoia.

Freda didn't like my father any more than she liked most men. To her they were good for sex, never for sustenance. But she never truly hated my father, never searched for his weak spots or called him a fool. John Earl she hated. She sensed his weakness, saw his cowardice, his shame, and said, mockingly, "And you from a poor, drunken daddy, what else would you become but a no-good. It's what you are. In your blood like poison."

It was hard to tell sometimes what set her off. She'd start yelling at John Earl about how he'd ruin her baby sister, stir her up with sex to confuse her, then take her away. Rita needed someone to protect her, Freda told him, a better man. My father, for instance. But my father sat sobbing in a corner of the room, one hand covering his face. I looked at him and wondered.

I watched the way Freda's eyes would get wild. I'd heard about people whose eyes changed color, but Freda was the only one I ever saw it happen to. When she was angry they turned purple, that murky, crushed velvet color. She told me once she could turn them all white if she wanted. I believed her. When Freda got worked up, it was as if the tongue had begun to speak in a revival tent. She'd throw her head back, the black hair heavy against her back, then clench her delicate hands into fists and howl. She did this for courage she told me later, the way Indians whoop in battle before the arrow rides off the bow.

We were in the high-ceilinged butler's kitchen, beer cans everywhere, whiskey spilled on the oilcloth-covered table. I was sitting in a small black rocking chair I pulled with me from room to room, watching, too excited to be afraid. When Freda took over, anything could happen.

"I should shoot you, you stupid bastard," Freda told John Earl.

She looked carefully around the room to see what we thought of this. Her eyes lit on me. I smiled at her, cautiously, afraid John Earl would see.

"Don't do it, Freda," my mother wailed. "That's not the answer. No. Don't shoot poor John Earl."

She was drunk. Her vote didn't count. Freda looked to my father. He pulled his hand away from his face and shrugged his shoulders.

Do it, I thought. It was so loud in my head I feared I'd actually said it. I put my hand to my mouth. John Earl was silent, but I could tell by the heat in the air that he was scared.

Freda started moving toward John Earl. He stepped back, and she walked past him through the narrow hallway into the bedroom. I could see her reach under her pillow, pushing aside the head of her snoring husband, and pull out an old revolver. The white of her hand looked so pretty against the dark wood of the gun butt. I remember thinking what a contrast it was, and how important her hand looked when her index finger slid alongside the trigger.

"You can't hurt my babies anymore," she was saying, walking steadily back into the kitchen, her movements calculated. She took a stiff-legged cop pose to aim, and it looked as if she'd been doing it all her life, creeping up, holding the gun braced and on target. Later in my life I would witness the precise skill with which she dropped birds from the sky. She was better than a crack shot, and maybe John Earl knew it.

"Go ahead," John Earl said, but his face didn't look as if it believed him. He was sweating, great big quarter-sized spurts of perspiration from his mottled forehead, and he licked his lips as if he needed a drink. I noticed his hands were shaking when he went to wipe the sweat away.

"So what's keeping you?" he asked, trying to put a fist to his hip as if he didn't care, but his hand was so slick it just slipped right past his hip and dangled by his side, twitching.

"I'm getting to it," Freda snapped. "I just want you to know why I'm gonna do it, is all. You know why, John Earl?"

John Earl didn't have an answer for her. It pissed her off even more.

"I'll tell you why," Freda was saying. "If I let you live you'll ruin these babies. Mark my words."

Once Freda had decided on a course of action she usually followed through, but I worried she wouldn't shoot John Earl if she kept talking, so I said real loud inside my head, SHOOT HIM, and crossed all my fingers for luck.

She turned real quick to look at me; it was the biggest mistake she ever made. She didn't see my father move up quietly behind her. Just as she squeezed the trigger, right in line with John Earl's sweaty forehead, my father hit her right arm from beneath and the bullet hit a whiskey bottle, shattered it, and lodged in the wall of the hallway. The shot sounded sharp as a whip cracking, and glass from the whiskey bottle caught John Earl full in the face. But that was all. My mother saw the blood on his face and fainted.

"I can't believe I missed," Freda was saying, staring at the gun that had clattered to the floor. "Let me try again. I won't miss this time," she said, but my father was too quick for her, grabbing up the gun just as she reached for it. "I might have thought you'd be on my side," she said, eyeing the gun as he emptied it of bullets.

I put my hands over my face and sighed. Then I pushed myself out of the rocking chair like an old woman and went to Freda, wrapping my arms around her waist, reaching up high so I could feel her heart next to me. She looked down at me and started laughing.

31

"Well," she said, to no one in particular. "Eva's vote counted. Say, Eva. It did, didn't it?"

I nodded up at her and sighed again. We gathered around my mother slapping her, shaking her, calling out her name.

Thirty years later I returned to Watson Chapel and ran my fingers over the hole the bullet had made that night, remembering the look on Freda's face when she aimed at John Earl's head. I never told her about the black rock I found a few years later in Mississippi, or how I'd rub it, wishing John Earl dead. It seemed it had fallen on me to do him in.

That night the cops came to arrest John Earl. Freda called them, saying he was dangerous when he drank and would they please take him off her hands. Men believed anything Freda told them, even cops. So did I. I had believed she would kill John Earl and had wished for it so hard there was no chance of it coming true.

F O U R

The towns had names like Big Cane, Leola, Star City, and New Iberia, places we lived, the sound of them evocative of the smell of gardenias on a summer night. We accumulated these names, my mother and I, as we followed John Earl through the South, never quite knowing what sort of work he did. I wrote the names of the towns in a book when I was older, trying to remember how many there had been before we came to Yazoo City. I spoke the names out loud and thought of the southern land, the way it curved and fanned, the Mississippi River delta black and rich with minerals, the water red as blood with clay. The names sound now like the constellations. I look into the sky at night and expect to find them spread out jagged like a broken heart.

We started out in Watson Chapel, after Africa and the divorce. I remember Freda's house but only vaguely the small apartment we moved to on Pine Street after Rita and John Earl married. It seemed dark all the time, but old memories often come to me in black and white. I played with a ballerina doll my mother had brought from Paris and caught a glimpse of John Earl in bed with my mother, her legs nearly up around his neck.

After Watson Chapel was Star City, where Rita and John Earl went to college. John Earl graduated with a degree in political science, taught one class, and quit. They were learning to drink then but saving it for the weekends when school was out. On those days I would leave by the side door of the small house we rented with a salt shaker in my hand. For hours I chased birds, scattering salt in front of me, believing what John Earl had told me—that to catch a bird I had only to get one grain of salt on his tail feather

33

and he would be mine. It was a ploy to keep me busy, that and throwing a fistful of pennies out into the yard, where I would grope on my knees and drop the pennies into my pockets until they were heavy. I would come home to find the side door locked and hear my mother moaning on the other side of the bedroom window screen, her "OH baby, Ohs," floating out into the thick summer air like poison. I'd bang hard on the side door and my mother would grow quiet, then John Earl would appear at the door with another handful of pennies, a towel wrapped around his waist.

My father passed through once when we lived in Star City. He was returning from Africa again, broke, asking for food and clothes. This time he'd killed thirty elephants, he said, slaughtering them not for money but for the pleasure of watching them drop. I remember listening as he told my mother, seeing her face fill with pain. I couldn't figure out whom she pitied more, the elephants or him.

It was a rampage, he told her, a bloody rampage. "Bloody" was his favorite word, and he used it—in an excited voice, with wild hand gestures—to describe everything. In Star City he was on the "up" peak of an illness that could take him just as far down in a matter of weeks. Later doctors would tell him he was borderline psychotic and treat him futilely with drugs for depressions that lasted five years at a stretch.

He did not know how sick he was when he was younger. I can tell by the pictures. I have one of him taken on the Star City visit, taped into a scrapbook with a Band-Aid. He looks very thin in my stepfather's big trousers. He wears them cinched up high with a broken belt and holds my white kitten tucked up under his chin. He looks afraid, barely able to face the camera, as if he knows it will pick up something he does not ever want to see. He is in his late twenties, just a baby, not much older than my daughter now.

I remember that picture more than the visit, and the stuffed lion he gave me, with soft yellow fur and shiny green disks for eyes. I slept with the lion at night, holding him close under my chin the way my father held the kitten. I had a dream about my father then, in which he pushed me high on the rope swing in Africa and I sailed into the dusk, flying over Mount Kilimanjaro and back into his arms as he stood waiting by the door to the camp. It was a dream of love, the unconditional kind where no one is dropped, forgotten, or left behind broken. He left soon after that, off to a sanitarium for two years, and I did not see him again until I was sixteen.

We moved to New Iberia, Louisiana, when I was in my last years of grade school, driving down from Arkansas with a U-Haul trailer lashed to the bumper of a two-tone station wagon my mother had bought from her first husband.

It was in 1957, the year Hurricane Audrey smashed the Gulf Coast. The delta land of southern Louisiana was flat, and I could smell salt the nearer we got to New Iberia. I had never seen a land so ruined by nature. The fields were soggy with floodwater, and cattle lay in them, dead and bloated, with flies and maggots covering their carcasses while turkey buzzards circled overhead. In the mangled, uprooted trees were rags of human clothing, colored prints and stained white cotton torn into eerie flags. A hound dog lay on his back by the road, his legs sticking straight out like the spines on a sea urchin. Three hundred people had died in the storm, some lost forever, their bodies submerged in the bayous where alligators would find them.

The force had been so violent families still stood in the doorways of their broken homes, stricken by the emptiness around them, children hanging wearily to their mothers' skirts, too young to comprehend the magnitude of death. And there was no clear sky to wash free the memory of a wind that had screamed for three days without stopping. I knew the clean blessing of a clear sky after a storm, the way it seemed to startle into hiding the violence that had come before it. But here the clouds hung low, the color of sulphur, and I remember a ragged fear that the more miles we drove the closer we were to being swallowed up. The smell of the Gulf had become oppressive, mixing with the sweet decay all around us. My mother breathed in deeply and said something about the smell of the ocean being intoxicating. I thought to myself it must be the beer she held tight between her legs. I pulled my shirt up over my head and held my breath.

We lived in a trailer then, outside New Iberia, immigrants it seemed, or migrants, rootless in our wheeled house with the cinder-block steps and plastic window curtains. My mother sold her dia-mond necklace, a wedding gift from my father, to buy the trailer. I knew this because John Earl had thrown a plate of spaghetti in her face at a roadside restaurant to get her to do it.

I went to a rural school, driven each morning to class in the back of a pickup truck one of the sugar cane growers used as a school bus. School is what I remember most clearly in New Iberia; that and the driveways covered with white seashells, the crunched-up dust of them smelling like brine and thick as chalk in my clothes after a day outside. The kids at school were from poor families, part Cajun most of them, and many went barefoot until the weather turned cold.

There was a boy who sat across from me in class, a freckled kid with flax-colored hair and a big head, his eyes narrow and pale blue. He wore no shoes in good weather, but when it turned bad he wore his sister's shoes, a pair of scuffed Mary Jane's, too big and strapped on the wrong feet. I could see he knew no better, that left and right were as incomprehensible to him as the alphabet. He was teased a lot, that boy, and hung his head pitifully there at the back of the classroom, too timid to look into the teacher's face when she called on him. I would try to catch his eye and smile, but I could tell he did not trust me.

One day another boy tried to make him drink muddy water from a sinkhole in the play yard. The boy was fat and obnoxious and stood pointing at my classmate's shoes, calling him sissy. As I watched, twisting up the ends of my sweater into a knot, I saw my classmate's lowered eyes filling with tears and the tears falling straight down into the sinkhole, steady as rain. It was the sort of thing that made me hot inside, blood filling my head as fast as the boy's tears dropped, and I could feel my heart charge into another rhythm, the beats quick and thin in my chest. When I felt like that there was no thinking to what I did. I grabbed a fistful of mud and ran at the fat boy, calling out, "Pig, eat this!" and crammed the mud into his mouth, upsetting his balance. He fell back into the sinkhole and his rear end filled it perfectly. He caught me, tore at my sweater, and pulled the braids from my hair before the teacher came and paddled him right there in the play yard in front of a crowd of hooting, contentious children.

After that the boy who wore his sister's shoes would find his way next to me in line, silently watching as I pushed my tray toward the lunch register. I would turn to smile and he would drop his head, embarrassed to be found there, too shy to speak my name.

We moved away before the year was up, and I remember that last day, going to return my books in the afternoon as if I were on holiday, exempt from the normal routine. I wore a pair of blue jeans with a hole torn in the seat, and as I walked into the classroom and up the aisle to the teacher's desk, I could feel a breeze and knew I'd forgotten to put on underpants. The boy smiled as I walked back past him, a big grin, then waved good-bye.

"Thanks, Eva," he called out, before I closed the door behind me.

I think of him now when I see ragged children on the streets, their pants too short, shirts stained, toes poking through their sneakers. I wonder if they are a different breed, tougher, and if their shame is easier with others like themselves.

We sold the trailer, hooked up the U-Haul again, and moved to Yazoo City.

I don't know if most adults can place a time when the world became different for them, a day when they woke up and knew that to rely on anyone else was foolish. I haven't asked around, but it can happen that way. One day you believe, or try to, that you are safe, protected by those wiser than you. And the next you wake up and notice yourself for the first time. How strong your hands are, how oddly real your body looks in the filtered light coming through the bedroom window, and how walking out into that light and not looking back will feel right. It was that way for me, as if I had slid out of a cocoon into noise and light and the way things really were, and understood I was alone. It was a good feeling. I can't deny it.

It happened in Yazoo City, the place we lived the longest, the summer I found the ravine. Rita and John Earl lived in their own world, one filled with and emptied by the liquor bottles they stacked in boxes in the carport, ready to take to the bootlegger when they'd gathered up two cases. Looking back, I understand the pain of it. I see my mother's face in my own. She was not a bad woman. I never thought she was, in my better moments. She was just sick in a way that ate her up. And lonely. I understand now how that is.

She would wake in the morning early, needing the alcohol so much by then that her long hands, once as smooth and strong as my own, would be shaking. The tremors jerked through her body, as if she'd been plugged in and set in a puddle of water. She had been a beautiful woman, so slender and young people had thought she was my sister. Now her once-bright hair was dull, and her small waist was pushed out by a swollen belly. The veins in the back of her legs stood out, and she had no ankles, just puffs of flesh between her calves and feet.

I would come to her in the morning when I heard the vegetable bin in the refrigerator slide open. It was where she kept her vodka. She would fill a coffee cup and then a tall glass, which she kept in the freezer. I remember the look in her eyes when she would see me walk into the kitchen and catch her stooped over the bin, her hands shaking so badly that the bottle banged the plastic as she pulled it out. It was the look that big-headed boy had when he wore his sister's shoes to school. Shame, burning so hot her eyes watered.

"Rita," I would say to her, looking right and then left, trying to avoid her eyes, "Can I play out all day?"

And she would tell me yes, I could, if I ate breakfast first and packed a lunch. I could see my leaving made things easier for her. Her hands wouldn't shake as hard and she wouldn't gulp the vodka she hoped I thought was coffee. She would tell me she wasn't feeling well that day—a back problem, she'd say—and I would say I was sorry and ask if there was anything I could do.

"No," she'd say. "Just don't get into trouble."

We had the same conversation for years.

She knew I was good at getting into trouble and that trouble interrupted her day, like the time I walked across the water pipe spanning the ravine while floodwaters pushed across it in waves.

I did it on a dare, the way I seemed to do everything, telling the neighborhood kid who'd called me a chicken that I didn't see him walking across any pipe.

"You do it first," he'd said to me. "Show you're not chicken."

It was a thick pipe, about two feet wide and half a city block long, tarred over at the joints, and was the only quick route to neighborhoods beyond the ravine. I walked it easily in dry weather, balancing and turning pirouettes when I reached the middle, impressed by my grace and lack of fear, and by the way my calf muscles knotted up strong and hard when I stood on my toes and spun with precision like some junkyard ballerina.

This day the floodwaters surged on the same level as the pipe, making it slippery. The next day the girl with blond hair would float past, her eyes open wide in that angry water.

I watched the whirlpools, wide, powerful vortices sprung to life by all the trash in the water. All it took was a good flood to sweep the countryside clean. I took my first step onto the pipe and thought how it would be to fall into a whirlpool and be sucked to the bottom. I imagined it would look like the inside of a tornado, the way Dorothy saw it from her bedroom window, a wild black wind spinning tighter and tighter. I thought about the tadpoles and where they had gone in the flood, and about the rocks that had been lifted and carried miles down the channel. The ravine would look different when the flood receded, that was certain.

I lifted my arms for balance and moved forward, turning each bare foot out as I stepped, feeling the pipe smooth and slick as oiled plastic. My toes ached when I tried to grip down. Two steps more and I heard the boy on the bank yell over the rush of water, "You're not a chicken, Eva. Come back now or I'll get your mama."

I could feel my feet slip and braced myself, knowing I would fall if I breathed too hard. The rush of the water grew louder, and I dared not look down. I was thinking of how that boy would find Rita, drunk in the middle of the day, and I wanted to turn around quick so he wouldn't go for her, but I couldn't. I slid my feet backward, a half inch at a time, and heard the boy call again from the lip of the ravine.

"I'm going now, Eva. Going to get your mama. You hear me?"

I looked straight ahead and watched the water toss a tree limb onto the far bank.

"Here she is," I heard the kid say. "You come on now, Eva. Your mama's sick. You come off that pipe. Right now. Your mama says."

I turned slowly, trancelike, and saw the trunk of an oak tree lurch in the water, heading straight for the pipe. My legs slid out from under me and I hit the hard surface, tearing something inside. The trunk smashed into the pipe on the far side of the ravine and caught on the metal, its tangled roots raised like arms above the water.

I could see my mother now. She had staggered and fallen to her knees at the edge of the ravine, the water soaking her as it splashed up the sides and over the bank. She was trying to stand, moving the way a fish flops when it's dying. I saw her mouth move, but I could not hear her. The kid stood over her, looking down. I wondered what he was thinking. She passed out there in the thick grass, and he waited beside her while I crawled my way back across the pipe, wishing she had fallen in.

Not long after that, I awoke in the morning to notice how strong my hands were, how black my hair. Soon I would be allowed to spend summers with my aunt Freda—Christmas vacation, Easter, any time school was out. And my mother would go away, dry out, come back. Each time I noticed another piece of her missing, as if one day I might hear her voice and not be able to see her at all.

There is an old picture of my mother, taken when she was eight years old. In the picture her head is resting on the lap of an old black woman who, Freda told me, was my mother's mammy. The old woman is sitting on a porch swing, and her left arm is resting on my mother's shoulder, her hand placed lightly on my mother's cheek. The woman's print dress is folded up into a pillow under the child's head. My mother's smile was sweet, timid, vulnerable, and in this picture that smile is on her face. I can forgive her. Seeing that smile in a picture in the bottom of a box of old black-and-whites in Freda's house, I can.

F I V E

Through Wabbaseka, Stuttgart, Altheimer, and Clarendon, the rutted blacktop of U.S. Highway 79 runs at a southwest diagonal down the state of Arkansas, taking the path of tornadoes. For over thirty years the towns have remained as I remember them, outposts built upon land so flat it looks as if somone had taken an iron to it. Cotton fields, rice paddies, and patches of soybeans creep to the edges of the towns and the railroad tracks that run parallel to the highway. When weeds grow too high along the tracks, threatening the crops, farmers set fire to the dry grass, and for miles there is a stream of flame running down the shallow gully. On a summer night the line of fire looks like a path of glory moving on to the edge of the Arkansas River where it stops abruptly. When I was young I swore I could hear it hiss where it met the river.

In late summer the cotton bolls split wide open, white against the deep green of the mother plants, and from the highway it looks as if thousands of handkerchiefs have dropped from the sky. Across the river, fourteen miles from the shantytown of Altheimer, is Watson Chapel.

I grew up seeing this land, summer and winter alike, from the window of Freda's '56 Chevrolet as we made the trip from Watson Chapel to Altheimer, Altheimer to Yazoo City, and back again. Off the road, deep in the cotton fields, were tar-paper shacks leaning southwest with the wind and the highway. They were the homes of sharecroppers, huge families of blacks who slept five to a bed and filled the fields at dawn. From the road I could see their colored kerchiefs, reds and yellows, bending deep into the rows of cotton, rising up and dipping down. Black faces in the sun shone smooth as polished onyx, and the children's faces were lesser stones, moving quickly down the rows, chasing fibers of cotton blown high on the wind. Sometimes a mother would tire of her child running wild in the field, and a small head would disappear beneath the rows of cotton, a strong black hand would raise up and lower, and from the open window of the car I might hear a high, indignant cry, sharp like a gunshot through the clear air.

There were always deaths along that highway, cars smashed against the low concrete bridges that spanned the bayous. It was the main topic of conversation in the cafés along Highway 79: who had died. When Freda and I stopped to get something to eat, I would listen with grisly attention, thinking often of the tattered baby doll my aunt Leta had taken from the car in her wrecking yard. I imagined one car alone on that flat stretch of blacktop, driving a hundred miles an hour, so fast you couldn't see the face behind the windshield when it went past, and how the car would hit a rut in the road and spin like a gyroscope until it met with one of the bridges.

I heard a waitress once tell about a man who had fallen from the top of the big bridge that crossed the Arkansas. He'd slipped off the scaffolding when the bridge was being built, down into the river and onto a pillar that had broken loose. In Arkansas "pillar" sounded the same as "pillow," and for years I imagined the man floating in the river, a pillow under his head, the thick brown water pushing him along to the river's edge where the gully fires vanished into the water.

On the way into Watson Chapel, Highway 79 passes the Catholic cemetery, its wrought-iron arch painted white and peeling. I asked Freda once if only Catholics were buried there, and she said, "They like to think so, but how do they know once they're dead?" And then she laughed, crazily, her eyes watering, and pounded the dash of the Chevy until I thought she'd hurt herself.

"You see," she continued, wiping her eyes, "what you do is this. You tell them, right before they die, according to their wishes and all, that they'll be buried here, right here in this cemetery. A *chosen* spot. A pretty one, like there, under that dogwood tree."

Freda pointed to a pink dogwood spread low over an empty plot.

"And then," she said, her laughter so out of control she was holding her sides, "you find a nice burlap sack, put some rocks in it—ever heard the term 'cement overcoat'?—then you stick the body in and pay a visit to the river. Saves money. I die, you do the same thing. Okay?"

I stared at her for a while, my mouth open. She was sitting up straight in the driver's seat, looking at me out of the corner of her eye. Freda was of the opinion I was too serious for my own good, and told me so.

"You don't think that's funny?" she asked me. "What's the matter with you, Eva, you don't think that's funny. You need a sense of humor. You been around my sister so long you forgot how to laugh. I want you to laugh. Now."

She stared back at me, wrinkling up her eyebrows. She made a pouty face.

I laughed. A little.

"Louder," she said, slapping the dashboard. "Just think how a nun would look in one of them cee-ment overcoats. Lead shoes. A stone habit. Ooooh, that's good."

I started giggling.

"You're strange, Eva," she told me. "Wonder where you get that."

Freda loved Watson Chapel, its dark downtown area built along the railroad tracks, old brick buildings set solidly on the dirty streets that ran along the bluff of the river. Outside town there was farmland and thick woods filled with ticks and chiggers. Freda bought a piece of land out there, dug a deep pond, and put in albino catfish that shone iridescent as I watched them from the edge, prodding their lazy bodies with a long stick I took along whenever we visited what Freda called The Land. She never lived on the land, but it was there, she told me, when she needed it.

On the edge of town the paper mill blew foul-smelling smoke into the air day and night. My mother hated that smell and said women could go for days without knowing when a baby's diaper needed changing because the air always smelled like shit. Rita hated Watson Chapel and said she couldn't see why Freda stayed there. Freda told her she was meant to be there, that once a place was in your blood you weren't meant to have transfusions, moving all over the place the way Rita did. It hurt your heart, she said, made you die early.

Freda's house was ruled by smells: cornbread soaked in buttermilk, black-eyed peas cooked in pork fat, fried okra, soaps in the bathroom stacked high on a pine shelf. I could smell the soap when I walked in the front door, lilac dust and rose, gardenia, and the sweet, clean scent of cold cream set out in open jars on the kitchen table where Freda put on her makeup.

She would sit there each morning before breakfast in front of a double-sided mirror, its round, delicate frame set on a porcelain base. From a silver box she'd take a tube of lipstick the color of black cherries and paint her lips with her little finger. Then she'd do her eyebrows, high and arched, with a black pencil. She smoothed the cold cream on her perfect skin and used no rouge. The Choctaw in her showed in her high cheekbones and strong jaw. I watched her as she did her face, the slow pressing together of the lips, the way she admired herself in the mirror, looking sideways to catch a studied look of arrogance. She knew she was beautiful and that nothing, not even age, would ever take that beauty from her. When she was sixty-six she could smile and look sixteen.

Freda was up at dawn each day, wearing a pair of white cotton men's pajamas with no bra underneath. I could see the flat side of her chest where she'd had a breast cut off when she was thirty-five. She took no care to hide the scarred, bony flesh when she bent down, and I would stare through the opening in the pajama top, remembering what she had looked like when she came home from the hospital. My mother and I were living there then, after we'd come back from Africa, in the apartment upstairs that Freda rented when she needed the money.

Once, when she was in the claw-footed bathtub in the bathroom off the butler's kitchen, she called out to me through the open window—out into the yard where I was bent on my knees picking wild violets, eating the stems because the taste was like green apples. She had a sweet, singsong voice, high and pretty and thick with a Tennessee hills accent that hadn't flattened into an Arkansas drawl. I heard her and ran through the back door, straight into the bathroom without stopping because there was never one thing I would not do to please her. If she called, I came. If she said do the dishes, I did the dishes. If she said sing to me, I sang. If she said believe me when I tell you this, I believed.

She lay there in the steep-sided tub, her long neck resting on a sponge, her black hair hanging to the floor. I saw the bandage then, what looked like yards of tape starting at her shoulder and winding around her back, crisscrossing her chest, the gauze of the bandage where her right breast had been stained pink. The other breast was round and full, the nipple as pink as the stain on the gauze.

"Eva, baby," she said, grinning really big so I wouldn't be afraid— she was the only person I ever knew who could grin and talk at the same time—"I need you to help me out, honey. I need you to hold my back, please."

I bent down and slipped my small hands behind Freda's warm back, feeling the tight muscles, pressing gently while she pulled herself up by the sides of the tub. I could see the pain in her face and knew it made her angry.

She never said anything about the breast being gone. She never cried. Years later my mother told me she had only seen Freda cry once. I could think of only one time, too, but it wasn't really crying she did. She wept, priming the tears from a place rusted out and hollow. The sound was like a mourning dove's or a single note blown on a flute.

Freda served breakfast at six in the morning, bringing the plates to the table prepared: four slices of bacon, grits, two eggs, and a slice of cornbread. She never asked if it was too much or too little, figuring it was just right. The four of us, her husband, Owen, who worked for the railroad, her anemic adopted son, Michael Paul, Freda, and I, would sit at the round table covered with a scarred oilcloth. I would look out the slats of the Venetian blinds onto the traffic on Poplar Street, waiting for Owen to stop with his talk of local politics. He was a boring man, and Freda had not listened to him since the day they were married. If he so much as called her name she told him to shut up. It was the way, my mother said, Freda liked her men. Obedient. Owen obediently handed his pay-check over to Freda each week, never asking questions. The son was a skinny boy who'd been born to a crazy neighbor. Freda couldn't have children, her ovaries scarred by a pelvic infection when she was young, so she'd taken Michael Paul from the neighbor who now lived in the state asylum. She fed him yeast cakes to fatten him up and gave him dolls to play with so he would not be tempted by rougher games. In puberty he began to show his homosexuality, and everyone in the family said it was Freda's fault.

Whenever I came to stay I was expected to be his big sister, a guardian angel, his only friend, but mostly I ignored the boy. I had a dream about Michael Paul when I was thirteen and he was ten. In the dream he clung tightly to the tall white posts of an old colonial house set deep in woods run wild with poison ivy. I could see him from my place on a narrow path that led to the door of the house, his arms wrapped around the post, his body pressed close to it as if he thought a rumbling in the earth might shake him loose. I called out to him in the dream, and as he looked toward me the pillar turned to snakes that wound thick around him until he vanished. I told Freda about the dream and she frowned, saying nothing. Years later Michael Paul hit a truck head-on out on the new interstate that looped around Watson Chapel. They cut a hole in his skull so his brain could swell, and he died not long after.

I remember Freda always in motion. She never sat at the kitchen table and smoked a cigarette or drank a cup of coffee when she was talking to me. She'd be pulling clothes from the washer, waxing the floor, spreading squirrel hides out to dry on an old window screen propped up against the back of the house. I would follow her from room to room, out the back door, to the alley where she burned the trash, watching her head shake when she laughed, her arms move in quick gestures, listening to her voice rise high and clear when she went on about what fools people were, particularly my mother. Rita was her favorite fool. It's not that she didn't love her. It had to do with respect, Freda said. How could you respect someone, she asked, who didn't respect themselves?

"How many TV sets you have at home?" Freda asked me one morning when she was scraping the breakfast leftovers into the bird feeder out back.

"Five," I told her, feeling vaguely ashamed.

"Fool," she yelled back at me. "Your mama is a fool and she's trying to make you into one. Five! What do you need with five of the goddamned things? Do you know what those things do to your mind? Do you?"

I told her I didn't. The truth was, I'd never thought about it.

"They're put on this earth to stop free thought. That's right. You can't think when they're turned on. You try it sometime. The next time you sit down to watch a TV set, just try to think about something important."

"Like what?" I asked her.

She glared at me.

"You'll figure it out," she said, tossing a handful of cornbread to the wind. "What was I saying? Now don't tell me you can think and watch at the same time, because you can't. You'll think of something—*important*—and then you'll be looking at the TV, so you'll stop that thought and just sit and watch like a fool. It makes people stupid. You remember what I say. You don't watch it around here, do you?"

I told her no.

"See?" she said, and laughed. "Now are you happy here?"

She didn't need to ask. Freda's was the only place where all the problems dropped away. There were no screams in the middle of the night there, no cases of empty bottles in the carport marking time. It was the one place I felt alive, and the older I got the more I would cling to the memory of her bullying me into shape, making me laugh, and coming to my bed at night to kiss me on each cheek and the tip of my nose. I loved her, dear God how I loved her, so much I can feel the ache of her being gone rise in me sometimes so strong I panic.

And I saw what she meant. No matter what she told me, I saw, because she made the point again and again if I didn't get it, yelling at the top of her voice. It scared people who didn't know her, especially children, who thought she was angry. But it was just the way she talked, loud, fast, and with conviction. Everything she said sounded as if it were some ancient wisdom that had been told to her and her alone.

Freda was a follower of the theories of Carl Jung, and she told me how people carried in their subconscious knowledge from the beginning of time. They were strange notions for a kid to hear.

She asked me once if I'd ever done anything I didn't understand but seemed right anyway. I told her I couldn't think of a thing.

"Well think, damnit, think," she said. "I'll just wait here while you think, and when it comes to you, you tell me."

I was sitting on an old crate in the alley while Freda pushed trash into a metal barrel with a broom handle, looking at me from time to time, wrinkling up her forehead as if she were trying to help me.

"Think. It'll come to you. Think of something. Anything."

And I did. As she lit the trash with a match, I told her about the time in Mississippi when I'd been in the woods and scraped my hand on the bark of a tree I'd been climbing.

"So what happened?" she asked.

The trash had caught good by then, and Freda stood with her back to the flames. I remember how the heat made her look as if she were floating.

I told her I'd taken an oak leaf from the ground, a big one, and let my hand bleed onto the leaf.

"Why?" she asked.

I told her I didn't know.

"Yes you do," she said.

I told her it was a silly reason. I didn't want to say.

"Nothing's a silly reason," she said with certainty.

She fanned the flames with her arms now, looking like a magician's girl as sparks rose into the air.

"Because," I said, feeling foolish, "I thought I'd give life back to something dead. My blood. I'd give it my blood."

"Aha!" she said, kicking at the flaming barrel. "See what I mean? Probably thousands of years ago all kinds of people were doing this, bleeding on leaves, you know. It's symbolic. It means something. It's tucked way back there in your subconscious until you have a time to use it and then, bam, there it is, and you don't know why unless you think about it. And maybe even then you don't know."

We went to church twice a week, to mass, and I asked Freda

why, if she believed in the works of philosophers and psychologists, she needed church.

"It's ritual," she told me. "Everybody needs ritual."

I remember walking into the church behind Freda, smelling the perfume of the votive candles lit in rows along the altar. The stained glass of the windows was deep blue and rose-colored in the candle-light, their steepness heightened by the vaulted ceilings, and I felt as if I was walking not into God's house but into his tomb. I knew a lot about the miracles of the church then, had listened to Freda tell me about Bernadette and her vision of the Virgin Mary. They spooked me, Catholics did, so quiet and sure and icy in their belief. Freda seemed too human to belong to them, too free to have been a nun until her thirtieth year.

She covered her head before entering the church, according to custom, not with a hat or a lace scarf but with a Kleenex anchored in place by a bobby pin. People stared at her for this and whispered, saying it was disrespectful. Freda told me God didn't give a damn, that she could wear a baseball cap if she liked, and that the purpose of covering the head was so the angels wouldn't get hot and bothered over the sight of a woman's hair. It was true. I read it later in a book of Jung's on religious ritual.

It seemed we knelt for hours in that church, Michael Paul next to me fidgeting, picking his nose, looking dazed and stupid. I often wondered why, if Freda would not suffer fools, she was so nuts about her son.

The summer of my thirteenth year I was allowed my first pair of stockings. I wore them to mass one day rolled tight around my thighs with rubber garters, the kind better used as slingshots. I knelt beside Freda and could feel my legs go numb as the priest called the congregation to communion. As she stood to walk forward I re-member seeing the smoothness of her black hair, thinking the angels would surely like it, and the way the Kleenex floated up off her head, free from the bobby pin. I reached up to catch it and passed out, falling in a heap on the soft brown leather of the kneeling bench. When I came to, Freda had me propped in a chair at the back of the church and was splashing holy water in my face, slapping me gently, breathing under my nose as if her breath were smelling salts.

"Those silly things choked off your blood, girl," she said.

That day she talked to me about sex, as if it were the thing to do after what had happened.

"You think," she said, "that to put some nylons on your legs makes you sexy."

I remember wondering where she got her ideas. I told her I hadn't thought about it, that I just liked the way the stockings mashed down the hair on my legs.

"So you don't think about it that way yet," she said, "but you start feeling it. The way you move. How you cross your legs. How good that nylon feels on you. Sexy. Then you start pushing your chest out, wiggling your butt. You start changing at your age. It's good, Eva."

The way Freda talked about it, it didn't sound so bad. She believed in sex. It ran in the family, she told me, the sex thing—needs so great they ruined people's lives. She said it was something I couldn't do anything about, if I had what she called "hot blood," except to let it boil.

"Your mama," she said, "cannot live without it. Did you know that?"

I told her sometimes it sounded like it was going to kill her. But I didn't think about it. Not with my mother anyway. I thought about boys, one in particular, meeting me under the pecan tree in Freda's yard late at night. I imagined how he'd run his hands up under the print of a new dress, and how my legs would loosen and fall open. What he'd do next I wasn't sure. Freda told me what that was, and I think I gasped, figuring it was just too strange to be true. But once I settled into the notion, I liked thinking about it.

Freda said in life there was hard work, expansion of the mind through thought and reading, and sex. I said what about death, and she told me, yes, of course, there was that, too, but not to worry about it. The way she presented the world, all you had to do was live and everything would take care of itself, but without the other two disciplines, sex would take over. If I minded my life it would all balance out. And wasn't I lucky, she said, that she was here to teach me.

Next door to the house in Watson Chapel lived a boy my age named Ronnie White. He was half Choctaw, too, with long arms and legs, skin the color of cured tobacco leaves, and eyes that closed halfway when he smiled. I'd seen him each time I'd come to stay and had watched him grow from a gangly kid to a tall boy who walked as if he were on a tightrope, hips pulled in, thigh muscles tightening when he took a long step. We would meet along the fence grown over with morning glory that separated Freda's yard from the Whites'.

I would wait each afternoon by the fence, pulling leaves off a fig tree that grew on Freda's side of the yard, breaking the stems open and rubbing the sticky milk on my fingers, pretending I did not see Ronnie making his way through the thick bushes next door. He always had a look on his face, like Elvis on the big screen, as if he knew something bad. I liked his eyes, their slyness, and the way his mouth opened partway when he ran his tongue along his bottom lip, as if he were hungry.

We went swimming in Chapel Lake that summer. Freda tied her white cotton top up under her one breast and dove into the lake from a tree stump along the edge. When she came out of the water I could see Ronnie watching her, curiously, wondering where the other one was.

I fell in love with Ronnie that afternoon, watching him swim across Chapel Lake. He was fourteen. In the dark water of the lake his body was invisible until he lifted his arms to make a stroke. In the sun they were wet and shining like the shells on pecans after a rain. He would roll his head with each stroke, open his mouth for a breath, then close it slowly as he lay his face back in the water without a sound. It confounded me that he made no noise, parting the water with his perfect strokes again and again, kicking his feet gently. I told myself I'd never seen anything as lovely as that long body moving quietly across the lake, black hair catching the sun like the faces of children in the cotton fields. Freda saw me watching and heard me catch my breath when Ronnie stepped from the lake on the other side, water running down his legs.

"He's a pretty boy, Eva," she said, looking at me knowingly. "He's a real pretty boy."

That winter I turned fifteen and spent Christmas at Freda's. It snowed for a full week, and Highway 79 blended white with the frozen cotton fields. Chapel Lake was solid ice, a foot thick, and for a month I stayed on, past time for school, until the thaw came. Freda gave me a black hat made of rabbit fur to wear when I stood at the fence waiting for Ronnie.

He never talked much when he came, and I could never guess if he really liked me, but being with him was something I was starting to need. I caught my breath a lot when he leaned close on the fence. I liked the way he smelled in the cold air, exotic and warm, like the jars of spices that filled his mother's kitchen.

We made plans to sneak out on New Year's Eve and meet in the alley that ran behind Freda's big yard and alongside the tiny gospel church that was packed with black people on Sundays. I left by the back door late that night through the dry snow that lay in small drifts against the house. In the alley, lit by a streetlamp, Ronnie waited for me, leaning against the stone wall of the gospel church, his hands bare, holding a box of firecrackers. He grinned at me as I opened the gate to the alley, then reached out and pulled loose the tie on my hat.

"Take it off," he told me. "I want to see your hair."

I stood perfectly still, afraid to move. I'd never been touched by a boy, except in fights. Had never been kissed except by my silly cousin, Michael Paul, who'd jumped on my bed one morning and held me down while he licked my face. He'd said that made us kissing cousins and I'd told him to drop dead.

Ronnie pushed the black fur hat back from my head and let it fall onto the snow. I looked down at the soft impression it made and said, "It looks like a cat. Just like a cat."

"No it doesn't," he said. "You do. You're the one who looks like a cat."

"Freda says it's heredity."

"Freda would say something like that," he said, moving closer. He took hold of my ponytail and pulled the rubber band loose.

"Why do you wear this silly thing?" he asked. "Your hair looks better down."

He ran his fingers through it now, pulling gently at the tangles at the end, smoothing it around my face, holding it to his mouth. He held his right hand cupped against my cheek for a moment and dropped the firecrackers into the snow.

"They'll get wet," I said.

"Who cares," he replied.

Ronnie stood staring at me and I felt my face go hot.

"You're pretty," he said. "No. Not pretty. Beautiful. Beautiful is better."

He moved close and put his mouth on mine, slipping his arm around my waist. I could feel him shaking.

"Open your mouth," he said. "Open it wide."

I did and felt his tongue press against the roof of my mouth, then slip down under my tongue. My back arched, against my will, and I cried out, grabbing at the shoulders of his thick coat to keep from falling. We stood there tight against each other, and the snow started up again. I could feel it melting in the corners where our mouths met, running down my neck, and soaking the cowl of my sweater. Ronnie slipped a hand up under it and I let myself sink toward him.

"You have two," he said. "That's nice."

"You knew I had two," I told him. "Don't be silly. You saw me at the lake."

"I thought maybe that was heredity too."

He pushed me back gently, gauging the look in my eyes. I was having trouble focusing and felt dizzy.

"Here," he said. "We'll make a bed in the snow."

He dug out a space the size of a coffin in the alley, brushing the snow up high along the sides with his bare hands.

"Eskimos keep warm this way," he told me. "It's really okay."

When he was done he pulled me down. I lay on my back as he fanned my hair out along the ledge of snow. I could feel him reach under my coat and work at my jeans, awkwardly, his fingers catching in the zipper. I pulled him to me as the fabric slipped away, hoping to ease the pain that had started when he kissed me. It pushed through my belly, an ache so dark and deep I had to move my hips to quiet it. I could feel the boy inside me, with a pain that was sharp at first, then warm. How much time passed I do not know, but we cried out together and I pulled his head close, smashing his mouth so hard against mine I could taste the blood.

Ronnie rolled into the snow when we were done and I sat up, looking down at the stain that looked violet in the lamplight. It seeped along my thighs and onto the caked ice beneath, reminding me of a grape Sno-Cone.

"Dear," he said. "Oh dear," something I did not expect a boy to say. "You're bleeding."

"Freda says it's normal," I told him. "It happens the first time."

"Freda should know," he said, and laughed. "How come I'm not bleeding?"

"I guess it's not your first time," I said.

"Do you love me, Eva?" he asked, brushing the snow from the firecrackers he'd picked up.

"Yes," I told him.

"Good," he said. "I love you, too."

We dried the fuses of the firecrackers on our coats and set them off in a string. Ronnie ran down the alley toward his house, yelling back, "Happy New Year."

I ran, too, through the snow to the back door of Freda's house where I turned the bolt quietly and walked in my socks to bed. I didn't sleep that night, and when Freda came in the morning to wake me I was sitting on the edge of the bed, feeling the sheath of dried blood tight on my thighs, thinking I'd never want to wash it off.

"It starts to smell after a while," she said, looking around the bedroom as if she expected to see something out of place.

"What's that?" I asked, horrified.

"How was it?" she said.

"Was what?"

I could feel my mouth hanging open.

"Your first time," she said matter-of-factly. "What do you think I mean?"

"How did you—?"

54

"Look here," she said, reaching behind me. "Presto. A leaf. A fig leaf. How symbolic."

She waved the leaf under my nose, tickling me.

"It's not a fig leaf," I said. "It's maple."

"Good. You pass leaf identification. And here, another leaf."

She had a small pile raked along the edge of the bed by now. She was enjoying herself.

"The leaves out there are under snow, Eva. Now how are you gonna get leaves on yourself, unless you're under the snow, *in* them, tell me. Frozen leaves get melted loose, you see, by body heat, or some other kind of heat, maybe firecrackers, or . . ."

"You didn't watch, did you?"

"Of course not. I don't have to watch. I remember what it looks like."

"Okay," I said. "You know. Are you mad at me?"

"Don't be silly," she said. "What's to be mad at . . . nature? So how was it?"

She folded her arms up over the place where her breast had been, not letting my eyes pry for the first time I could remember.

"I don't know," I said, embarrassed. "Nice. Very nice."

She rolled her eyes at me, looking disappointed.

"Nice? Is that all you can say? You been in training all these years and 'nice' is all you can say? You lose your virginity, something Mary kept until the day she died—that was tricky. Think about it sometime—and it's just nice. You're a woman now and it's nice. *Nice.* What a dull word. Nice nice nice nice nice. Oooooh. Boring. Say it five times and see how boring it sounds. Go on."

"Nice," I said.

"More," she said.

I spoke the word again.

"Five times."

"Nice nice nice nice nice," I said, laughing now.

"Think of another word."

"Different," I said. "It was different."

"That's better," she said. "Different from what? Root beer floats? Hockey? What?"

If it had been anyone but Freda I'd have gotten angry, said shut up and mind your own business.

"Different from anything else," I told her. "How should I know? I'd never even kissed him before. Never kissed any boy. And now . . . all this."

"How did you feel, Eva?"

I thought about it for a while, knowing I didn't have to hurry with an answer. I watched her face, the way she looked older all of a sudden, and wished for a moment I were her and had gotten past all the bad things that were to come. It was just in that one moment I knew it all and then it was gone.

"I felt," I began slowly, "as if I were on a small boat on the river, rocking with the wind. And then a star fell straight out of a constellation and burned a hole right through me."

"Hmmm," she said. "I got nothing to say to that. I guess it was as good as I said."

"Better."

"Were there fireworks, Eva?" she asked, laughing, pulling a leaf from my hair. "Did you give some blood back to the leaves?"

"Don't tell my mother," I said.

"You know better than that," she said, reaching over to hug me. "Rita has enough to handle with her own sex life. You think I want her in competition with you?"

I winced. Thinking of my mother that way always put an edge on things.

"Don't say that," I told her. "It doesn't sound good."

"Sorry," she told me. "Just a fact of life."

I told Freda I didn't want to go home, that back in Mississippi it was as if everything was on fire, Rita and John Earl angry all the time, and when they weren't they were passed out. I said I was never sure what to say to them, how to treat them, and that back there I couldn't really talk at all. She said that was okay, I could save it up for when I came back. I said what if there was nothing to save up?

"There will be," she told me. "There always is."

Freda drove me back to Yazoo City when the thaw came, down Highway 79, past the barren cotton fields and across the high bridge that spanned the Arkansas River, on into the South I loved, back to Rita who had two breasts. I wondered if she had dried out while I was gone.

I called Ronnie when I got home and he asked when I was coming back.

"Summer," I said. "I'll be back in summer."

The Arkansas branches off from the trunk of the Mississippi like the twisted arm of an old oak. From the banks of the river outside Watson Chapel it spreads out broad like a plain, meeting up with gully fires, dead wood along the shore, young boys gone for a summer swim, and swallows them whole without ever asking their names. It has a life, that river, and you can hear it sometimes in the dead of night like a train whistle low and clear on the wind. I thought I could hear it at Freda's, covered up to my neck with quilts in the safe bed. It whispered in my dreams the meanings of things, calling out the names of trees and stones, birds, plants, and the craters of the moon, lovingly, as if they were all its children. I could hear it sometimes in Freda's voice, its strength echoing up into the words she spoke with no apology. And when I was standing on its banks I knew it was all true, that I was not crazy but in some strange way in rhythm with its waters.

We took a picnic basket to a grove of cottonwoods along the riverbank one Sunday morning in that summer of my fifteenth year. Ronnie was away visiting his grandparents on a reservation some-where in North Carolina. I missed seeing him at the fence each day and wrote to him dutifully, and when he wrote back I discovered he couldn't spell, not even my name, which he wrote out as *Evie*. I never asked if it might be a nickname, afraid it wasn't. I showed Freda the letters and all she said was, "Good looks *and* brains, at least in men, aren't all that common, Eva."

It was clear and hot already, and I could smell the clay damp along the banks from dew that had settled. It smelled like the ravine at night in Yazoo City, wet earth and minerals so potent my mouth watered when I breathed deep.

I had eaten great handfuls of river mud when Freda had taken me down to the water when I was younger, and had smeared what I didn't eat on my body, watching it dry orange in the sun, so tight on my skin it cracked and fell off in chunks as I ran. When I was a little older I sat for hours by the water mashing the clay into shapes; human heads with hollow eyes, cups and bowls and saucers into which I would splash water, letting it soak deep into the clay and turn it soft again.

This morning it was just the two of us, Freda with her cotton pajama top tied up high in a knot, drinking ice water from a fruit jar while she stared out across the river. The store manager had kicked her out of the Safeway once for that jar of ice water, insisting it was corn liquor, and when she'd thrown it in his face so he could smell it I'd stepped real hard on his instep. That was the day she'd said we were a team.

I was spread out on the blanket we had brought, eating a meatball sandwich, one of Freda's specialties. She wasted nothing. When the sauce was gone, out of the pot came the meatballs. She'd crumble them up on eggs, or mix them with the fried okra; this morning they'd been sliced dry onto two pieces of Sunbeam bread, the kind you can mash into a ball, throw at the ceiling, and have it stick.

Freda turned around to look at me, smoothing out the blanket with her hand as she leaned forward. It was an old Indian blanket, something her mother had given her, all orange and green and purple in a crazy pattern that looked like giant eyes on sticks.

"What are you thinking about, Eva?" she asked.

It was hard to say. Something was happening to me that summer. Whatever it was, I couldn't put my finger on it, but it had to do with how I felt inside, as if something was breaking loose from me, not exactly the way a bad cold would, but that was about as close as I could come to explaining it. And even then it didn't make any sense. I expected Freda to tell me what it was, or give me something to fix it. It scared me. I felt like I needed medicine, but that couldn't be right. I wasn't sick. Not sick, at least, in the way I was used to thinking.

"I don't know," I said, poking a finger deep into the Sunbeam bread. "I guess I want to feel good all the time, like that night with Ronnie. And not just when I'm here. All the time. I can't fight feeling bad anymore. It takes over. I don't like it."

"That can't happen—feeling good all the time," she said. "It's unnatural."

"So what do I do?"

"You'll know one of these days," she said. "Just finish school and then you can come live here—for good."

"Promise?" I said, wanting to believe it would happen, but knowing it never would.

She never got a chance to promise, which for a long time is what I thought had jinxed my life for the next twenty years. I believed that if she'd only said "I promise"—those two words taking hardly any breath at all—everything would have worked out fine.

"You hear that, Eva?" Freda asked me, turning away quickly.

"Hear what?" I asked.

"Listen."

I listened, thinking maybe it was the river noises.

"I don't hear anything," I said. "What am I supposed to be hearing?"

"*That*," she said impatiently, moving her arm out in a direction upriver from us. "Listen," she said again, more emphatically, "Just listen."

There was no wind, and sounds came up on you suddenly. I could hear something now the way you do when a radio knob is turned up slowly, the music coming closer and then nearly filling my head. I thought I could feel the ground start to vibrate beneath me.

"What is it?" I asked, excited.

"Ssh, quiet," Freda said. "Quiet now."

I had heard the sound before, rising up on a Saturday night from the tiny church that fronted the alley behind Freda's house. It was a gospel song—not a hymn, slow and reverent—and the voices yelled at full timbre and harmonized, Glory! Glories! It grew stronger and stronger, moving through the cottonwoods with such force I saw birds scatter from the trees. When I listened to that chorus of voices from my bed at Freda's I'd be covered in gooseflesh, the hair on the back of my neck pricking up, throbbing with the pulse of the music. I loved that sound, so close to the heartbeat of the river.

"Here they come," Freda said, pointing in the same direction, "Right through the trees."

I looked down at my arms and watched the skin rise up.

I saw them now, a whole congregation of black people, maybe two hundred, coming down the bank through the cottonwoods, their long white robes trailing across the red clay until they looked as if they'd been dipped in blood, their mouths open so wide as they sang I could see the soft pink of tongues and the flashing of gold teeth in the sun.

"Lord Jesus meet us by the river," I heard them sing in full-bellowed voices, not one timid note among them.

> *"Wash us in the blood,*
> *in the blood,*
> *oh the blood, dear Jesus,*
> *of the lamb."*

Several called out "Hallelujah" and fell to their knees on the shore.

I looked at Freda and she put a finger to her lips.

"If we're quiet," she whispered, "they won't go away."

Like wild animals, I thought.

The head of the congregation, a big man the color of jet, held his arms up high and spread them wide. He looked as if he were ready to ascend, his robe blowing back from a wind that had quickly risen. He called out to his people in a deep, full voice, "Brothers and sisters, walk with me now. Let these waters re-*leeve* the sins of this earth. Be saved, in the name of sweet Jesus, by the miracle of the water. By the miracle, children. Let the Lord hear you children, shout 'Hallelujah,' brothers and sisters."

He took a breath, his arms still raised high, and I could see his chest swell beneath the robe, full as a ten-year oak.

"Into the water, sisters. Into the water now, brothers. Cleanse your souls shiny white as these robes, white as the light of Jesus. Sing Hallelujah, children."

"Hallelujah!" they shouted back, so long and loud I could see the ice in Freda's water jar rattle.

My head was light with the sound of them, "*Hallelujah*"s rising in my own throat, choked back and then free again. I wanted to sing with them, thrash on the bank and roll limp into the river. The feeling was so strong I coughed and sputtered until Freda slapped me hard on the back.

They started into the river then, dozens of them, beckoned by the preacher who called out as they passed, "Bless you sister, bless you brother, sweet Jesus, bless you all. Taste the Glory, children. Submerge your souls in the Light. Praise Jesus. Hallelujah!"

"Praise Jesus," they sang back. "Praise the Lord."

And the gospel blues pulled them straight toward the water as if they had been born of it.

I watched as their robes billowed up around them, pockets of air caught in the fabric carrying them up high over their heads, and then they went down, swaying with the current, one by one, the preacher laying his broad hand atop each head, crying out, "In the everlasting blood of the lamb, I baptize you."

As they went under, their robes caught in the water like dying swans and went down with them. Some held their arms up as they went under, and I thought I could hear a "Praise Jesus" bubble to the surface.

For an instant, I moved to stand up, the call in me so strong I had to fight it. We watched them struggle up out of the water, singing as they came onto the bank, their robes heavy now and flattened against their bodies. I noticed some of the women had huge breasts, round as melons beneath the wet fabric, and that the men looked like boys, shy, surrounded by all this womanhood. They sang louder when they were clear of the water, clapping wet hands together and moving like a black and white snake, single file through the trees. In their retreat I could see the women shake their hips in rhythm to the music, and I felt a sweet pain low in my belly. If they had seen us they had not let on.

I looked down at my arms, at the gooseflesh risen up in dark points on this hot summer morning, and wished I had followed them in. I turned to Freda sitting there on the old Indian blanket, her bright, beautiful face lifted high, a peculiar smile on it that made me happy.

"I'm going in." She nodded as if she already knew.

I didn't sing as I moved down the bank toward the water, looking across to the other side where two young boys fished with cane poles. I didn't know anything to sing except "Honeycomb." But I could still hear them far down the river and imagined I was part of their congregation, about to be made pure and simple, washed free of something whose name I did not yet know. I'd seen their faces when they'd come out, lost in something that brought amazement to their eyes. They were free. Oh yes. I could see it. A miracle had taken place in that water. I swore to myself it was so. I'd seen that same look they'd had, once, in an airport, on the face of a tall black woman. She wore a two-inch-high rhinestone pin on her jacket that read JESUS. I remember reaching out to touch her as I walked past—wanting to touch her—and how she turned around quickly and smiled at me, her eyes patient and understanding, filled with a notion of heaven.

The water felt warm at first, like in Africa, then cooler further out where the bottom started to slip away. I looked back toward the bank and saw Freda watching me.

"Should I hold my breath," I called out, "or did they just go under singing?"

"I think you better," she called back. "Hold your breath, that is."

I went down slowly, the thin cotton of my T-shirt turning wet against my breasts, reminding me of Ronnie's cold hand inside my sweater.

I stayed down as long as I could, my cheeks puffed out like a guppie's, feeling the current pushing between my outspread legs, my toes gripping the firm river bottom. I felt like a reed in some underwater wind, not sure what I was doing. The water was cool and heavy with the current, and I imagined it was deep as outer space. I spread my arms out the way the preacher had done, and a thought came into my head so loud and clear my eyes opened in the dark water.

"Help me," it said, over and over, first deep, then high, then as meek as a child's plea. "Help me." My mouth opened in surprise and I tasted the rich blood of the water, choking me; and the voice grew louder. I burst into the air, taking a deep breath, wanting to be rid of it. The sun was so bright I clapped a hand over my eyes and shook my head until the thought went away.

"You baptized yet, Eva?" Freda called out.

"I think so," I said, stumbling back to the blanket, coughing.

"Finish your meatball sandwich, then. Rats come here."

"Don't you want to talk now?" I asked. "Don't you want to know what I was thinking?"

She looked serious now, and I thought of how she knew things, saw them in dreams—sometimes in broad daylight with no warning at all. I thought to myself she had heard the river.

"Say," I said to her. "Say what you know. I want to hear."

I was getting panicky, afraid she wouldn't tell me. She could be stubborn that way.

"Sometimes, Eva," she began slowly, "you have to keep your thoughts to yourself. But you'll be fine. One of these days you'll be just fine."

"What do you mean?" I demanded. "Tell me what you mean. You know something, don't you? Don't you! Say what it is."

She knew I was afraid and that I hadn't come out of the river changed or free. My time was yet to come.

"Forget about it," she said, getting up to shake the blanket. "Some things just are, Eva."

That was the last I saw of Freda for a few years. And from that moment on my life began to explode, in short bursts sometimes. In others, boom, right through the wall.

S E V E N

Before Rita sent me away to the hospital I was allowed to see my father for the first time in ten years. I was the one who had asked to see him, and I had my reasons. We'd moved from Yazoo City by then and left behind the land that had sustained me. I called it the true South and was loyal to it, believing for a long time afterward that if I'd never been torn from its sanctuary the world would have stayed as dazzling as the night sky from my bedroom window. There were no more summers in Watson Chapel with Freda working her magic. We wrote to each other faithfully but it was never quite the same.

We moved to Raleigh, North Carolina, making the trip in a fancier car that had no trailer hitch. Raleigh's rich, tree-lined streets seemed filled with well-dressed teenagers driving shiny cars bought by Daddy.

John Earl had become a big shot by then, the executive of a textile manufacturing company, and now he drove a black Lincoln and kept his liquor in a monogrammed flask. My mother kept drying out and getting soaked again, but now she had a battalion of psychiatrists who fed her pills and gave her shock treatments for depression. Freda wrote to me that shooting electricity through the brain wasn't her idea of the best way to cheer a person up. I agreed. The more Rita got zapped the slower she became, wandering around the house in a daze so thick she might as well have been drunk.

We lived in a big place with imposing white columns that were supposed to support the front porch but were just decoration, like everything else in that town. The house was a suburban colonial monstrosity meant to suggest the antebellum days of the South, prefabbed right smack in the middle of a housing development called Tree Haven. We lived on Hickory Road, which intersected with Cherry Lane, which gave way to Willow Avenue. It was a regular arboretum.

It was in Raleigh that Rita's brother, BQ, found us one rainy night. Freda had said it would happen, that one of these days he'd show up and I'd see what drinking had done to the family. I told her I knew already, but she said I didn't *really* know how bad it could get, that BQ had actually killed a man for a drink.

I remember the night he came. I was looking out my window on the second story, thinking about the ravine in Yazoo City and how on a night like this the water would be rising. I saw a man stagger up the old brick walkway, and I could tell right away it was BQ from pictures Freda had shown me. In every shot I'd ever seen of him he was skinny, dirty, and hollow-eyed. Out there in the rain he looked like a scarecrow wandering in from the field. He needed a drink badly and rammed his fist hard against the front door, so hard the banging could be heard over the fight Rita and John Earl were having. I ran down the stairs and stood behind my mother as she held the door open and looked out at BQ in the rain; his eyes were as wide and wild as a dog's stranded in the middle of the road at rush hour.

My mother didn't say a word and left me standing at the door with him while she got her purse. I wanted to say something but he spoke first. He asked if I had seen his daughter.

"She's your age," he said, and I saw spit form in the corners of his mouth as he tried to talk without slobbering. Freda had told me when the craving got bad enough, BQ's whole body went haywire.

I told him I had never met her and looked down at his dirty pants, yellow stains running from the crotch to his socks. He smelled and in his eyes I saw the hunger of a lion, something that wouldn't let go until it was fed.

"I guess she's dead," he said, seeming to believe this about his daughter, his body shaking harder now from the dampness.

My mother appeared with a check, the expression on her face uppity, as if this big house made her better than her own brother. I peeked and saw that it was for twenty-five dollars and thought to myself that three of those would pay for an hour with the psychiatrist, and three hundred of them would do for two months' drying out in the Virginia sanitarium. I was good that way with figures.

BQ's hand shook as he took the check, as bad as my mother's in the morning, and I saw the way he cast his eyes down to avoid looking at the fake white columns and his sister's face. It was ten o'clock at night, and I wondered where he'd be able to cash a check at that hour, so I found my own purse and gave him all the money in it—a lot of change and some wadded-up dollar bills.

Rita had left the door by then, not having spoken one word, no "Hello, good to see you," nothing, and when I handed BQ the money some of it spilled through his shaking fingers and rolled into the cracks of the brick walkway. He got down on his knees then, right there in the rain, and ran his hands over the bricks. I closed the door and knelt beside him on the walkway, picking up pennies and dimes, and a buffalo-head nickel I told him might be worth some money. He looked over at me and I think for the first time he really saw me. His eyes teared up all of a sudden, the way it happens when something grabs you so quickly you don't have time to stop it, and said, "I hope you never have to do this."

When we were done BQ thanked me and walked off into the night, down well-groomed Cherry Lane, and I wanted to scream— bad. I did it, high and crazy like Freda, beating my fists against the bricks until they bled.

"She's doing it again, John Earl," I heard my mother say from an open window on the first floor.

It was seeing BQ that made me want to find my father. I thought about the way BQ had said "I guess she's dead" when we talked about his daughter. I didn't want my father thinking I was dead, whether I liked him or not, I just didn't want him thinking that.

I found his address on a letter he'd sent to Rita and she'd never answered. It took a lot of looking. In the letter my father asked why my mother wouldn't write and tell him about his *only* daughter, this underlined as if it were truth, when in fact he'd already fathered another. He said he missed me. Rita never knew I read the letter. I wrote to my father and he wrote back, sending a large check, enough for a plane ticket to Fort Lauderdale with some left over for clothes.

In his letter he said I must have misconstrued his silence all those years. *Misconstrued*. It sounded high class to me so I looked the word up and wondered why he hadn't just said I must have misunderstood. He wrote about how Rita didn't want him to see me and he didn't understand why. I took this to mean he didn't construe why. He said I sounded like an intelligent young woman. I had no clue what had given him that idea, except that I had used the word *provident* to describe my decision to write to him. That may have made a difference. I was to learn my father was very big on intelligence and any display of it. He liked his children to impress him— he had five or six before his spawning days were over—and seemed to believe their smartness was a direct result of his genetic input. His bright ones were done favors from time to time, and those not so bright were ignored.

When I told Rita I was going to Florida to see him she said I would be sorry, that all the years she had tried to protect me from him would be wasted.

"So who's protecting me from you?" I asked her.

She became quiet and got that hurt look she'd get when I rattled her fragile belief that she was doing the best she could. When the doubt was really strong she made daily trips to the psychiatrist and the liquor store. By that time she'd been hospitalized ten times for alcoholism and depression, although when she was drunk she called her condition "schizophrenia." She liked the sound of an exotic malady.

John Earl told me I'd be an ingrate if I left, and of course I looked up *ingrate* and added it to my daily list of ten new words. It was something I did to kill time and so I could smart-mouth the teachers, and it fit in with Freda's notion of discipline. The *ingrate* stayed with me. I couldn't figure how a kid who was too embarrassed to open a Christmas present could be an ingrate. I had a hard time accepting gifts and never knew how to say thank you. But that wasn't what John Earl meant. He meant I wasn't grateful for what I had with him and my mother. He was right about that.

Part of the money my father sent I spent on clothes—short

dresses, skirts, and lavish underwear—and I spread everything out on my bed so my mother would be sure to see.

"You'll look like a little whore," she told me, hinting at the beginnings of her jealousy of me. Something about being a chip off the old block flashed in my mind, but I didn't say it.

On the plane to Fort Lauderdale I ended up in first class—a fluke—next to a drunk lifeguard who worked at the Fountainebleau on Miami Beach. He was returning from his father's funeral in Greensboro, maudlin and sloppy, and kept trying to make a pass at me.

"What's your name?" he asked, pouring half his drink on the seat tray and the rest in my lap. I was wearing a white A-line dress, one my mother had picked out. It was polyester and melted when I spilled cigarette ashes on it and, I noticed, turned green when bourbon soaked through it.

I told him my real name, which was a mistake.

"Eva," he said. "What a beautiful name," and then passed out with his hand on my knee. I threw it back at him and watched it slide down his leg and dangle near the floor.

The stewardess asked if I wanted a drink and I said yes, matter-of-factly, a gin and tonic. I was already practiced in siphoning John Earl's liquor supply and watering down what was left to a weak tea color. He just kept wondering why he couldn't get drunk as fast, the stupid bastard.

It was the only drink I took on that flight.

I waited for my father at the airport gate. In my purse I carried the picture taken of him in Star City, the one in which he held the kitten up under his chin. My mother said that after all these years I would still recognize him, the resemblance between us was so great. I thought maybe that was why she didn't like me, because I reminded her of him. Maybe I looked even more like him when I put on makeup and heels. Once, when she was drunk, she'd told me about his dressing up and how she'd come to know about it when she found her shoes stretched. I found a negative a few years back of my father dressed in one of Rita's girdles, his legs crossed carefully so it looked like he had nothing down there. I tried to imagine what it would be like for a man to want to do such a thing, but the harder I tried to picture him putting on a brassiere, the more confused I became.

He was a tall man, James, and he had put on weight. The first things I noticed were his legs, very muscular, his greasy hair, and the way he smelled, which was not good. He had an accent that carried the weight of an upper-crust education—the way he drew out his syllables, his voice purring and rumbling. When he said my name, waving from behind the gate, the *E* was sharp and high-pitched while the *Va* rolled out in a long, deep sigh. He sounded as if his mouth were full of something warm.

I saw him with his hand resting on the gate and wished I hadn't come. It was instinct more than anything else, one of those hardball-in-the-gut feelings that had no words to it. He had green eyes, dark as a northern sea, and in them I saw a sly craziness that had grown over the years. He looked out of whack, as if too many thoughts were going in his head at once.

James hugged me awkwardly, pressing his cheek next to mine, and I held back a gag.

"Recognized you immediately," he said in that peculiar accent.

Behind me the lifeguard was bellowing my name, pushing past people to get to me.

"A new friend?" James asked, and raised an eyebrow to indicate he questioned my taste. It was something we both did, unconsciously, shooting the left eyebrow up to show disapproval or doubt, so far it nearly crawled up the back of the head.

"He looks like a typical Miami Beach goon," James was saying, pulling at my arm. "Inbred probably. Retirement-center babies. They're really all eighty years old, but the permanent tan keeps the skin in place."

He looked at me as if I should laugh, and I raised my left eyebrow, tentatively, and said, "Really."

A crazy thought started up in my head as I moved with James through the crowded airport, watching the Latins with their heavy gold bracelets and necklaces rattle past me: This man wasn't really my father. The woman in Raleigh wasn't really my mother. I couldn't shake the thought.

"He's not my father," I heard my head say. "I don't belong here."

And I started to feel panicky, as if I didn't know where I was. My hands and feet began to sweat and my mouth went dry. I tried to attach the greasy man walking by my side to my memory of Africa, and all I could see was the back of a neck and the front seat of a jeep. I kept willing the man in memory to turn around and look at me, but his head was fixed straight ahead. The man next to me, I didn't recognize. I'd never seen him in my life. I could feel the grimace on my face and the racing of my heart. All around me things seemed to be melting. I wanted to bolt and run for the door before it melted shut. I tried to think of a way to stop what was happening and heard myself say out loud, "I don't know. I just don't know."

It helped, so I said it again.

"What's that?" James asked, turning around to look at me curiously.

We were in the parking lot now and things were starting to look right again.

"I don't know," I said, honestly.

I took a deep breath and felt the heat rise from the asphalt and scald my throat. I coughed, bracing myself against my father.

"You all right?" he asked.

"Sure," I lied.

My father's car was a rusted red Corvair, filthy inside with moldy, smelly beer cans, banana peels, fast-food wrappers, and no air-conditioning. Even with the windows down, the July sauna of Fort Lauderdale suffocated me with the man's smells. It had to have been a week, longer, since he had bathed. His was the kind of odor that comes with layers of sweat and dirt, exhaust fumes, garlic, and beer. I could taste it in the back of my throat and wanted to vomit. I kept the window all the way down and hung my head out like a dog, pretending I was sightseeing.

He didn't seem embarrassed by all the years we had spent apart, or it may have been that he was not quite aware. He had his own circuits. I wondered for a moment why he had been so anxious to see me. He began talking about my mother, a rehearsed quality to his words, as if he'd imagined how it would be having me here to listen. I sat back in my seat and tried to concentrate on his voice.

"I left your mother because she was very unstable," he was saying. This was delivered in educated, measured tones, his voice growing deeper and slower for emphasis, his eyebrow raising occasionally.

This is it, I thought, he wants to set the record straight. It's someone else's fault he left.

"And she will always be unstable," he continued. "You must have realized this by now, at your age. Schizophrenia with paranoid overtones. I suspect she's been diagnosed by now. I knew early on and told her so."

So that's where she got it. I told him, sure, she had seen psychiatrists and been hospitalized. I had a feeling this would excite him.

"Aha!" he said. "So it's confirmed. Well. It might be a good idea for me to speak with her doctor. See if you are living in a fit environment."

I wanted to say I wasn't but wouldn't be inclined to trade it for this one. But I kept my mouth shut. An unexpected twinge of loyalty to my mother began to tug at me.

"Your mother was always jealous, insecure," James went on, the Corvair doing eighty-five now on the turnpike.

"I think a lot of it had to do with the way she grew up, an orphan almost, and that crazy sister of hers raising her, what was her name, the crazy one, you know, who tried to kill your stepfather."

Now the loyalty really kicked in, and anger, the kind that made my face hot. I frowned and turned my head away. No one had said I had to like this man. I'd wanted to, but something was wrong here. This wasn't Africa and he wasn't pushing me high on a swing. That had been a dream, I was certain of it now.

"You like her, do you?" he asked, seeing my face before I turned away. "That crazy aunt? That's not good. She's the dominating sort. Oh. We needn't talk about this bloody kind of thing now."

I looked down at my left hand and noticed my fingers rubbing together the way they did when I kept the obsidian in the pocket of my jeans. Right, I thought, don't talk about it unless you want to die.

"Maybe I shouldn't have come," I said, startled to hear my voice.

I'd given no thought to saying it, but there it was. I rubbed my forehead, trying to ease away a growing headache.

James looked over at me, worried, as if he'd really fucked up now.

"No no no, Eva, darling, don't say such a thing. Sorry if I tread. You like that aunt of yours, that's fine. Why, I hardly know her. Right?"

"Right," I said, sullenly. "She's good. Freda's good."

"I'm sure she is," he said cheerily, but I knew he didn't mean a word of it. "Let's talk about something else. My wife now, right here in the present. We'll talk about her. How'd that be?"

"Fine," I said.

"She's like a breath of spring air, Eva, after that last woman."

She would have to smell like spring itself to keep from gagging with this man, I thought.

"The last woman I was with was bloody mad," he went on. "I cannot tell you how mad. Far worse than your mother. I had to have her committed. She rolled around in the front yard without a shred of clothes, in the middle of the day, for God's sake. Shock treatments didn't help. She was galvanized by them, like Frankenstein."

"How many have you had?" I asked, out of the blue.

"What?" he said, his jaw dropping a bit, surprised to hear me speak another full sentence.

"Shock treatments," I said. "How many?"

"They're a good pick-you-up," he said, regaining his composure. "I have them when I need them. I don't keep count."

In the ten years since I had seen my father, he had become a marine biologist, a profession I would later think odd for someone who became seasick with such ease. To hear him talk about his work he was on the brink of winning the Nobel Prize, and once in a manic phase would make that very claim, along with the belief that he could win the Boston Marathon despite his habit of smoking four packs of cigarettes a day. I listened to him and thought of how he'd pushed me on the swing in Africa. It was a silly thing to keep remembering. I was beginning to think he could be something of an embarrassment, given time. So I sized him up instead of trying to know him. It was easier that way.

"We'll fly over to Eleuthera tomorrow," I heard him say. "Your visit comes at a time when I'm trying to make a marine lab work over there. The research possibilities are staggering."

Jacques Cousteau, I thought. Dear old Dad.

"We'll have fun, too," he continued. He looked to me now for approval, and I gave him a smile, not wanting to appear ungrateful. "Go fishing for marlin. I remember the first time my father took me."

From the air Eleuthera looks like the bleached carapace of a turtle, surrounded by water the color of pastels in a Monet painting. The water was so clear I could see the silvery fins of fish reflecting light as we dropped in a seaplane thirty feet above the shallow water. The plane felt as if it had been put together with rubber bands and wire, and when the pilot shifted gears the engine groaned and bumped in the belly of the plane. I looked to my father to see if I should be afraid and saw an impassive face, eyes looking past the scenery into some other dimension. As we touched down in the harbor, water rose over the windows and rushed off in sheets when the wheels settled on the ramp.

Eleuthera seemed a transitory place. The natives, who had once been British subjects, worked their trade in fish, charter-boating, and ramshackle tourist accommodations. They were generally happy people, unconcerned with the passage of time—at least until the drug trade moved in and time became money, and money became so plentiful the natives carried it around in paper sacks. That was when the cars showed up on the island, moving at twenty miles an hour, sometimes faster, down the narrowly defined dirt road called King's Highway, occasionally leaving dead children and stray dogs behind them.

The island was only eight miles long, and if you stood in the middle of King's Highway you could see the harbor on one side and the white shell beach to the west. On the ocean side the land rose gracefully and then dropped slowly into the sand at the water's edge. In the brush giant banana spiders stretched out as big as the palm of a man's hand, the yellow and green of their bodies iridescent in the light. On the beach were empty conch shells, and during a storm they would rattle in the shallow water like bones.

The beach is where I spent most of the five days of my visit with my father, except for one day. He disappeared almost as soon as we arrived, after checking us into an old frame-and-stone hotel on the beach side. It had been built by the English in the late 1800s and had stood through five major hurricanes. The heavy oak of its walls was saturated with the smell of salt. I was given a room of dark-paneled wood with a basin that stood under a hole in the ceiling. A window with a warped frame and half a pane of jagged glass faced onto the ocean.

At night I watched storms move in from the Gulf Stream. The light over the purple water would turn green for an instant before the lightning struck, and then the sky would become a silver web of light.

One night a bolt struck the tin roof of the hotel and moved in sheets of frantic current outward into the air, and for a moment the entire structure looked as if it had been plugged in. That was the night my father knocked gently on my door, and when I opened it I saw him standing in the hallway, drunk. I asked what he wanted, confused by his ghostlike demeanor and the way he had slipped off so quickly. At first I had been relieved, but after a few days his absence had troubled me and I had begun to believe it was his guilt that kept him away.

He looked at me curiously, not the way a man looks at a woman but the way a woman looks at a woman, assessing my femininity, the way I had my thick hair pulled back from my face with a red scarf. It made me uncomfortable.

"Would you mind," he said, bracing himself with one arm against the doorway, "trying to call me Father."

I said no, I wouldn't mind. Then I told him to get some sleep. He waved his hand at me, passing off the suggestion, and staggered away from the door. I closed it slowly, walked over to the window with its broken pane, and thought about hitting it with my open hands. But they had just finished healing from the time I beat them against the bricks the night BQ came.

The next morning I walked down King's Highway, looking for a place that served breakfast. There wasn't much along the road: an outdoor bar with a thatched roof where an old white man sat drinking rum and milk; a vacant straw market; a black-painted frame building called The End of the World Bar; and Aunt Cora's Crawfish Pot, the only place along the road with an open door.

Inside the stone building, one of the few that had stood during the 1936 hurricane, it was dark. On the chalkboard menu there was one item, conch fritters. I saw my father sitting at the bar with a black man in a captain's hat, and he grinned as if seeing me for the first time. Where had I been? he wanted to know.

We would go fishing this morning, he told me, with Captain Ben, the black man next to him, who wore a gold shark's tooth on a heavy chain around his thick neck, and gold rings on every finger but his thumbs.

We left for the harbor, having had no breakfast, and my father talked to Captain Ben about starting a lab on the island. I trailed behind them, staring at the coconut palms as we passed, thinking that nothing had seemed real since I'd stepped off the plane in Fort Lauderdale. The thought that seized me in the airport started to push its way up again, and I fought it off by thinking of Freda out in the alley in Watson Chapel, burning trash, telling me how sometimes people do things and never have a clue why.

We moved slowly out of the harbor on Captain Ben's forty-six-foot billfisher complete with tuna tower and outriggers, a depth finder, and shiny fishing rods as thick as a thumb joint. Captain Ben told me about all the gear, proudly, as if he had bested his brothers who still fished the waters in cracked wooden boats.

I sat in the fighting chair as we crossed from the pastel water offshore to the purple ink of the Gulf Stream, which cut like a river through what my father called "the normal ocean." I surveyed the water as we moved over it, feeling the wind gather moisture to fuel the storms that crept toward the island like thieves in the night. But today the storm would not wait until dark. I could see the cumulus clouds building in the southwest, their bottoms starting to flatten out and darken.

My father rigged a pole and let the line out so the bait would skip behind the boat as we trolled. His greasy hair was glued to one side by the wind, showing a bald spot. His skin was the color of putty, and I thought it must have been a long time since he had been on a boat in the sun.

I liked him a little better out on the water and watched him as he worked the baits, thinking how well he had tied rope knots in Africa. When he was working, the darkness seemed to be driven from him. He warmed up to me a bit and smiled as he put the pole into the gimbal in front of me—straight up like a lightning rod.

"You get a hit," I heard Captain Ben call down from the bridge, "you set the bait and reel. That's all there is to it. No fancy instructions. How else you gonna learn except to do it yourself?"

I didn't like Captain Ben. I could tell he thought my father was a joke, plying him with "yessirs and nosirs," then shaking his head when my father's back was turned. I wondered why he bothered, hiring himself out like this.

"Have you ever fished?" my father finally asked, looking surprised by his own question, as if he weren't sure why an interest in me had taken hold of him at that exact moment.

I told him yes, in Mississippi, all the time, for catfish, bass, and crappie.

"Well, marlin are bigger," he said, "by about four hundred pounds."

I thought about his passion for elephants in Africa and the time he'd come through Star City skinny and sad-eyed, and told my mother of the rampage, the way he'd slaughtered elephants just to watch them drop.

"You like to kill things," I said, my heart shuddering in my chest at my boldness.

He was leaning against the gunwale, trimming bait, and I thought for a moment he hadn't heard me. I took a deep breath, relieved. Then he looked up slowly, as if he had been thinking, and I could see that he had heard. Two red marks gashed his cheeks as if I had slapped him.

"No," he began slowly. "No no, Eva. That's not it at all. I don't *like* to kill things. It's more as if I have to."

He was looking past me now.

"I don't expect you to understand," he continued. "In my family it's kill or kill yourself. Oh, God. Forget I said that. It's a sport. Nothing else."

He'd meant it though, that line. I could see the self-hatred turn his features hard as the shell on a locust. I wondered what his life had been like long before I'd been born. The only thing my mother had told me was that his father had killed himself, pushed a gun so far back in his throat it had stuck there even after the bullet discharged. Suicide. It's something that ran on his side of the family like a pastime.

The wind was picking up, churning the water into steel-colored waves, and I heard Captain Ben call down from the bridge, "She's a quiet one, sir, but pretty."

I looked up and saw him grinning at me wide enough to show four gold-capped teeth. I knew that look. I'd seen it on the bootlegger's face. I turned around in the chair and kept my back to the man.

My father stood alongside the chair now, watching the water as if he knew what he was doing. But he was beginning to look unsure of himself, as if he'd realized it had been a mistake to come.

"Are you happy, Eva?" he asked, close enough now so Captain Ben couldn't hear. "I mean, are things okay for you at home? I never know, you see, how they treat you. Your mother never writes."

I thought about it for a minute, how it was good of him to ask, and yet how it would hurt my mother if I betrayed her. Those were words she should hear from me, not from him.

"Sure," I told him. "I'm happy."

"Good," he said, sounding relieved. "I just needed to know."

The boat was rocking wildly now, and I liked the way it pushed and pulled me in the chair.

"Not being seasick is a true test of your water legs," my father was saying. "I meant to give you some Dramamine back at the hotel. Are you feeling sick?"

I told him no, I wasn't sick at all. As the boat moved up over the white crest of the waves I was feeling relaxed, almost sleepy.

"I've been sick a few times," my father said. "Everyone has their time."

I heard Captain Ben laugh behind me.

"More than a few," he called out.

I looked up at my father's face, saw the huge pores of his oily skin up close, the way his eyes blinked slowly as he stared at the water. I remembered the picture I'd brought with me—the skinny young man, the fear in his eyes, the white kitten under his chin. For an instant, and it happened so quickly I felt the pain in my throat, I wanted to tell him I loved him. It didn't matter that he had gone away, that he was no use to me now. None of it mattered for that moment, not a bit.

"I love you," I said low and into the wind, my head turned away. "I love you, Father."

He stood alongside the chair with me for two hours. His breathing grew shallow and his face took on a pallor that alarmed me. I asked from time to time if he was all right, but he did not respond. The clouds in the southwest were building higher, and their color had turned from bruised to black. I thought of the skies in Mississippi in July, a wall of black moving across the cotton fields. I had never been to sea and seen such a sky, but I knew the demon it could spawn, a tornado real as Dorothy's Kansas twister. The Gulf Stream had turned a slate color, and the waves were cresting higher, slopping over the back of the boat as Captain Ben called down, "We'd better go in. It's getting bad."

"She needs a fish," my father said, the first words he'd spoken in two hours. He was frozen to the side of the chair, his left hand gripped on the armrest so tightly his knuckles were white. On his thumb I saw what I thought to be a cut, a red vertical slash across the nail.

"You've hurt yourself," I said, pointing.

He looked down and hid his thumb quickly under the armrest, shaking his head no, unable to talk.

I sat dutifully, ignoring the fat drops of rain that had begun to fall like water balloons onto the deck. There was a roar then, the sound of a freight train moving through the sky, and I looked to see a cloud wall bearing down on us. Narrow as a finger at the base, a water spout was dropping toward the water on line with the boat. The pressure in the air dropped and a flying fish spun onto the deck of the boat, its wing broken from the impact. Everything went haywire then, the wind of the spout deafening as it approached. Captain Ben gunned the motor and my father threw up in my lap.

"It's okay. It's okay," I said to him over and over, stroking his sticky hair as he held his head over the armrest.

It was the last I would ever see of him. I returned to Raleigh to be locked away, and when my psychiatrist called my father to ask if he would come to visit, my father said I was incurable. No hope for me at all. He told the doctor that if they were smart at that hospital they'd quit wasting their time and send me on to the state asylum. I wondered for a long time what had made him say such a thing and came to figure it was his own shame.

E I G H T

Rage is a personal thing. It belongs to that *sanctum sanctorum* of the spirit, deep in there where no trust lives. I knew its color well: black, boiling up like a storm cloud on a day when the ground temperature is a good hundred and ten degrees and there's nothing that will cool the air but a full-blown electrical holocaust. It had built up over the years, grown in the night like deadly spores, and I could taste it, dark and hot in the back of my throat. It was never simple anger—that mild, distant cousin that could relieve itself with a "damnit" and an "oh shit"—I knew nothing of that anymore. There was no wild heartbeat to warn me of the strength of it and no damp palms to let me know I was about to act on it. I would come to in the middle of a rage so pure I'd know nothing of what had come before. Around me things would be broken, splintered, smashed, and there I would stand, cleansed somehow by the destruction of it all, my hands bloody and my face white. They had called me murderous when I was younger. They hadn't been far from wrong.

Soon after I came back from Eleuthera, Rita took me to her psychiatrist, my hands bandaged in thick mitts of gauze. I'd broken all the windows on the first floor of the house on Hickory Road. My boyfriend had dropped me off at two in the morning, and I'd found the doors locked, the lights out. Those locked doors had reminded me of times I had stood in some greasy carport in some new town listening to my mother inside moan, "Oh baby OH Oh, it's so good."

As a kid I'd wanted to cry when I heard her talking like that, or scream because it scared me. Now it just made me sick. I knew all about sex. I'd come a long way since that night in the snow with Ronnie. My boyfriends had taught me things; ways to move my tongue, my hips, and how to let the back of my throat relax. I never understood how they knew what I should be doing and figured another woman could probably teach me better. I was standing on the front porch rattling the locked screen door and thinking about these things, and the next thing I knew I was standing in the front yard, my arms loose at my sides, blood dripping onto my new white shoes.

There was so much blood when I was done I couldn't see the deepest cuts, and the odd thing was there was no pain. A day or so later, maybe, when the skin started to tighten and heal, but not when I did it. My fists were all I needed. I felt powerful then, strong as any grown man, and quick, but mostly I had no fear.

Once, when we were living in Mississippi, I cut open the bottom of my foot on a heap of broken glass hidden in some weeds. Chunks of skin hung loose from my heel as I walked home, leaving a half-mile trail of blood. I knew this because I looked back as I walked, thinking of Hansel and Gretel and their bread crumbs. I stood in the carport and banged hard on the door when I got home. It was locked as usual, and I remember the look on John Earl's face when he opened it. Anger. And how that look changed when he saw the widening pool of blood beneath me.

"What have you done?" he asked, and I held up my foot to show him the raw evidence. The glass had cut clear through to the muscle. He gagged, covering his mouth, and went to get my mother. I heard him whisper to her over and over, "She's not even crying, Rita. She's not crying. That's not normal."

On the night of the broken windows Rita and John Earl came staggering out into the front yard and dragged me screaming up the stairs to my room, so neatly kept there was no hint a lunatic lived there.

Along one wall were my books: philosophy, psychology—the complete works of Carl Jung—Shakespeare, erotica, books on astronomy, botany, zoology, geology, physics—I'd read them all by flashlight, with my head under the covers, often staying up until four in the morning. I didn't have to read that way, I just liked to, as if what I learned from those books would be safe only if I kept it dark and quiet.

On another wall were shelves that held my rocks, feathers, tree branches, dried flowers, lumps of red clay, and an authenic Indian arrowhead taken from the banks of the Yazoo River. My clothes were hung neatly in the closet, my shoes lined up in rows.

I remember how that room looked—down to the copy of *Man and His Symbols* lying open on my desk—as Rita and John Earl pushed me through the door. John Earl had a good choke hold on my neck and was trying to avoid my bloody hands. He never liked blood, and seeing too much of it in one place was liable to make him faint.

It was bright in my room that night, and the moon through the uncurtained window illuminated everything in detail, especially my mother's face. It hung over me, huge and pale, and I kept staring at it, wondering how it would look when she was dead. She kept rubbing a place on her hand where I had bitten her. And there was John Earl's face, bright red with anger. I remember how tight the muscles in his jaw were as he strained to hold me down, and how I wished I had a knife so I could shove it right through his pointy Adam's apple.

I thought about what I'd do to him as he held me there, hitting me hard across the face with his fist when I struggled. No, I wouldn't go for his throat. I'd hog-tie him, gag him with a sock, and then start at his crotch, the knife point jammed an inch into the testicle skin, right in between his nuts. I'd jerk the knife up then with a lot of pressure until I hit the pelvic bone, slicing his dick in half on the way. My mother wouldn't cry out anymore after that. No sir. Then I'd do his belly, all the way up to his chin, a nice clean, deep gully. It was like watching fire, thinking about cutting him up. I was breathing hard and wanted at him so bad I could feel part of me rise up, like they say the soul leaves you when you die. I'd tear so much blood out of him the white carpet would be soaked with it, so much he'd be choking on it, and then I'd stand back, look down at what was left of him and say, "Fuck you."

I started to laugh then. It was too much, the thought of saying "fuck you" to John Earl, hacked to pieces.

"What's wrong with her, for Christ's sake?" he said to Rita, when he saw I was laughing. "She's nuts."

My mother whimpered at the foot of the bed, shaking her head.

He hit me again and I started yelling at him, spitting through the blood that was running out of my mouth, "Fuck you. I hate you. I hate you both. Go ahead. Kill me, you stupid bastard. Stupid bastard. You fuck. You shit. Fuck you, you two-bit piece of shit. I'll tell Freda what you did. She'll kill you, slice your fucking throat open, and then what will you do, you chicken shit? Go ahead. Do it. Rot in hell. You're not my fucking father. I *hate* you. Every goddamned day of my life I hate you, and there's not a thing you can do about it."

I got it all out before he let me go, and he didn't hit me again, not even a slap. I like to think he saw something in my eyes then. Fate, maybe.

And then I blacked out. Someone tried to hypnotize the events of that night out of me once, but it didn't work. When I came to, the covers of my books lay on the floor, the pages ripped from them. My dresses and shirts were in shreds, and even the soles of some of my shoes had been torn loose. Red clay lay crumbled on the white carpet like dried blood. The shelves with the artifacts had been pulled from the wall, everything smashed or crumpled in heaps, the arrowhead the only thing left intact. I was holding it in my right hand, my arm raised high. Rita sat crouched in a corner of the room, her face and arms covered with deep scratches.

John Earl was gone and I wondered quickly if I had killed him. I looked to the floor for a trail of blood. No luck.

"He's left," my mother said, her voice hollow. "You ran him off, Eva. Are you happy? Damn you! Look what you've done. He's right. You *are* crazy."

I watched as she turned her head and pressed her face against the wall, huddled there in the corner of the room like an animal driven to retreat. That's why I'd hurt her. Because she had cowered; from John Earl, from life, from being my mother. I wanted loyalty from her, the kind that makes you say, "Get away from my kid, you bastard, or I'll kill you." The kind she got from me.

But I was fresh out. And as I stood staring down at her, my arms fell limp, the arrowhead dropped into the wreckage on the floor, and all I felt was tired. And hungry. Hunger so absolute I thought I could eat an entire jar of mayonnaise if it was what my hand found first.

John Earl came back of course, and I was the one who was sent away. Rita told him she'd do something about me if he promised he would never leave her again. It wasn't normal the way I'd been those last two years, she said, and did he remember how when I was younger I bit my fingernails to the quick and chewed my knuckles until they were raw? I must have been disturbed early on, she told him, and yes, what I needed was professional help. I should have known enough to get myself out of there then, but my mother worked quickly.

Psychiatrists' offices are all the same. The atmosphere anyway. It's like walking into a motel room when you're on the road. There, presto, is a tiny room filled with things you recognize: bed, chair, lamp, TV, sink, and for this you should feel comforted. Never mind it's not *your* bed, *your* lamp, *your* sink. And never mind that in the morning you'll leave it all without a second thought. For a while the motel room is yours, and you can tell yourself you live there, and that something good will come of it.

In the psychiatrist's office there is a desk, a chair, a couch, a leather-bound notepad, a tray of pens, and a lamp with a low-watt bulb. A large potted plant takes up a corner of the room. The beige room. Always beige. Or off-white. And the psychiatrist, in my experience, is male, wears tortoiseshell glasses, button-down shirts, and V-neck sweaters. Oxford loafers, no pennies. A wedding band, plain gold. Five gray hairs on either temple. He never smiles.

This was Dr. Roberts, my first psychiatrist, and something of a prototype for all who came after. I remember sitting in the thick leather chair in front of his desk, my bandaged hands resting stupidly in my lap like a couple of cones of cotton candy. I'd go to scratch my nose and be eating gauze. My right eye was swollen nearly shut where John Earl had hit me, and the skin around it felt like hard rubber.

I didn't much like this circumstance. It had become too dangerous. My mother had enlisted the help of my boyfriend in getting me to Dr. Roberts's office, telling him how I'd broken all the windows, and that if he really loved me he'd convince me to see a doctor. He told her he wasn't surprised, that I was a very angry young woman. This amused me. He was that sort of guy, the kind who would ass-kiss a parent because he was afraid not to. I didn't put a lot of stock in this particular boy, but he was all I had at the time, and I listened to his advice, wishing for a brief moment I were just an average kid like him. Straightforward. Untroubled. Dull.

So I went, thinking it could be no worse than jail, which is where my mother said I was headed if my behavior didn't change. I told her it would change all right, yes indeed, it would definitely change. This seemed to scare her, and she drove at a good fifty miles an hour down residential streets to get me to the doctor's office. I never had time to consult Freda about any of it, but I could guess what she'd have said: "A psychiatrist, Eva? Bullshit."

So here I sat, more confused and belligerent than I'd ever been, watching Dr. Roberts peer over the rim of his glasses at me.

"You've hurt yourself, Eva," he said, noting the obvious, something I hated. I wondered if he'd noticed that my eye looked like the inside of a pomegranate. I sat back and sighed, annoyed by the sudden familiarity.

"Do I mind if you call me Eva?" I said, and he looked up, perplexed.

"What? Do you mind if I call you . . ."

"Eva," I said. "Do I mind? No, not really, but it would have been polite to ask, don't you think?"

Now Dr. Roberts sighed, a nice, full, "I know what teenagers are like" sigh. He didn't like me right off. I could tell. It was that way a lot with certain men, older ones. They'd look at me first because I was pretty, and then they'd look again and a change would come over their faces. Instinct. Something that said, Keep away. She's stronger than you.

And meaner.

"As I was saying. You've hurt yourself."

"Right," I said. "I punched myself in the eye."

"I was referring to your hands," he said. "Your mother tells me you broke all the windows in the house."

"Just the downstairs," I said, trying to sound hurt by the additional blame. If I'd wanted to break them all, I thought, I would have.

"Okay, Eva. The downstairs. Why did you break *all* the downstairs windows?"

I told him I didn't know. "What do you think?" I added.

"Pardon me," he said. "Are you asking me to tell you why you broke the windows?"

That's the thing about psychiatrists. You ask a question, lob the ball into their field, and they whack it back at you. I enjoyed it for a few minutes.

"Yes," I said, "because I really don't know why I did."

"Are you angry, Eva?"

"What do you think?"

It went on like this for a while. I wasn't about to tell a man I didn't know what had been growing inside me for years, that I feared I could murder John Earl and not blink an eye. In fact, it was unlikely I would ever tell any man. It was none of his business, and something told me the more he knew the less likely I would be to leave his office with my hands unbound.

He gave up on the window question and asked me about voices and visions—hallucinations, he called them—had I heard or seen any lately? I thought of my uncle BQ and wondered how he would answer the question.

"No," I answered honestly. "Have you?"

That did it.

"I'm *not* the patient here, young lady," he said, his irritation showing. "This won't take long. Just try to answer honestly."

I hated being called "young lady." I had no conception of what it meant. There were no ladies in my family. It was a silly word when you thought about it long enough. Lady.

"Eva."

"Huh?"

Dr. Roberts was rolling a pencil back and forth in his palms, studying me closely.

"Answer honestly. I can't help you if you don't."

"I am," I said. "I'm being very honest."

"Okay. Fine. I just wanted to make sure you understood. Tell me something then. Have you ever had the feeling things are not real?"

"What things?" I asked. "How do you mean?" I was honestly stumped.

"The way things seem to you, your surroundings. Do they ever seem unreal to you?"

"How could they do that?" I asked.

I thought briefly about how I'd felt in the Fort Lauderdale airport when I'd gone to see my father, but I dismissed it. It seemed insignificant now.

"Just answer the question. Think about the question and then answer the question."

"You must get paid a lot to do this," I suggested.

He sighed again, and I could see Dr. Roberts getting old before his time, sighing at every exasperation—his wife, his kids, me.

"You're old enough to go to juvenile detention, Eva. Is that what you want?" He spoke this precisely, with just a hint of anger.

"Okay, okay," I said. "I might have felt that way when I took drugs."

He scribbled furiously on the pad, looked up at me for a long moment, and then wrote some more. I wondered how he could stare at me and not notice my eye, which was beginning to feel as if it were filled with hot sand. I lifted my hand to rub it and the gauze mitt grazed my cheekbone. Piss, I thought, I'll kill that bastard yet.

"What sort of drugs, Eva?"

"Listen," I said, truly annoyed. "I'm tired of this. My face hurts, my hands hurt, and I feel sick. I want to know why I'm here. What you're going to do. Something."

I didn't expect him to drop the drug question. It was too good. But he did. That's another thing psychiatrists do, let you off the hook when you least expect it and then save the good questions for later when you're worn down, pliant, trusting.

"I'm going to ask you that very question, Eva. Why do you think you're here?"

I wasn't prepared to tell him, didn't *want* to tell him. The question scared me, and I felt all fluttery inside. How could I say I didn't know where to go, what to do, how to do it? I didn't know. I had friends who had goals, places they wanted to be, and sometimes I'd try to imagine how they figured these things out. It had to be difficult to *really* know what you wanted to do with your life. If I pondered long enough I'd imagine a little cabin in the woods where I would live, alone, and that's as far as it got. I knew only one thing. I wanted to leave. All my life I'd thought about doing it and now I didn't know how. That had to be it or I'd have left by now. Lots of kids did it, packed up at three in the morning, walked to the highway, and stuck their thumbs out. I told myself I had to know what was coming, that I'd end up here, answering stupid questions, playing wise-guy games, staring across the desk at my future. How could I tell this man that the only way out that I knew was to destroy everything around me?

I looked at him straight on, wanting to say something he'd believe. My head was really hurting now, and I wanted to get back under the covers with my books. But there weren't any books left. I'd taken care of that. In bed with my boyfriend then, trying out a new technique. That was no good either. I'd be nothing more to him now than the girl who breaks windows. The girl who sees a shrink. In Raleigh it wasn't good to be seen with someone different. Crazy. That's what they'd call me behind my back. Once it got all over the school no one would have anything to do with me. And I had the sort of boyfriend who talked, the fool.

"I think I'm here," I started slowly, "because I'm a pain in the ass, and if my mother doesn't do something about me John Earl will leave her."

"That's it," he said.

"You're right," I said quickly, proud of myself.

"I wasn't done, Eva. I meant, 'That's it?' That's the only reason you can think of?"

"I think it's the real reason. The real reason beyond the obvious reason."

I didn't know. I didn't know anymore what the goddamned reason was. What's the reason? I asked myself silently. I don't know, I answered. I don't know. I don't know. I don't know.

"What's the obvious reason?" I heard Dr. Roberts say.

I had to think hard. I'd forgotten what he'd asked me.

"The obvious reason for what?"

"The obvious reason you're here, Eva. You said there was a real reason beyond the obvious one. What is it then?"

"Oh," I said, rubbing the gauze across my forehead. "Because I broke the windows. And I hit things. I bust up my hands when I'm angry."

I gazed over at the potted plant and saw myself uprooting it from the ceramic container and slamming the dirt ball upside Dr. Roberts's head. I laughed.

"What's amusing, Eva?" he asked, sitting back in his chair.

"That's a good question," I said. "What's amusing Eva. Not much."

"Eva," he said, wanting me to be serious, the tone of his voice suggesting that if I were, he just might be able to help me.

"Eva," he said again, "you hurt your mother. You scratched her up very badly. With an arrowhead, I'm told. Do you remember that?"

"What about me?" I said. "You think I ran into a doorknob? That's what all the housewives who get beat up say, isn't it? What about me? He hit me. With his fists. And it's not the first time. It won't be the last. He'd kill me if he could. He hates me. She hates me. *That's* why I'm here."

I screamed the last at him, like a revelation.

I heard myself then, really heard myself, and I wanted to cry. I heard the voice in my head over and over. What about me? Huh? Say. Tell me. What about me? I'm not so bad, am I? Tell me I'm not. Not so bad they'd have to hate me, get rid of me. But I *want* to leave. Help me leave, mister. Get me out. Just say you understand. Say you know it hurts when a two-hundred-pound drunk backhands you when you're eight years old. Say you know it hurts now, sitting in this chair, with that eye all funny-looking and those hands starting to throb. Please.

"Your mother told me what happened, Eva. Do you remember what you did to her? To your stepfather? Do you remember? That's what I want to know."

What about me? Come on. What about me? The voice slowed down, like a heartbeat, fading out.

"No," I said quietly, my voice dead now. "I don't remember what happened to her. And I don't care. Does that satisfy you? Or anything happening to my room. Anything. Nothing. I remember nothing."

"Does that scare you, that you don't remember?"

"It's better than remembering," I said.

And I meant it. I didn't want to know what happened when the rages came, or how I looked, or what I said. What lived in me then, I suspected, was a guardian angel, someone who went to battle when I needed protecting. And I knew in my gut there was no way to stop it except to run. Run the way I would if I were in a flat field and saw a tornado coming. And then what?

He gave me a lot of tests, Dr. Roberts. Inkblots, personality tests, an IQ, and he asked me to finish sentences.

"I would love to . . ." he said, looking up hopefully from his list of unfinished sentences, as if I might say, "have an ice cream cone."

"Chop up John Earl," I said flatly.

Why lie? I thought. It felt good to say it, even better to see Dr. Roberts's reaction, a double raising of the eyebrows and a quick, deep sigh, as if he couldn't quite get his breath.

"When I'm older I'd like to be . . ."

"Any place but here."

I did best on the IQ test, and the rest of it I guess I flunked, although I could have done a lot worse and been diagnosed with something as gloriously aberrant as hebephrenia. But that wasn't what I was, according to the tests. Nor was I schizoid, haploid, diploid, or paranoid. My mother broke the news to me, going against Dr. Roberts's suggestion that I be kept in the dark. She said I had a sociopathic personality. I looked it up. It seemed to mean I had no conscience. They were wrong about that.

I wanted to ask if you could be locked up for having no conscience, but the answer came soon enough. That night, after the visit with Dr. Roberts, I pulled a butcher knife on John Earl. We were at the supper table and he was saying something about how I wasn't nuts after all. I was just spoiled. An ingrate. A sponge. Useless. Rotten.

I got up from the table slowly, pretending I had something caught in my throat, and walked over to the sink where the knife rack was. I remember it all clearly, no blackout this time. I had my back to John Earl, and he didn't notice when I pulled a knife with a two-inch-wide blade from the rack and tested the point of it with my thumb. I figured it could carve a path through an oak if put into a strong enough hand. I liked the way the blade caught the light as I tipped it up. It was hard to hold in my bandaged hand, and when John Earl saw me coming at him, he said, "You've got to be kidding."

But just for an instant I saw that same look he'd had when Freda pulled the gun on him, like he was at the mercy of crazy women and his days were numbered.

I'd gotten about halfway to John Earl when my mother got up and ran toward the phone on the wall, screaming, "I knew this would happen. I knew it. I just knew it."

A squad of medics came and they were really dressed in white coats, just like in the movies. John Earl had me to the floor by then, his only wound a ripped shirt pocket. I'd been aiming for his heart. He held me down while one of the guys in the white coats gave me a shot. When I came to, I was in Virginia.

N I N E

Padded rooms do exist. Freda told me about them when I was a kid. She said it was where they kept BQ when he had the DTs. I'd imagined a room covered in spongy quilts, a place where you could do somersaults, back flips, and then run headlong into the wall and not get hurt. But not if you're wearing a straitjacket, which is what they had me rigged up in like a burrito. I'd heard Houdini had gotten out of them on a regular basis, even underwater, but no matter how much I twisted and sucked in my ribs, I couldn't manage more than an inch of movement beneath the thick fabric.

When I came to, I couldn't focus at first and everything seemed a dull yellow. As my sight cleared I could see that the quilted walls were indeed yellow. Years of rank breath, untempered fear, and crazy thoughts had probably turned them that shade. I breathed out my own fear and felt it settle in, right at home. I didn't scream, although I considered it. Who knew what fierce keeper paced on the other side of the door that had one meshed glass window at the top. A porthole of sorts. Instead I lay where I had been dropped—every muscle in my body aching and my neck stiff—in the corner of the room on a single mattress, no sheets beneath it. I was trying to make sense of the straitjacket and get a clear thought going at the same time. How much time passed before I locked on to one I do not know. It could have been an hour or a minute—the drugs had been potent enough to warp time—but when I remembered what had happened I tried to sit up straight. It was no use. I flopped back like a fish tossed up on the riverbank. I wriggled and inched my way off the mattress onto the quilted floor, and lay there staring at the ceiling. There was a bare bulb poking out of it, protected by a little wire cage. Why was it covered? What was I supposed to throw at it? There was nothing in the room but quilts nailed to the walls, and I was trussed up like the Christmas goose. I lay there for a while and tried to think. It wasn't easy. I'd get hold of a thought and then it would be gone. It was better if I closed my eyes, so I did. I saw my mother's face and opened them quickly.

I'd never feared her before. Now I did. I'd pushed things too far and here I was, signed, sealed, and committed by a woman who liked to play Russian roulette with a busted revolver and who would do anything to hold on to that lousy husband of hers. For a man. For a no-good, wife-beating drunk. That's why I was here. At least it's what I told myself over and over. It helped keep my eyes open, get the blood going, thinking about how wrong I'd been done. My legs felt heavy and my hair hung tangled in front of my eyes. I wanted a mirror, something to tell me I was real.

I heard the door click like tumble locks in a safe. Of course it was locked. And if it hadn't been the chances weren't good I'd be able to turn the doorknob. A male attendant stepped inside the room tentatively and looked from wall to wall as if he expected to see the place in shreds. I blinked back at him. He was young, perhaps twenty, and quite nice-looking for a blond.

"So you're finally awake," he said, smiling.

It wasn't what I'd expected, his smiling so wide and friendly.

"Where am I?" I asked, inching my way toward the wall so I could try sitting up.

"Your doctor will be here soon and fill you in."

"It's a simple question," I said. "Where am I? I have a doctor? What for?"

He looked a little hurt and I was sorry for being mean.

"Everyone here has a doctor," he said. "He'll be here soon. I'm going to cut you loose now."

He said it the way he would have if he'd been alone in the woods and come upon a wild animal in a trap. There was some pity in it, but it didn't bother me. I felt pitiful. I looked up at his face as he walked across the room and bent down to loosen the straps on the jacket. There was compassion there, the way his eyes softened when he saw me try to blow the hair out of my face.

"How do I look?" I asked him.

I had a lot of vanity then. I'd been told by enough boys that I was beautiful. Hearing the words, I felt good inside, proud, but after a while the feeling went away and I needed to hear someone say it again just to prove it was true.

"Actually," he said, "you look pretty good for someone who was wheeled in at two in the morning, limp as a rag doll."

I was loose from the jacket now and rubbed my shoulder joints where they'd stiffened up. I stuck my fingers in my hair and they caught in the thick snarls. The boy asked if I needed to use the bathroom. I told him yes.

"I'll wait here for you," he said, and opened a partition in the padded wall that had been invisible to me before. In the tiny bathroom was a jailhouse-type toilet and the kind of mirror you see at rest stops. I looked into its scratchy surface and could see that the swelling had gone from my eye.

When I came out the boy asked if he could do anything for me before he left. He said I could have breakfast after the doctor came.

"They do that to war criminals," I said.

"What's that?" he asked, looking worried.

"Keep you hungry till you break."

He didn't laugh and asked again if I needed anything.

"Could I have a comb?" I asked. "Or a brush? Anything. A toothbrush."

A very strange look passed over his face, as if my request required a major decision.

"You could hurt yourself with those things," he said. "You aren't allowed anything like that, at least for the first twenty-four hours. Observation period. It's the rules."

He hadn't said no yet.

"No," I said. "No. No. Of course not. I won't hurt myself. They brought me in because I tried to kill my stepfather. I don't want to hurt *myself*. Think about it. If I were suicidal would I want to brush my hair?"

My presence of mind was blinding. Here you are, I thought, God knows where, and you're trying to convince this guy you're sane.

He laughed, seeing my point, and said, "If I bring you a comb, you have to promise you'll put it under the mattress when you're done so I can get it when I clean the room."

"They're not going to keep me here?" I asked, hopeful.

"Not usually," he said. "Not unless you act up."

"I promise," I said. "Right under the mattress. Thank you."

He left to get the comb, and I stood in the middle of the room and stretched, feeling my muscles resist. I stretched some more and started to feel pretty good. I was hungry. Okay, I thought, I'm ready to leave.

"What's your name?" I asked when the boy came back.

He really wasn't bad-looking at all, now that I was even more awake. He was built like a ballet dancer, with legs that moved as if they were made of hot metal, and a nice tight rear end.

"Roy."

He acted shy now, as if my knowing his name changed things between us.

"I'm Eva."

"I know. It's a pretty name."

Oh, I thought, that's close. That's real close. Pretty soon he'll tell me *I'm* pretty.

"Here's the comb," he said, stepping up to me and holding it down low as if he were passing a lid of dope to me on a street corner. Such an illegal thing, this comb. I could smell him. Clean, not antiseptic, but like outside. Real air. Sunshine. And like a boy, musky and wet. It was a nice combination. I felt my belly ache and caught my breath, wanting to fall right up against him and forget everything.

"Remember," he said. "Under the mattress." And he left.

To this day I still wonder about that comb Roy gave me. It was hard-edged steel with teeth like the points on a saw. I stood holding it in my hand after he closed the door and then crept over to the mattress so I could sit in the corner and inspect it more closely. It would have taken a bit of doing to saw through my flesh with that comb, a couple of hours maybe, but it was definitely possible. Messy, sure, but what else had they given me to do? The teeth were close together, and I ran my thumb along them and heard a tinny sound like a cheap music box. Should I kill myself? I wondered. Here I am alone with this comb. This deadly comb. I laughed, thinking this is what people in padded rooms think about. It was part of the territory. You're in a padded room, you think about the other one hundred and one uses for a comb. It's the only thing in sight that has any potential. That and the light bulb, now that the straitjacket was off. I wasn't suicidal though, so I tried combing my hair. The metal teeth scraped my scalp and got knotted so tightly in my hair I thought I'd never get it out. Roy would like that, having them find me with the comb stuck to my head. I worked with it slowly, still thinking about what a peculiar gift it was. How many metal combs could there be? Two? Three? A dozen? I'd never seen one. And what did Roy expect? To come back later and find me combed within an inch of my life, scalp fragments stuck to the wall? I slipped the comb under the mattress when I was finished and waited for their next move.

It was a long time before anyone came. I looked at the window now and then, expecting to see some horror-movie face pressed up against it, but all I could see was the dim yellow light I had glimpsed in the hallway when Roy had opened the door. I had time to think. It's what came naturally, the way I expected it would when I died. It had that sort of feeling to it, and the clarity with which I remembered gave me comfort.

I'd had friends in my life, a few good ones, but Jennie Whately was the one I thought of right away. She lived down the street in Yazoo City. I could see her young brown body in the moonlight by the ravine where she would meet me some nights. Jennie was a Lolita. I knew it the first time I read the book. Humbert Humbert knew how to spot a nymphet. So did I. There was that quality about Jennie, twelve years old at the time—I was thirteen—the long lashes and downcast eyes, the way she moved like a colt when she walked, awkwardness and grace mixing into one heart-stopping gesture. Like the way she brushed her long, honey-colored hair from her face, absently, unaware of the beauty of it when it fell back across her shoulders. Or the way she tiptoed up to the edge of a diving board and dove in cleanly, never making a splash. And like Lolita she looked best in grubby clothes, her long legs growing straight down from the bottoms of tattered shorts. I loved Jennie Whately the way young girls love each other.

I remembered one night I spent at her house in summer. I'd waited for Jennie to go to sleep on the narrow twin bed, and when her breathing came slow and deep, I slipped my hand beneath the thin sheet. She was wearing a gauze nightshirt with an open throat, and I could feel beneath it, not much bigger than my thumb, the beginnings of her breasts and the way the nipples came erect as I rubbed my fingers over them. I was shaking so hard I fell off the bed and woke her. She mumbled thickly, something about sleeping closer, and I crept back into bed with her, shuddering as she wrapped her arms around my waist and lay her head on my belly. When we woke in the morning we were in the same position, not embarrassed at all, but limp and content as puppies. I thought of her now and wished that she were next to me and that I could smell her summer scent, as warm and thick as gardenias in the heat.

I thought of my mother and how she had cried the day my new kitten had died. The kitten was pure white, a gift from my aunt Leta, and I'd brought it all the way from Watson Chapel to Yazoo City, feeding it droppers of milk in the front seat of Freda's Chevy. It had a habit of sleeping in the wheel well of John Earl's car after it had been around for a few weeks. One morning John Earl backed out of the carport and the kitten, terrified, had clung to the wheel and been mashed beneath it so its insides came out through its mouth. I never knew why John Earl showed it to us that way. Rita cried all day and into the night. I remember her standing in the kitchen, trying to make a salad for supper, and how she doubled over the cutting board and sobbed so hard I thought she'd collapse. John Earl came in from the living room then and said, "Why you

crying, Rita? 'Cause the cat got the butter squeezed out of him?"
And then he laughed.

That's how it looked though, exactly. After he said it Rita just
sat down, right there in the middle of the kitchen floor, tears stream-
ing down her face. I remember thinking as I stooped down to hug
her, what a good heart she had. I thought of that now, starting to
believe somehow, some way, she'd have a heart for me. She'd understand why I'd done what I'd done and set me free.

I thought about Freda's laugh and her bright, beautiful face held
up toward the trees, and the sun as we sat that day by the river,
the last summer I saw her. I thought of her saying, "You baptized
yet, Eva?" and I could feel myself smile.

I remembered the sound of the gospel singers crying out their
salvation in Hallelujahs so loud they rang out now in this padded
room.

Ronnie was in my thoughts, that poor half-Choctaw boy who
couldn't spell, couldn't write, but could feel. I remembered the touch
of his hand cold and sharp under my sweater that New Year's Eve,
and the way the black rabbit fur hat looked in the snow, warm and
alive as a full-grown cat.

I ached. In my heart, my throat, my belly, I ached, so bad it felt
like someone had hold of me from inside. I wanted some of it back,
those times that were good or bad or painful. It didn't matter which,
because if I could be someplace else and know what I knew now,
maybe I could change. Go back and make myself not want John
Earl to die. Go back and turn the rage into something good. But
it was too late. I knew it. I wished the pain would go away. I'd
never felt it like this, so vivid and relentless. Getting mad usually
kept the tears from coming, but now I could feel them hot behind
my eyes and thick in my throat as if I had swallowed lead. I doubled
over the way my mother had on the floor in Yazoo City and wept
until my stomach hurt. I remembered Africa and the lion and I
cried harder. I thought of the boy who wore his sister's shoes. Of
my father's face in the picture taken in Star City. And finally, I
thought of myself when I had come to that morning—had it been
morning? Roy had said there would be breakfast—tight inside the

straitjacket, my hands burning from old wounds, locked in this room—mistrusted, hated, alone. And I stopped crying, quick as pulling up the handle on a well pump.

I heard the door open then but stayed crouched in my corner, my hair tangled again and wet with tears. Soft footsteps moved across the padded floor toward me.

"Hello, Eva," I heard a deep voice say. "I'm Dr. Fox."

T E N

The name suited him. From beneath my hair I could see a man whose ears were swept back and pointed at the top like a jackal's. They looked as if hair should be growing out of them. His face was narrow and his jaw square, his eyes the color of the Gulf Stream off Bimini, a grayish purple that looked unreal. His hair was crew-cut and steel-gray, topping off a body that looked to be well over six feet tall. He grinned at me and I saw the pointed incisors.

"So, Eva," he said, sitting down cross-legged on the floor. "You mind if I sit down a moment?"

His accent was pure Virginian, lazy and snobbish. I didn't want him too close to me, so I pressed harder into the corner.

"Go away," I said. "Just go away."

"How are you feeling?" he asked, ignoring my request, leaning back on his elbows as if he planned to stay awhile.

My head was spinning. They're going to ask me this a lot, I thought. How do you feel, Eva? What do you feel, Eva? So how *did* I feel? Scared. So I said it.

"Well, I can imagine I would be scared, too, Eva. Do you know where you are?"

I wondered for a moment if he would be scared, this jackal-man, if he were tied up in a jacket in a rubber room. I couldn't imagine it. He wasn't the sort to be captured. I could tell by his eyes.

"Eva," he said again. "Do you know where you are?"

"A hospital."

"What hospital?"

"I don't know. They didn't bother to tell me."

"They?"

"Anyone. I'd guess it's where my mother goes."

I wished he would hush up. I had no energy left for questions. Trying to follow him made my head hurt. All I wanted was to be left alone so I could come up with a plan.

"That's right," Dr. Fox was saying. "You're in Virginia at Blue Ridge, so you must know, then, what sort of hospital this is."

"Funny farm," I said, remembering the comb under the mattress. It wasn't as good as a butcher knife, but it had possibilities.

"Psychiatric," he said, and smiled.

I didn't like it when he smiled. I wondered if he had a wife, and, if he did, how she managed to kiss him around those teeth.

"How long will I be here?" I asked, moving out from the corner a little now, trying not to look helpless. It wouldn't do to look helpless if I was talking furlough.

"That depends."

"On what?"

"You, Eva. It depends entirely on *you*. How you progress."

"I'm fine," I told him, noticing the scars on my hands. I tried sitting on them so he wouldn't see. "Just fine."

"No no no, Eva," he said, with some passion. "You are *not* fine. People end up here for different reasons, and none of those reasons is because they are fine. You're sick, dear, and you need time to get better."

Dear, I thought. He called me dear. That word had such an odd effect on me. It's the sort of word a grandmother uses, quaint, soft, forgiving.

"Do I *have* to stay here?" I asked.

He pulled his knees up to his chin and pressed a finger to his sharp nose. I thought perhaps he was giving the question some thought.

"Yes," he said finally. "You've been committed by your mother for ninety days, and beyond that time she has the right to keep you here until you're of legal age. I'm not saying that will happen, but it's a possibility. I want to be honest with you."

"That's a year," I said. "A year. A whole year!"

"It's time to concentrate on helping yourself, Eva, not on how long it will take."

I didn't hear anything he said for a while. A year. Oh, I had been stupid. Very very stupid. Jail couldn't have been any worse. I should have killed him. In his sleep. They let juveniles off for that sort of thing. And I could have run, gone to court and then skipped out the back door. To where? Freda's? No. That's the first place they would look. California. How would I get there? Hitchhike, that's it. Find a boy and hitchhike with him. Then what? I looked around the room. They'll have to let me out of here sooner or later, I thought. There has to be a way out. Give it some time, I told myself. Don't screw it up.

"Eva," I heard Dr. Fox saying. "What are you thinking?"

"What?" I asked.

"Where did you go? You were deep in thought. I don't think you've heard a word I've said."

"I was thinking about taking a bath," I lied.

"You can do that today. I'm going to have you moved to another section. And after that we'll visit three times a week. You'll have group five days a week, every morning."

"Group?"

"Group *therapy* with some of the other patients."

It hadn't occurred to me there might be others.

"Oh," I said, thoroughly disinterested. "What else?"

"Breakfast, dinner, and supper. The food's not so bad. I eat it."

He laughed at himself then, such a funny man.

"And occupational therapy with one of the attendants twice a week. I believe you met him already. Roy."

I could occupy myself with Roy just fine, I thought, giving Dr. Fox an evil look. I wondered if he had any clue what went through my head.

"Do you have any other questions, Eva?"

Any other questions. He sounded like the captain on a cruise ship. I had other questions all right. One special one that started forming in my gut and chest, a horror pushing its way up—something so frightening my mouth went dry and my palms and feet started to sweat. What else was it they did here? I felt the fear before I knew what had started it. My head was still fuzzy from the drugs, and I was having trouble remembering. It was something terrible. Worse than being tied down. I remembered, and at that moment I could feel myself shaking, cold all over, and I needed to go to the bathroom. Shock treatments. That's what they had given my mother. Forty of them. She'd told me all about it. How they'd dragged her screaming to the treatment room and jammed a rubber bit in her mouth, and held her down while they turned on the juice, electrodes pasted on her temples, the wires running to a control box. How she'd felt like she was going to suffocate, and then she'd wake up all sore from the convulsions and not know where she was. She told me how the nurses held her legs and how she tried to scream past the rubber bit but couldn't make any noise. And I'd seen how she'd been afterwards. Confused, wandering from room to room, picking up things and putting them down, asking what day it was, who I was. Buttering her fingers at the supper table. And the way she talked about it when she came out of the fog, over and over, how bad it was. It had scared the life out of me. Electricity through your brain. Dear God, don't let them do that to me, I thought. Don't let them. I'll be good. I promise.

"Eva, what's wrong?" I heard Dr. Fox as if from the bottom of a well.

"Shock treatments," I said, my tongue sticking to the roof of my mouth. "You won't give me shock treatments, will you? I won't be needing any of those."

I looked him straight in the eye now, the way the condemned must stare at the eyes of the executioner, looking for some last hope of reprieve. What I saw was resignation. I could feel the sweat run down the inside of my shirt.

"Eva," he said, very seriously now. The initiation talk was over. "We do everything here within our power to help people. Electro-convulsive therapy is one of our treatment tools."

Oh God, I thought. It's got a nice name. It's a tool now. They will. They *will* do it to me. Oh Jesus, get me out of here. I was starting to hyperventilate. My hands felt numb and my ears were ringing. It was my worst fear. The beginnings of it came from summer storms in Mississippi, seeing lightning split whole trunks of trees and blow out television screens. It was a power more magnificent and deadly than any other. I'd heard about a boy who'd been struck by lightning near the river in Watson Chapel and how he'd danced around after the bolt hit him, shaking like a mad dog, foam coming out of his mouth. And then he'd just dropped dead into the water, and it hissed around him he was so hot. I used to pray each night it would never happen to me, and then later, after I'd heard Rita's stories, I'd pray they'd never wire me up the way they had her.

"Are you saying yes or no?" I shouted at the doctor. "Yes or no? You said you'd be honest. Yes or no? Tell me."

"You're obviously afraid of ECT, Eva," he said very calmly.

Certainly he'd never had any himself or he wouldn't be so god-damned calm about it.

"There's no need to be. And I can't give you an answer at this point. But when we decide on a course of treatment, and if ECT is part of that treatment, I'll be sure to tell you."

I hated him. Where was that comb? I wanted to tear his face off with it, hack him up, spit on him. But fear came up to drive away the anger, and it was as cold as the bottom of a grave. I was trapped and there could be no heroics. I *had* to be good. And if I'm good, I thought, they'll notice.

"Okay," I said, taking a deep breath. "Okay. You just tell me what I need to do here and I'll do it."

Dr. Fox stood up abruptly and held his hand out to me. I looked at it for a moment and then extended my own. It seemed such a silly thing to do.

"I'll see you in a few days," he said. "It's been good talking to you. You'll be moved to Section Fifteen later today."

"Good talking to you, too, asshole," I said after he closed the door.

E L E V E N

Section Fifteen was a hole, a damp prison of a basement with little individual cells that were fitted with metal doors, locked tight at night. In each cell was a twin bed, nearly as wide as the room.

A nurse had taken me there, out of the padded room and through halls that wound through each section of the hospital. I was checking carefully to see where the exit signs were located.

Section Three was where they kept the really bad ones, the nurse told me. She didn't say this to make me feel better. She wasn't that sort of woman. I could tell by the way she wouldn't look at me directly, talking out of the corner of her mouth like a tour guide. She was young, maybe five years older than I, and not pretty. She wanted to be. I could tell by how much makeup she wore, the pancake kind that clots up in oily pores and streaks orange when you sweat. She had it laid on thick, like cement off a trowel. Her name tag read MISS HECK. And the false eyelashes, very popular then, gave her a startled look, as if the world bewildered her. She probably wished my nose were a little bigger and my eyes a little smaller. I wondered if it made her feel better, thinking I was crazy. Some girls in high school were that way about me, trying to find something wrong so they could dismiss me. I fucked their boyfriends anyway.

As we passed through Section Three I noticed a woman whose age I could not determine, immobile against the wall. She wasn't *leaning* on the wall, she was part of it, stone still, her eyes the same color green as the paint. What surprised me was the freshness of her hair, bright blond curls poofed out like Orphan Annie's, and those same cartoon eyes, blank as holes punched in paper. I imagined she was the girl who'd floated in the ravine years ago, grown up now. Her mouth hung open, and saliva puddled around her lower lip and gathered in the corners. I stopped right in front of her and studied her face, thinking if I looked close enough I might see dust in the lines beneath her eyes. I asked if she was okay, hoping her eyelids would flutter or she'd suck in the spit.

"She won't answer you," Miss Heck said. "She can't."

I asked why that was.

"She's catatonic," the nurse said. "She's sick. Just like you. And the doctors are trying to help her, just like they'll help you."

The bitch. So nice and slow and easy, right out of her mouth with that Virginia accent. "She's sick. Just like you." *Not* like me, I thought. I'm not pegged to a wall, peeing down my leg, waiting to be wheeled off like warehouse stock. My eyes aren't dead. I can see what's around me, better than you think, lady. I wanted to pop Miss Heck right across her ugly face, not a slap but a good backhand fist to her pancaked jawbone. I imagined it would feel like wet clay, oily and pliable, and that I'd have to whack it real hard to make a dent. Then I thought about the shock treatments and shoved my fists into the pockets of the limp cotton robe they'd given me. Control. That's what I needed. And patience. I gave the nurse an evil look but she missed it.

"Fresh air might help," I said softly, right into the blond woman's face so she could feel my breath and maybe jumpstart right there on the spot. Let me breathe some anger into you, honey. I wanted to help her. I thought about her stiff and cold at night and wondered if those long, shapely legs of hers had ever been wrapped around a man. Or if anyone had ever said to her, "You've got the prettiest head of hair I've ever seen."

Did she think? Or had that landscape inside her been leveled by wildfire, smoke coming out her ears when it happened? Had some man put her here? I looked into her moss-colored eyes, the tip of my nose nearly touching hers as I stretched up on my toes, and said, softly again, "I'll be around if you want to talk."

The nurse had a firm grip on my arm by then. I could see the dull edges of the fingernails she was trying to grow.

"You're not to worry about her," she said, and steered me off down the corridors, past gibbering, frightened-looking women, raving with their private pains.

"Where are the men?" I asked, as we took the first flight of stairs leading to the basement of the hospital.

"Men?" the nurse asked, looking bothered.

"Men," I said. "Patients who are men. Where do you keep them?"

"They're in a different wing," she said, pressing a fingertip to the rim of one of the fake eyelashes. By midday she'd sweat through the glue and have to duck into a toilet to paste them back on. I could tell by her face she was worried they might fall off right there, drop like a couple of spiders down the breast pocket of her uniform.

"Do we ever get to see them?" I asked as we entered the gloom of Section Fifteen.

"Is that all you're worried about?" she said, huffy now. "Men?"

"What's your first name?" I asked, knowing before I got the words out that it was Audrey. Insignificant things came to me that way. Freda had said it would get stronger as I got older.

The nurse was silent.

"Well, Audrey," I said, seeing her jump just a little, "I like that fellow Roy.

We were standing in front of the glassed-in nurse's station now, and I could see her face grow disturbed right there in the reflection.

"He's not bad-looking, wouldn't you say?"

Chances were, she liked him. He was the sort of boy nurses had crushes on.

"Roy," she said. "Roy. The attendant Roy."

"Right," I said, looking around. "Roy. He's what my aunt Freda would call a real pretty boy. Nice body, too. You ever notice the way his hips move when he walks?"

She flushed red and her hands started to shake. It must have killed her to keep control, all that insecurity pushing up, eating at her, telling her to do something with me quick. I could feel it coming off her like heat.

"There is a hospital policy," she began very carefully, her voice cracking, "and if Dr. Fox hasn't told you about it already, I will. Hospital policy states that the patients are not to fraternize with staff members. And vice versa. It's important to keep this in mind. You are here to get well, Miss Elliot."

"What's 'fraternize'?" I asked.

"I think you get the meaning."

Yes, I know what it means, you moron, I thought. It was fun to get under her skin, I couldn't help myself.

"You like Roy, don't you, Audrey?" I said, thinking she'd probably decided someone had told me her name. Maybe Roy. Yes. Maybe Roy had said her name to the new girl: "I like this nurse, Audrey Heck. She's a fine woman. The best."

She'd had enough of me and said so. Her eyelashes were all droopy now, and I was beginning to feel sorry for her.

"I'm not crazy, you know," I said, leaning toward her as if I were giving a confidence. "I just get mad a lot."

She looked at me then, straight on, and I saw intelligence in her eyes. She was thinking I might have a point. After all, I didn't look crazy. I didn't pick at my face or wring my hands. I'd combed my hair. I was young. How could you be so young and so nuts? I saw it working in her, this notion, and then it was gone, dismissed, just as I would be when she was done handing over the thin folder she'd kept tucked under her armpit. There was a damp stain on it where she'd sweated through the uniform right onto the chart.

"Nurse Hayes," she was saying to the tired-looking black woman behind the glass of the station, "this is Miss Elliot. Dr. Fox has assigned her here. I'm sure you have a bed waiting."

"Sure I do, Audrey," Nurse Hayes said, leaning forward from her slumped position.

Nurse Hayes looked up at me as if she wished I were the very last person she ever had to see. I've heard since that that's what happens when you work with the insane. Something goes out of you. Desperation is contagious.

I don't remember anyone else in Section Fifteen but Nurse Hayes. Not one ghostly figure slipping past those metal doors, left open during the day. I try hard, but nothing comes.

I stood by the station after Nurse Heck left. I was cold. There were low, mesh-screened windows in the long room, but they let in only a faint sulphurous light that hung close to the windows and did nothing to push its way in. A green vinyl sofa was at the center of the room, and an upright cigarette stand was bolted to the floor.

"Can I smoke?" I asked the nurse, watching her fill in my name and age at the top of an official form.

She looked up, still not seeing me, and said, "You gets one cigarette an hour, on the hour, and I lights it for you."

There was a clock behind her in the tiny station, and it read three o'clock exactly. I wondered whether to push. A cigarette sounded like the one thing in the world I wanted at that moment, so I said, trying to sound cheery because she seemed to need some cheering, "Hey. Look at the time now. What do you know, it's three o'clock on the nose."

She smiled a little, the creases in her dark skin pushing up like folded leather.

"Where your cigarettes?" she asked, not looking behind her.

"I don't have any."

"Then you leave some money so I can give it to Roy. He brings smokes once a day."

"I don't have any money."

"What?" she said, coming to life. "They send you here with no money?"

I pulled the empty pockets of my robe inside out and made a pitiful face.

"No ma'am," I said. "I's broke."

"Make fun of me, will you? I can talk regular."

She was smiling though. Nurse Hayes was the sort of woman you could tease.

"Here," she said, leaning off the edge of her chair and fishing in her purse. "You can have one of mine."

All of a sudden I felt I liked her more than I'd ever liked anyone.

"It's a Kool," she said, tapping it out from the bottom of the pack so I had to pull it out butt-first.

"Why do you do that?" I asked.

"Do what?"

"Take out the cigarette that way. Tapping the bottom."

She rolled her eyes, indicating she'd heard it all now.

"Don't you know, girl?" she said. "It's the only polite way to offer a smoke. You want a smoke with my germs all over the filter?"

"I never thought about it that way," I said.

I held the cigarette between my teeth and stuck it through the little round hole in the station window so she could light it.

"Why do you have to light it?" I asked, exhaling the smoke in a big rush and watching it fan out across the window.

She looked at me now, pushing the wiry gray hair back from her forehead, and smiled real sweet. I liked her smile. It was a little sad, but there was amusement in it, too. She knew things, I could tell that. I saw by her tag she was not a full registered nurse but an LPN. They'd probably stuck her down here years ago and forgotten about her.

"Because," she said, almost grinning now, "a lighted match can be a *very* dangerous thing in the hands of a confused person. That's why we got that puke-ugly vinyl sofa. Five years ago some woman set afire the old sofa—horsehair—and I like to never got that fire out. Matches is hospital policy. Audrey done already *told* you about hospital policy?"

"Is hospital policy why you're down here?" I asked, hoping she'd keep talking.

"You smart," she said. "You real smart."

The cigarette was half gone and it was only three minutes after three.

"Go on now and finish your cigarette," she said, "and I'll get you checked in here."

I moved toward the couch and could feel the cold cement of the floor beneath the thin slippers they'd given me. Nurse Hayes was watching me, not suspiciously, but like she was putting words to me in her head. I could tell she thought I was pretty, or maybe I was just imagining it. I must look like hell, I thought. At any rate, if Nurse Hayes did think I was pretty she wasn't threatened by it, not the way Nurse Heck had been. It was always good to know where you stood with a woman.

I was sitting on the cold sofa thinking about leaving, when I noticed that the cigarette was gone and that Nurse Hayes was standing over me, holding out another.

"Go ahead," she said. "You had a long day."

I took the cigarette and sat back on the couch, trying to figure. I knew my mother. Once she had a mind to put me in here it would be tough getting out. Rita put a lot of faith in the opinions of psychiatrists. It's not that she was deep-down mean as much as she was scared, but the difference between the two didn't mean a hell of a lot now. Not from my little perch. Everything would seem better to her now that I was gone, at least for a time, or until she figured out, if she ever did, that I was not the problem.

I couldn't leave by the front door now, out into the hot Mississippi night and down to the ravine where the moon shone like a lantern into the seething life of the potholes. I couldn't tell myself home was not a prison if I could just walk away from it. I looked over at the door by the nurse's station. It was metal, too, and locked. I looked across into one of the four rooms in Section Fifteen. No windows there. The low windows with the meshed wire were possibilities, but it would take a lot of tearing with bare hands, and then Nurse Hayes would conveniently have to turn her back. There was no plan yet, but I felt one coming, just the way I could smell rain when I stood under a clear blue sky.

TWELVE

Ophelia Hayes was her full name. She'd told me so when Roy brought in our supper trays.

"We going to sit over supper together," she said. "Might as well know who we is."

Roy smiled at me when he brought the tray over to the couch where I sat, smoking yet another of Ophelia's Kools. It was the sort of smile a boy gives when he thinks he's taking good care of you. He'd brought another couple of packs of Kools for Ophelia, and some filterless ones for me, saying, "I just figured you'd like this kind."

They seemed to get along real well, Roy and Ophelia, joking with each other, Roy telling her a dirty story I could just manage to overhear.

"And then the guy shouts up to his brother," he was saying to Ophelia over by the station, "through the window on the second story of the house, says, 'What you doin' up there, Rufus?' "

Roy poked Ophelia in the ribs with his index finger, getting her ready for the punch line.

"And Rufus, he shouts down, 'I's layin' linoleum, brother.' And the brother, he calls back up real serious, 'Say Rufus, she got a sister?' "

Ophelia laughed at that one.

"Come sit with me and Eva now," she said to Roy. "While we eats."

Roy said he had to go, Section Three supper trays were waiting.

"That woman who won't talk," I said from the couch. "Does she eat?"

Roy said yes she did, and he fed her, made sure she ate every last bite. Just like that, like he already knew I cared. He said he'd see me in the morning and waved as he slipped his key in the metal door. I waved back, raising my left eyebrow, feeling stupid. It was that cruise-ship atmosphere again. It didn't fit. How could they yuk it up and wave to each other when they knew what went on around here?

"Achhhh," I said, as Ophelia sat down on the couch and pulled her supper tray toward her.

"What?" she asked. "I can eat at my station, you don't want company."

"No," I said. "That's not it."

"What then?"

"I just feel so stupid," I told her. "Sitting here on this crummy couch in a locked room, for Christ's sake, smoking your cigarettes, having a tray brought to me like I'm sick or something. And you and Roy so cheerful. What's the matter with you anyway? Doesn't this place get to you? And how can you let him make racist jokes, and *laugh* at them?"

"Well," she said, picking up a pork chop with both hands and holding it poised in front of her mouth, ready to bite, "that's a lot of questions. First off, *is* you sick? Maybe you ought to answer that one."

"No," I told her, without hesitating. "No. I'm not. I've been thinking about it a lot and I'm not."

"I didn't think so," she said, the pork chop mushing up her words.

"Oh yeah?" I said, picking up my own pork chop, noticing there was no knife. "How do you know?"

"You been around crazy people long as I have," she said, her eyes getting big, "you knows. You don't do any of them loony things. Like the way you looks around. You don't looks spooked. Crazy people looks spooked, like they got hemorrhoids in their brain. A lot of them talks to themselves, which ain't crazy in itself, but they says strange things."

"Like what?" I asked.

"Oh," she said, shrugging her shoulders up real high.

"Well . . . if I said 'em it wouldn't make no sense anyway, would it?"

"Guess not," I said, seeing her point.

We ate our supper in silence for a while. There was okra on the plate, but it was boiled, so I pushed it aside.

"You, too," Ophelia said. "I hates boiled okra. Give it to me fried any day. But boiled . . ."

She made a face.

"What about you?" I asked.

"How's that?"

"What brought you here, to this place?"

Ophelia, so long in this dark corner of the hospital, and me her only customer, felt like talking. Her man, she told me, had run away almost fifteen years ago. I asked if "man" meant husband, and she gave me a surprised look, saying, " 'Course he was. What else you think a man is?"

She had two sons, one in high school and one in prison. The one in high school was no angel, she told me, but she could say one thing for him, he wasn't in prison. The one who was in prison had robbed a local gas station.

"Now *that's* crazy," she said. "I told him, when he gots to trial, I says, 'Arnie, why you didn't just wait and see if that gas station man would *give* you the money? He didn't need to know you had no gun.' Looked at me like *I* was crazy, my own son."

She'd been working at the hospital ever since her husband had left and had been one of the first black people they'd hired.

"So why'd he leave?" I asked.

"Oh," she said. "Same old reason."

"What's that?" I asked. "Did he beat you up?"

"Don't be silly," she told me. "Nobody beats me up. I'd like to see him try. That woulda been some fun. No no no. It was another woman, some red-haired thing in a red dress he met at one of the joints, and if she be with him still . . . Hell. I don't care what they doin'. You know how many black women they is without husbands? More than stars in the sky, I bet you."

"I'm sorry," I said.

"Don't be. It's good riddance. That's all it is."

She got up to clear the supper trays, and when she came back she handed me a cigarette, saying, "And you just ended up in the wrong place, huh?"

"You serious?" I asked, eyeing her.

"Serious as a heart attack," she said. "I already says you ain't crazy, ain't I?"

So I told her sure, I was in the wrong place, and if my mother had done what normal people do, I'd be in jail just like her son. But I wasn't sure if they tried you as an adult in the state of North Carolina if you were my age.

"But you ain't killed him," Ophelia said. "I'd've heard about that."

I told her no, but I'd wanted to so badly I sometimes thought I had.

"Why's that, honey?" she asked. "Why you want to kill him so bad?"

So I told her.

I told her how it was from the time I was a little kid, how I'd rub the stone wishing he were dead, and about how Freda tried to shoot him once, but missed. I told how Rita's face looked swelled-up and purple when he'd done with her, like she'd died and lost all her air. I said how I wanted to jump on his back like a monkey when he did that, tear his throat out, and sometimes it was all I could do to hold myself back. I told her about Freda, too, and her pretty singsong voice, and the one breast, and how Freda said we were special, being part Choctaw, and that one day every-thing would be all right for me, but sometimes I didn't know about that. I told her about Rita getting drunk and trying to kill her-self, how I was afraid one time she might just do it right, and then I'd feel like hell because I hadn't killed him and saved her, and how would I live with myself after that? I told her about how I got angry and blacked out, coming to with my hands all bloody and my belly feeling so empty I could eat for days. I told her a lot of things, and in the middle of all the bad stuff she stopped me for a minute, holding her hand up in the air like she wanted to be called on.

"Say one thing," she told me, "not no person—but one thing you can think of makes you feel good just remembering it. Just one thing, and don't think about it. First thing out your mind."

"The river outside Watson Chapel," I said. "Those cotton fields off Highway 79. Stars outside the window in Yazoo City."

"That all?" she said.

"The way my aunt Freda laughs."

"Not no person," she said.

"I said the way she laughs. That's not a person."

"Okay," she said. "Go on now. Finish the story."

It was funny, after I'd said that about the river and everything, I was done. Nothing seemed quite so bad as it had when I was talking about it. I looked at Ophelia, puzzled.

She looked back at me for a long time, her face kind and reassuring. Finally, she said, "You know, Eva, your life ain't been a lot worse than a lot of folks'. I knows people could tell a story like yours and a lot worse. You know what they does?"

I shook my head.

"They gets away. No person wants to put up with craziness. Sooner or later, you be crazy too. Look at your hands, child. That's the beginnings of crazy, hurting yourself like that. And that man what raised you, that John Earl, well, did you ever think about how he'll just go on being miserable for the rest of his life and someday you be just fine? 'Cause that's what he is, miserable. No person acts that way he's not miserable. You just got to get out, find your own life. You old enough now. Your aunt Freda's right, you be fine. I knowed kids fourteen years old on their own, and just fine they are. You got a place to go?" she asked.

I told her Freda. I'd go to Freda.

"She sounds like a good woman, your aunt. A little strange, maybe, but good. She look after you till you know which place you really going."

"Will you help me?" I asked.

"How you mean?" she said.

"Get out of here," I told her.

"Why, we just met," she said. "That's a big favor to ask. I don't make decisions like this just out the blue."

• • •

I was thinking what group therapy would be like my first night in Section Fifteen as I lay on the hard slab of a bed, tucked in safely behind the locked door. Ophelia joked that it was for my protection and not hers that she locked it. That room smelled—of what I was never able to pinpoint, but it was strong enough to keep me awake. Before she turned out the light Ophelia told me I had group the next morning, and when I asked her what it was like, she said she'd never been and honestly couldn't tell me.

"From what I hear though," she said, "they yells a lot. Gets out frustrations."

"They" were neurotics, I suspected. Freda had told me about neurotics, how they blew everything out of proportion. My mother, she'd said, was one.

I'd asked if she thought I was one, and she'd said, "You have to understand what proportion is first, Eva."

I had to be escorted to the new building—that's what they called the low, pink-brick structure off to the east of the main building— by Roy, for the morning session.

Ophelia had given me a brush from the few belongings my mother had packed and had let me borrow one of her old eyebrow pencils and some dark, cherry-colored lipstick. I'd outlined my eyes with the pencil, touching the tip of it to my cigarette so it would melt and go on strong and black, and then I'd used the lipstick as rouge and put a good, thick dose of it on my lips. I didn't look too bad, all in all. I studied myself in the warped, stainless-steel mirror outside Ophelia's station, looking back over my shoulder the way Freda did, holding my head high so my neck arched in a long curve. Ophelia stepped outside to look at me and said, "Whoa. Is you exotic."

I was allowed some clothes, finally, a pair of jeans and a black sweater. I always wore black if I could. It was autumn now, and in that Virginia mountain country the days were cool.

"You look nice this morning," Roy said as he led me across the parking lot. "Nice" was pretty mild for the way he was looking at me.

"You, too," I said, flattering him more than I'd expected. He reacted with a big thank you and his face turned red. It's the one thing I hated about blonds, the way they blushed purple at the slightest excitement. I took a deep breath and looked around.

"It's pretty here," I told him, and he looked back at me, enchanted.

That was the word those high school girls used when they talked about me. They said I enchanted boys, put a spell on them. It was my eyes, one of them had told me once in a fit of anger, my eyes were wicked.

Right outside the little town of Pilot, the hospital sat on a hill overlooking a river. Hills covered in hardwood trees rose up beyond the water, and I could smell wood smoke.

"The name of that river," I said, pointing. "What is it?"

"The New River," Roy said. "N-E-W. Pretty, isn't it?"

A high bridge spanned the river from the hospital side and disappeared into the trees on the other. I thought of the bridge that spanned the Arkansas.

"Anybody ever die on that bridge?" I asked Roy.

He stopped right outside the door to the new building and looked at me once again as if he were trying to decide whether I could handle certain information. His look said I was just fine.

"Suicides," he said. "Once in a while a patient gets loose and that's where he heads."

"Huh," I said. "That's too bad. I heard of a man fell from a bridge once. An accident though. Or so they said."

Roy motioned through the door to someone inside.

"I'll be back for you in two hours, Eva," he said, placing his hand very carefully on the small of my back, so light that if I'd called him on it he could say it was a mistake.

"You'll do just fine," he was saying. "Relax and don't let them get to you. They're just a bunch of diehards."

I started to ask what he meant, but Dr. Fox opened the door and waved me inside.

The "group room," as obviously named as the new building, was soundproof and rigged with video equipment and a TV monitor. It was state of the art for the sixties, and not the sort of thing in popular use then. The patients, about five or six of them, sat in straight-backed vinyl chairs around a huge round table that held boxes of Kleenex, strategically placed, the tissues elegantly peeking out of the tops of the boxes like so many white flags. Dr. Fox showed me to an empty chair. I selected the one next to it.

"We have a new member today, group," he said, raising his eyebrows and smiling sort of cockeyed when he noticed where I'd sat. "Please welcome Eva. This is her first session."

Something about the way he said it gave me the creeps.

Dr. Fox took his place behind the video camera and signaled the group to begin. It was not what I'd expected, being taped like a sideshow.

No one spoke for a long time. There was no embarrassed fidgeting or sighing, just silence, as I studied the woman sitting directly across from me. She was tall and straight, her hair dyed jet-black and her skin tinted that godawful Q-T orange.

The woman stared back at me, haughty, sizing me up.

A chubby man, fiftyish, sat next to her, and there were others, meek housewife types, a couple of them probably in their mid-thirties. Thirty seemed ancient to me then, and forty beyond comprehension. It was an age to which my mother belonged and one in which everyone seemed to suffer crisis. I didn't know then that menopause could put the screws to you in a way not unlike having a song stuck in your head for two years straight.

I stared at my hands as the silence deepened, noticing how thick the skin was where it had scarred over. I'd heard you couldn't sweat through scar tissue; the pores were destroyed. I turned my hands over and inspected my palms. They were damp. Roy had said he'd be back in two hours. That must mean I would see Dr. Fox when the session was done. I looked over at him. He was watching me. Fine, I thought, get an eyeful. I can outwait these idiots. I was beginning to wonder what these jokers did with their full hour of therapy when the voice of the woman with the fake tan came loud across the room like she had a megaphone.

"You're very pretty. I bet you fuck a lot of boys."

My chin shot up as if I'd taken an uppercut.

"Yes, I'm talking to you, Miss Hot Pants."

"What the hell . . ." I said, the words out of my mouth before I knew I'd said them.

Swell, I thought, this is all I need, after being drugged and hauled in here like damaged goods. I raised my eyebrow and looked at the woman. She grinned maliciously, showing two straight rows of expensive-looking teeth.

"Betty says you fuck a lot of boys. Do you like them well hung or does that really matter? I think it does." It was the chubby old guy now, in an affected Jack Benny voice. When I looked up he had his right elbow cupped in his left palm and was brushing at his face with the free hand, just the way Benny did on TV.

"Leave the girl alone," one of the housewives said.

The rest of the group ignored her, but I thanked her silently, looking to Dr. Fox to see his reaction. He was impassive, moving the camera from face to face.

"What's going on here?" I asked, finally. "Is this some kind of a joke or something? What are you people doing?"

Bingo. It's all they wanted, just a little rise out of me.

"I knew your mother," Betty said. "She *was* your mother, wasn't she, the one with the sex problem? Rita? Was that it? Tried to fuck all the doctors, even my husband, the bitch. We had a name for—"

"Oh, I remember her," the chubby man interrupted. "Tall and slim like a young boy. Nice hips."

"Charlie, shut up," Betty said. "I'm trying to talk to her. There's something I want to ask, so just keep the fuck quiet for a minute."

Charlie hung his head.

I knew they wanted me to take this personally, that much I could figure. After all, I was probably the only new game to come along in some time. But I started wondering what they'd do to the woman with the Orphan Annie curls, if the orderlies wheeled her in all stiff and blank, propped her up next to the table, and left her. Would these people tear into her as they had me and then go haywire when she sat there like a stone carving? I waited.

"You like to fuck like your mama?" Betty was saying.

That did it. If there was a rule that said I had to take this, I was about to break it.

"Shut up," I said, giving them that haughty look I'd seen Freda practice in the mirror each morning. I leaned toward the table and placed my palms on it, challenging. "You don't know a goddamned thing about my mother. So shut the hell up, both of you, or you'll regret it."

"Testy," Betty said. "Isn't she?"

My hands were hurting. They had started to do that now whenever I got angry. I rubbed them hard.

"That name we called your mother," Betty started up again. "It's just a common name, really. We called her a—"

She didn't get the rest of it out. I picked up the nearest Kleenex box and lobbed it at her. The corner caught her square in the right eye. She fell back in her chair, batting at the air, yelling, "You little bitch. Why you low little bitch. Dr. Fox! I pay good money to come here."

Dr. Fox sat still, but I could see his eyes moving from Betty to me and back again. I wondered how far he would let it go.

"A *whore* is what we called her," Betty said indignantly. "What do you think of that?"

I got up from the table, the blood sounding in my head now like a train roaring down the tracks at midnight, its speed unchecked. And above the roar an overlay of sound, my mother's voice through the window in Star City, crying out, "Baby that's so good. Do it some more." I could hear her behind the locked door of the carport in Yazoo City. I could hear her in Watson Chapel, New Iberia, Big Cane, and Raleigh, the same moans over and over, a sound that made me so sick I wanted to puke.

I got to Betty as she was standing up to back away and reached my hand out to her cheek, as if to stroke it.

"Come here," I said, sweetly, coaxing her. "Come here and I'll fix that face of yours."

"Eva, sit down now. Now!"

Dr. Fox was behind me, so quick I hadn't heard him leave his chair.

"Eva," he said, very quietly, consoling, the way you do when people are out of control. "Eva, we let our emotions out here, but we don't get physical." He placed a hand on my shoulder.

"The hell you say," and I turned on the idiot, biting hard into his thumb joint. I kicked at his shins with the pointed tips of my boots.

"God, that hurt," he said involuntarily, reaching down to rub his leg.

I kneed him in the head and he grabbed hold of me but couldn't keep me for long. Charlie came forward to help the doctor, just as I got a grip on the back of a chair and swung it in front of me, yelling out, "Get the hell away from me or I'll kill you all. Let me out, goddamnit! I'm sick of this bullshit."

"Okay, Eva," Dr. Fox was saying. "Just put the chair down now. Just put the chair down. That's it. No one's going to hurt you."

"You're goddamned right," I hollered. "You let me at her for what she called my mother. That's all I want. Just let me at her."

I started crying. God I hated it when people saw me cry.

"That's good, Eva," Dr. Fox kept on. "Sit down now. Good girl. There you go. No one means you any harm."

This was as good as I could be. As much as I could take. It was pretty pitiful when I thought about it. All that resolve to avoid the shock treatments—gone—and over some dirty-mouthed, neurotic doctor's wife. How good could I have been if she hadn't crossed me? Could I have sat for months in Section Fifteen, smoking Ophelia's cigarettes, watching the clock for the hour to pass, wondering if anyone on the outside remembered my name? What would have set me off then? The unfairness of it all? The monotony? A vision of John Earl's fist hard against my mother's jaw? I didn't know. I just didn't know.

They let me be for the rest of the hour. Dr. Fox said I could stay if I behaved myself. That's the word he used, "behaved," as if I'd just shot a rock through his bedroom window and he'd let me off easy if I made good the damage. Betty excused herself and went home, her hand cupped over her eye as she shot me an evil look right before she slipped her skinny butt out the door.

"I'm going home now," she'd said to Dr. Fox once I'd calmed down.

"I understand, Betty," he'd said.

Home! Just like that, gone, no one waiting to put a latch on her. She'd get home, check in the mirror to see if her cornea was scratched, and then lie down after her trying morning in group. It killed me—she actually paid money to come to this place.

All the anger I'd felt was gone with her, poof, out the door, and I sat there thinking if only I could get away from everything that reminded me of my life, I'd be great. I stared across the table and watched Charlie fiddle with his zipper. The housewives started up, feeling safe now. They talked about depression, very civil exchanges, and I wanted to yell at them that they wouldn't be so goddamned depressed if they got divorced. Just left the bastards and took a vacation, something with a little more life to it than six weeks in a head shop.

"But I'm better since the shock treatments," I heard one of them say.

I folded my arms on the table and lay my head down, trying to think of a prayer Freda had taught me long ago.

Dr. Fox's office looked a lot like Dr. Roberts's, but smaller. Even the plants were smaller. I sat, once again, facing a shrink across a desk. I didn't wait for him to speak.

"You punish people with shock treatments here," I said.

He held a pencil between his palms, rolling it back and forth.

Vuja-de, I thought, when you *know* you've been someplace before and you never want to go back. I laughed.

"What's funny?" Dr. Fox asked.

"You're all alike," I said. "Aren't you?"

"Who's that, Eva?"

"You. Dr. Roberts. Shrinks. Never mind. Answer me. I want to know if you're going to punish me for what I did in there."

"Eva," he began, rubbing his forehead where I had kneed him, "that seems to be your major concern since you've come here. ECT. Of course we don't punish people with ECT. But your behavior does suggest a lack of control. You forget that's why you're here. You can be a danger to yourself and others."

"A danger to yourself and others," I mocked him, making my voice high, bobbing my head back and forth.

He shook his head regretfully, as if I'd disappointed him.

"I'd like an answer," I said. "To this. Answer this. Tell me, just once, honestly, one human being to another, if you think I didn't have a right to kill that son of a bitch after all those years of watching him beat my mother to shit. Tell me that. That's normal, isn't it? Don't people break after a while? They have to do *something*, don't they? Something. Leave. Get angry. Something. Doesn't that make any sense to you? And then I come here and some loony woman gets her rocks off talking about my mother that way, asking me who I like to fuck. What's the problem? you wonder. Wouldn't you get a little angry? I'm sane. As sane as you. If I don't believe that I *will* go nuts. I used to wonder—I admit it—but I don't now. Not after seeing what really passes for crazy."

"In a way," Dr. Fox said, very slowly, the way he did when something seemed to impress him, "that's a very healthy attitude. But you can't blame others for your reactions, Eva. You can't put your sickness off on someone else."

"Oh quit," I said, exasperated. "Just quit. Didn't you hear me? I'm not sick. I just need to go away. Wouldn't that be a healthy thing to do? Find someplace else to live?"

"Run away, Eva? Is that what you want to do?"

Dr. Fox sat back in his chair and lit a cigar.

"Mind if I smoke?" he asked, drawing hard on the cigar, his lips wrinkling up around the end of it.

"Mind if I don't?" I said, irritated.

"There are certain fields of thought, Eva," he said, measuring his words again, "that suggest that everyone carries a certain strain of neurosis. Genetic, almost."

"You'd like that, wouldn't you?"

"Eva," he said, ignoring me, "let's talk about something else now. Let's talk about your sexual encounters. What Betty said seemed to bother you greatly."

"Go to hell," I said.

He pushed on.

"Do you want to be kept, Eva? Is that what you want? To be a kept woman? That's very often what happens to girls with sexual patterns like yours."

"How about this," I said, watching the smoke from his cigar hovering blue in the air between us. "How about I just like to do it. Ever think of that? Instinct. My aunt Freda says it's instinct."

"Hmmm," he said, behind the smoke. "I understand your aunt is somewhat unbalanced."

"Where do you get that?" I asked, not too calmly.

"Family information your mother provided during one of her stays with us."

"Such as?" I said, biting the bottom of my lip now, tasting blood.

"Your aunt is not the patient here, Eva. You are."

"Oh thank you so much for reminding me. No. She's not, and she never would be. You know why? Because she's too damned smart to ever get in a mess like this. She tried to kill John Earl. Years ago. And she would have, too, if my father hadn't stopped her. And you know what else? She wouldn't have regretted it. Not one day, because she knew it was right."

"Right to murder someone, Eva?"

"Fuck you. Fuck you or I'll—"

"Or what, Eva. What will you do to me. Will you hurt me? Is that your solution to everything, Eva? To strike out? Hurt before you get hurt?"

It was as close as he'd gotten yet.

Dr. Fox picked up the clock on his desk and inspected it.

"Do you want to get well, Eva?"

"I want to get out of here."

"That's not what I asked you."

"Are you going to give me shock treatments?"

"That again, Eva," he said, waving his hand now through the cloud of smoke. It had gotten so thick I was feeling dizzy.

"Listen," I said. "I just get upset. That's all. No big deal."

"You're minimizing, Eva."

I slumped back in the chair and closed my eyes.

"I can tell you, Eva," he continued, "as with all our patients who seem resistant to treatment, ECT is a definite possibility. Does that answer your question sufficiently?"

"Go ahead and do it," I said, my eyes still closed. "Just do it. Get it over with so I don't have to worry about it."

"I'm going to consult with Dr. Presley this afternoon about that very thing, but not because you say so, young lady. I'll be talking with you again tomorrow after I have more time to review your records. Try to enjoy the rest of the day. Roy is probably here now to take you to OT."

I glared at him as I stood to leave, thinking This is what old feels like, so tired your legs felt like two sacks of cement grinding forward from the hip joints.

"How was group?" Roy asked as I walked into the outer office.

"I think I flunked," I told him.

He laughed.

"How's that?"

"Forget it," I said. "It doesn't make any sense anyway. And why the questions, Roy? What do they do, hire you to take notes afterward?"

I shot him a look and saw I'd hurt his feelings. Christ, I thought, why do I do that?

"I'm sorry," I said, looking at the shadow of a huge oak as we crossed the lawn to the recreation building. Its leaves were a clean scarlet in the autumn light.

I remembered how I'd gathered leaves in the autumn in Yazoo City, pressing them between waxed paper with crayon shavings. I'd take a hot iron to them then, and the crayons would melt in wild colors, soaking through the leaves and preserving them. I'd label each leaf according to shape and name. I liked the smell of them, warm and dusty, and once the crayons were melted on, they smelled just like the first day of school.

Roy had stopped beneath the oak and was looking at me.

"What?" I said. "I already said I was sorry."

"Forget it," he said. "And yes, they do ask me to tell them what you say."

"I thought so."

"You're in a lot of pain, aren't you, Eva?"

I sat down beneath the oak and started laughing.

"They tell you to say that, too, don't they? Who am I supposed to trust here?"

"I said it because I think it's true. I thought you might want to talk."

"Well I don't. Not about that anyway."

The air felt so clean it made me sleepy. I stretched out on my back and stared past the oak to the sky. Roy stood over me awkwardly, looking back over his shoulder.

"You should get up, Eva."

"Why's that?"

"It doesn't look good."

"Oh . . ." I said, "I see. Okay. I'll get up if you tell me something."

"Sure."

"Do you like me, Roy?"

He was getting nervous, shifting his weight from one foot to the other.

"Please get up," he said. "Listen, Eva. I work here. It's hard to answer questions like that. I have to think about my job."

"Forget about your job for a minute," I told him, "and just answer my question. You answer it, I'll get up."

"I guess so," he said. "You sure get awfully angry though. I mean, I haven't seen you that way, but it's what I hear."

I stood up, brushing leaves from my jeans. Roy looked relieved.

"Only when I'm pushed," I said. "Besides, all you've done is help me. How could I get angry with you? You gave me that comb. That was a big risk."

"Thanks for putting it back."

"So," I said. "Answer my question again. 'I guess so' isn't any kind of answer. I've never heard a boy say 'I guess so.' "

"You're sure of yourself, aren't you?"

"Certain situations," I said.

It smelled wonderful out here under the tree, and I could see smoke rising on the far side of the New River. It was a good name for a river, and I wanted to walk along its banks right out of the state of Virginia, through woods and flat country, past log cabins and yards filled with goats, hound dogs, chickens, rusted old trucks. I remembered the way the river had made me feel when I was younger, seeing it on a summer morning, mist rising in clumps so thick it looked like an army of bodies was floating above the water. In those moments I couldn't separate myself from it. I trusted every action it took. If it took a life by flood or drowning, I trusted. Breathing in its air, it was all I could do to keep from running to it. I was ready to go. Now.

"Yes, Eva," Roy was saying. "I do like you. How can I help it? I don't think I've ever seen another girl like you."

Oh, I thought. That. I'd forgotten the boy was with me.

"So you'll help me get out of here," I said, bending to pick up a leaf the color of a strawberry. "Say you will."

"I can't do that, Eva," he said, not meeting my eyes.

"Yes you can," I told him, stubbornly. "You know what they'll do if I don't get out of here, don't you? Shock treatments. They do it all the time."

He nodded.

"So help me. I'll take warm clothes, whatever money we can come up with. I know where I'm going and I know how to live outdoors."

"This is crazy. I'll lose my job."

"No you won't. I promise."

"Eva," he said. "I hardly know you."

He put his hand on my face then, and I could feel how much he wanted to kiss me.

"You're sweet," he said.

"No I'm not," I told him. "But I will be sweet if you want me to be. Help me out and I'll be sweeter than anyone you've ever known."

I spent the afternoon in occupational therapy making a bowl. Roy gave me a big lump of clay, smoother than the red river mud I used when I was a kid. I was reminded of those times—Freda sitting on the riverbank watching me pour brown water into the thick basins, my hands too small to shore up the sides well enough to hold more than a few tablespoons. She would call out to me from her blanket on the bank, "Eva, you make a clay face now. You do those so well. Those big hollow eyes you make are so *pretty*, sugar. Reminds me of archetypes."

I laughed, remembering how silly it had sounded.

The folks at OT weren't exactly threaded through the needle.

Roy told me they'd come from all sections of the hospital. A fellow at the table next to mine ate most of his clay before Roy caught him. A gray-looking woman worked on a prefab belt, snapping links together until the belt was a good five feet long.

I concentrated on my bowl, looking up now and then to catch Roy staring at me. He'd smile and pretend he was watching the other patients, but I knew he wasn't. It was that old magic working on him, Freda would have said. The woman's belt kept getting longer, and the guy with the clay started shoving it in his nose.

"Nice work, Eva," Roy would say every now and then, nodding at my bowl. I stained it orange, and dropped little black pellets of glaze all over the wet surface so it looked pockmarked like the moon, and dug my initials in the bottom of it, deep, so they'd be sure to remember me.

"What does this bowl mean to you, Eva?" Roy asked, staring over my shoulder now.

"Come on," I said. "They train you to say that. Hey! It's a bowl."

"Well, sure," he said. "It's a bowl. You're right."

"You ever here at night, Roy?" I asked.

"Thursdays and Fridays."

"Come see me Friday night."

"How?"

"Just come talk to Ophelia."

"Okay," he said. "I will."

He kissed the inside of my neck then, quickly, but I still felt the charge, a line of heat straight up from my thighs.

"Do it again," I whispered.

There was no Friday night, at least not the one I imagined in my head. A Friday night where you got all dressed up and fixed your face, and a boy came to the door looking nice, his hair combed so neatly he looked a little silly standing there, not quite natural, like his mother had spray-painted him before he left. And sometimes he'd have put on a good shirt that itched his neck, and he'd try to scratch when you weren't looking. The air always smelled right on those Friday nights, like it did on the state fair grounds in autumn. Pure. Freedom waiting out in that night. Possibilities. Sex. The way the boy's body looked in the back seat of the car, or on a blanket in the middle of a field with the moonlight polishing his muscles like warm oil. Oh, I'd seen boys like that so many times, and I could still smell the soap on them, could still see the way their neck muscles tensed when they moved over me nice and slow. I liked the way they got stiff beneath their blue jeans. I wanted them with their clothes on, their clothes off. It didn't matter. On those nights I'd wear dresses so the boy could push the skirt up high on my hips. I'd look down and see how nice that looked, the way his hand slid up along the inside of my thigh, and I'd get a charge up my spine when he'd moan, feeling how wet I was.

I wanted Roy to come to my cell in Section Fifteen, in his clean white attendant's coat with the set of hospital keys jangling in a loop at his waist. I wanted to feel his weight on me, help me pretend I was somewhere else on some other Friday night. And when we were done I wanted to go for pizza or just lie still until the desire came back. And after all that he'd look at me and say, "Come on, Eva, we're going to get you out of here."

That's the way I thought it should go.

I remember how Ophelia let Dr. Fox into my room that next morning. She knocked on the door very deliberately, saying, "Honey, Dr. Fox here to see you."

I knew it must be bad, his coming to my room that way, before breakfast, before I'd even gotten out of bed. I could feel my heart kick into high gear and my palms start to sweat.

"Good morning, Eva," he said, standing at the foot of my bed, reminding me of John Earl that last night in Raleigh.

"What's up?" I said, pulling the covers high as I sat up, feeling how the bottoms of my feet were damp against the sheet.

"We're going to start your series of ECT today. Just eight of them. The minimum. Dr. Presley and I feel it's best to start them immediately. We usually get better results that way. I know you must have some questions."

Eight. Just the minimum. Like a minimum death sentence. I couldn't speak. I tried and nothing came out. I couldn't cry. I tried that, too, feeling the tension like a hot rope of fire pulled tight around my neck, and if the tears had come they would have helped. Crying was always the last resort, the thing you did when it was all over.

"Eva," Dr. Fox said, from some land far away, his voice rising up from a crack in the earth where all hope had fallen. "Eva, listen to me, I know this frightens you. There's no need to be afraid. Most people don't even remember the ECT."

I could feel myself breathing now, in and out, that was good, but my hands had gone numb and my head was a wad of cotton. I thought of the electric chair, the hideous skullcap strapped to the prisoner's head. I closed my eyes.

"What gives you the right?" I finally said, my voice sounding astounded, betrayed. "I'm only seventeen years old."

"We have a boy here thirteen who's just received a series, and he's much improved."

"Improved from what?" I asked. "From what? What did he do? Talk back to his mother? I hate you. I'm underage. You can't do this?"

"Your mother has signed the consent form, Eva. She is your guardian, after all."

"Where is she?" I said. "I'll kill her."

"She signed the form on your entry, Eva. She's not here. Listen now. The attendant will be here for you in an hour, and after today you'll be picked up at 8:00 A.M. until the series is completed."

I did something then I regret. The fear was so great I thought I had no choice. I remember how I felt sitting in that bed, wet all over from fear, the front of my gown soaked with it, seeing Dr. Fox's face in shadow, backlit by the yellow light coming from Ophelia's station; how great my humiliation was; how ugly and small I felt in the green hospital gown; how the cheap slippers were tucked neatly beside the edge of the bed; how Dr. Fox did not look at me with compassion but with a certainty that I must be taken in hand and changed. That was the scariest part of all, and I swore to myself I had no choice.

I begged.

I got out of the bed, swung my legs over the side, and dropped to my knees. Carefully, I clasped my hands before him on the edge of the bed, looked up into the man's face, and said, "Please don't do this to me. Please don't," as earnest as I have ever been. "I'm begging you. Please give me another week, a little more time. I'll get better. I promise. I'm begging you. See?"

I sank down farther on the floor and bowed my head.

"Please," I said, my voice cracking.

"Get up now, Eva. I have to finish my rounds."

Just like that. Get up now, you silly little fool. Get up now.

Dr. Fox moved toward the door, and I could see Ophelia standing there, head down. It must have hurt her to see me like that. Ophelia believed in pride. It seemed I had, too, long, long ago. I lunged for Dr. Fox's coattail, held on tight, and said, again, "I'm begging you, please, Dr. Fox. Listen to me. Just listen. This is a mistake. My mother said they never helped her one bit. I saw what they did to her. Please. Help me. Don't do this. Please."

He shook me loose and didn't even look back as he strode past Ophelia to the locked metal door, where he let himself out with a key that was part of a ring of keys so fat he seemed to lean to one side as he walked. I remember just how that key looked as it went in the lock. It had one scoop and one point, and the top was perfectly square.

Don't ever let them tell you it's not so bad. Don't listen when they say, "You'll feel nothing." Cover your ears and hide your eyes when they try to get you to trust. It's a lie. I swear to God, it's a lie.

It came about in a slaughterhouse, years ago. A couple of men were observing what happened to the hog-tied animals when they were hit on the head with a sledgehammer. They went into convulsions, and those that didn't die seemed calmer afterward. It got the men to thinking. How about doing it to people? No. Not with a sledgehammer, of course—too barbaric—but with electricity, finely tuned, the voltage just enough to cause a seizure, but not enough to kill. They've never quite known what it does to the brain. The patient becomes confused, the memory goes, and sometimes the depression and the anger with it. But the effects don't last long. Maybe two weeks. And all those brain cells are gone. Zap. Thousands at a pop.

They did it in the basement, right around the corner from Section Fifteen, in a small cold room where they had the box and the headband with the electrodes set up on a gurney.

Ophelia hugged me and blessed my soul when a big, fat orderly came to get me. She said it when I went with him quietly: "Bless your soul, child."

Roy wasn't on this detail. I like to think he refused. I didn't fight, not once. Why give them the pleasure? And what's to fight for if you're doomed? I didn't cry. I prayed. Freda's Hail Mary's coming to me like a song almost forgotten.

"Blessed art thou amongst women . . ."

I'd never seen the doctor before or the nurses who attended him. He didn't bother to say good morning, perhaps knowing the irony of such a kindness, and the nurses did not smile or look at me. I damned them all.

"Pray for us sinners, now and at the hour of our death."

They strapped me to a second gurney and wheeled the one with the box up close. It was gray metal with a large black dial. I saw the cord leading from the box to a heavy-duty outlet along the baseboard. There was a mobile unit of oxygen at the head of my gurney.

"Open your mouth, please," one of the nurses said.

I held it open wide as I would if I'd been in a dentist's chair, and the nurse said, "Not so much. Just bite down."

It was a hard piece of rubber, and the taste reminded me of the hot tar that would bubble up from the street in Yazoo City. I would scoop my fingers into it, put it in my mouth, and chew as if it were bubble gum. I thought of Jennie Whately and how she said I was as bad as a pickaninny.

I said to her, "Explain what that means."

And she said, "You know, a little black child."

It made me feel good, thinking I was behaving that way, as if it were instinct and not just because the tar looked like chocolate fudge.

They tied me by the ankles and wrists with soft leather straps, but the nurses held down my arms and legs anyway, all four of them, like points on a cross.

The doctor put salve on my temples and adjusted the two flat, cold disks on the leather headband. Out of the corner of my eye I saw the cords that ran to the controls and the voltage meter on the box.

When his hand moved toward the box, I looked at his face. He was not a kind man. He looked down at me as if I had no name, no fears, no breath, no passion. How could I hate him? There was no way to stop what was going to happen, and hate did no good. I tried to scream out "No!" before the last line of the Hail Mary came to me, but the bit kept my tongue from moving.

I don't know if they heard me at all, but the sound filled my head. No-ooooo-ooo like a train whistle, long and low and insistent, growing louder the closer it came, straight past the gullies full of fire, and on to the Arkansas River where the sound echoed from bank to bank and rose free into the air and blew hard like a southwest wind through the windows on Poplar Street in Watson Chapel. And there it found an ear. I could see Freda sit up straight at the breakfast table where she was putting on her makeup and look back over her shoulder quickly, as if someone had tapped it.

And then I felt it, a force so strong it was as if I had been knocked back against the wall. As if they were pushing three hundred pounds of lead onto my chest. I remember trying to breathe, trying to remember what it felt like to breathe, how it looked when people breathed, so easy, in and out, no effort at all. How did they do it?

I was being borne away on a black river, no sight, no sound, death around the bend heavy and deep as a flood. Breathe, I thought. You'll die. Breathe. It grew heavier by the second, all that weight, so much of it. Breathe. World without end. Breathe. And then there was nothing.

I came to in another room, and there was a box of cornflakes, a bowl, and a carton of milk on a tray beside my cot. It was the first thing I noticed, like an absurd still life. The terror of the electrodes came back, and for a moment I felt the weight again and the screaming in my head. Breathe! I gulped in air. It felt dense as mercury. I tried again, relaxing. It began to feel right. Dr. Fox had lied about that, too. Maybe older people got confused and didn't know what the hell had hit them. But I had fine memory banks, very nearly photographic, and it would take a lot to pop my fuses. And all the weight I'd felt was nothing more than my diaphragm being paralyzed by the surge of electricity. They'd tried to kill me. The oxygen was to bring me around once I'd died.

I hurt. Not the sort of blinding headache I would have expected, but my back, arms, legs, and neck felt as if they'd been whacked with two-by-fours. The convulsions had done it. When they sent the electricity through you with no muscle relaxant to loosen you up, the body jumped and twitched like a dying chicken, jolts so powerful they could snap your spine.

I was still strapped down, this time with a chest and leg belt. And I was getting mad again, although I knew it didn't matter anymore how mad I got. I was getting out of here.

"Get me out of here, you fucking morons," I hollered, and didn't let up until a nurse came running to my cot.

"You idiots. Fiends. Bastards. Bitches. Cunts. Fuck you. You tried to kill me! You think this will help? I'll show you who it's gonna help. Come 'ere. Now! Let me out! Get me loose, you fucks. There's nothing else you can do. I'm not scared anymore. You hear me!"

I bucked and strained against the straps, trying to lean forward to bite at them, but I was tight in the wrap.

"How am I going to eat these goddamn cornflakes, you morons? You're sick. Come feed me then, you stupid shits."

"Miss Elliot," I heard the nurse with the fake eyelashes say. "Calm down and I'll let you eat with the straps free."

"Oh, it's you," I said, looking up. "You little twat. You'll let me eat with the straps free, will you? How nice. That's smart. Why don't you just put it in a fucking feed bag and strap it to my face? I've had it with you people. I'm not afraid anymore. What else can you do to me here? Hook up a wire to my crotch? Burn my tits? Fuck you. Here. Let me feed you some cornflakes."

I aimed at the cereal bowl and spit hard. My face felt as hot as if it had been branded with an iron. If she loosened the straps I'd tear her tits off.

I heard someone moaning to my right. I turned my head, feeling the deep bite of pain in my neck, and saw a cot next to mine, a full head of blond curls splayed out on the pillow.

"Stop," the voice said. "Just stop. Okay? Stop. You stop now. Come on. Stop, will you?" Quiet and sweet, not demanding at all. I liked the sound of that voice. It calmed me some.

"You okay?" I said to the woman who only a few days ago had hung like Christ from a post in Section Three.

"What?" the woman said, trying to move toward my voice.

"Okay?" I said. "Are you okay?"

"Well," she said, as if she were thinking about it, "if he just stops, you know, just stops—that's all I'm asking—I'll be fine. I'll be okay. Yes. Okay. A-okay. You say that well. Okay. Will you stop now?"

"Sure," I said, "I'll stop. It's good to hear you talking."

"Yes," I heard the young nurse saying, "the treatments certainly have helped."

I swung my head around.

"If I were talking to you—Audrey, isn't it?—you made-up little snatch, I'd let you know."

She looked as if she'd been slapped. Home run, I thought. Hit her where it hurts. No more feeling sorry for people.

"Miss Elliot," she said, "if you keep this up you'll have to go back to your section without breakfast."

I could see her face turn purple under the pancake makeup. What control. I admired it.

"Oh, too bad," I said. "And after all I went through to get this breakfast. Do me a favor, Audrey. Just feed it to me. Please. I'm really too sore to do it myself. Come on. I'm hungry. And I promise, I'll be quiet now."

She mixed the milk in with the cornflakes, eyeing me the way she would a rattlesnake, and took a plastic spoon from her uniform pocket.

"Hold your head up," she said.

I obeyed.

"Open wide."

"Second time I've heard that today," I said.

She spooned some cornflakes in, and I felt the soreness in my jaw, like two hinges whose seals had cracked. I chewed the food up really good, mixed a decent amount of saliva in with the milk, and spit it all back at her. One eyelash drooped and then fell to the floor, suspended in the air momentarily by a web of saliva.

"You little . . . ," she said. "You . . . you . . . little . . ."

"Bitch," I said.

"I'll get you fixed for good. You'll be sorry."

She dropped the bowl of cornflakes on the tray and brushed wildly at her uniform while the other eyelash slid down her cheek.

"Too late," I said, and started crying, sobs that came out of me like that first morning in the padded room. They gave me a shot, then. And when I woke up Ophelia was standing over my bed in Section Fifteen.

"You all right, honey?" she asked, brushing the hair off my forehead with her hand.

"Yeah," I said, my mouth thick with drugs. I felt dirty all over. Heavy and caked with something filthy. I wanted a bath, long, hot, and unsupervised.

"Roy been asking about you, sending little notes under the door. They took his key away. Seems they knows something's up."

"They're bad, Ophelia," I said to her. "The treatments. It's like they suck out your body, and crush it at the same time."

"I knows. I heard. I even seen it once."

"I don't want to know how it looks."

"I ain't tellin'," she said, putting her finger to her lips and smiling.

"You think I need them, like Dr. Fox says?"

"No."

"Then help me get out of here."

"I'll do what I can," she said.

I hadn't heard her right. It had to be the drugs, a dream, something gone haywire after they'd zapped me. I'd come to and she'd be standing there, sweet Ophelia with her tired face, saying, "I's sorry, honey. I can't lose my job. Some things just can't be helped."

"You will?" I said, testing her.

"Sure enough," she said, conviction in her voice as strong as the heartbeat of a river.

"I will, but listen, you and Roy gonna have to make it look like just you did it. Otherwise I lose the job. Roy says he can get another. I might anyways. Come to think of it, that don't scare me much."

I couldn't believe it. I had died, and in this new life people were merciful.

"Rest now," she said, smiling. "I hates to say it, but you probably have to take more treatments before you gets out. Don't want to arouse no suspicion. But you took it good today. I's real proud of you."

They gave me the rest of the treatments back to back, and it was the same each time, except now when the jolt came I held my breath and pretended it was my own free will causing all that suffering. And when my breathing stopped and everything started to go black, I saw Freda sitting there at the breakfast table, saying, "Just a little more, Eva. You can take it. Just a little more." And then there would be cornflakes, and a new nurse now because the one with the eyelashes had disappeared. The lady with the Orphan Annie curls was gone, too. I asked about her but no one would tell me anything.

The treatments are supposed to confuse you, once they really start slamming you with them. The doctors don't come around to see you then, preferring to wait until you're making sense. I suspected it was the guilt that got to them. But I never did get confused. Maybe it was my age. Or maybe, like Ophelia said, God just wouldn't let them take, and the opposite would happen to me, I'd just get more clearheaded by the day, and come time to leave, I'd know I was doing the right thing.

She packed a bag of clothes for me late one Friday night, long after the rest of the hospital had been put to bed, and gave me twenty dollars.

"Tuck it in your brassiere," she told me.

I told her they only did that in movies.

"Right," she said. "That's where I seen it first."

I thanked her, seeing how neatly she had folded the money, two worn ten-dollar bills that smelled of damp earth, and said, "You can't afford this. I can't take your money, Ophelia."

"You can't afford not to," she said. "I gets my reward later on, when you is safe."

We'd looked at a map the night before, in my room with the door closed, and I knew that the path of the New River cut across the western tip of North Carolina. I'd keep to the river for as long as I could, then pick up Highway 40 and head west into Arkansas.

Ophelia wanted me to take a bus once I was out of Pilot. I told her I would so she wouldn't worry, but the money wouldn't go that far, and I planned to hitchhike after I was off the river path.

"You go easy now," she said, "and takes a sweater under your coat. And don't let no men bother you. When you gets to your aunt's you call me at home."

She'd written the number in tiny digits on the map and pointed to it as she spoke.

I told Ophelia I loved her. It was funny how it sounded, as if I were out of practice saying it. I wanted to hold her tight and tell her that some day she'd know how right it was, helping me. I asked her Why, out of all the people who came through this place, why me?

"Because God tell me to," she said. "And I done it before, long time ago, and don't you ask no questions 'cause I ain't telling you about it."

The next night I stood outside Ophelia's station with the sack of clothes, waiting for her to get comfortable in her chair. I was nervous.

"I feels silly," she said. "Ain't nobody gonna see me here pretending to be asleep. This be silly."

"Do it anyway," I told her.

"You knows which key to take?"

I told her yes and slipped the square-headed key from her ring.

"You does study hard," she laughed. "Come kiss Ophelia goodbye now."

I ran into the station and hugged her right there in the chair, nearly knocking her over, holding her so tight I felt all her goodness covering me like a blanket. Tears came to my eyes, a sharp stinging pain that let me know I was alive.

"That oughta hold you," she said. "Now go. Go. Be quick about it. Roy be out there now. He doin' this for me, you know, not just you. Go, girl."

And she leaned back in her chair and closed her eyes.

"I's asleep now," she said. "Go break out the hospital."

The key worked fine, as smoothly as if it had been greased with mink oil. The tumble locks clicked and dropped, and I pushed open the heavy metal door to find Roy on the other side, his back flat against the dark basement wall, a finger to his lips. He said nothing as I followed behind, holding on to the tail of his jacket, down a short flight of steps and through a side door he opened easily with a key held ready.

We were outside now, on the west side of the hospital, maybe fifty yards from the banks of the New River. Roy put a finger to his lips again, and we crept across the west lawn until it merged with a grove of oak, and then, farther down toward the bank of the river, with cottonwoods.

It was cold, well into October, and drifts of fallen leaves lay black and silver in the moonlight. I could hear the sound of them, soft whispers as we pushed through the piles, knee-deep at times, down the slope toward the river. I felt the gooseflesh on my arms beneath the heavy piling of the coat and breathed fast, tasting the smells of smoke and leaf mulch. I looked behind me once and saw the hospital built upon the rise of land like some ancient prison, its dark brick walls broken occasionally by small, screened windows, the light of Section Fifteen glowing a dim yellow and then blinking out.

"Eva," Roy whispered to me fiercely. "Hurry."

We ran now and I did not look back again, not even when we heard a male voice call out, "Roy Atkins? You out there?"

"Who's that?" I asked Roy as we kept running.

"My supervisor," he said. "I told him one of the patients had left the badminton set out."

"Badminton?" I said. "They play badminton here?"

"Hush up, Eva. Keep moving."

We had reached the bank now, a smooth, sweet slope edged with sparsely set cottonwoods. It would be easy walking for a while.

Out of earshot of the hospital we talked now, cautiously.

"You have the map?" Roy asked.

I told him I did, patting the breast pocket of my coat.

"You sure you'll be safe?"

I nodded.

"Eva," he said, grabbing the arm of my coat as we approached a small hollow in the bank, "Stay with me here just a few minutes."

The moon was full that night, as bright as it had been that last night in Raleigh.

Roy looked very young in the faint light, his blond hair loose and curly from the river air. He had pretty eyes, like a girl's, long-lashed and pale blue. In the light they looked almost silver. I wondered if he'd ever tried to grow a mustache. I could feel him reach under my jacket the way Ronnie had just two years before and knew I did not want him in the same way I'd wanted Ronnie. Still, I let his hand move freely. And when he lay me down on the leaves I didn't resist. I owed this boy.

"Eva," Roy said, his voice tense with excitement. "You are the most beautiful girl in the whole world. You are. I swear you are."

He had my pants down around my ankles and the ground was wet against my backside. It was a familiar feeling, reassuring almost, as if I'd just stepped out into the backyard and spread my legs and there he was, this boy, as ready as any. I could feel him come, something that didn't always happen, way back inside me. He'd remember this, I knew, and I wanted to tell him something sweet so for the rest of his life he'd hear my voice whenever he stood beneath a full moon in autumn.

"I love you for this," I whispered in his ear, and he thought I meant the sex, which is how I meant him to take it. I doubted any girl had ever told him so.

"Oh Eva," he said, compassion in that voice. "You are sweet. I don't just like you. I love you. Let me go with you."

"No no no," I said in a hurry, standing up, panicking at the thought of him tailing me to Arkansas. "Don't be silly now. I have to go. They'll come looking soon. I'll write you. I promise."

We said good-bye there on the riverbank, and Roy reached into his jacket and pulled out a bag and a small packet of folded bills.

"Lunch and lunch money," he said, handing them to me. "I think the lunch just got mashed."

I smiled and kissed him on the mouth, full, pushing my tongue so far back I could feel the fillings in his molars, rough on the edge like little pieces of tin can. I held onto him for a long moment, not wanting to hurt his feelings, then bent to pick up the knapsack, turned, and started to make my way up the river.

"I won't forget you," I called back. "I promise."

All my life I had sought the comfort of the night and stood bound by some quiet understanding to the earth, staring up at a sky chained by its ancient constellations, pointing to them, calling out, whispering their names. Theirs were the voices beyond my bedroom window, a million solar winds that blew wild through my heart, beckoning night after night so I would know, somehow, there was a gateway to the meaning of those heavens. For a moment I knew that meaning as I watched the New River move beneath the moonlight, saw the dusty ash of the Milky Way that seemed to pulse like an amoeba as I stood, my head thrown back, studying its scape as if I were a surveyor strapped to the blazing tail of a comet. It had to do with owning yourself. Had Freda said that? It didn't matter. The stars claimed ownership to God only. I did the same as I slipped my arms through the straps of the knapsack, knowing that now I was finally going to do something that mattered. Not run, not hide, but move through the world as if I belonged here, straight on into the night without fear because I knew its habits.

I loved the smell of the damp riverbank, rich as pork frying over a campfire. I reached down into it, held it to my lips, and sucked as if I were drawing juice from a Sno-Cone. I cupped my hands and splashed the icy water on my face, tasting the minerals in it and smelling the flat, soapy scent of musk. Animals swam in this river, were born, bred, and died here. I thought of the beavers tucked safe into their wood dens for the night; of the owl come out to call the name of its prey, feed like a king, then fly to its roost to contemplate this darkness.

When I was small, people would ask what I wanted to be, the one question all children are asked and so few understand. I always had one response. Staring at the scabs on my knuckles, I would answer, "A hermit."

I suspect folks worried about me when they heard that answer because no one ever said, "Oh, come on, Eva. Think of something else."

They would look down at their own smooth hands and change the subject, or the direction of their attention altogether. And I would smile, thinking how it would be to live alone in the woods with all those wonderful things to do. Search for rocks, plot stars at night. Tame bullfrogs. Tap trees. Feed the animals. Loop a hammock made of vine from one tall bough to another and sleep high in the trees like a cat.

It was where I belonged, right out here in the heart of nowhere, where everything had its own rhythm. The hospital didn't matter, and Rita and John Earl were phantoms who couldn't catch me now because how could you catch a girl who smelled your blood on the wind and raced like an animal, poof, into another dimension?

I was going to Watson Chapel, but until I got there the sound of the river, whose hand I could almost hold, was all I knew.

THIRTEEN

Sometimes, when I was a kid, I would wake in the middle of the night, panicked, and hear the wind outside my window. I thought I could see its form move across the walls, black and writhing, up into the corners and across the ceiling where it would hang upside down like death. It was my fear hanging there, as pulsing and alive as a full sac of baby spiders. I knew the shape and sound of it, not during the day when the sun drove beasts to rest, but at night when the dreams of being alone came—dreams in which I stood in canyons with walls two miles high, crying up into air I could not see.

"I'm down here! Can't you see me? I'm down here."

And then, when I woke, the sheets would be wet, twisted around me so tight I bucked like a mule to get free.

For now, that fear was gone. As each night passed I dreamt of stars floating like globes of light down the course of the river.

For a week I followed it, the water's path steadier than the marked blacktop I glimpsed from time to time when it ran parallel with the river. I had a knife now, one I'd found along the banks the first morning, tangled in some fishing line. It was a good one, the blade maybe eight inches long, and it worked like a switchblade with the push of a sturdy button on the genuine bone casing. That's what it said—GENUINE BONE CASING—and I wondered, Whose bone? Had it held a cow upright, or was it the rutting tool of an elk carved now into this perfect sheath? I pressed the button and watched the blade flash out, the spring action on it so strong the knife jumped in my hand. I liked knives the way I liked fire, and I was fascinated by the two images together: swords gleaming in the light of a red-yellow blaze on some dark shore. There was kinship in their talents.

When the edge on a knife was good you could cut smooth through the grain of wood to its heart. And fire could down a tree as fast as any chainsaw.

This knife needed work. I could see dimpling on the blade from its being left too long in the water. I took river mud, mixed it with the sand farther up the bank, and found a flat stone on which to whet the blade, moving it back and forth across the stone, through the gray mixture of sand and mud that sparkled with flecks of mica. When I was done I raised the knife high and came down on the limb of a thin cottonwood tree as if I were moving through the woods, cutting a path. It sliced through easily and the bough dropped at my feet, its cut edge smooth.

I carried the knife in the right hip pocket of my jeans and practiced as I walked along, whipping it out as if it were a six-shooter, shouting to the trees along the riverbank, "Put 'em up!"

In my front pocket was the money from Roy and Ophelia, forty-three dollars. It touched me, thinking how they had come up with that amount—not a stiff, sterile fifty-dollar bill, but four soft tens and three ones gray with use. I'd sat on the riverbank that first morning, counted the money, and added the two digits together, making seven. Freda would have said it was good luck. She believed in the power of numerology, a practice of witches and sorcerers. She'd added the numbers of my birthdate together once, saying, "You're a seven, Eva. Pay attention to that."

I wasn't sure what sort of attention I should pay, other than keeping a running tab in my head. It was the number of the Pleiades, she told me, a group of stars called the seven sisters. The Choctaws prayed to those stars, believing their spirits had drifted down from them one dark night, back at the beginning of time. I could find them in the eastern sky some nights, flung out across the blackness like a necklace of fine white stones.

I blinked at the money in my hand and shrugged my shoulders. My aunt, the witch. What would Dr. Fox think about that?

I hadn't needed the money yet. There had been eight sandwiches in the sack Roy had given me, plain peanut butter, and I'd gotten by on one a day—half when I woke and half before I found a place to make my bed. Ophelia had even packed a toothbrush and five packs of cigarettes. Stuck to the first pack of Kools I opened was a little note that read: *One smoke a hour, girl.*

Making a bed was easy enough. As I moved west toward the autumn sun I would scout for hollows along the bank, the kind Roy and I had slipped into that last night, and they were usually sandy and warm. I would fall asleep almost immediately, tired from the day's walk and the hypnotic, rushing sound of the river. I had never known a calm as deep as this, and I whispered thanks before dropping off, knowing full well that I could have been slobbering over my supper tray in Section Fifteen, the shock treatments taken hold.

The weather had been good, the last edge of an Indian summer so brilliant it was like a bell rung once on a clear, cold morning. I had seen eagles rise on the wind currents of the river, then drop in a dead dive, their wings folded back. They would spread them wide a few feet before impact and glide off at right angles, precise in their play. There were bobwhites that cried out their two-toned whistles from the tops of cottonwoods. I'd call back the way I used to when we visited the land outside Watson Chapel, remembering how I would stand in the woods waiting for their cries, for the chance to answer back, and hear them call again—to me, I thought, always to me—those jumpy two notes that sounded like their name.

I kept to the river path for three days, not knowing yet if I had crossed into North Carolina. I drank the free-running water when I grew thirsty. It was cleaner than the Arkansas but still tasted of earth. I reasoned the animals drank it and I was no different from them, in a circumstance so like theirs now that I howled at the moon at night to proclaim the bond. They, too, had to dodge the telltale sign of captors. In their world it was the crack of brush, the heavy footsteps; a shotgun discharged in cold air; the barely perceptible whoosh of an arrow riding off the bow. I listened for the sound of my own name, called by some white-coated witch doctor high up in the hills, net in hand, his voice full of a need to catch hold of me, quick, before I disappeared. But they couldn't get me here. You didn't send posses downriver. To bus and train stations, maybe, and out onto the roads where real people traveled. Not here. I wondered briefly how they were taking it back at the hospital, and in Raleigh. Was Dr. Fox humble now, shaken by my defiance? Had he thought, for one instant, that I was more than a screwy teenager? I doubted it. Was my mother worried now, not for my safety but for John Earl's? Did she fear I might come in the dead of night, slip through some window she had forgotten to lock, take that knife down from its block in the kitchen, find her husband, and murder him while he slept? Did she fear or did she hope? Perhaps her senses were still alive in her somewhere, keeping pace with me in her dreams, knowing somehow that the danger or hope grew less the farther west I moved.

On the morning of the seventh day I took to the highway. The trees along the river had grown too thick to make a passage, and I was running low on peanut butter. The meager diet had been good, keeping my head clear, and my muscles felt strong. I checked the map in my jacket pocket, guessing that I was somewhere on the edge of the Great Smoky Mountains, in the Cherokee National Forest. The trees continued thick along the two-lane road, and I could hear the feeble buzz of cicadas holding on to the ghost of summer. It was their season now to die, and I wondered if they felt death coming, putting up a call to mask their fear.

The trees were mostly bare of leaves, and those that were left hung like delicate bright ornaments. They reminded me of the old crazy lady outside Watson Chapel, who lived in a shack made of scrap lumber, the boards lashed together with rope and wire. Michael Paul and I would walk past her house on our outings, stopping to stare at her yard, grown wild with honeysuckle and blackberries. We would stand and stare up into the oaks and sycamores where she had hung the lids of more than a thousand tin cans. In the sunlight or by the light of the moon they shone with a platinum luster, rattling in the wind, twisting in circles. I would grow dizzy watching them.

"They're magic," I would say to Michael Paul as he tried to grab hold of my hand, afraid when the old woman walked into the yard to stare back.

We took a picnic basket to her one Christmas Eve, filled with tins of food Freda had packed—and a bright red apple because I had insisted it was the one thing a witch would want—set it beneath one of the glowing trees, then ran like mad back to the '56 Chevy where Freda waited, laughing, making chicken noises. The next day we snuck back and caught her opening the tins and emptying them into a low trough where dozens of cats gathered and fought as the food dribbled out. When she was done with a can she'd take the severed lid and place it in the pocket of a workman's apron she wore. Finished, she looked up once, held both arms over her head, and waved back and forth like a sapling bowing to the wind. Then she turned her back and walked, the tin lids rattling in her pockets, into the hovel that was as crooked as she.

I thought of her now as I watched the trees, wondering how she had stood the cold. It hadn't been so bad for me, these few days, but I thought I'd never be as tough as that old woman. It worried me, not being tough.

It was my plan to hitchhike now, or at least until Altheimer, where I could hook up with the river. I had a frugal streak that made the promise of a free ride appealing. Plus it seemed magical, to stick out my thumb—a gesture of intention innocent and in-dependent at once—and by that gesture take hold of my destination.

I knew enough about hitchhiking to figure there wasn't a lot I could do until a car came along, so I sat down on the shoulder of the road, opened the knapsack, and dug out a pack of cigarettes. I'd smoked only one pack so far. I lit one now and thought about how natural it felt to smoke outside. I watched the tip of the cigarette grow an ash an inch and a half long, holding it straight up like a smokestack to see how long it would stay. It dropped when a bird flew past, a bluejay, who dove down too low, screeching at me. They were mean, bluejays, so protective of their nests they'd aim at your eyes if they were threatened. I couldn't blame them. You watched over your own.

I saw a car approaching on the upgrade, an old white sedan, and it looked so real in the afternoon light, no mirages in the cool air to interfere. I stood up to assume my duty, hoisting the knapsack onto my right shoulder, which felt good and sore now. I stuck out my thumb and smiled.

The car sped up as it passed me, and I caught a glimpse of an old woman peering over the steering wheel, studiously ignoring the fact that I was the only other human for miles.

"Huh," I said out loud, disappointed the magic hadn't taken. "You probably have a granddaughter my age."

Now that I was up I started walking downhill in the direction of the sun. I walked for a couple of hours, up and down the contours of the hills. I'd head up an incline and start counting, seeing if I could make it to the top of the rise before I reached five hundred. If I reached it at four hundred and ninety-nine I was miserably out of breath, but if I hit it at five hundred and fifty or so I was okay. Then I tried to figure how many yards it was down a hill, stepping in three-foot strides, half running from the pull of gravity. It was a weird feeling, being self-propelled, and I imagined what I'd look like to a bird perched high in one of the trees, as if I were making a crazy attempt at flight, lurching faster and faster down the hill, my arms splayed out for balance. They had to be laughing at me, I thought, as my knees buckled and I took the sort of fall I hadn't taken since grade school. I lay face down on the shoulder of the road, the knapsack flung far in front of me. I could tell without looking that my knees were skinned good.

I got up when I heard a car coming and stood there brushing at my jeans, noticing the thin blots of blood on the knees.

"Shit," I said. "That hurts."

It was another old car, this one beat-up and blue, with a large patch of rust on the passenger door. In it was a man, probably in his thirties, and he wore his black hair slicked back in a ducktail, the way Elvis had done when he first stepped out of Memphis.

"Afternoon," he said out the open passenger window, pulling alongside me.

I started walking real slow, trying to get the kinks out of my knees.

"You need a lift?" he asked, keeping pace with me.

If it had been summer I would have been sunburned by now, waiting so long for a ride, but I didn't tell him so. Looking through the open window at his dull face, the particular smallness of his eyes that were maybe brown, maybe gray, I didn't want to tell him anything. He was the sort referred to in high school as a loser, one of the great multitude of men who were just plain trouble. And it's not that they were all bad, really, but I couldn't tell right off about this one. He might just be stupid, and stupid could be harmless. He had a nervousness about him I didn't like, the way he kept shifting in the seat, leaning around the steering wheel to get a better look at me. My knees really hurt now. It would be dark soon, and if I camped at the river tonight I would make no progress.

"Where you going?" I asked, still walking, stiff-legged now.

"You hurt?" he asked.

"Fell down. Where you going?" I repeated.

"On to Knoxville," he said, trying to look bright and happy about it. "Will that put you anywhere close?"

Even I knew Knoxville was a good distance. I told him any place west was closer than here, and he laughed, not as if he were amused but as if he wasn't used to doing it. He had a scar on his upper lip that puckered when he smiled, twisting up his mouth so he looked simple.

"Come on," he said, friendly. "Keep me company for a while."

He patted the seat beside him. It was the sort of thing John Earl had done once, the year I was fifteen. He'd been drunk at the time, and the look he had in his eyes was the same as when he looked at Rita's backside. "Come keep me company for a while," he'd said, patting an empty spot next to him on the sofa, and I'd left the room in a hurry.

"I don't know," I said.

"Come on," he told me again. "Rest your legs."

I got in and rested the knapsack between my knees, on the floorboard. It was good to be sitting, and I felt sleepy right away.

"Have a beer," he said, cracking open a sixteen-ounce can. He had a six-pack by his feet, and I could tell it was fresh by the tight little beads of moisture on the cans. I looked at him as I took the beer and figured he was the homeliest man I had ever seen.

"Thank you," I said and turned to look out the window, thinking that sometime, way back in my childhood, my mother must have taught me to say thank you like that—so natural.

I confess to being naïve, or gullible, or both. "Gullible" is the word I've heard used over and over in my life, meant to describe moments of weakness or lapses in judgment. "You're gullible, Eva," I've heard people say, and for years I protested, seeing myself as the hardest cookie ever to come out of an oven. I can still sense danger and walk right into it, telling myself it's just the weather makes me feel that way, like when the clouds are low and the barometric pressure is dropping, and everything feels so heavy you can't quite breathe right.

That's the way I felt when I started drinking that beer.

"You like beer, do you?" he said.

I told him it had been some time since I'd had one.

"Why's that?" he asked, running his tongue along his lips, keeping his eyes more on me than on the road.

"Watch out!" I yelled, as he veered onto the shoulder.

I'd decided I didn't like him, not at all. It was awkward to be civil to someone you couldn't stand. I zipped my jacket all the way up to the collar. It didn't matter to him whether I liked beer or not, and he wasn't used to talking to women, that was obvious. He struck me as the kind who walked into a bar and grabbed for what he wanted and then grunted over it later. It would have to be a pretty sleazy bar, I thought, for him to have any pickings at all. He probably thought he'd done a real cagey thing, getting me in the car. I wasn't worried though. The beer was making me feel calm. If he tried anything all I had to do was throw open the door and jump.

I looked around the car. Lots of empty beer cans. No luggage; a pair of scuffed leather shoes with broken laces in the back seat. Women's shoes. I looked at his feet. He wore work boots.

"You live around here?" I asked, watching the dim shapes of trees out the window, the fading light turning them a pale yellow.

"Nope," he said, opening another beer. "Don't live around here."

I saw his face in profile, an eye narrowing, the puckered corner of his mouth turning down. He looked like a rogues' gallery portrait, angry at the camera, trapped in a lie. He forced a smile as he turned toward me. Whenever he tried to look nice his face got scary.

"Why," he said, light as he could, "I been visiting a buddy. Don't need nothin' when you go see a buddy. How about you? You got folks in—where was it—Oklahoma?"

"Arkansas," I corrected him.

I'd told him I lived in Sultan, North Carolina, and was going to

WALKING INTO THE RIVER

drive my sister's car to Arkansas, but it had broken down, so I'd decided to hitchhike.

Never heard of Sultan, he'd said.

I hadn't either.

And then he asked what my sister looked like, was she as good-looking as me. I told him she weighed two hundred pounds and had bad hair. He looked disappointed, as if this made-up ugly sister of mine had anything to do with him.

"Tell you what," he said after a while. "I may just take you all the way to Arkansas. I got nothing going for a few days. What do you say?"

I say fuck you, I thought, but I'd had another beer by then, and the thought of being driven all that way and not having to spend any money sounded good, so I asked him, "You want me to help pay for gas?"

I look back on it now and see how hard he struggled trying to look normal, how the veins on his forehead stood out when he said, "Hey. No problem. It's on me. Ladies don't have to pay."

It was the biggest lie I ever heard anyone tell.

When I told him yes, that driving me all that way would be swell, he had stepped hard on the accelerator out of plain anticipation.

"Have another beer," he said now, all chummy. "Eva, isn't it. You said your name was Eva."

I told him yes, regretting it, hoping he wouldn't remember once the night had passed.

"I'm Bob," he said.

If it was an alias, boy was he inventive. A simple name, spelled the same forward as backward. A million of them out there, teeming on the back roads like maggots. Bobs, everywhere, waiting.

I'd been thinking about men some when I was walking the river. All sorts of thoughts came to me there and I paid them a good bit of mind because Freda had said the river gave up secrets if you took the time to listen.

"You listen, Eva," she'd said, "and you'll know a lot more when you leave this water than when you came."

The way it went with men was like this: They couldn't be trusted, not most of them anyway. You took the one thing from them they wanted to give—sex—and figured out the rest on your own. I thought about all those boys I'd known in the back seats of cars, how their eyes got faraway when they were done, and there wasn't much to say. Ronnie had been sweet, and Roy, helping me the way he did, but they were exceptions. A lot of them said they loved me, but usually when my bra was down around my waist. And I hadn't wanted them *all*—I had my standards, ways of picking and choosing. They had to be pretty boys, the kind who turned heads, but even then they could be rotten. There'd been a pretty boy once who'd scared me, who'd said right when he was getting my panties off, "Act like you don't want it, you little bitch." I'd tried, figuring it was a new twist, and the more I acted like I didn't want to, the rougher he got, until I really *didn't* want to and started screaming at him to stop. He didn't stop and I never saw him again.

I say now that what happened wasn't my fault. I look it over the way I would an old scar, inspecting the depth of it, remembering how much it hurt. But when it started to happen I thought that if I hadn't been out looking for trouble, well, maybe it wouldn't have found me.

Ophelia had warned me. I see the look in her eyes to this day— so serious and stern, the way a mother is supposed to look when she wants you to listen—saying, "Don't let no men bother you." But what was I supposed to do that night when it got out of hand so fast I barely had time to be scared, to say, "Hey, don't bother me, you. Stop, will you? Just stop. Please. Stop." It was the lady with the Orphan Annie curls who'd talked that way when she came to from the shock treatments. I knew later what she was talking about and what had shut her up all those years like a ruptured drum.

I'd had part of another beer and was starting to doze off as night came on. It was clear and I could see the starlight beginning to dawn through the windshield as I lay my head against the door.

Bob reached across and patted my thigh.

"Don't!" I said, my voice thick.

"Whatever you say E-va."

I looked over at him once before I closed my eyes and noticed he was looking out the driver's window, scouting the countryside.

I wondered what he could pick out in the darkness with those tiny eyes.

There was no way to keep my eyes open any longer. I dreamt in stops and starts, none of it making any sense. Dr. Fox was there with a key ring hanging from his lower lip, his hands bound in front by electrical cord. I saw Freda in the river, naked, with three breasts, all of them welted up and bleeding as if she'd been beaten. Then the gospel singers floating in rowboats around her, silent as the air before a storm. And then there was a crow, its talons caught in my hair, beating its wings so hard the sound filled my head.

I woke up when I heard the screech of the parking brake. Slumped against the door, I sat up quickly.

"What's going on? Where are we?" I asked. I had to pee.

He was moving across the seat toward me, unzipping his pants, and I hoped for a crazy minute he had to do the same.

"Come here," he said, his voice rough. He grabbed hold of my arm and yanked at me. I could see him start to stroke himself with his left hand and noticed it was a pitiful size. He had his thumb and forefinger wrapped around it as if he were a kid holding a pencil. It made me sick. I was thinking it was a lousy thing to do, like some flaccid pervert in a movie theater, and right out here in the middle of nowhere—where was I? I tried to stick my head out the window and felt his fingers digging into the back of my neck. He pulled me away from the window, yelling in my face, "Don't you try to get away, bitch, don't you even think about it. You try, I'll kill you!"

"Stop it!" I screamed. "You're hurting me. Let go!"

He was excited now, angry. God knows what he had been thinking all that time I was asleep. I grabbed for the door handle and it spun in a full circle. Then I lunged for the window and felt his hands around my neck, pulling me down.

"Suck it you little whore, you little piece of trash."

He had a good hold on my neck, and I thrashed from side to side, trying to break his grip.

"Suck it!" he screamed at me, digging his fingers into my hair and smashing my face up against the dashboard. It was like falling down on a cold piece of concrete. He slammed me down again and

I could feel my eye starting to swell, the same one John Earl had busted.

I was scared, as bad as with the shock treatments. There was something in his voice I'd never heard before, not even from John Earl. It brought back the bootlegger's face, staring at me in the back seat, searching for something, sniffing, his eyes yellow and runny. The things those eyes would do once they had you pinned and locked away.

"No no no," I started screaming, trying to kick him. "No! You can't make me."

It just made him madder. I started crying.

"Please," I cried, as he jerked my head down toward his crotch so hard I felt something snap. I saw a flash of white then, hot like lightning.

"Please don't. Please. Just let me go." I could hear my voice breaking into little pieces, pleading. "I don't want to. Please."

"I can hurt you, little girl," he was saying, his voice deadly. "You don't stop fussing I can hurt you real good."

He had hold of my head so tight it made me dizzy. My mouth, open to scream, was up against his crotch, all nasty smelling, and I thought I'd gag if I had to take him in. I fought hard, as hard as I'd fought that night in Raleigh, but John Earl had been stronger, bigger. This man wasn't much taller than I and I could tell it was wearing on him. If I could just fight long enough he'd get tired, and I'd try for the window again. I could see it out of the corner of my eye, wide open.

My right arm was free, and I doubled it back, ready to strike at him, when all at once I remembered the knife and hoped he hadn't lifted it when I was asleep. I imagined I felt its weight there, pressing against my hip. I was on the floorboard now, the knapsack jammed up against me.

"Suck it you little slut, you cunt, suck it."

He was having trouble breathing now, or was it me? I heard the panting in my head, loud and fast and full of something gone crazy, my thoughts focused now on the knife, my hand nearly to the pocket. He pulled one hand loose from my hair then, balled it into a fist, and struck me square on the cheekbone. I heard something pop again and saw an explosion of silver. I tried to shake it clear, but he had his fingers knuckle-deep in my hair again, pushing and pulling.

"That'll learn you," he said, so out of breath his voice rasped.

When he's done, I thought, he'll kill me. He's either got a gun or he'll bash my head in. He's going to kill me. The thought roared now, drowning out the sick sound of his breathing, the sight of the open window, my own disgust. It's all I heard, as if it were a familiar song being played over the cheap car radio.

My face felt heavy and full of blood and throbbed each time he pulled me against him. I felt the butt of the knife now, the metal tip of it hooked up under my fingernail. I pulled at it slowly, felt it move a hair, and lost the grip.

"Bitch!" he was yelling. "Open your mouth wider. Open it!"

I tried again and my fingernail caught good this time. I inched the knife up slowly, wishing my pants weren't so tight. My hand was shaking like crazy. Had he noticed? What if I dropped it? What if he got it? What if . . .

HE'S GOING TO KILL YOU, EVA.

It wasn't my voice, or my thought. Or Freda's. It came big and hollow like a gong rung from a mountaintop. He was pushing my head up and down wildly, the way I used to see my grandmother scrub clothes on an old washboard.

WHEN IT'S OVER HE'LL KILL YOU.

"That's good, bitch," I could hear him saying. "But you can do better. Suck it harder. Harder now," the words coming in great chokes.

I had the knife flat in my palm now and brought it around slowly, carefully.

"Suck . . ."

I bit down as hard as I could. It was no bigger than a Tootsie Roll. I tasted blood and cum, thinking I would vomit. I let my throat relax, and swallowed.

"Ahhh, my God, Jesus," he cried and pulled his hands from my hair as if he'd touched fire. He shoved my head aside and was grabbing at his bloody cock, doubling over like he was going to be sick.

I flipped the button on the blade, my whole body shaking now, my vision blurred through the swollen eye. I leaned away from him and drove the knife into his side, a downward motion, erratic, the blade tilted too far to the right.

I looked at his face when I did it, saw his mouth open in a big O and his neck muscles go stiff. He started beating at me with his fists, trying to pry the knife free from his gut where I still held it, pushing with all my weight, down on my knees. I clasped my left hand over the one that held the knife and twisted. He cried so loud I could hear it echo in the trees.

"Stop. Stop. Please. Just stop. I'll let you go. Please. Don't."

I didn't believe him. I could see the blood soaking his yellow shirt. There was enough of a moon to see the pattern of it, spread out like oil across his belly. Where he'd unbuttoned the shirt at the bottom I could see a full dimple of blood in his navel. I pulled back and got the knife out, biting his hand as he tried to hold me, and jammed it in once again, hitting his crotch. I hadn't aimed for it. There *was* no aiming, just pushing and pulling and the fierce voice outside me, screaming full tilt now, HE'LL KILL YOU IF YOU DON'T KILL HIM. HE WILL, EVA. HE'LL KILL YOU.

I stabbed him twenty more times, in the chest, in the leg, the face, wherever I could hit, hoping I'd struck his heart. I'd imagined what it would be like to stab John Earl. I'd thought I would hear the sound of bones cracking and cartilage popping. But it wasn't that way. It was like stabbing a pillow. The flesh gave like a soft casing, or the papery shell of a cocoon. It felt like feathers and air underneath where the blood swims in its thousand little channels, so soft and vulnerable you want to take it all back and say, "I'm sorry. I'm *so* sorry." And the lungs made a screaming sound when they were punctured, an eerie wheeze like the word "Oh" drawn in sharply.

HE'S DEAD, EVA.

I turned quickly to look for the voice, the hair on the back of my neck rising, fully expecting to see a face fill the open window.

He lay still now and I crept up on the seat, fell against the passenger door, and sobbed. I shook until my teeth rattled. It reminded me of the sound the conch shells made in the shallow water off Eleuthera. I reached my foot over tentatively and pushed at him with my shoe. His knee wobbled back and forth once and then stopped. I thought I could still hear blood bubbling out of the holes in his chest. I held my breath and pushed again, and his legs flopped all the way open, the blood on his crotch a matted nest of purple.

I looked away. The blood was slamming through my head so hard I could see it red behind my eyes, a dense clot of tiny veins blinking on and off with each heartbeat. I thought I might die anyway. My head felt huge, spongy and hot, my pulse so out of control it made my throat ache. I tried to think about Eleuthera again, tried to remember the way the sun had felt as I lay on the shore, so hot my muscles were languid and loose as a cat's in deep sleep. I had felt so good and clean there on the sand. My heart slowed. Another thought. Find another one.

There was the river the night before, much warmer than the cold autumn air. I'd waded in it before making my bed, feeling slick, algae-covered stones beneath my toes, and had reached down to pick up a handful and found they were as white as the fur of a rabbit's foot. I'd rubbed them between my palms, loving their smoothness, tucking them into the pocket of my jeans. They were there now, a lump as big as a handful of gumdrops. I dug my hand in and pulled the stones out to hold them flat on my palm. There were seven of them, hot as coals. I held them to my forehead and swore I heard them hiss. Then I jammed them back in my pocket, quickly, coming to life.

I wouldn't look over at him again, couldn't, so I closed my eyes, felt for the knapsack, which was sticky with blood, and pulled it into the back seat as I edged carefully over. I reached for the door handle, lifted it up, then stepped out into the night and started running.

FOURTEEN

It was night and I'd crept up quietly, wanting to surprise her, but I was so tired I just sat down and held my head in my hands, breathing in the smells of Poplar Street. The old Chinese restaurant up the block owned by Harry Si pumped out chow-mein aroma day and night, and it mixed with the deep, sugary smell of Homer's Barbeque next door. Harry Si, if he was in a good mood, told his customers they could take the fried rice next door and let Homer put some gravy on it. I remembered when I was a kid, holding the paper bucket out to Homer—a big black man who didn't smile much, didn't laugh, and kept his head down even when you asked him a question—and watching him spoon gravy on carefully, as if he were measuring its worth.

"Five cents," he'd say, and I'd hand him a nickel and run out the door.

It was Halloween night. I realized that as I sat on the cool grass. Trick or treaters were passing one another on the other side of the street, heads peering intently into their bags of candy as they stumbled along. A tiny witch with a high peaked hat and a glittering cape stopped and turned in my direction. "Trick or treat," she yelled across Poplar Street, waving her free hand.

"That's the truth," I said to myself, but I called back to the girl, "Same to you," wondering if she had seen my face and thought it was a mask. She smiled and walked on.

It didn't take my aunt long to come to the door. I had my back to her and she spoke from behind the screen.

"I thought it was probably you."

She'd been waiting, she said, ever since she'd heard I'd gotten loose.

"And you took your sweet time," she added, guiding me into the house.

"Try walking thousands of miles," I said, trying to shake off my jacket, my arms so stiff I had to hold them straight in back of me while she pulled at the sleeves.

The big front room was lit by candles, a hundred of them at least. On tables, suspended from holders near the ceiling, and tucked into corners of a bookshelf that ran the length of one wall—everywhere my eyes focused I found a soft point of light. On one wall a crucifix shone red, then gold and white as the air in the room stirred the flame beneath it. I watched it for a moment, remembering how when I was twelve years old I had lain in my bed at Freda's, studying the crucifix she had placed on my dresser, thinking that if I was brave enough I could see Jesus standing right there in the room. As I studied the cross it began to glow white, the light spreading out across the room like metallic gauze, and I did not feel fear but a silence inside me so profound it was as if I were floating in that white haze, lifted up into the room, my breath nothing more than the rhythm of the light. And at that moment everything I had ever known made sense, and just as quickly the light disintegrated, dissolving like so much effervescence in a glass, and I was back on my bed staring at the cross of wood and metal.

I told Freda the next day, and she said it was a doorway I had seen, a hole punched in the universe by my willingness to believe.

"Believe in what?" I asked, thinking that all I had wanted to do was spook myself.

"Why in things you can't see, of course," she said, looking at me funny. "You want that, don't you, Eva?"

I told her yes, wondering about it, skeptical, and finally decided that what I couldn't see probably held the best possibilities.

I remembered how it was on Halloween nights when Freda would walk from room to room with a long taper, lighting the candles silently, bowing her head as she went. She said it was the ritual that was important and that it had no tie to any religion, although some nights she would swing an incense holder by a chain, in great wide arcs, just the way the priest did at communion. Freda mixed spiritual practices the way she did vegetables in her soup, and no one pot tasted or looked the same as the next. The whole house would begin to smell of perfume as she lit the candles, mixing with the scent of soaps stacked high on pine shelves in the bathroom. I would tiptoe behind her through the house, a willing shadow, a miniature ghost in her image, wanting to know the dimensions of her odd faith. Or was it faith as much as instinct, a way of knowing how to move through the world and not be snagged by the ordinary and the cruel? I would study her closely and see something close to rapture in the silhouette of her face.

When the candles were lit we would sit on the floor, surrounded by a full halo of light, and she would take both my hands in hers and tell me to close my eyes.

"See those candles, Eva?" she would say. "Remember how they look, all that light moving around you. When it's all you see, ask your questions."

"What questions?" I would say, and she would put a finger to her lips, quieting me.

Now, in the shifting candlelight, she saw my face as I had seen it in the mirror at the bus station, my right eye as purple and soft as bruised fruit, the flesh across my cheekbone a dark yellow.

She lifted her hands to my face, slowly, as if she beheld a beam of light she could catch if only she were careful enough, and placed them, cupped, cool against my skin. "Baby, what have they done to you?"

Her voice was so tender, so steady. Her eyes shone with the light of candles. I stared at her, at that beautiful, exquisite face, loving her as I had when I was a girl, eager to please and helpless to know if it could ever be enough. I could feel my tears start to come from way down deep, an ache so vast it rocked my heart, pulled at the moorings until I could not hold it still. I sat down in the middle of the floor, tears soaking into the split flesh of my eye, burning, healing. If I had to lose my mind, I thought, better to do it here. Let the hinges snap where I was safe. It wouldn't happen though, I knew it. I was like one of those sand-weighted plastic clowns, life-size, and the only thing that might change me was a punch hard enough to make all the air go out of me, whoosh, so fast they'd have to post gale warnings.

I could hear Freda in the kitchen, taking ice cream from the freezer. I looked up through tears that splayed the light into bands of color. She was making a root beer float, scooping the ice cream into a fruit jar, snapping the root beer cap, and pouring until foam rose in the glass and spilled down the sides. She had made floats when I was young, always before bedtime, telling me it made sleeping manageable. And then I'd wake at three in the morning, craving another, reaching for the glass by the bed so I could lick the foam that had dried along the rim.

I felt silly sitting there, a grown girl now, sucking the soda and ice cream through a straw, sobbing, trying to get the spoon to my mouth as my hands shook, snot running onto my upper lip, the fruit jar cold and slippery. And it was Halloween, for God's sake, the weather outside so cool frost had started to settle on the grass. Ice cream weather. I laughed, choked, and sprayed the mess down my sweater.

"You finish your float now," I heard Freda say as she wiped root beer off her face, "and then you tell me."

"You know something?" I said, looking around the room, spotting shapes that were surely chairs or tables but looked to me like bodies crouched, ready to spring.

"What's that?" Freda said, ready to hear me out now.

"When I was a kid I never thought about how strange this place really is. And you . . . I mean . . ."

"It don't strike me that way, Eva," she said, her teeth glowing pointed in the candlelight.

"I mean . . ." I continued. "I don't mean it unkind. I don't mean it critically, you know . . . it's just . . . you're just . . . *odd,* when you think about it."

"Well don't then," she said, dismissing what I thought to be a revelation. "Forget that and tell me what happened, clear, so I see it from beginning to end. And don't leave anything out."

It took a while to go through it all, and when I told her about the shock treatments I had trouble breathing and sat up straight, reaching out to her. I could see her face getting serious, then angry, then disgusted when I got to the part about highway Bob, and when I finished I had the strangest feeling none of it had happened. How could it have? Did the rules of nature truly suggest that one bad thing followed another? I sat rocking back and forth on the floor, swearing to myself it was a lie.

I imagined it was a Halloween night past and I was sitting in this same spot, waiting for Freda to call on the spirits with her singsong voice, high and sweet as if she were calling cats to a supper dish.

"Speak," she would say on those nights. "Give a sign."

And from the walls, the ceiling, the floorboards would come faint sounds of tapping—maybe just the wind against the eaves—that grew louder and more insistent as Freda whispered. "There is no fear here," until the noises became deafening and I could feel the air vibrate and catch in my throat when I took a breath.

"What do they want?" I would say in a squeaky whisper, grabbing for Freda's hand, and she would answer softly, her arms opened wide in a gesture of welcome, "Communion, Eva. They want communion."

"Eva," I heard her say now, her voice penetrating the memory. "Your poor face. He busted up your pretty face. I'd take the gun to him for that."

"Too late," I said, stretched out flat on the floor, exhausted now. "I already killed him. He's dead. Probably still in his car."

I shuddered, reached into my back pocket, and felt the knife still there, then pulled it out and let it rest on my palm.

"Murder weapon," I said absently, letting the knife slide to the floor.

Freda stared at it. "You don't think that's wrong, do you, what you did?" There was some respect in her voice, a certain awe. Her niece had killed a man.

"Maybe," I said. "Murdering someone is wrong. I know that. It doesn't mean I didn't want to do it, but it's wrong."

"Come on, Eva," she said. "Talk sense."

I shrugged.

"Remember John Earl?" she said. "How I close to killed him?"

I nodded, remembering as if it had been yesterday the look on his face when she'd pointed the gun at him. I smiled. "You scared the hell out of him," I said.

"You liked that, didn't you?" she said. "Tell the truth. You wouldn't have cared if he'd died."

"No," I said. "I still wouldn't. It's not the same though, actually doing it, putting a knife in someone. It doesn't feel the way you think it will."

"How's it feel?" she asked, her eyes wide.

Where did this thirst for blood come from? I wondered, rabid as the sex thing she always preached about. Freda tickled me, her wanting all the details.

"It's like stabbing a pillow," I said. "That's what I figure. Just like that."

"Is that so?" she said. "Huh. I wouldn't have guessed. Well. It was self-defense, that's for certain. And you stepped right in the middle of fate and changed it. You changed your *destiny*, Eva. Think about that."

"Right," I said. "Suppose I was meant to get away? Suppose it happened exactly the way it was planned? Suppose you missing John Earl was planned? What am I talking about? It just happened. That's all."

"You get a little older you'll change your mind about that," she said, her voice clipped the way it could be when she thought I was talking nonsense. "Those dreams that come true. How you explain those, tell me that, if it's not all planned? And then some dream comes as a warning to tell you it'll happen that way unless you change it. I know these things. I *know* them."

She was excited now, the way she got when she was making a point, her eyes glassy and focused somewhere deep inside herself. She was confusing me. I thought about how she had always talked about respecting life, what a gift it was. I was tired, that much I knew.

"If you got a conscience about this, Eva," I heard her say, "you're wrong."

"I didn't say I had a conscience about it. You did." I yawned.

"Well look at it this way." She wasn't hearing me. "Not many people get second chances. His time was up. Way way up. Way out past the time-space barrier. Kaput. Someone pulled his number. He bought the farm . . ."

Once she was like this I couldn't stop her. She was giggling now, slapping the floor with her palm.

"How does it feel," she asked, grinning at me cockeyed, "to be a murderer?"

I ignored her.

"He had a date with destiny and you were his escort, oooh Lord, he'll never drive that lonesome highway again. He's real stiff now and you're the cause all right."

"You're sick," I said. "And not very funny."

"You got it, honey," she crowed, raising both fists in the air. "Don't mess with us, we'll cut your wang off. Ha! He's dead as a doorstop, the bastard, and he won't hurt you or nobody ever again. You think he'd have stopped with you?"

"It gives me the creeps to think about it," I said.

"Sorry, baby," she said, contrite. "Come on now. Laugh a little. Smile! I'm just trying to cheer you up. If you laughed you'd feel better."

I laughed, sounding phony, deliberately.

"Harder," she said, tickling me.

I rolled over on the floor, trying to get away from her, yelling, "Stop! It makes my face hurt."

"Sorry, baby," she said again, her face serious now. "So tell how you got here. You left out that part."

I'd run for miles that night, counting over and over in my head up to five hundred and then starting over, trying to keep the picture of him lying in the front seat of that car, all bloody, out of my head. My knees gave me a lot of trouble and I'd fall, get up, and fall again, my clothes torn and bloodstained when dawn broke. On the afternoon of the next day, I found a town—some spit-in-the-dust-hollow in Tennessee, I can't remember the name.

They'd been nice at the local store that doubled as a bus depot, and I'd bought a ticket straight on to Watson Chapel. I'd changed my clothes in the bathroom before the bus came, and that's when I saw my face, knew instantly why the woman who ran the store had been so kind and helpful, saying to me maybe five times, "Are you sure there's nothing I can do for you, honey?"

And then I'd gotten on the bus and some old pervert had tried to sit down next to me, leering so hard I thought he must practice it, but I put my knapsack on the seat and gave him a pure look of hate that seemed to scare him because he stepped back as if he'd been pushed.

"Men can't be trusted," Freda was saying. "A few, maybe, the sweet, dumb ones, but you've still got to bend them to your will. Then you don't want 'em after you've done that." She sighed. "It's a dilemma."

"I guess," I said, too tired to talk anymore.

"Eva," she said, holding my chin with her hand so I would look at her. "I'm not making fun of what happened. You know that, don't you?"

I nodded.

"It's just that you been through a lot, and if you don't laugh and see the other side of it, something might freeze up in you for good. You understand?"

I told her yes, trusting her. It always surprised me how easy it was to do.

"And there's nothing wrong about not feeling bad about what you did. Nothing at all. There's even pride in it. You saved the state some money, Eva."

I smiled, thinking how complete was her logic.

"They called here right away," she said, changing the subject. "After you left the hospital. They thought I'd know something. I did, you know, from the first time you called out to me, I knew. But I couldn't tell where you'd gone, except that you were near water. And I wouldn't have told if I *had* known. You know that, Eva. I *will* protect you. Well, you got a head start, I'll say that, but they'll come looking soon enough. Maybe. I don't know what it's worth to them anymore, but they might."

"I know," I said. "John Earl doesn't want me loose. Rita, either. They think I'm dangerous. You think I'm dangerous, Freda?"

I gave her a scary look.

"Ha!" she said. "Only to yourself. You don't scare me."

"Who does?" I said, getting up and following her to the back of the house, watching the rooms fill with smoke as she blew out the candles one by one.

I slept in my old bed that night, back in the room off the butler's kitchen. Freda had pushed the bed up under the window the way I liked it. She kissed me goodnight, pulled back the curtains and said, "Looks like rain."

"It's dark," I said. "How do you know?"

Her shoulders shrugged in the dim light and her teeth flashed wide and white as the Cheshire cat's. It was all I could really see, her teeth glowing like pieces of marble, floating there above the bed.

She lit a candle on the nightstand, said, "Sweet dreams," and floated out.

I thought a lot about Bob as I lay there. Now that I started to remember how he looked when I'd left him, I was sure I'd poked one of his eyes out. I worried about that for a while. It felt worse than killing him, taking one of his eyes. I reached out to the nightstand, gripped the sheath of the knife, and pushed the button. The blade flashed a dull silver in the candlelight, and I could see there was hair stuck to it. What if they find me? I thought. What if he's still alive? No chance, I told myself. Don't be silly. Better to wonder what if I *hadn't* killed him. Well, I'd be dead. And then what? Would I have seen that light again, brighter than dawn, clear and blue-white as lightning? What had he seen? Where had I sent him? Christ. It was no good thinking about it, working on myself to get at the guilt. When I was a kid I used to wonder what it would feel like if I actually did kill John Earl. How would I feel when I woke the next morning? Who would I see in the mirror as I stood brushing my teeth? A murderer? A crazy girl? Or someone who had just had a bad dream? Now I'd know. But I didn't feel that different, really. Just tired to the bone. And hungry. Self-defense, Freda had said. I could live with that.

There was singing from the church that night, soft at first, and then the rhythm picked up, hands clapping, feet stomping on the old worn boards.

I'd been inside once, for a Saturday-night service with one of the black girls from the neighborhood. The church was just one room, filled with rickety pews that creaked when you sat on them, the floorboards spongy with wear. I'd held my friend's hand when the adults—all of them big, black, and serious about their Jesus—started up the chorus of "Just a Closer Walk with Thee," salting the melody with moans and cries, swaying back and forth so the whole room seemed to move.

I liked the way that music made me feel, charged up inside as if I could fly with it. I pressed my hand to the window so I could feel the vibration of their voices, and then the rain started up, hard and heavy, washing across the window in sheets and frosting the pane. I thought then that whatever came later, no matter how good or how bad, I would remember how I felt at that moment, caught inside those voices, my hand against the cold glass, safe, certain no one would ever find me if I just closed my eyes.

FIFTEEN

I stayed on through the winter at Freda's. Both the hospital and my mother called. Freda told them she hadn't heard from me. I'd listen when she answered the phone, watch her lift the heavy black receiver from the cradle as if it were a weight, suspicion on her face. She never trusted telephones, saying they were for idle people and the only time you should ever use one was in an emergency. When I was a kid and the phone would ring, she'd pick the receiver up and drop it into a tin bucket she kept close by. Then she'd go to banging it with a hammer, yelling down into the bucket, "I hope that hurts your ears you go bothering me like this when I'm in the middle of my work. Ain't you got work to do?"

And then she'd kick the bucket for good measure and walk away. People didn't call often, never knowing what to expect on the other end of the line. So when the phone rang that winter we could pretty much guess who it was.

I'd watch as Freda crossed her fingers behind her back when she said, "Eva? Why no. I'd have let ya'll know if I'd heard from her. Here? Of course not!"

She was so believable, so sincere, and I could imagine Dr. Fox melting on his end of the line, listening to that sugary, throaty voice. It worked. No one came to check. I asked if she thought they really believed I wasn't with her.

"Doesn't much matter, does it?" she said.

She had a point. It was like graduating from some institution, she told me. I just had to move on and leave that part behind me, or take a little of it, whatever I'd learned there, and use it when I needed to. She asked what I thought I'd learned.

How to run, I told her.

I still wondered about the murder and if they could pin it on me, but after a month I stopped worrying. Freda said in that wild country some animal was bound to come on Bob, crawl right in the car and take what was left of him. I tried to imagine how it would be, a bobcat stealing in on him, thinking he was asleep, then coming closer to the true scent, his eyes getting wide, his breathing faster, until he'd be all over the carcass, tearing at the wounds where the blood had congealed, pushing his thick tongue into the eye sockets, drawing life from a stale kill. I liked to think of it that way. Like bleeding on the leaves. Giving life back to the wild. I slept easier after that.

Sometimes I couldn't sleep. I'd lie in the back room with my eyes wide open, staring at the ceiling where the wallpaper had peeled. I thought about my own death then, wondering what it would be like when it happened, and if it wouldn't be a hell of a lot easier than what I was doing. Once I was dead I wouldn't know it, despite what Freda said about a consciousness in the afterlife, and I would be freed from having to deal with other people. I'd started to believe they could tell just by looking at me that something was wrong, as if the word *defective* had been stamped across my forehead, bled into my skin like ink from a tattoo. I had strong suspicions I was a truly evil girl, especially when I looked back on all the evidence: stealing boys from other girls, wishing people dead, killing, hating, running away. Maybe I ran before they could figure out how really bad I was. But if that was so, if I was so bad, why did Freda love me? I decided it was because she had to. No one else ever could. It was one of her duties, a discipline of sorts. I never asked her, though, afraid she might say I was right. The more I thought this way, the closer I came to deciding I didn't want to live. I held on to the notion and kept it close, the way I would a blanket on a cold morning.

We had a good winter and Freda hunted squirrels on the land, something I could never bring myself to do. I'd stare down the barrel of the gun, trying to look professional about it, then put my finger to the trigger real easy the way she'd taught me, but at the last second I'd swing the barrel around and fire high at an empty piece of sky. Freda would shake her head and say she guessed it was different with me when it came to animals. I took this to mean I could slice up a human any old time I liked, but when it came to killing creatures I was fluff.

We'd tote the gutted carcasses home and hang the hides on the clothesline to dry or freeze, depending on the weather. Each Sunday we went to the river and stood along its frozen banks, watching, listening, but no one came. Too cold for baptizing, Freda said, and I agreed, taking off my shoe and touching a bare foot to the icy water, feeling the electricity of it all the way up my leg.

Some days we'd take the Chevy out Highway 79 to Altheimer, past the bare cotton fields, stiff and brown in the winter light, strewn here and there with stray bolls blown loose at harvest. I remembered how that land had looked in early autumn, so thick with white the air was hung with the dust of it. Cotton blown high into the limbs of trees, snagged on the splintery boards of old wooden fences. Cotton rolling like tumbleweed down the rutted Main Street of Altheimer; caught in the brief and violent spin of dust devils that swept through the gullies and out into the fields. Cotton clogged up against the screen-porch doors, floating like shredded lilies across stagnant catfish ponds. It made me think of death, all that cotton loose on the wind, left to fly in the void until it met with something that had substance.

As we drove past, Freda nodded in the direction of the fields as if they were talking to her, and I thought about being buried out there, how good it would feel to be down deep in earth, tasting its minerals in the back of my throat. I held my head out the window, taking in the sharp winter air, knowing this was where I belonged, aching to open the door and run through the fields to where the river awaited me.

"What you thinking?" Freda asked me. I could feel her staring. It was something she did when she was driving, and it unnerved me.

"Watch the road," I said. "You'll hit a skunk."

"No skunks in daylight, and don't change the subject," she told me, veering off toward the gully, giggling. "Say what's on your mind, Eva."

"Death," I told her. "Death and sex."

"Two big topics, those are," she said.

Freda pulled the Chevy over and stopped the engine. She sat up straight behind the steering wheel, her long fingers locked tight around it. I didn't want to talk. I hoped it wouldn't be a time when she made me.

"Go on," she said. "I'll wait here."

I turned to her, disbelieving, feeling foolish, wishing she didn't understand so often what went through my head.

"Go on," she said again, pushing at my shoulder. "And button up your coat."

"It has a zipper."

"So zip it."

I started out slow across the field, feeling the crunch of the brittle cotton vines beneath the soft leather of the moccasins Freda had given me. The ground was cold, but not frozen. It looked so much bigger close up, great clods of earth mounded on top of each other by the tiller, forming perfect rows with valleys in between.

I stooped to pick up a clod, put it to my mouth and bit it, feeling it turn to gritty dust. I loved the taste of it, the smell and texture, and the way my mouth filled with liquid from wanting it. I stuck a cotton boll in my pocket as I moved off toward the stand of trees that fronted the river. I looked back once and could no longer see the Chevy or the road. When I made it to the middle of the field, I stood there motionless, my arms limp at my sides, thinking that it must be what a scarecrow sees day after day and that if I stood in the middle of that field long enough I wouldn't be able to tell myself from the rest of it. When the wind blew I'd bend and rustle like the plants, the cotton stuffing inside me exactly like the cotton in the field, raw and coarse. If the wind blew hard enough some of my stuffing might blow free, but it wouldn't matter—I'd be with my own kind. The sky would grow dark and when the rains came my head would tilt up.

I stayed out there a long time, still as I could be, trying to match my breathing to the wind. If I opened my mouth a little I could feel it push in, the way it does when a balloon backfires, a quick whoosh, a lightness inside. I let the wind catch me and tumbled onto my side, down into one of the grooves between the rows. It felt safe there, as safe as being in my bed in the back room at Freda's with my hand against the cold glass, listening to the gospel singers.

This is where I would stay, I told myself, next to the ground, hidden from the bright assault of each passing day. I was getting old. I'd felt it coming on, a state of mind as forlorn as a naked scarecrow in a barren field. But down here I could smell the dirt and taste the iron. I clawed at it with my fingers, loosening great chunks, rolling it back and forth like a cat, feeling the ache in my loins so sweet it was better than any man. I pulled my hair loose from its band and ran my fingers through to the ends, rubbing the dirt into it, feeling it grow thick with dust. I stretched out flat on my belly, feeling my heartbeat through the tight muscles, boom, like a fist slamming into the skin of an ancient drum. I pressed my ear into the dirt, listened for an answering beat, and heard the thunder of a train moving along the tracks by the gully. The louder it grew the more it sounded like my heart, a roar nearly deafening, and then silence. I lay there breathing hard, feeling depraved. Had I snapped this time, turned some psychic bend in the road, ending up deranged in a dead cotton field in winter, my legs splayed out, my mouth open? If I *was* crazy out of my head, I didn't want to know.

I rolled onto my back and looked up at the sky.

"You're crazy," I whispered. "They didn't know when they locked you up, but they'd know now."

I got slowly to my feet, brushing at my jacket, my hair, the front of my jeans. I looked around and saw I'd made it only halfway to the river. It had gotten dark, the winter light fading quickly in the east. I could see, way off toward the road, the dim headlights of the Chevy blinking on and off. I'd forgotten all about Freda. Forgotten where I was. I ran now along the length of a furrow toward the car, careful not to stumble, frantic as I watched the last faint glow in the western sky snap out like a light. What was wrong with me? I ran faster and called out, "Freda!"

I stopped at the edge of the field and listened, breathing hard, remembering the dark night I had run from Bob. Dead Bob, blood running out of him thick like syrup. Was she there? Did she hear me? I called again.

"What's the matter with you, Eva!" She said it real slow, each word like a drumbeat in the still air. "You crazy?"

She stood leaning against the Chevy, a hand on her hip, her long hair blowing out behind her, the silver streaks in it glowing platinum in the dim light.

"I didn't say go for the rest of the day, worry me sick, did I?"

I was too out of breath to answer.

"Get in the car," she said. "Supper's late."

She opened the door and I collapsed on the front seat of the Chevy, a small dust cloud growing up around me.

"You know what you need, Eva?" she said as she started up the car.

"What's that?" I asked, peering out the window in the direction of the field.

"You need a boy."

"I'll say," I told her.

"Blood so hot it boils," Freda had said once about the women in our family. That blood did something else, too. It ran out of me into the land and back in again, charged with a passion that bound me to the South as strong as anything I've ever known. I didn't understand, though, until I'd torn myself from it, hemorrhaged near to death, and then returned weak, needing a fix. I didn't understand how it figured in my life, not until I threw myself out into the wild, deep into ravines where even pain grew dark and thick, more personal.

"You need a boy." Such a simple answer. Freda was wrong when she'd said that, the only time I ever think she was dead wrong. It was a sore point with me later on, and I tried to blame her for it, but the truth was it took a long time before I knew what I needed. Sometimes, even now, I wonder if I really know.

•   •   •

I saw Ronnie once before he went off to school, which is where
Freda said he belonged, permanently, because to educate him would
be a life's work.

He stood at the fence one afternoon, and I could see him from
the kitchen window where I stood with my hands in the soapy water
of the dishpan, doing the sort of chore Freda said built character.
I was beginning to tire of her dictums and her railroading me into
shape with housework, but it kept me from thinking too much.
Freda wasn't liking much of what I thought these days.

I could see him looking over toward the house and thought how
tall he had grown, his arms too long for the rest of him, his skin
dark against the sheepskin collar of his coat. He jerked his head up
the way a horse might, in the direction of the window where I stood.
I was wondering if I should go to him. I didn't believe I was pretty
anymore, but Freda said that wasn't the truth. I'd stand in front of
the bathroom mirror and look at my face, at the two scars that
looked like one, running from my right eye down the side of my
face. How could it have scarred like that, with no stitches? I asked
her. And there were other things that were different. Like the way
I jumped at loud noises. And the way I felt tired most of the time.
Old.

"Go on now, Eva," I heard Freda say behind me. "Go out and
see that boy. He may be dumb but he's still pretty. And sweet. He
brought me flowers on my birthday."

I went to him as she said to do, holding my head down as I crossed
the backyard, pressing my fingers to my face where the scar was,
feeling a heavy ridge that was the color of half-cooked steak. Why
did they always go for the face? I wondered, looking up when Ronnie
spoke my name.

"Eva," he said. "It's been a long time, hasn't it?"

"Sure," I said, looking up at him now, hoping to scare him a
little. "What? Three years."

"Still as pretty as ever," he said, holding his hand out and brushing
the hair back from my eyes. "Pretty as a cat."

"Cats scratch," I said, backing away from the fence. "Don't you
know that?"

He looked confused, unused to meanness, and I was sorry for him.

"I've thought about you, Eva," he said, lowering his voice. "All the time."

"Really," I said.

"Want to go for a walk?"

"I should stay. I have work."

"Come on," he said. "I'll hold your hand, and if anybody says howdy and asks how it's going today, we'll say we just got married and they'll be happy for us. What do you say?"

"I say you're crazy," I told him, wondering what the hell was going through his head. "I wouldn't marry you. I don't even know you."

"Sure you do," he said, looking honestly hurt, the smile on his face disappearing. "All these years, what's not to know? And I didn't say we *were*," he continued, sounding as stern as I'd ever heard him. "I just meant we'd pretend. For fun. What's with you, anyway, Eva? You're cranky."

"What if they want to see my wedding band?" I said. "Suppose that happens? Who's gonna believe I'm married to you if I got no wedding band?"

He crossed to my side of the fence now in a quick jump, swinging both legs over so nice and easy I remembered the grace that had drawn me to him the summer I'd watched him glide across the lake, back before everything went haywire.

"Here," he said, taking off his high school class ring and slipping it onto my finger.

"Hey," I said.

"There," he told me. "Now just turn it around and it looks like a wedding band. Genuine gold-filled. It says so inside. Look. Take a peek."

I laughed. "You're silly," I told him.

I could smell him now, just the way I remembered him, like cinnamon and nutmeg and clove oil, the warm spices from his mother's kitchen clinging to his hair, his clothes, rich in the cold air.

"I don't mean to be," he said. "I just love you. Ever since you were a little girl out playing in the yard. I used to watch you from my side of the fence and wish I could take you inside with me at night, pull your ponytail loose and spread your hair out on my pillow. Have you sleep all cuddled up next to me. That's what I thought all those years, Eva. At least until I figured out what to do with you."

He nuzzled me, pushing his mouth against the back of my neck, nibbling.

"Stop," I said. My head felt light and my belly was starting to ache so, I wanted to move against him. But I had a flash of Bob, moldy and rotten now, and felt sick. "Stop it!" I said again, angry.

"Why?" he said in my ear, still holding tight.

I shivered, pulling away from him. "Because," I said. "I've changed."

"I'll say," he told me, running a hand inside my coat, squeezing a breast.

"That's not what I mean, you idiot. Look at my face."

"Don't call me names, Eva," he said, his voice breaking. "Please don't."

He stood back and put his hand to my cheek now, as gently as if he were stroking a baby. He smiled down at me, his eyes kind, not seeing what I meant. "It's beautiful," he said. "It's always been beautiful. It always will be. Don't you know that?"

I sighed, shaking my head.

"Eva," he said. "I'm not so dumb I can't see what's happened to you. But what does that matter? And I know something about you, Eva. Something even you don't know."

"What's that?" I asked, curious.

"Things aren't as bad as you make them, Eva."

He smiled, proud of himself.

"Ha!" I said, sitting down on the ground, tired now. "Oh whoopee then. Things aren't so bad. What do you know. Well I'd better get busy then. Just what do you—"

"Calm down," he said. "I hear about you, Eva. Freda tells me. I don't say it's fair the things that have happened. It's not fair at all. But I do know you can be happy if you just let yourself."

For a long time I'd believed there were two kinds of people in the world. Those who thought everything would be fine no matter what happened, and those who knew better. I was one of the ones who knew better. I was bitter, cynical; there was an edge to me now. I wanted to smack this boy. Fool, I thought. Mama's boy. *Happy?* What was that? A warm bed and an aunt who loved me? How long could she keep me from facing myself? Two weeks? A month? A year? It was already wearing thin.

I stared at Ronnie for a minute, trying to figure if I should say what I felt, and decided against it. He'd just get hurt. I could count on it.

"Come on," I said, getting up.

"Where?" Ronnie asked. "Take a walk?"

"Over to the church," I told him. "There's no one there now."

"What for?" Ronnie asked as I pulled him by his coat through the narrow alley behind the house, pushing open the rotted wood door in back of the church and stepping into its cold, dark chamber. I couldn't see and pulled Ronnie up close to me, pushing his free hand inside my sweater.

"This," I said, running my tongue along his lips. "This is what for."

"Eva," he said, his voice shocked, "you don't have to be so rough."

"What do you want then?" I asked. "The way it was when we were kids? Just shut up. You hear me?"

I pushed and pulled at him, telling him where to put his hands, how to move his hips. I grabbed at him the way men had grabbed at me, not caring if I hurt him.

"Fuck me!" I yelled in his face. "Just do it."

I pulled him to the floor and felt a splinter from one of the old boards drive into my knee.

"Come on, Ronnie. Fuck me. That's what you want, isn't it?"

I had hold of the back of his neck and bit him hard there until he cried out.

"You bastard. You fucking bastard," I kept saying over and over until he started to cry. He tried to pull my head up against his chest and I bit him again.

"Stop it, Eva." He was sobbing. "Just stop it now. You don't mean that. Say you don't."

"I do mean it," I said up close in his ear. "I do. I hate you. I hate you all. Why don't you just fuck me?"

I felt useless.

"Because I love you," he was saying. "You don't have to do this. I love you. Don't be mean now. Remember how it was, that first time, in the snow? Remember, Eva? How you said you loved me? Say it now, Eva. Say you love me."

I was looking at him now, at his wide brown eyes made huge by tears spilling onto the perfect edges of his cheekbones. Such a face. I'd seen girls stop on the sidewalk when they saw him standing there at the fence, and they always had the same look—one of wonder that any boy could be so perfect. I did remember how it was that first time and wanted to cry, too. Where had that feeling gone, a longing so sweet and illicit I ached to feel it again? With a hundred boys I had tried to feel it and never had. I was the one who had changed all right, laughing at his letters all these years, thinking him simple, starting to hate so deep there was no room for anything else.

"I'm sorry," I said, meaning it. I looked into his eyes when I said it, hoping he'd believe me. "I really am. I don't know what's wrong with me."

I rolled onto my back and held his head against my breasts, stroking his hair, feeling like I'd poison him if I held on too long.

"What do you want to do?" he asked, his voice small and sad. "Just tell me what you want to do. I'll do anything for you, Eva. You want to get married? I will. Today. We're old enough. All we have to do is get a license."

I leaned closer to him and kissed his eyelids. They were warm and salty.

"I had a dream about you, Eva. We had a baby. We named him Spike."

He laughed now, rolling his eyes up to see if I had smiled. I could see it was all he really wanted, to have me smile.

"Spike," I said. "Spike." I giggled. "What kind of name is Spike?"

I ran my hand along the soft wood floor and wondered how many feet had worn these boards to near dust. Feet stomping for the Lord.

"No," I said, weary now. "What good would that do, to marry you? I'm not right. You'd see that soon enough."

"I love you, Eva," he said again. "That's what good it would do."

"Well," I told him, standing to dress, "if it makes you happy to think so. But it won't do. It just won't do."

Ronnie went away to school and started writing to me again. His spelling had gotten better, and it bothered me that it mattered. I asked myself what he saw in me. I'd stand in front of the mirror, studying my face, and figure it was something invisible. Was it something that lived behind my eyes? All I could see in there was blackness, and all I wanted was to get to the heart of it, slip away, and never feel a thing.

S I X T E E N

We were sitting in the living room under the portrait of Jesus, his eyes all soft and milky as if someone had just stepped really hard on his foot. Freda had finished the portrait of the Manson family that day, and it was propped beside Jesus, drying. I looked from the pictures to Freda sitting on the floor with a black shawl draped around her shoulders, her eyes dark with makeup, and tried to reckon what sort of person could place the two side by side and not think it peculiar. I was beginning to wonder what kind of snakes lived in her head and what she did when she went off to the land by herself, sometimes for days at a time.

"So tell me about you," I said, slamming shut a copy of *Man and His Symbols,* sick to death of hearing about anima and animus, archetypes and the Catholic church. It was enough to make me batty.

"Why?" she asked, suspicious. "What difference does it make?"

It made a difference all right, and in this way: I had always thought about her impact on me, how she'd managed to get me to listen to her from the time I was a little kid, but I'd never wondered what had formed her, thinking she had always existed whole and with no past. Now I was curious.

"It just interests me," I said. "That's all."

I knew I had to play her a little. If I was too eager she wouldn't tell me a thing. If I pushed, she'd push back, harder. Come to think of it, I couldn't remember her telling anyone about herself. Not one soul. People came to her to talk about themselves, and that's the way it had been for years.

"Not much to tell," she said, looking around the living room as if she were bored and distracted by the subject. "How you feel tonight, Eva? Feeling better?"

Turn it back to me, I thought, just like always.

"Come on Freda," I said. "Just tell me something. Anything. How you grew up. What it was like? Like a bedtime story. Tell it like that."

She had a dark look now, as if she were at war with something old and powerful.

"A bedtime story, is it?" she said. "That what you want?" Her tone was snappish.

"Sure. Whatever you like."

"I was raised in an orphanage. What do you think of that?"

"I think that's too bad," I said, careful now, hoping I would pick the right response so she wouldn't blow up and send me off to bed.

"Do you now?" Her voice was cold. I didn't like it when she turned mean. She could scare me with that voice of hers, turn it down a notch and make my blood run cold. "You think everything's too bad, Eva. That's *your* problem. Some things just are, you know. My mama had no money when Daddy died. She had no choice."

I didn't like her answer. Didn't like her making excuses for someone when she was so quick to tell I shouldn't make any for myself.

"You believe that?" I asked, knowing I was going to make her angry, but not caring now. It was exciting the way a room felt when she got mad.

"How can you believe that?" I kept on. "Your mama had no choice. My mama had no choice. I have no choice. Everything's predestined unless it suits you otherwise, unless you want to tell me I'm feeling sorry for myself, then *I* have a choice. Which is it? You say live with it, get past it, go on. The way you see it I have no choice but to sit here night after night listening to you change your mind. What is it then? Do we have a choice or not? Why didn't your mama look after you instead of locking you up with the nuns? You got locked up, too, didn't you? Didn't you, Freda? And you didn't like it one bit, and it bothers you to this day the way your mama tossed you off on somebody else."

I'd never spoken to her this way. Each word out of my mouth rattled me, made me want to take it back as soon as I'd said it.

When I finally looked straight at her, her face had gone black. I'd seen it happen maybe twice in my life, as if all the light in the room had been sucked into her.

She was standing now, her hands on her hips, her head thrown back. I couldn't help but notice the graceful arc of her neck.

"Damn you!" she said, the words spit out like a mortal curse. "Where you get your information? Tell me that, Eva."

"She didn't love you, did she, Freda?" I said, knowing I was asking for murder.

She kicked at a chair and sent it tumbling backward into the room.

"Eva!" she growled at me, her voice vibrating as if she were trying to gargle while she spoke. She threw off the shawl, yanking so hard it ripped clean through. "You think that! You think mamas don't love their children because they make decisions that hurt them? I tell you, *she had no choice.* I learned some valuable things in that orphanage. It was the beginning of a path, Eva. A *path,* you hear me? You think I could make money all these years out of nothing if I hadn't learned there how to pinch the smallest bit off of *nothing?* And discipline, how to order my life so I could see that path? Your life's a fairy tale, child. What's hardship to you? What's neglect? Learn from it, Eva! I was there until I *came of age.* You learn what you can, take what you can out of what you're given. And don't you *ever* make fun of what I try to teach you. You'll be lucky to remember it the next time you're in a corner. And if you bad-mouth Mama again I'll slap your face. She had no choice. You hear me?"

She was out of breath, angrier at me than I'd ever seen her. I dare not speak as I watched her stalk off to her bedroom, grabbing at her shoulders where the shawl had been. I could hear her pulling out drawers, cursing, slamming the doors of the big double closet, yelling out, "Goddammit! Where are they?" as she rummaged around.

It hadn't taken much to get her going. I'd felt it building for weeks, the way she eyed me when I sulked, her exasperation when I took no interest in her teachings, challenging her at every turn.

"Here," she snapped, walking back into the room with a tattered cardboard box. "Here's your family. Come look. Just take a look.

Generations of people who had less than you. You want to look? You want to know so much about us? Take a look. Here's your heritage. Here's all the misfits you been wondering about. You go prying, Eva, you better be ready to see."

She threw the box at my feet. Old black-and-white prints scattered about the room. I looked up and saw how shiny her eyes were, as if she might cry, and it hurt so much to see her that way I hung my head, ashamed. A print had fallen into my lap, faceup, and there was my grandmother, the woman everyone called Big Mama, her Choctaw features strong and prominent, staring back at me. On her hip she held a little black-haired girl who was grinning. Without asking, I knew it was Freda.

"I'm sorry," I said, not looking at her. "I really am."

She didn't answer.

I reached for one of the pictures that lay facedown on the floor and turned it over. It was my mother in a print dress, skinny, standing in the middle of a field, her hands clasped behind her back, her face unsmiling. It was a desolate picture, the field just stubble, and my mother's figure stark as a scarecrow.

"How old is she here?" I asked Freda softly, looking up at her, trying again to show I was sorry.

She peered down as if it were an effort. "Your same age," she said biting the words off, folding her arms up high on her chest. She looked cute like that, all pissed off, and I laughed.

"Come on," I said. "I'm really sorry. Honest. I don't know anything, you're right. And I'm selfish. Come on. Sit down. Sit down and tell me about her in this picture. Please. I'm begging you, okay?"

"Like I said, she's your same age," Freda told me, sitting down warily as if I might start something up again. I could feel her trembling as I tried to hug her. She pointed at the picture.

"This was right after that sorry bastard from Ripley slammed Rita's head up against a tree, tore her clothes all up, and raped her. Mama said she was a mess, the skin on her head split open like you'd cracked a coconut. I was already married to that idiot Owen by then."

Freda glanced toward Owen's room where we could hear him snoring, and rolled her eyes.

"Idiot," she hissed under her breath.

"What happened?" I asked.

"She came to and made it back to Mama's. Mama had married Mr. Jones by then so she had money. That's why Rita didn't have to go away. Mama took her to the hospital and they stitched her head up, never asked what happened. Ever notice how Rita's hair grows cockeyed? That scar on her head's the reason. The next year she came to live with me so she'd stay out of trouble. Never did though."

I picked another picture off the floor. It was of a red-haired girl, maybe six years old, in a ragged dress, her hand clasped tightly by the hand of a man with Indian features, his black hair long and slicked back.

"Who's this?" I asked.

"Rita and Daddy."

"She had real red hair? I always thought it was fake."

"And blue eyes. The only one in the family. Daddy never believed she was his, but she was. He used to hit her, say she wasn't."

"Sounds familiar," I said.

"She was sweet, Rita was. You had to know her then to see how really sweet she was. She used to do this crazy turkey imitation, wobble her neck in and out. I still don't know how she did it. She was funny."

"You make it sound like she's dead," I said.

Freda didn't answer, just kept looking at the picture of Rita and her daddy.

I looked closer now at the stern look on the father's face and the sad eyes of the child—*my* child, *my* mother—how she looked like poverty and anger and desperation just standing there, the free hand hanging limp at her side, no tension in the muscles. She looked defeated even then. I looked again at the picture when she was my age, at those same eyes grown older now, no expectation in them of anything but trouble. I held the photos together on my lap, placing my hand over them as if that could warm them up.

"How come—" I started, and saw Freda watching me now, curious. "Why, exactly, is she so screwed up? The drinking? Letting John Earl beat her? Why?"

Freda leaned back on the sofa and placed her hands on top of her head. I could see the flat place beneath her pajama top where she had no breast.

"It's what she wants, Eva. Pain and suffering. It's what she knows how to handle."

"I don't believe it," I said. "How could she want to be miserable?"

"You're one to talk, Eva. I tell you, it's what she knows how to do. She never got past it, just let it eat at her until she felt she didn't deserve any better. I'll tell you one thing though, you can't save her, and if you don't get free of her this time she'll hurt you worse than anything they strap you down for. She wants you unhappy. She can't help it. She wants you to suffer. Just like she did."

I was confused. My mother had no choice, but I did. If that was what she was saying, none of it made sense.

"That's sick," I said.

"You see the difference now, Eva?" Freda asked me, "between Mama and Rita? How Mama did what she had to do and Rita does what she's driven to do? After you make your own mistakes you won't judge so harsh. You'll forgive her. Just like I forgave Mama."

Never, I thought. Not in a million years. I tried not to think about Rita, and most of the time it worked. But now I was looking her life dead in the eye, and could see it was not so different from my own. It made me angry. She could have done better.

"She's weak," I said.

"Maybe," Freda said. "Maybe she is. Maybe you are. Maybe I am. I don't know, Eva. I'm tired of thinking about it. I've done all that and I'm tired of it."

I looked in her face now and saw pain, years of watching people she loved be destroyed. No wonder she'd taken on my life as if it were a mission.

I'd taken another picture from the mess on the floor. It was Freda walking across a cotton field, her right hand held up to her head to keep a straw hat in place. The cotton shirt she wore had blown up on one side and a breast was exposed, round and perfect, with no bra to cover it. She was smiling, her head turned in profile, as seductive as a movie star.

"Look here," I said, holding the picture out to her. "What a body."

She was wearing cutoff shorts in the photo, and you had to look only once to see what a knockout she was.

She frowned as she pushed the picture back to me.

"That's a long time ago," she said.

"Your breast," I said. "The one you lost . . ."

"It wasn't *lost*," she said quickly. "They cut it off. It was cancer."

"I know," I told her. "I remember when it happened."

"You couldn't," she said, disbelieving, as if she'd thought it had been a secret all this time.

"I do," I told her. "I remember you all wrapped up and the blood on the gauze. It made me sad. I thought it must hurt and wondered why you didn't cry. Every time I was hurt after that I'd force myself not to cry. I wanted to be as brave as you."

She was quiet, studying my face. She let her hands fall into her lap and sighed. "I didn't cry, Eva, because there was no use to it. What would it get me but swollen eyes? You can live without a breast. I mean, all it does is *hang* there, and hang lower and lower the older you get. I don't miss it now. At first, when I'd wake up, I'd put my hand where it used to be, thinking I'd had a bad dream, but after a while it was like I was born that way."

"Is that why you don't sleep with Owen?" I asked. "Because of—"

"Hell no!" she said, her voice loud. She started laughing. "I don't sleep with that fool because if I didn't watch him every minute, he'd put it in my ear. That's how dumb he is."

"I'm sorry I made you mad," I said, relieved to hear her laugh. "I really am. I just wanted to make you talk for a change. You always ask the questions."

"I don't like to talk about me," she said. "I already know all about me. Find another picture now. Let me have that old one."

She sat there smiling at her old reflection, a young woman loose on a summer day, and I could tell by the look on her face that she liked who she was. Not just then, but now. I envied her that.

I reached into the pile again, imagining it was a tarot pack and

I could pick the card that told my future. I flipped the picture up as if I were taking it from a deck. BQ's gaunt face stared back at me, his eyes big and yellowed, trapped, as if someone had run him into a corner before taking the picture. I remembered him that night in Raleigh, down on his knees in the rain picking up the change I'd dropped, looking up and saying, "I hope you never have to do this."

"Who is it?" Freda was saying. "Who you got now?"

"BQ," I said. "I got BQ."

"Poor BQ," she said quietly. "Poor old BQ. Put him back in the box, Eva, and come sit by me. That's enough for one night. Next thing I know you'll drag your cousin Emma out of there and I'll have to explain her, and I don't know if I could. Put him back, Eva, and come here."

I tossed BQ back into the box and crawled up next to Freda on the couch. She smelled like lilac soap. I saw her smile as she pulled my head to her shoulder. I let it rest there as she stroked my hair— and as the fear overcame me. Somehow, some way, I was going to have that look BQ had, drained and cornered, with no room to back up. No place to run. I could see it as clear as Jesus hanging on the wall, clear as the Manson family huddled under that rock. It was what I'd felt that day in the river when I'd come up for air, but now it was closer and I could almost smell it stalking me.

"Don't be scared, Eva," I heard Freda say. "They're just pictures. Old pictures. Don't be scared."

"You know," I said, my voice breaking. "You know what's going to happen to me, don't you? You knew it before and you wouldn't say. Say it, Freda. Say now! Tell me."

"Forget about the pictures, Eva. Forget about all that. It's time for you to have another life. Your own life."

"I'm not talking about the damn pictures. I'm talking about *me*."

She was silent.

"Answer me this time," I shouted, pulling back from her. "Tell me what to do. I don't know what to do, Freda."

I started crying.

"What do you *want* to do, honey?"

"Be a hermit," I said, feeling like a big baby. Her baby.

"That's what you always say."

"It's not a lie," I told her, rubbing my face up against her sleeve. "I mean it."

"Well maybe we ought to get you a boy, Eva. Maybe that's what you need."

"Sure," I said. "I'd probably kill him."

SEVENTEEN

I was never surprised that it was Freda who brought Eddie to me, the way a mother cat brings dead mice to her kittens, pushing at the kill with her paws, standing over the body, yowling, until the kittens wander over to take a look. Men were like windfall fruit to Freda, and because she had no use for them, she never fully understood how deadly they could be. None had ever dominated her. She wouldn't let them. How could she know?

And they were curiosities to her, like wind-up toys or the suction-cup feet on tree frogs. She looked them over, up and down, as if they were an alien breed, and smiled sometimes at how cute they were. She'd watch the way they went about their business and mimic it, raising her voice authoritatively, trying it out for size. Basically, she hated them and would strike with her tongue if they got in her way.

"Shut up," she would say to Owen when he sat down to breakfast, "and don't say one word to me."

He was a shadow in that house, sliding from room to room, looking up with wary eyes if he passed his wife in the hallway. Her son, too, never seemed to materialize fully, although I believe she loved him, desperately, in fact, protecting him as no one ever would again. She treated him as she would an invalid, coddling him, until he walked out the door one day with a man twice his age, a lover who would be the first of many.

It was in the spring when Freda found Eddie at Harry Si's, just another college boy working in a restaurant to raise money. When she brought him home I was sitting on the swing in the big front room, watching through the window as she walked up the steps with him. She was grinning, holding his hand, and I could tell by the way his eyes were all soft-looking that he'd half fallen in love with her.

"Eva, look what I found," she said, pushing him through the front door.

He looked to be my age, a little older maybe, and was handsome in an ordinary sort of way, with wide hazel eyes and brown hair that curled around his ears. He had a good build and was tall enough for my liking, but as I looked him over I had a flash of Ronnie standing by the fence in his sheepskin coat, his thick black hair hanging over the collar, his head turned up to smell the winter air, and I knew this boy standing before me wouldn't smell like Ronnie, wouldn't taste like him.

I really hadn't been thinking about boys one way or the other except to zero in on the memory of Bob laid out in the car. Even that was fading. Freda said I was in the middle of a fallow period and it would pass. I imagined myself bare like the cotton field in winter, unconcerned with anything but climate, and thought maybe it was good to lie fallow. I tried to explain the notion to Freda, and she said that was fine, but cotton fields didn't have hormones. I told her if I ended up with anyone it would probably be Ronnie, and she said that wouldn't be so bad except he had no vision. And I said Who does, those starched and pressed boys I went to school with and fucked in the back of their mothers' station wagons? She promised she'd find someone *real* for me. A real boy, making it sound like something you could take apart and wash when it got dirty.

Here stood her real boy, holding out his hand for me to shake, saying, "Pleased to meet you, Eva. Your aunt told me you were beautiful, but I had no idea."

They never did. It's as if beautiful, before they saw the real thing, was some teased-up hairdo and a pouty mouth, big tits and a tight little skirt. When they saw me they always stopped and turned around. Maybe that's why I smiled and said thank you to Eddie, getting up from the swing to take his hand. It had been a long time since I'd really believed I was.

I remember how his eyes looked as I stood there holding his hand. Scared.

Eddie and I started dating. Freda said it would get me out of myself, and when I told her Eddie was no prize, she said he was the best she could find in Watson Chapel, and not to be so stuffy.

He would come to the house in an old green Ford and take me off to the Rendezvous, a roadhouse out by Highway 79. I remembered going there with my mother when she was dating John Earl, sitting on one of the high bar stools watching her dance close, filching the olive out of her martini. I liked the clean, sharp taste of it, and as soon as I finished one, the bartender would drop in another. My mother was the only person in Watson Chapel I ever saw drink a martini.

I drank beer and Eddie would order Scotch, a liquor that turned my stomach just to smell it. It made me feel good to drink, as if a fire were lit right in the pit of my stomach. When it wore off I usually wanted more, counting the hours until it was time for Eddie to pick me up. He said he liked me when I drank, that I was more interesting then. The truth was, once we got in bed, I'd do anything he asked if I'd had a few.

Freda warned me to watch the drinking, and when I insisted that I could handle it, she told me, "That's what they all say."

Eddie liked to put on airs, trimming the edges of the southern accent he'd been born to, using big words as if he'd looked them up just before coming to get me. I'd looked up plenty of words in my life and knew that a cynic wasn't the same thing as a cryptic, but he used cryptic that way, as if it were a noun.

"You're a cryptic," he'd say, trying to put me in my place for being negative, and I'd want to bust out laughing. I'd stuff a napkin in my mouth instead, pretending to cough. I felt sorry for him, trying so hard to be smart. I didn't hear the paper-mill workers who hung out at the Rendezvous trying out big words on their dates. The most they got out was, "Hey baby. Nice tits." So I guessed maybe Freda was right. Eddie probably was the best Watson Chapel had to offer, now that Ronnie was gone.

Eddie talked a lot about finishing college, but never what he'd do after. "How do you plan to make a living?" I asked him one night as we sat in a dark corner of the big, barnlike room.

"I don't know," he said, avoiding my eyes, something he was good at. "Maybe I don't have a plan. Go on the radio, maybe. Be a disk jockey."

"It's not good not to have plans," I told him. "I never had any and look at me."

"I look at you a lot," he said. "I like what I see."

It was something he'd started saying—"I like what I see"—and it gave me the creeps, the same way it did when he'd start grinding his teeth right before he kissed me. I like what I see. What did that mean?

"Stop it," I said. "If you want to say something like that, say I'm pretty . . . or beautiful. I'm not a piece of luggage."

"Okay, then," he said. "You're beautiful. That make you happy? You're so beautiful I want you to run away with me . . . before they pull my draft number. We'll go north. How's that for a plan?"

There was something desperate about Eddie, starting with the way he'd gotten stuck on me from the first. Not like Ronnie. Ronnie had loved me and I'd felt it. With Eddie, it was as if he needed to get hold of me real quick, like *I* was going to be his career. I think he knew he could charm Freda into letting me go with him, sensing I'd do whatever she said.

When he came over to the house he was nothing *but* charming, slick and polished like the kind of boy you end up hating but your parents love. Freda said he was smart and that counted for something. I said Why, because he used words so creatively? I think it made her feel better, believing this was a boy who would take care of me. She'd walk around him in a circle, looking him up and down, saying, "Eddie, you're not too bad-looking a boy. What you want to do with your life?"

And Eddie would answer back, smooth as could be, "It all depends on what I'm offered."

Freda liked that answer. It meant Eddie had vision.

"Well," I said, looking past the empties that were collecting on the table, "what if I don't want to go? What if I have other plans?"

"Be serious, Eva," he told me, using a patronizing tone he'd begun to take with me lately. I had to admire him a bit for thinking he could talk to me that way.

"What are you going to do here? Wait until the happy wagon pulls up out front one day? Or wait till you get beat to shit again?"

I looked across the table and noticed how he held himself when he was trying to convince me of something. His shoulders got tight, and he pressed his elbows close together on the table as he leaned toward me. I don't know. Something about his anxiety appealed to me.

Eddie knew all about my life. Freda had told him some and I'd told him the rest. It was what I had to talk about. Having killed a man was a great conversation piece. I liked the way Eddie crossed and uncrossed his legs when I said what I'd done to Bob. The things that were really important, though, I kept secret, like the way the river talked to me late at night sometimes, and the feeling I got when I was near the cotton fields. That was none of his business.

"I'm safe here," I said.

"You're bored with here," he told me, sounding sure of himself. He did that a lot, too, telling me what I thought, and I had to admit that sometimes he made sense. And he had Freda to back him up, to tell me it was time I had a life of my own, someplace fresh that didn't hold so many memories.

"Maybe I am bored," I said after a while, not wanting him to believe I couldn't think for myself. I'd stopped thinking about killing myself by then, and without that I guess I *was* bored.

Eddie and I started sleeping together in the back bedroom. Freda said it was the practical thing to do, having him close by so I wouldn't risk my health out in the woods or on the cold floor of the church where someone might walk in on us. I felt funny about it, though, as if when he got into that narrow bed, naked, I was seven years old again and he had no business being there, sliding his hand up under the weight of my breast, saying things like, "The French say a perfect breast will fit inside a champagne glass."

Who'd want to put it there? I would think, and what did he know about the French anyway, this insubstantial boy who'd never gotten to like fried okra? When Freda fixed it he'd move it around on his

plate like it was radioactive. He didn't like pig's feet either, or black-
eyed peas, and it made me suspicious. On the other hand, I enjoyed
being irritated by him and keeping it secret. It made me feel stronger,
like I had a power over him, information that could destroy him.
It was a screwy thing to think, but I'd thought screwier things.

I'd roll onto him and try to get him hard, which was a job because
half the time I couldn't find it. He wasn't so bad once he got excited,
and I could close my eyes then and think of Ronnie, how good it
had been with him and how he'd said afterward he loved me. Eddie
said it, too, but he was always so serious about it. He'd take me by
the shoulders in the dark and say, "Eva. I want you to know something. I love you. I want you to know that. Do you understand I
love you? Do you believe me?"

And I'd say yes, I believed him. It was the same as saying Yes,
I believe cows give milk. What was to doubt? He made such a point
of it.

In the morning Freda would call us to breakfast and I'd feel silly
dragging out of the back room with Eddie, as if I'd had some oversized
friend stay the night. We'd sit at the table with Owen and Michael
Paul, waiting for Freda to serve our plates, and I'd think about how
it had all gotten too strange for me. It was as if I'd gone to bed a
child and awakened forty. Michael Paul was still nibbling at his
yeast cakes and picking his nose whenever he got a chance. Freda
was still telling Owen to shut up if he breathed hard. And I was
waiting for Freda to tell me what to do. I was starting to catch on
to how she liked rounding us up at the table, as if we were worshipers
in some tiny church waiting for her to speak the word. She gathered
the uncertain around her and offered up solemn declarations, so
when one morning she said, "You two should go away, make a life,"
I thought, Why not? What's to lose? And if this was how she saw
my future, with this cocky boy from Watson Chapel, someone to
take care of me, a full bingo card, then who was I to doubt her
instinct? I'd gotten irritated by her and wondered if I understood
her logic, but I always trusted her. I believed, too, that I wasn't as
strong as she was, fearing that without her my head would go haywire
and I'd be all alone, wondering how to make it stop. Maybe Eddie

would know what to do if she took him off in a corner and explained it, gave him instructions.

"What do you think about that, Eva?" I heard Freda say that last morning. "Going away and making a life."

She made it sound as if we'd wander off into America, like God's blessed children, ready to forge something dim and hopeful out of sheer need. That's what Eddie and I had in common. Need. I don't think we knew it then, but it took hold quick enough.

"Why not?" I said, looking to Eddie.

His face lit up, and he even put a forkful of grits to his mouth to show approval. "It's what I've been trying to convince her of all this time," he said.

All this time. One month. Eddie had a knack for exaggeration.

I remember how Freda looked the day we left, rocking on the porch swing with a book propped open on her lap, her beautiful, intelligent eyes as studious as a child's. For years I would remember her that way, like a Madonna, a new lace shawl draped over her head, strands of black and gray hair showing through, and how she stood to kiss me on the forehead, saying, "You'll be back some day, Eva. I promise."

Her voice cracked a bit when she said it, and I turned to wave as we walked to the car. I'd given up asking her what would happen. She wasn't telling.

E I G H T E E N

Wе made it all the way to Washington State. It was as far from the South as I had ever been, in a section of the country so brutally serene—its weather as mild as the expressions on people's faces— that I hated it from the beginning. I saw no true rivers here, wide and slow arteries that cut through the heart of a state or formed its sinuous boundaries. The streams—not rivers at all, to my mind— moved fast and shallow, noisy all the time. The trees were mostly evergreen and I found no comfort or kinship in them, no tie to their enduring mantle of green, never altering except to grow taller and more ominous. The forest had no bed of leaves for its floor, no glorious open spaces that let the sun heat the air with the sweet smell of sap. Dense stands of trees were nurtured by incessant drizzle and grew thick with ferns and mushrooms, creatures of the dark, and I could smell decay in those woods long before I entered them.

We lived in Eddie's old green Ford for a summer, sleeping in roadside parks, picking fruit in a border town because the Canadians didn't want us crossing over with just ten dollars in our pockets. It was an excuse to turn away the draft evaders pushing at their borders.

We took to the fields at dawn before the flood of workers came, hoping to get a spot in one of the rows so we'd be guaranteed a flat or two of berries or cucumbers that would net us no more than seven dollars for a day's work. The cucumbers were the worst, with rubbery spines that itched when they caught in my fingers. I had to pick them on my knees, not knowing I was pregnant at the time, disturbed by the heavy sickness in my belly as I crouched forward. I thought it must be how the cotton pickers felt when they bent deep into the rows, and I began to see that what I once had idealized was backbreaking work.

Eddie had told Freda grandly that what he did with his life depended on what he was offered. For now, this was it. I would watch him in the row up from mine, leaning forward as if to receive some punishment, and I could see his eyes, anxious and resentful. He tried to hide it, but I could see clearly that taking care of me wasn't what he'd bargained for. He'd wanted a pretty doll on his arm, no matter how many times he'd told Freda, Yes, he knew the meaning of the word *responsibility*. He would tell me that when we found a place to settle, I should find a job so he could go back to school.

"Be reasonable, Eva. I'm the one who can make the money," he'd say. "In the long run, if you look at it, you have no skills to offer."

He was right, I had to admit, but I didn't care for his saying it to me. Eddie was big on reason, or logic, or rationales, whichever word popped to his mouth first. He talked down to me a lot, as if I were a slow child with no conception of the world. He could be sweet though, and this kept me off balance, making me wonder sometimes if I really liked him more than I thought.

In the car at night we would climb into the back seat together and lie beneath an old Indian blanket Freda had given me when I left. It was then, in the dark, that I liked Eddie, the way he felt warm and solid pressed up next to me. He would run his hands through my hair, kiss my face, and tell me everything would be all right. He'd say it was just the two of us against the world, and when I told him that wasn't very rational, he'd say maybe I was right. He told me he'd never really had a girl of his own, someone who wanted to stay with him, be loyal. Sometimes I'd watch him walking toward me, his head hung down, and I'd notice how his hair curled around his ears like a little boy's, and I'd want to pull him to me, suckle him like a baby. He couldn't look me in the eye when he caught me watching him like that, and I figured it was from some shame that ran deep—maybe because he'd been poor all his life, or because his family wasn't educated or because his daddy was a drunk. We had more in common than I knew at first, a lot of ugliness. Sometimes I wanted to be nice to him just for that.

At the end of the day we'd cash in our fruit, standing in line with the migrants—hollow-eyed, hungry-looking people, who brought their tattered children with them, trying to double the day's income. I would watch them hold dirty palms upturned while the field boss counted out bills from a tin box, and think of the black children in the cotton fields in Arkansas. That memory was still pierced with nostalgia, coming from a land I loved. Here, where the sun shone less, I couldn't see into the hearts of people and call forth the compassion I had known as a child. Now I was just one of them, poor and dirty, and my outstretched hand looked no different than any other.

We moved on to Seattle when the season was done and continued calling the car home until Eddie got a job selling furniture at a wholesale house. We put together enough money to rent a place, and when I found out I was pregnant, Eddie asked me to marry him. I don't remember feeling one way or the other about it. I believed I'd cared enough for Ronnie to tell him no, but with Eddie it was like an experiment, something I could try.

We went to the big courthouse in downtown Seattle and stood before a justice of the peace, Eddie in his stretch jeans and I in a peasant dress that hid my growing belly. We had two court clerks as witnesses, and Eddie gave me his high school ring for a wedding band. I studied it and thought of Ronnie.

We moved into a tiny frame house set in a big yard full of fruit trees and flowering bushes. It was the yard I liked, how the afternoon sun played through the leaves and cast shadows on the mossy undergrowth. I'd pretend the house was set deep in a southern wood and I could walk out the front door and see cardinals perched high in the sweet gum trees. But there were no sweet gums here, and certainly no bird as bright as a cardinal. Instead I saw brown sparrows and mottled pigeons, starlings that screeched and dove, and gray squirrels whose coats were thin and ratty from city dwelling. I fed them all to fatten them up, but it never changed their colors, so perfectly matched to the temper of the weather. At times I'd catch a smell just like the ravine when I was young and would creep through the yard looking for the source, never finding it, figuring I was just crazy.

Eddie and I talked about how our lives would be if he had a chance to finish school. We'd buy a house someplace else, down South, maybe, and I'd have a big feather bed beneath an open window where I could watch the stars at night and have the sun warm on my face in the morning. We'd call the child Olivia. I knew it would be a girl and told him so.

I liked being pregnant. It was as if the life inside me absolved all that was dark and deadly and made me good and pure. When the doctor first told me, I had trouble believing him, thinking it must be a tumor that had taken root and given me a feeling of fullness. I felt good for a change, magical almost, and dreamt often of a little dark-haired girl standing beneath a sky fractured with constellations. It was the finest dream I had ever had.

At night I would lie in bed with Eddie and ask him to listen for a heartbeat in my belly. He'd get the oddest look on his face then, as if there were no connection to him and what pushed and curled beneath the tight skin. I asked him if he was happy we were going to have a child, and he said sure, who wouldn't be, but I knew it didn't mean the same to him. I didn't mind. The baby was the one real thing I had ever done, and I started praying, unused to the practice, that I would be good to her.

I thought often about what it would mean to be a mother, presto, with no clue how to go about it. It seemed a gift not to be conferred upon the ordinary, and I thought seriously about how I would be with this little girl. I would talk to her from the time she was born and not let up until I heard her speak her first words; if she needed comfort I would hold her until she slept. I'd stare at the empty crib in the corner of the tiny bedroom and imagine Olivia asleep inside it, safe and secure.

It had been two years since I had talked to Rita. I dreamt of her, seeing her as I had in those pictures at Freda's, standing alone in the middle of a cotton field. I'd awake wanting to touch her, just reach out my hand and stroke her face to make sure she was alive. I wrote to Freda asking if my mother was well. She wrote back that Rita was the same as always, just sicker, and that if the booze didn't kill her, John Earl would. Freda warned me to keep my distance, but I couldn't help it this time. I had to talk to her.

I thought a long time before I did it, picking up the receiver and putting it down, pretending to dial the number with the button depressed, saying, "Hello, Rita. This is Eva," into the dead mouth-piece, feeling my palms turn sweaty and my heart race.

What was so hard about calling your own mother? I wondered. People did it every day. What went through their heads before they picked up the phone? Did a cold fear take hold of them? Did the words "She'll hurt you, don't do it" run through their minds? Did they wonder if she'd be sober or even sane? Or did they just pick up the phone as if it were an everyday thing and dial the number? I took a deep breath and tried it that way.

When she said hello I told her right off I was pregnant—no "This is Eva," no "How are you," just "Rita, I'm pregnant," my voice tight as a highwire.

"I'll call you back," she said. Confused. I gave her the number and she hung up.

I stood in the tiny living room looking out the window at the deep gray of the Seattle sky, the receiver dead in my hand, and wondered what was so urgent that after two years she had to call back. It wasn't saving me the price of a phone call because she would have called back right away, and I waited a full hour to hear from her. And it couldn't be that she was contacting the hospital—screaming all the way to Virginia, Hey, I found the little bitch—because I was of age now, married and living in another state. She couldn't touch me that way anymore.

The phone rang and I stood staring at it for a moment, thinking I'd made a mistake. All I had to do was ignore it, she'd give up eventually. But I had to dive back in. It was like slamming your hand into a wall until you believed the wall hurt as bad as your hand. I reached for the receiver.

"Eva," she said, sounding half drunk. "I called Dr. Roberts and talked to him. He says you should have an abortion."

Just like that. Whack, from three thousand miles away, so hard I saw stars. Didn't I tell you? I heard Freda saying. Don't you know any better by now?

"What?" I said, stunned into ignorance. "What's that?"

I could hear her breathing heavy on the other end, ice rattling in a glass.

"You're too unstable to raise a child. Dr. Roberts says so."

I felt my face go hot with shame and anger. Shame that I had believed in my own goodness, that this was one thing I might do right, alone, without dragging anyone else into it. Anger that that weasel of a doctor could pretend to know me. Too unstable. I remembered him sitting behind that desk in Raleigh, rolling a pencil in his palms, studying me as if he had a microscope trained between my eyes. I remembered what it felt like to hate. I hadn't had such strong emotions for some time now. It came back to me the way breathing does when you've come from a depth of one hundred feet. I took in a sharp breath.

"Abortion," I said. "No. No. I can't. I won't. I'm too far along. I don't want to. I'll be a good mother. I really will."

"Adoption, then," she said, her voice thick. She could get drunk faster than anyone I knew.

"It's all I have," I said, hearing how pitiful I sounded, hating myself for it. "You can't make me. I won't."

"Be reasonable, Eva," she said. Hearing that from her, I almost laughed.

"Adoption! Abortion!" I yelled at her now. "It's what *you* should have done."

I hung up then, slamming the receiver so hard it cracked.

When I told Eddie about the call he was quiet for a long time, tipping back and forth in a rocking chair he'd smuggled out of the furniture store.

"She's crazy," I said to him, waiting for a response. "Don't you think so? To say that to your own daughter?"

I looked to him for affirmation now, for the conspiracy he was so fond of—me and Eddie against the world—but he could turn the tables on me and take the other side when I least expected it.

"Well, Eva," he said, pressing the tips of his long fingers together the way he did when he wanted to make a point. It was the tension I saw in those fingers that made me nervous. "Did you ever think about the practicality of a decision like that? I mean, financially. One less mouth to feed and all that."

My mouth dropped open.

"It's your child, too," I told him. "How can you say that? How can you?"

"Just a practical thought, Eva," he said. "No one said you had to do it."

"Go to hell," I said, and watched the tips of his fingers turn white.

N I N E T E E N

All hospitals reminded me of Blue Ridge. When we were driving across the country I'd see them in cities we'd pass through, the wide emergency doors that could open like a maw and suck you in. I knew that once you went through those doors it was all over. It didn't matter what was wrong, they'd find a reason to keep you. A ruptured spleen or a broken toe, it was all the same, and pretty soon they'd come for you and take you to that dark room in the basement where the shock machine hummed, so hot with voltage it practically jumped off the gurney.

When it came time to have the baby, Eddie had to yank at my hair to get me in the door of the hospital. I locked my knees and refused to move, and he started pulling at me, his face growing red, saying, "Don't be a baby, Eva. This is where you have to go. You have to."

But once he got me to the delivery room, Eddie decided to wait outside. They lay me flat out on a table and strapped my feet into stirrups. It scared the hell out of me, and I kept trying to raise my head to see what they were doing before a contraction would slam me back down, take the wind out of me and leave my upper lip slick with sweat.

"What are you going to do now?" I'd ask the doctor in a panicky voice when I could breathe right. "What are you doing? What are you going to do to me?"

I know he thought I was nuts because he turned to a nurse and said, "Doesn't this woman know why she's here?"

The nurse thought I was crazy for sure. When she lay a damp towel on my forehead, I felt the pressure build up in my chest, and

I pulled away, yelling, "Don't! Don't touch my head. Leave my head alone! I know what you're trying to do."

I had a fear of anyone touching my temples. Eddie had tried massaging me there once, and I'd run from the bed screaming, the memory of the electrodes and the rubber headband unbearable.

I kept telling myself this was different from Blue Ridge, but the panic came on so strong I couldn't breathe. It was as if someone were standing on my chest, and I guess I passed out because I don't remember the rest of it, not until Eddie came walking into my curtained room with the baby wrapped tight in a blanket. She was dark as a papoose, her hair a shock of black that strayed almost to her shoulders, tiny bumps that fluttered like a bird's breast when she breathed.

I took one look at her and cried, lifting my hand to a face smaller than my palm. She was soft as a kitten, perfectly formed, and as I looked at her I couldn't comprehend what I had done, whether it was good or bad, and I kept crying until she started up, too. I opened my gown and let her mouth rest where it belonged. I felt clean then and didn't need to look to Eddie to see what he thought about it all. I didn't even hear him slip past the curtains and walk away.

A fat nurse with a hypodermic came in that night to give me morphine for the pain. I'd torn something when I delivered Olivia and could feel the ache dragging like a knife down my belly. Eddie told me later it was when I was high on the drug that I called my mother.

I don't remember what I said, but it was enough to mend the damage caused by our last conversation. When Olivia was a few months old, Rita showed up on our doorstep.

T W E N T Y

I was feeding Olivia when I heard the knock at the door. I had been laughing, watching her mouth tighten up around my nipple until her lips turned white. I eased her away from my breast and wondered who it was. The only person who had ever come to visit since we'd moved in had been Mary, the next-door neighbor who had a boy barely a year old. But it wasn't her knock. Mary was loud and forthright and banged at the door to make herself heard. This was a tap tap tap, timid and secretive, and if I hadn't been sitting close by, I never would have heard it.

I opened the door, holding Olivia on my hip, and saw her standing there, her eyes nervous as a squirrel's. I'd remembered her eyes as blue, bloodshot, yes, but blue. Now they seemed to swim in her face like eggs with the whites gone bad. Her skin was a peculiar yellow color, like a faded tan, and the flesh hung loose on her arms. She looked a lot like BQ now, the Indian features prominent in her face. I wondered if it bothered her. She'd never liked being Indian. Her hands were so shaky she kept her fingers to her mouth to steady them, chewing at the stubs of fingernails. Her hair was dull and thin. I thought I might have seen her look worse, years ago back in Yazoo City, but she would have been very young then, practically a girl, and so I must have been mistaken. I was afraid that if I let her stand there too long she might buckle like a pile of sticks.

"I quit drinking, Eva," she said, as I opened the door wider, motioning her in. I couldn't get my voice yet so I just waved her past.

I wanted to say something, quick, afraid that if I didn't I might scare her off, but all my throat did was squeak, making useless sounds the way Olivia did in her sleep. I never remembered hugging her, not once in my life, but I tried now as she stood inside the door. It had taken something for her to come all this way—seven hours on a plane without a drink if nothing else. She'd had to leave John Earl in favor of me.

She jumped when I put my arms around her and I could feel her tremble. "Hey," I heard myself say. "Hey. That's really good." And I thought out of the blue of the ceiling above the shock table.

I asked her to sit down on the couch Eddie had brought home the week before and took the small shoulder bag she carried. I shook it instinctively, listening for a rattle or a clink.

"I told you," she said, not looking at me. "I quit."

"That's right," I said. "You did. That's good."

I noticed I was talking to her as if I had to keep her calm.

She reached for the baby, her arm trembling. It was a gesture of supplication, the kind you find in paintings of beggars fallen at the knees of Christ. It made me sad to look at her.

"Could I hold her?" she asked.

"Why?" I said.

"She's my granddaughter."

"No," I said. "Not that. Of course you can hold her. I meant why did you come?"

It *wasn't* okay though. I had a lightning fear that Rita might steal Olivia's breath, suck the life right out of her. I handed her over carefully.

"You asked me to come, Eva," she was saying. "Don't you remember?"

I told her Eddie had said something about it, but I was high on morphine when I made the call, and drugs made you say things you wouldn't ordinarily say.

"I see," she said. "I thought you needed me. It's what you said, anyway. I quit drinking so I could come see you and the baby."

So it was my fault she'd quit. There could be hell to pay for that. As far as needing her, Jesus, I'd always *needed* her.

She held Olivia on her lap carefully, as if she were a piece of crystal, and the baby's fat cheeks jiggled as Rita tried to keep her arms steady.

"Sure," I said, trying to picture myself asking her for something. It was unbelievable, but I guessed I'd done it. There were witnesses. "Of course," I continued. "Yeah. Every girl wants her mother around after she's had a baby."

It sounded stupid and phony. I didn't recall ever saying something so idiotic. I'd said it because I didn't want to hurt her, because as she sat there, looking as if she'd walked through a car wash, all the pity came rushing back.

"She looks like you," my mother said. "Baby baby baby. Hi, baby."

She chucked Olivia under the chin and smiled, sweet and crooked, her eyes kind. I'd seen that smile in a picture of her—the one where she lay in the porch swing, with her head on the lap of an old black woman. It was nice to see her that way, but as suddenly as the smile appeared it was gone, and she handed Olivia back to me.

"Eva," she said, trying to look me in the eye. She'd look up, catch me studying her, and look back down, like a kid trying to confess to something bad.

"Yes?" I kissed Olivia on the lips and licked the end of her nose. She giggled.

"Eva, I'm sorry. I came to say I'm sorry."

"You don't have—"

"No, Eva. Don't stop me, because if I don't say it now I won't ever do it. Just let me. Be quiet and let me talk . . . this is hard. I . . . I have to."

I didn't know if I wanted to hear an apology from her. If she was sorry, who could I blame? If she said "Forgive me," what would I do? I didn't know forgiveness. It went against my nature. And I felt comfortable with blame. I nodded and sat down on the edge of the couch, feeling my jaws go tight.

"There are a lot of things," she said. "I mean, I didn't write them down or anything—I should have—so I won't remember it all, but I have a list in my head, sort of. At least I did. Oh . . . God." She put her head in her hands. "It's hard to believe I've been so bad."

"You aren't bad," I said, feeling sorry for her. It's the way it always went. Anger. Sorrow. A little more anger, then hate. Pity. Confusion. I never knew how I'd feel about her.

"Hush now," she said. "Just let me talk."

So talk, I thought. Do it.

"Eva. Could I have a drink . . . of water? Water would help. Sometimes I put lemon juice in it and pretend it's wine. Isn't that silly?"

I stared at her and saw how sheepish she seemed. A bad little girl.

"No lemons," I said. "Sorry."

I got some water for her and watched the ice crash around in the glass as she put it to her lips.

"Doesn't that get a little old?" I asked, "shaking like that? Doesn't that get to you? I bet if you leaned against the wall the paint would peel."

"It calms down after a couple of weeks. You remember how it is. It takes a while. Jesus, Eva. I can't think. I'm sorry. Sorry for what I've put you through. Sorry I've been such a wreck all your life. When I'm sober I see how bad it's been. Then I want to drink to forget it. I like to forget. It's what I do best. Can I just say I'm sorry for all of it? Can we just let it go at that? Will you forgive me?"

She took a sip of water, and I could see tears spilling into the glass.

"Of course," I said, quick as I could, trying to get it out before my throat closed up. "Of course I forgive you."

It was a lie, the biggest one I've ever told, and when I said it I tried to imagine how it would really feel to forgive someone. I suspected it would feel clean, the way I had felt after Olivia was born. Why now? I wondered. Why was she sorry now? It was strange enough to see her sitting in my living room, this woman I loved and despised, pitied and worried over, tried to kill for, ran from, denied, and in the end, in some crazy way, feared. I feared what caring for her would do to me now. It bled me dry to love her.

Rita and Eddie got along as if they'd been born to the same litter. Thinking back on it, I see there must have been something I missed, like the way my mother looked at Eddie when she thought I wasn't watching. Or the way he deferred to her as if she were as important in my life as Freda. They were soul mates in no more than two days' time, and Eddie would take me aside at night, saying, "This can't be the same woman I heard about back in Watson Chapel," or, "She must have had a good reason to lock you up, Eva. I can't believe she'd deliberately hurt anyone."

Oh no, not her, I thought, not this woman. She didn't know word one about hurting people. And thanks for the vote of confidence. I looked at Eddie as if he were a traitor, and he just shrugged his shoulders. He was right about one thing though. She wasn't the same. The longer she stayed the stronger she seemed to get, the more she talked—to Eddie, mostly—the less her hands shook, and the more frequently she smiled. At first I thought it was a miracle, one of those magic acts that visits ordinary people, transforms hopeless wretches overnight so that in the morning everyone's walking around saying, "What the fuck happened?" and the person who's been changed just sits there grinning like a chimp. After a while I saw it was nothing more than Eddie that had come over Rita.

I'd wake in the morning and my mother would be in the kitchen making pancakes, telling me I couldn't send Eddie off to work on an empty stomach. I'd tell her it was enough to get myself up after the baby had cried all night, and she'd say that was no excuse, a woman should look after her man. I'd raise my eyebrows and keep my mouth shut, wondering what her next trick would be. Eddie ate it up. The most he ever got out of me was supper.

She spent more than a week with us, cooing and fussing over the baby, making me wonder at this maternal instinct that had come to her suddenly like a virus, like some week-long flu that would run its course. I tried talking to her about something other than what would please my man, about why, for instance, she had fought with John Earl all these years if pleasing a husband was such a goddamned easy thing to do.

"He's not so bad, Eva," she said. "If you knew him the way I do you'd understand."

"What's to understand?" I said. "That he wants your nose somewhere besides in the middle of your face?"

She said it wasn't very kind of me to talk that way after John Earl had supported us all those years. Excuse me, I said, just what ought I to have done to repay the stupid bastard? And what had happened to my feeling sorry for her? I wondered. Sorry had gone out the door the minute Eddie had walked in and said, "Pleased to meet you. Eva told me you were beautiful, but I had no idea."

Same old line. Slick Eddie in his stretch jeans, showing off his crotch. It worked every time. Eddie was the sort who appealed to desperate women, and Rita fit the mark. And if that was the case, then what was I?

Soon I was being shooed out of the kitchen at suppertime because Rita wanted to make something special for Eddie. A surprise. I told myself it shouldn't bother me—after all, she was sober, for Christ's sake.

But at night I would lie in bed after fixing up the couch for her and feel the tension growing. The longest I'd ever seen her make it without a drink back home had been two weeks. She'd be busy for a few days, full of hope, and then she'd crash. I tried to remember the way I saw it coming on—the telltale dryness of her mouth and the way her eyes got real scared-looking, as if she'd just realized she was going to die someday and there wasn't one damn thing she could do about it. I thought I'd seen that look when I'd told her goodnight, could have sworn she was starting to crack again and I'd had a glimpse of the woman my mother really was, one so whacked out by fear she'd do anything to nail it back tight in its box.

What had scared her? Me? She'd asked if I was happy, and when I said yes, fibbing because I'd never been quite sure what happy was, she'd looked disbelieving, as if I couldn't possibly be. It bugged her I'd said I was, lying or not. I could see it. And when Eddie would kiss me in front of her, she'd stand up in a huff and say, "Well. You should keep that sort of thing in the bedroom."

Since when did she get so moral? I wondered. If I remembered correctly, to her the bedroom might just as well have been all of the great outdoors. The longer she hung around, the more my patience dissolved. I asked politely one day when she might be going home, and she said, "Day after tomorrow, Eva," as if she'd had it in her head all along.

The afternoon before she left she walked up to the convenience store on the corner and came back with half a case of beer, a drink she wasn't partial to, but it would do in an emergency. I can't say I was surprised, not even disappointed, really, but I remembered clearly how she was when she drank, and I wanted to shoot her on the spot.

"Want a beer?" she asked, heading for the refrigerator, which was really nothing more than an icebox, one of those squat little white jobs, circa 1930. It had come with the house and kept Olivia's formula at an even room temperature. It would turn Rita's beer lukewarm in a hurry.

"Put it in the freezer," I said. "Like you used to. Go on. Hide it. Remember how you used to keep that glass of vodka in the freezer, thinking I didn't know what it was? Go ahead. Stick a glass up there. Make yourself at home."

"I'm nervous, Eva," she said. "You understand that. So much excitement with you and Eddie and the baby. You remember how I used to get nervous. What can it hurt? I'm leaving tomorrow. I'll just have a few."

At least she hadn't said, "I'll just have one." Why in the hell would she have just one, or even a few, when she had twelve racked up there at eye level, calling out, Come and get me, drink some more and you'll feel better. Better than what? The piece of shit you felt like when you walked in the door? Yes. Better than that. I could see now. It had been a strain on her all right.

"I shouldn't let you bring it in here," I told her. "I should just put my foot down. This is my house. Mine."

She settled herself on the couch and cracked a beer.

"Nice couch," she said. "Someday Eddie will fill this house with furniture."

Sure he will, I thought, piece by stolen piece.

"You hear me," I said. "This is my house. And what will Eddie think when he comes home and finds you drunk? He likes you. Why don't you just leave it that way?"

"I'm your mother, Eva," she said. "And if I want to have a beer, I'll have a beer. Maybe Eddie will have one with me."

I rolled my eyes at her. He probably would if he got home before she was half wrecked. I could always count on Eddie to do exactly as he pleased.

"What happened to 'I'm sorry'?" I asked her. "What you said when you got here? You're nice when you don't drink. I like you then. Come on, Rita, put it away."

She ignored me and I let her drink. All day long I let her drink, and when she'd finished the last of it, slumped down in a corner of the couch, I covered her up with the old Indian blanket and thought of her beautiful sister sitting on that same blanket with me by the river. They were night and day, those two, born of the same mother. How could it be? I looked at her face, the skin slack and wrinkled as a frog's belly, and hated her.

Eddie came in late, and I was in bed listening to Rita's fitful sleep, to cries and moans that sounded so hellish I felt blessed to be free of them, afraid that if I slept I'd walk right into the middle of her nightmare.

"What's wrong with your mom?" he asked, getting into bed, and I noticed how white his skin was, not a freckle on it. He reminded me of one of those salamanders who spent their lives in caves.

Mom, I thought. It was a word jumpy little sitcom kids called their mothers. Mom. It made her sound like someone else.

"My *mother*," I said, "is an alcoholic. Or did I mention that?"

"Oh," he said. "I get it. I'm sorry, Eva. I really am. Why didn't you stop her?"

I pulled up close to him and asked him to hold me. Eddie wasn't fond of outright displays of need, but sometimes he'd oblige.

"Stop her?" I said. "Stop her? You've got to be kidding. Nothing stops her. Not me. Not hell freezing over. Not guns. Not knives. Fists. You name it."

I fell asleep that way, with my head on his chest, and the next thing I remember is Eddie screaming, "Stop it! You're sick. Get away from me."

I woke to see my mother, naked, her hands under the covers of our bed, grabbing at Eddie, whispering, "Come on, baby, let me in there. Come on."

Olivia was screaming in the other room, and Eddie was swatting at my mother as if she were a big, persistent dog. I thought it was a dream. It had to be. She couldn't be that low.

"Stop it, lady," he was saying. "Stop it or I'll have to hit you. Leave me alone. Go back to bed. You hear?"

Eddie shoved her off onto the floor, and I could see her swollen belly, her tits flat and sagging, her scrawny legs. I'd seen her naked a lot when I was a kid. She liked to walk out of the bathroom that way, as if she'd accidentally forgotten her robe, but I always knew better. She was just trying to heat up the house so that sick fuck John Earl would come sniffing for her. But back then she'd had a body. What I saw now was pitiful. I was going to be sick. I grabbed at Eddie and said, "Let me by. Quick. I'm gonna throw up."

I tried stepping across her when I got out of bed, turning my head so I wouldn't have to look at her, but she caught hold of my foot and tripped me. I fell facedown onto the floor, flat on my nose, and it felt like the time John Earl had backhanded me. I shook her loose and crawled toward the bathroom, hearing Eddie wrestling with her, listening to her call out again and again, "Come on, baby, come on. Do it, baby."

Then there was a crash and she was quiet. I was too busy being sick to care what he'd done.

I went to Olivia's room after and picked her out of the crib, sitting with her in the rocking chair I'd dragged in just that day. I sang to her, trying to keep her quiet, and heard Eddie outside the door telling me Rita was getting sick all over the place and I'd better come help. I told him to clean it up and held Olivia closer to me, smelling the baby powder I'd rubbed into the folds of her neck.

"Then just come back to bed," I heard him say.

I never answered him and stayed in that chair with Olivia the rest of the night, my eyes wide open, my nose dripping blood onto Olivia's nightgown. I thought about how the ravine smelled in Yazoo City on a hot summer night; the way the cicadas buzzed so loud I could hear them even now, if I clenched my jaw really tight.

The next morning I woke her roughly, pushing her from side to side on the couch where Eddie had carried her after she'd passed out. I told her what she'd done, screamed it at her, saying she was jealous of me and couldn't stand to see me happy. Her eyes came open halfway, and her mouth was dry and sticky when she tried to speak.

"Need a drink," she said.

"Fuck you."

"Please."

"Say you're sorry," I shouted at her. "Say it. Repeat after me: 'I'm a drunk and a whore and a slut and a lousy mother.' Come on, say it! Say 'I'm sorry I tried to fuck your husband.' Say it."

"What?" she said, coming to a little more. "What's that?"

"SAY YOU'RE SORRY, RITA. Rita. Rita. Why did I have to call you that? Huh?" I pushed her again. "Tell me. Was it so people wouldn't think I was your kid?"

"I'm sorry," she said in a whiny, thin voice, so pathetic she reminded me of those shaky, neurotic chihuahuas old women carry under their arms. Squeal. Squeak. I'm sorry, Eva. Squeak. Whine. So sorry, Eva. I wanted to hit her.

I put her on a plane that afternoon. We didn't speak on the way to the airport, and when I let her off at the main door, she looked as broken and nervous as she'd been when she'd stood on my front steps more than a week before. Nothing would change, I told myself as she opened the car door and started to walk away. It wasn't worth it, all the emotion. I had to understand that. But I rolled down the window and screamed out at her anyway, "I hope you die, you bitch."

People turned to look at her then, a wreck of a woman making her way through the door, shaking so badly she could barely stand.

It didn't make me feel any better.

It wasn't long before Freda called, and I knew it had to be an emergency to make her use the phone.

"What happened out there?" she asked when I answered. I could hear her stomping her feet up and down, running in place. She always said if you had to talk on the phone you might as well do something constructive at the same time.

"How do you know anything happened?"

"She's in the hospital, Eva. She might die. John Earl called to tell me. Can you beat that? I knew it had to be serious."

Rita had gone back to Raleigh, Freda told me, and disappeared. A janitor had found her unconscious in the back lot of a church two days later. In the ambulance the medics had broken her ribs trying to get her heart started and had punctured both lungs. The stomach pump showed it was sleeping pills she'd taken, dozens of them, and still she hadn't died. That's how the janitor had found her, "sleeping," he'd said, right in the middle of the parking lot. Freda thought maybe she was trying to make it inside the church to die.

I didn't know what to say. I remembered the last thing I had shouted at her and flinched. So many times I had thought it would happen and had been ready for it, drilled from as far back as I could remember. I'd make plans about what to do: how I would act, where I would go. Now I couldn't recall any of it. All I could think was maybe it was best if she died. Then there might be an end to the pain, and not just hers. But how could I stand it? There would be guilt, and that scared me more than anything. Guilt was what had given me those thoughts of dying back in Watson Chapel, so much of it accumulated for the price of nothing. Guilt that I was a bad girl, and that I couldn't help it. Guilt that I could wish one man dead all those years and then put a knife to another one and walk away. Guilt because I hadn't saved my mother from a man who tried to beat the will out of her. I knew how guilt felt—ugly, heavy, and constant as grief. I didn't care if I slept or ate, and each day it was there, accusing, saying, "You're bad, Eva. You know you are." And no matter how right it felt to point my finger at someone else and say, "There goes the reason," I would always slink back to the belief that a black heart beat inside me. If she died, that guilt would be my legacy. If she died, I'd remember for the rest of my life what I'd yelled at her, and I'd believe I'd made it happen.

"I warned you," I heard Freda say on the other end of the line.

"I said stay away, honey, didn't I? Don't you trust me anymore, Eva?"

"Of course I do."

"Tell me what happened then."

I tried to go through it for her, how she'd gotten drunk and come after Eddie, but it made me sick. Whenever I thought about it, I was standing outside again, listening to her moan and beg for it, and I told Freda I had to go before I lost my breakfast.

"I told you, Eva. Kiss the baby for me."

"You did tell me," I said. "I know you did. Just let me know what happens."

But she never got the chance. It was Rita who called, sounding weak but definitely alive. She amazed me. When I heard her voice, I crazily imagined a steamroller moving down the street at high noon, my mother standing right in its path; it would flatten her out like a cartoon cat, and she'd just pop back up after it passed, full of poison, and walk away.

"Eva," she said, "I'm sorry for what happened. What you said happened. I really don't remember, but I'm sorry."

There had to be a trick to this, I thought, saying you were sorry over and over and then doing something worse than what you'd been sorry for in the first place. It had to be a game, like chess, where you had the king in the back corner, cried stalemate at your opponent, and then said, "Whoops. I'm sorry, the game's not really over. I was only kidding. I'm going to beat you silly again."

"What's that?" I said, wanting to hear her say it again.

"For . . . for . . . you know what I'm talking about. I'm sorry for the way I am . . . when I drink . . . Eva. Eva? You there?"

"How's that?" I said, proud of the dead tone in my voice, hoping she hadn't a clue how relieved I was she was alive.

"Listen," she said. "I want you to know something. I want you to know it wasn't your fault I tried to kill myself."

I pulled the receiver away from my ear and stared at it.

"Eva . . . Eva . . . ," I heard her saying from far away. "It's not your fault. Eva?"

I didn't get it. How could she know I'd blame myself if she died? How *could* she know unless she'd studied me all those years, gotten such a strong sense of who I was, she could pin me like an insect on a board? When I'd thought she'd been drunk out of her mind had she really been watching me, calculating what to do with that fragile sense of duty I brought to her each day? Had she really known I would kill for her, and was she just waiting until I tried so she could box me off and be rid of me? Was I the one mistake she couldn't face? Was I her biggest threat?

She was sounding frantic now. I put the receiver back to my ear.

"Eva? Are you there?"

"I'm here," I said. "I'm here all right."

"I was jealous of you. You were right. I was jealous of your happiness. Jealous of your baby. Of Eddie. It's true. I was wishing I could be happy like you."

She was crying now and I felt nothing. What a goal, I thought, to be happy just like me.

"So what are you going to do now that you know that?" I said, stiff as the cotton fields out Highway 79.

"What? Eva. What do you mean?"

I was silent.

"I'm sorry," she said. "I won't bother you anymore."

I hung up the phone and went to my baby who lay asleep in her crib. I watched her perfect lips blow out like a goldfish mouth with each breath. She looked at peace, and as I reached my hand in to touch her I thought maybe I could steal some of it if I just stood there long enough.

TWENTY-ONE

When I was young I believed I knew no fear, only anger. It was the belief itself that kept my fear tame and meek. But it had rested deep within me, reaching out with claws toward my heart, waiting for the right moment to seize and strangle any vestige of boldness, any show of rage. It moved through me like an iceberg, gouging out channels where panic could move freely. It seems now that I awoke one day and it was what I had become. Fear. A thing as palpable as rage, but deadlier.

It was in the years after Rita's visit that it started to take hold. I began to have a hard time remembering why I'd married Eddie, and an even harder time figuring why we'd come to Seattle. None of it fit. Not the city. Not me. Not Eddie. Even Olivia looked like an orphan to me some days, as if I could pass her on the street and wonder whose child she was. Sometimes it seemed I'd been born right there on the spot: a full-grown woman with a child on my hip and a husband who had a passion for smuggling furniture out of dark warehouses in the middle of the night. I spent weeks at a time wondering how I had come to be with them, watching Eddie sit on the couch in his polyester jeans, wearing a pair of slippers, eating, always eating. He'd gained a lot of weight and looked now like the redneck that had been living in him all these years. By now the house was choked with cheap furniture, chairs and tables and night-stands that looked ready for the junk pile even when they were new. Eddie's future took shape every time he walked in the door with a new piece of fake mahogany. It was the one thing he really did well.

He wasn't too bad with Olivia. She was growing up to be an

inquisitive girl, sturdy and dark-haired, and she could keep Eddie's attention longer than I could.

I thought it curious that he could even tolerate a child after he told me stories about his own daddy back in Watson Chapel, a drunk who called Eddie stupid at every turn, always expecting too much of him, and of how it finally wore him down into leaving one day, right out the door and straight to Harry Si's, where he worked and slept in a back room while trying to go to school. There was a lot I hadn't known about Eddie when I met him. It turned out he wasn't really a college man; one credit in psychology and one in bonehead math were the only ones he'd completed. Eddie's mother had drowned herself in the river one Saturday night when Eddie was ten years old. It's all he ever told me about it, just that it had happened. Eddie grew fond of telling me what a hard life he'd had, and we took to competing with each other about whose past was sorrier. I started thinking Eddie was making some of his up to get an edge on me. My father beat me. Well, I had shock treatments. Top that. We were a pair no matter how you looked at it, both of us shot through with doubts. Olivia would watch us sometimes, arguing about who'd had it rougher, and just shake her head. It unnerved me when she did that, as if she could already see what was coming.

I tried going to school, taking science classes at the university, but it didn't last long. In a chemistry class I had to give an oral report, which meant standing before a class of one hundred students and making sense, not something I'd been accustomed to doing in my life.

The teacher had said it was a proving ground for our ideas, and if we couldn't explain something to someone else, the information was of no use to us. I had a good clue what he'd meant by that. I'd tried to explain to Eddie why, out of the blue, I broke down in tears and couldn't breathe right. I told him it felt like I was choking inside, and sometimes it got so bad I wanted to run, anywhere, it didn't matter, just run as fast as I could. He didn't get it though. He'd just look at me funny and walk out of the room.

The day I had to speak I took my report—ten pages on the effects of full-spectrum light on plant response—to the front of the class and placed it on the podium. I looked down at the words I'd typed, thinking all I had to do was read them and it would be over; that's when the choking feeling started, and I couldn't get my mouth to work. I looked out into the wide room filled with people my own age and younger—most dressed in jeans and sweatshirts, just a regular crowd—and they all started to melt together, like a mirage of water on an asphalt highway on a hot summer day. There were tears in my eyes, and as I looked back down at the paper I saw nothing but straight black lines, row after row of them, and then a splattering of teardrops in the middle of the page. I noticed how the paper puckered as the tears soaked in. My legs started to shake and I had to hold on to the podium to keep them from buckling. My chest and throat felt hot and my hands started to go numb. I don't know how long I stood there, but I remember a face in the front row through the blur—a fat boy with pimples—and he looked from my face down into his lap, too embarrassed to stare any longer. After that, everything turned the color of mercury, and the next thing I knew I was outside the classroom and running. I never went back.

I asked Eddie what was wrong with me. I did that a lot now, thinking this was the time I had feared would come, when I'd lose control and Eddie would have to call Freda and ask, "Now what do I do with her?"

"Come on, Eddie," I said to him, following him around the house, getting nervous all over again thinking about what had happened. "Tell me what's going on."

He finally sat down and started playing with the tips of his fingers, pressing them against each other, letting me know he was about to make a point. He sat there for a long time, his belly edging out over his jeans, studying me.

"You're a neurotic, Eva," he finally said. "I read about it. You can't deal with things so you just fall apart."

I'd depended so on Freda to instruct me, to say Here is what it's all about, now do it. I was looking to Eddie for the same thing. He was a poor substitute, but like the dull, shoe-flapping boy I'd known in high school, he was all I had. I thought myself weak for coming to him again and again, asking pitifully for answers, saying, Please, Eddie, explain. Make it better. Make it go away.

I nodded my head now, pretending that what he was telling me was good news, just what I needed to hear.

"You see, Eva," he continued, "what you're afraid of isn't real. Not real at all. It can't hurt you."

So why does it boil up in me like lye, burn my throat, turn my hands to ice? Huh? Eddie? Answer me that.

"So what do I do, Eddie?"

"Just don't be afraid, Eva. That's all there is to it," he said, looking full of himself in his candy-ass striped shirt with chicken gravy spilled down the front. I hated how it pleased him to give me advice. It made his day.

So why did I run to him in the first place, say to him, Make sense of this, I can't? I couldn't figure it. My head was full of noodles— I worried I was going nuts. I couldn't go to school. That was out of the question. Every time I thought about it I felt the humiliation creep up my neck and burn me like a rash. I wasn't like the rest of those people, hell no. I was defective, an emotional fuck-up. What do I do with myself, Eddie? I can't just stay here all day when Olivia's in school. Get a job. Try that, he said. Maybe that will help.

So I got a job, taking care of old people in their homes. It took all the nerve I had to go to the agency and fill out an application. They wanted to know what experience I had, so I lied and said I'd worked in a psychiatric hospital in Virginia. What's to lose? I thought. It sounded impressive, and I had a quick fantasy about how it would have been if I had worked there. I'd have stripped the wires to the shock machine and taken a baseball bat to it, then walked through the hospital with Dr. Fox's twenty-pound set of keys, opening doors right and left, calling into the rooms, "Time to make a run for it. Time to pack up and get the fuck out of here."

The agency never checked. They said they had. They lied.

Olivia was in school by then and had a miniature life of her own. Eddie had his work. And I was the one still looking, baffled by the day-to-day, frightened of what stirred inside me.

I took the bus to homes all over the city, and the old ladies I visited could have been the same blue-haired woman with a different dress. I'd go in to fix their meals, talk to them, let them talk, and it always seemed like the same conversation, how things had been when they were young. It was a reverie that held promise in the telling, but the reality sat before me and her face was wrinkled, her wedding band loose on her skinny finger. They'd drag out pictures and point to fresh, tight-skinned faces, saying, "This was me when . . . ," and I would remember Freda's box of tattered pictures. These women's lives seemed empty, their contacts so few I was the bright spot in their week. Had life been so good to them once, I wondered, that the memory was without pain? It seemed cruel to ask, and I understood how they needed to believe there had been a better time.

After a couple of months I had to quit the job. I'd started to panic when I rode the bus. I'd be sitting there, looking out the window, and realize all of a sudden how far away I was from home— from Olivia and Eddie and from the way the house looked with all the furniture jammed into it—and I'd try to remember what they looked like, as if remembering them made me real. But sometimes I couldn't remember, as if it were all a dream, and pretty soon I'd start thinking it *was* a dream and I was stuck on a bus in a city I didn't know, and I'd try to think of the name of the city and it wouldn't come to me. I'd remember how Dr. Roberts had asked, "Do things ever seem unreal to you, Eva?"

And my hands would start sweating and my mouth would feel as if it were stuffed with wadded paper. I'd think, This isn't real. No. It's not real. And what can I do about it? What can I do? Remember Olivia's face. Remember Eddie. What does the house look like? You live there with your girl, do you? And what does your husband do? I'd start shaking all over and try hard to cry because I knew if I didn't I'd scream, and if I started I might not stop. But I couldn't cry. And the panic grew. One day I just got up out of my seat and started screaming.

The bus driver put me off in a neighborhood I'd never seen before. It took me five hours to get home, and by the time I did Eddie was there with Olivia, who was crying. When I asked her what was the matter, she said, "I thought you'd died, Mama. I thought you'd gone crazy and died."

"Where'd she get that, Eva?" Eddie started up. "You want to tell me where our girl got that business?"

I knew where she'd gotten it all right. She'd gotten it from watching me wring my hands and pace the floor, tear at my hair and scream at Eddie that I might as well kill myself I was so confused. She'd gotten it from listening to her mother.

There was a sudden, cold piercing in my heart.

"What am I going to do with you, Eva?" Eddie said after I told him what happened. "You're not making any sense anymore. Afraid to ride a bus. Afraid to go to school. Maybe you need to see a doctor."

I told him to forget that idea right away. I'd had enough of doctors, and if I couldn't go to school and I couldn't work, then I'd just stay home, cook, and do the laundry. It was plenty of work for anyone, I told him. The truth was, I never wanted to walk out the front door again.

I swore to Olivia secretly that I'd never hurt her. I'd whisper it to her while I sat in the rocker, holding her, staring at her face, thinking there were so many things I could do wrong. And she'd say to me, looking up with eyes as black as Freda's. "I know you won't, Mama."

My big girl, the one I'd talked to from the moment she had opened her eyes, loved to hear about the ravine and the way the floods came pushing through it wild as horses. Holding her face close to mine, I would tell her about the rocks I'd found there, the names of the birds, the trees, and the way the river looked in summer. She absorbed it all, and by the time she was ten there was no child who knew the outdoors as well as she—what there was to know in this gray city. She'd come in the front door holding a fistful of leaves saying, "They're maple, Mama. I know. I know because how you told me."

But, oh, there were so many things I could do wrong, so many accidental things—out of fear or ignorance—and I worried I would do them. I'd read about a mother who'd put ground glass in her child's food. When the doctors asked why she did it, she said, "I didn't want her to suffer." And when told the child had hemorrhaged to death, she said, "Once is not so bad."

I worried I could damage Olivia just by being near her.

At night, when Eddie was asleep, Olivia and I would walk out into the yard filled with fruit trees. We'd stand and look up at the sky, waiting for the clouds to part so we could see fragments of constellations and pieces of the moon. I'd name the stars for her, and she would mimic those ancient sounds, saying "Antares" over and over again because she liked the way it made her feel.

"Like I can float," she'd say. "All the way up to the stars."

I would tell her how the sky had looked from my window in Yazoo City, broad and certain as the flow of a river, and that all I wanted to do when I was a girl was step into it and be carried away.

"That would be fun," she'd say. "Let's try."

And we'd stand there in the yard, flapping our arms, pretending we could fly.

I loved Olivia, her soft sweet smell and the way she held to me tight. I never had to try to love her. As the years passed I tried to anticipate her needs and fears so that she wouldn't worry, afraid I might care too little, afraid I was too damaged to be trusted. It didn't work. I couldn't shore up what did not exist. I couldn't reach into a pile of riches and say, "Here child, take all you want. I have plenty to give," when all there was in me was dust. But I know I loved her. No one could ever tell me that wasn't so.

T W E N T Y - T W O

Eddie was different. I can't say now I ever loved him. I couldn't love him. Wouldn't. Not even if you paid me would I say I had. It's not that he was such a bad man. He ate too much and was as lazy as any other man, but that didn't make him bad. I realized too late that you can love anyone just a little, if you keep your distance.

I told myself I needed Eddie and began to believe it so strong I couldn't imagine being alone. After I'd left the hospital and made it back to Freda's, I didn't want anything but certainty—to wake each day and have the same person there, someone who would say, "Time to get up, Eva"—and when I went to bed to be able to glance over at that person and say to myself, See, it's okay, nothing has changed today. I had discovered I could function if there were no surprises thrown into the order of things. I needed someone as steady as the river. Eddie was what I had.

I used to think it was all Eddie's fault we didn't get along because he was easier to blame, and I remember his words more clearly than I do mine. The Listen-to-me-Eva, I-know-what's-bests, that became more and more frequent. And then later, when he'd had enough, when it had gotten hard for me to step outside the front door without my hands sweating, "You're stupid. Incompetent. You can't do anything."

The more I stayed at home, the more Eddie said that was where I belonged.

Looking back on it, I see how my dependency on Eddie grew like a tumor, its roots deep. It choked off the blood that once sustained me, even if that blood had been as deadly wild as napalm. I woke in the morning next to a man I didn't know, had never known,

227

with a fear in my gut that if he left me I wouldn't want to eat or sleep but just wander from room to room, or sit and stare, because there'd be nothing left of me anymore, not as daughter, whore, wretch, wife, failure, or any of a hundred names that meant and always would mean that I could not move through the world alone, no matter how much I tried to keep the rage alive.

When Eddie was around we fought—about Olivia, about my ragged bathrobe, about who had a tougher life, about what I cooked or didn't cook. It didn't matter. We would square off in the beginning, equals it seemed, but I would always back down because in my heart I really believed the cruel things Eddie said.

When he said I was weak and didn't have a mind of my own, I believed him. When he said the only thing I knew how to do was fuck, I tried to take a vague pride in it, but I felt like a leper.

He didn't have solid reasons for what bothered him about me. It's as if he'd gotten sick of me by degrees and saw that the odd, pretty girl he'd married was really a despicable woman with snakes crawling in her head. He started doing quirky things to let me know he had the upper hand. I'd wake in the middle of the night and he'd be inside me, pushing so hard I thought maybe he was trying to make me feel it for once. I'd told him during one of our fights that he was a lousy lover and that I'd seen chihuahuas who were better hung. It was the truth, and I guess poking me in the middle of the night was his revenge. Freda had told me once that an insult to the genitals was the one sure way to hurt a man.

And I'd told him I hated the way he wouldn't bathe for two weeks at a time, or how he'd set a piece of fried chicken on the arm of a chair until the grease soaked in. Mostly I didn't like the way he lied, coming home late at night, never looking me in the eye, saying he'd gone out for drinks with a friend. I might have believed him if he'd had any friends. But Eddie always alienated people with his know-it-all attitude, and although it bothered me to feel sorry for him, I did.

I always said I was sorry. I'd crawl up next to him on the couch while he sat watching TV, a big console model he'd lifted from the store, rest my head against his shoulder, and say I wouldn't know what to do without him. I'd notice how his hazel eyes stared straight at the screen, the way his brown hair curled around his ears, and would imagine how it would feel to run an icepick straight through to his eardrum, saying all the while, "I love you, Eddie. I'm sorry, Eddie. I need you, Eddie."

I'd thought about leaving him but wondered how far away I would get before the panic took hold. I imagined standing on a roadside, Olivia next to me, staring in one direction and then another, and seeing nothing. It's the way the future looked, dim as that in-between light right before dawn, never changing in intensity, never black one day and blue the next.

Make a new life, Freda had said, with this boy I've found for you. This boy you can wind up and make do what you want; all you have to know is how many times to turn the key. But I didn't know. She hadn't said what to do if he started telling me how to think, if he said, "Eva, just listen to me and do what I say, and you'll be fine."

I wanted to believe it was that easy, but there are lies, and then there are bigger lies.

And she hadn't said what to do when my marbles started falling into the slots on the wheel, one after the other.

The panic had gotten so bad I'd be standing in a grocery store, in the middle of an aisle of canned goods, and my head would start feeling like it was made of gauze. My hands would turn wet and cold, my heart would race, and colors would grow brighter, as if a high-intensity switch had been tripped. They'd start to blend to-gether into one great pulse of silver, and I could feel people passing by me, staring. I'd see their faces staring right through me, bright as spotlights, and want to scream. One day, when the walls of the store began to close in on me, I ran outside so I could breathe. I slammed head-on into a postman and knocked his leather sack off his shoulder, scattering letters across the parking lot. When I grabbed him by the arm, he looked at me funny, really funny, and said, "Is there anything I can do, Miss?"

Miss. It sounded so impersonal.

"My name's Eva," I yelled at him. "Eva! I have a name."

I wanted to scream "Help me!" until he really understood what I meant. "Help me!" until he got the grasp of what it felt like to be me, packed to my eyes with fear, scared to stand still, scared to run. "Help me!" until he ran off in his own panic, yelling, "Come quick. This woman needs help. I swear to God. Come quick before it's too late."

But I didn't. I let go of his arm and looked around, dazed, remembering I'd left Olivia inside, too afraid to go back in. If I went back everything would start melting again, and maybe this time I wouldn't get out. I told the mailman I felt sick and needed some air, and would he please go find my daughter.

He brought Olivia out to me, his arm around her shoulder, and I wished for a moment he were her father, or my father, this nice man we didn't know. Her face was streaked with tears, and she was pressing her shirttail up to her nose, trying to blow it. It broke my heart. I remember how low I felt, how incompetent, just like Eddie said, afraid to do the simplest things. How could I say I was a mother to my girl when I'd run screaming from her, pushing people out of my way, leaving her as alone as I'd been left, in front of those locked doors on those black nights back in Yazoo City? What did she think of me, this shaking wreck of a woman standing in a supermarket parking lot, letters scattered all around? She moved next to me and put her arms around my waist.

"You all right, Mama?" she asked. "I was worried about you."

I told myself I didn't have to do it, that Eddie would do the shopping and the laundry if I just slept with him more, or tried to please him, or was just nice once in a while. If I listened to everything he said, he'd take good care of us, and I could be sweet to Olivia the way a mother should be. That would be enough.

When Eddie saw the panic was getting worse, he said I needed to go to a doctor and get some pills.

"I can't take it anymore, Eva," he told me. "It's starting to drive *me* crazy."

His name was Dr. Faust. I'd liked the sound of it when Eddie and I found it listed in the Yellow Pages, thinking a man with such a name would know something of evil and the means to purge it.

I remember how he looked at me when I walked into the office— that standard, carpeted square of a room where everything was just so. The potted plant, the thick chair, the honest-to-God mahogany desk, the desk lamp turned on low beam—as if he didn't need the light to see right inside my head, clear through to the stripped gears that strained with the turning of each thought. He had black eyes, black hair, and a black moustache. I looked to his fingernails when I sat down to see if they were black.

This is a mistake, I thought, as I tried to get comfortable in the chair. Not in a million years should I ever agree to this, no matter how nuts I get.

Dr. Faust leaned back in his chair.

"Tell me what the trouble is, Eva," he said, personal right off the bat. "I like to know right away what's going on. We can waste time later with tests."

His way of being chummy, I guessed. So I told him, as best I could, what real panic felt like. Not the ordinary fear a person had when, say, a snake crawled past him, but fear so total it was impossible to breathe, to think, to speak. Unspeakable panic, that's what it was. I gave him a chance to peek through the window and see what it was like to believe that the world was going to swallow you whole and never make a sound. When I was done, he was looking at me differently, as if suddenly my life was of great interest to him.

"It has a name, Eva," he said, looking at me intently. "Your fear has a name."

"What's that?"

"Agoraphobia," he said. "Displaced fear."

He was rolling a pen in his palms, looking as if he'd said the magic word.

"And this fear goes deeper than you might have guessed. We need to get to the source of it, Eva. It's in your past. I can help you with that. Have you ever been hospitalized, Eva?"

I sat up very straight in the chair, folding my hands in my lap gently, trying not to give anything away.

"No. Of course not," I lied. "Why do you ask?"

"I ask," he said, "because hospitalization is always an option for my patients, and I need to know your background."

I got up very slowly from the chair, appreciating how soft and cushiony it was. Eddie had never brought home such a nice chair.

I reached down for my purse and placed it very carefully on my arm. Everything slow, easy, no need to panic. Just take it easy. Push back the chair. Smile. Turn around and walk toward the door.

I had my hand on the doorknob and saw how easily it was turning, just about to open, when I heard him say, "Where are you going, Eva?"

"Bye," I said. "I'm going home now."

No, thank you very much, I won't be needing any of your special therapy today, doctor. I won't be checking into any hospital to-morrow to have my battery recharged, but I may just have my head examined for coming to see you.

No. They weren't going to lock me up again. I'd die first.

I told Eddie it had been a stupid idea in the first place to think a shrink could help me, and I promised to get hold of myself. I'd buck up, be strong, be tough. Things would get better, I told Eddie. But they didn't.

A couple of years passed and I stayed right in the middle of it. It got so I couldn't sleep from worrying about the panic, when it would come, how I would feel when it took me over. I lost weight and clung to Eddie so much he said I was disgusting. He threatened to leave and I begged him not to, crying, whining, saying I didn't know what to do and couldn't live without him. He said what else was new and hit me. I'd grabbed hold of his shirt as he tried to get out the door and saw the back of his hand before it hit my jaw.

I remember touching my fingers to my lip and feeling how sticky it was, then seeing the blood on my hand, bright as a cardinal's feather.

"You said you'd never hit a woman," I cried at him as he pushed me out of the way.

"You make it easy," he said.

He gunned the motor of the car and pulled out of the driveway. Olivia had come out of her room, and I heard her behind me but couldn't turn to look at her, knowing what I would see. I knew what resentment looked like now. I had seen it in Olivia's eyes many times. She'd grown tired of trying to comfort me, tired of seeing her mother cry and beg. She had come to hate me.

"What's wrong now, Mother?" I heard her ask, sarcastically.

"Nothing," I told her, not turning around. "Nothing. I'm just a little nervous, and your father needed some fresh air."

"Don't lie," she said. "Just don't lie to me."

"I'm sorry," I said.

"I'll bet," I heard her say as she slammed the bedroom door.

Eddie came back in a few days to apologize, saying he felt sorry for me. I let him. It was the only defense I had. But I always got a lecture about how it had gone on long enough, and how I should take a look at our girl, see what it was doing to her.

"Do you want her to hate you, Eva?" he asked me. "Is that what you want? For her to grow up seeing her own mother afraid . . . afraid of . . . everything? Tell me."

I told him, no, it wasn't what I wanted. And I didn't want help, either. I just needed time. Something to calm me down. If I were calm, I told him, everything would be better.

He'd brought home some beer that night. There hadn't been any in the house for years, since Rita's visit, and it was the one rule of mine Eddie had continued to respect. Now I didn't care if he brought in a truckload.

"Let me have one," I said.

"Sure," Eddie said. "Why not? Maybe it'll help."

Halfway through the bottle, I felt as if warm honey had been poured into my veins. This was it. This was the medicine I had needed. I told Eddie how it felt and he said, "Good. Have another one. It'll help you sleep."

TWENTY-THREE

Back in Yazoo City on those summer nights so hot my nightshirt clung to my thighs, and my hair lay against my back in wet strands, I would open the front door steadily, quietly, so they wouldn't know I had gone. I'd walk across the street, the blacktop warm beneath my bare feet, toward the ravine, my arms held out like a sleepwalker. I would imagine a cool wind blowing up under my nightshirt and out the sleeves, so forceful it could carry me off my feet.

I believed in beauty then, in magic, in the oasis of constellations above me, watering holes for the universe where there was light and comfort and music so clear and precise it could make your heart stop.

Down at the ravine I would run my hand deep into the potholes, feeling for the life there. I would think often of the blond-haired girl who'd floated by in the flood, a dead girl I knew now, carried by the river of water onto some higher ground where her body would be shoaled, snagged against a tree trunk by the leftover rag of a print dress, a pretty thing her mother had dressed her in before she went out to play. And her body would lie there, forgotten, still now after the madness of the water, no memory of the drowning, no consciousness to prove it ever happened, just her arms and legs splayed out like broken sticks there in the trash, her open mouth round and blue.

"I'll never be like her," I would say to myself, there on my knees in the dark, the ghostly white of my nightshirt muddied down the front. "Never." I'd repeat, and I said it as much of my mother as I did the drowned girl.

I would try to forget my mother's face when I was in the ravine, the way it looked bruised even when she hadn't been hit, and sometimes, if I lay on my back and counted the stars, I could. There were so many of them I wouldn't be able to count them all if I stayed there one hundred years, but it would always come back to me, and I would say again how I'd never be like her, feeling like a traitor somehow, sad not to honor her. I used to think it might have been all she ever needed, to have someone say what a fine woman she was. It might have made a difference.

I came to the moment in the history of my own fate where I stood looking into the mirror at a face so like my mother's, defeat and pain mapping the surface, that I cried out "Oh," as if I had seen a ghost, but one that still lived, caught between life and death, making promises to both sides but edging closer to the darker one. I saw the bloated creases beneath my eyes, skin the color of parchment paper, an upper lip swollen like the purple flesh of a plum where Eddie had smacked me. All of it as familiar and real as certain dreams. What was it that brought me here, the bad-joke committee laughing in my head, saying, "This is what you get. This is what you deserve. Did you think it would be any different? Did you? What were your plans, fool." Or was it genetics, maybe, a simple package, bound tight as cells and chromosomes, defective as the lie it was? Freda had said a lot of us were doomed that way.

Before she died, I asked her.

"Tell me," I demanded, self-pitying and morose. "Tell me why I ended up this way."

"It's a path," she said, her eyes half closed, heavy as the death that stalked her. "A path right to the center, Eva. Don't you know by now?"

It takes years to kill yourself if you don't do it the quick way. A knife in the throat is cleaner, and a gun can do the same amount of damage in ten seconds that it took me five years to do. I thought I'd found a way, finally, to stay calm and sure and steady. And blind. That, too.

When I drank, everything went away. I remembered how it had been back in Watson Chapel at the Rendezvous with Eddie, how easily it went down and how warm and good I felt afterward. The only thing that took away that good feeling was taking away the booze, and I wouldn't let that happen now. I had found the medicine I needed and understood why my mother swam in it, craved it, begged for it. No matter if she drowned. No matter if I did. Floating in that calm was the only sensation I wanted. I took it as a second blood and let it pump and push, telling me what to do. Have a drink. You'll feel better. Have two. It'll make it easier. Have more. More, until you're so soaked your skin is tight and there's nothing you can do but let it take you.

It took away the panic that caught in my throat when I woke, and the quicker I could get a drink down, the more distant the fear grew, like thunder in a receding storm. I loved the taste of it, bourbon straight, or gin, vodka, beer—it didn't matter—seductive as the tip of a man's tongue on my breast. Better. Because no man could wash me with a hope so pure.

And at first everything *was* easier. I could go places with Olivia and not run screaming like a madwoman through the first open door. I could meet men who were better in bed than Eddie. I'd bring them home with me when Olivia was in school, but Eddie always knew. He said he could smell them on me. I didn't care. Eddie was nothing more to me now than a fat, dumb hick from Arkansas. If he knocked me around, there was eighty-proof painkiller in the kitchen cabinet. I could even look in the mirror and believe I was beautiful again, usually at three in the morning when I was taking a last drink, the one, I told myself, I needed to make me sleep.

I'd think of Ronnie then, of how I'd seen once in his eyes everything that might have been good in me, and I'd look in the mirror and shout, "Hey! Eva. You're beautiful. Just like a cat."

Like a cat, that lion in Africa felled by the hunters, who was surely drawing a circle with his own blood to lie down in the center of it, tired, alone, waiting to die. Did I see it when I took that first drink, how two ounces of blood seeped through the capillaries for every ounce of liquor? Did I see the hemorrhaging behind my eyes, in my heart, down in my gut each time I lifted the bottle? Did I know and still walk blind into a river running wild across rocks sharp as razors? How could I? It felt too good each time it went down, sure as fire in a dry forest, strong as those gospel voices echoing by the river.

But that sense of power doesn't last forever. The poison takes hold, the body starts to die. It dies if you feed it what it wants. It dies if you don't.

I took to drinking as if Jesus himself had written the prescription. It was what I knew how to do, what I was born to do, and fuck all the rest of it. I had a capacity greater than any man's, drinking Eddie under the table early on. I thought at first it was something we might do together, but I was too serious about it for Eddie. It was my calling.

By the time Olivia was fifteen I was drinking all day, every day, and into the night, oblivious, almost, to Eddie's anger—to him— now that I was nothing but a useless drunk, a leech, an ingrate. Oblivious, almost, to my daughter's vague weariness, the way she looked at me when she came home from school, wary, as if I might reach out a tentacle and pull her to me. I would remember Rita's face and pour another beer, or a shot of vodka, to make it go away. It was the plasma that washed through me now. Six beers took the shakes away and made my tongue work. But I had less and less to say.

I worked at it, even before I got out of bed in the morning. It was my career, the one thing I did better than anything else, ever. I was predictable, dependable about it, relentless. At night, when my head felt thick, and I stumbled and slurred my words, I never forgot, not once, to put a bottle by the bed. When I came to in the middle of the night, I would reach for it, hands shaking so badly half the booze would spill before it reached my mouth.

Olivia got herself off to school alone in those days. We had stopped talking and no longer snuck out into the yard at night to watch the stars. She had come to me once, in the morning, kneeling beside the bed, and I had looked up at her, startled by how old she had become, my baby girl with the jet-black hair that hung to her waist now, my child who had a woman's figure. I had reached out to touch her hair and she had slapped my hand away, saying, "I want you to get help, Mama. Do you understand? Before it kills you."

I had nodded, promising I would, waiting for her to slip out the front door so I could put the bottle to my mouth.

It had started to make me sick, so sick I had to drink fast, outwit it, so the nausea would go away. Sometimes I made it to the sink in the bathroom before I threw up, and I'd think what a waste it was, all that booze I'd swallowed, useless now.

I stopped going out. The panic hadn't come back, but it had been replaced by something different, an apathy so final I did nothing but sit and drink all day in front of the television, the one thing Freda had said would make a fool of me. I had news for her. There were other things that worked just as well. I'd drink a beer an hour, or two, to keep the feeling level and my hands steady. I sat through game shows, talk shows, soap operas, saw Reagan picked off by John Hinckley, watched the *Challenger* turn into a ball of vapor. It was all the same show, really.

Eddie brought me what I needed. It reminded me of the metal comb Roy had given me at Blue Ridge—a tool both deadly and useful. It's the way I looked at the booze Eddie toted in by the sackful. I asked him why, if my drinking disgusted him so, he kept me supplied, and he answered, sulkily, that it was the only thing he knew to do. What if I killed somebody out there? he wondered. What then? But I knew it was what he wanted.

"It's payday, Eva," he would say, walking in the front door with a sack of imported beer, and he would toast me, clinking his bottle against mine as if it were some special occasion and not the beginning of another night of fighting.

The fights were no different than the ones I remembered when I was a kid. They could start with a look or a word or a movement, the sound of a bottle cap being unscrewed.

"You drink too much, Eva."

"You bring it to me."

"You think I want you out in public the way you are?"

"You don't think shit, Eddie."

And I would be off. I loved the drama, I swear to God I did. Loved telling Eddie what a worthless bastard he was, how he came from nobodies, just a poor hick in a big city. All that hate would come out of me, sure and strong as fire, and I'd watch his face, hoping to hurt him, waiting for him to fight back. It was a dangerous game, and if he'd had enough, he'd come at me with his fists. That's when I could hear Olivia crying in her room. I'd tell myself it had to stop, but it was like watching a movie you'd paid to sit through before you were born.

I hated Eddie, really hated him now, and couldn't figure why he stayed with me. He'd still take me by the shoulders when he wasn't mad and say, "I love you, Eva. Do you believe me?"

And I'd say no, I didn't believe him at all, not in the least, not for one minute or one second or ever. No sir. I said he only wanted to be with me because it made him feel better about what a failure he was, a man who had worked in the same furniture store for fifteen years, no degrees, no nothing. And he would scream it was me who kept him down all these years—being scared and sick and drunk—and that I'd been right, I couldn't be alone because just look at me now when I had a perfectly good husband to care for me.

"So leave," I'd say.

When I was drunk it didn't matter who left.

And he'd ask me, the oddest note of concern in his voice, "Who will take care of you if I do?"

I took a shotgun to him one night, one he'd bought when we were first together, back when we talked about having a house in the woods and how he would hunt our supper, pick the buckshot out and skin the animal right there in the kitchen.

He was in bed and I put the barrel to his temple, jamming it hard so he'd wake up. When he opened his eyes he was as scared as I'd ever seen him. "Open your mouth," I said. "Either that or get the hell out."

He had no notion the gun wasn't loaded. He grabbed it by the barrel and yanked it from my hands, pulling me down onto the bed, then rolled on top of me and pressed it against my throat. I don't know why, but it struck me as funny, and I laughed, expecting him to crack my neck with the weight of the barrel. He started crying then, so hard he rolled off the bed and just lay there like a kid, sobbing, the gun resting on his chest.

"It's not funny, Eva," he kept saying. "It's not funny. You think I want to kill you? Is that what you think? I love you. I just want you to be happy. That's all I've ever wanted, and you screwed with it. You got what you wanted, didn't you, Eva? Didn't you?"

I walked from the bedroom into the kitchen to get a drink, leaving him there. It was no good when he cried.

After a while I quit eating, except a cracker now and then. Eddie would bring home big boxes of them and place two on a plate in the evenings with a fresh bottle of beer. I guess it was the only thing he knew to do.

"You should eat your crackers, Eva," he would say. "You're losing weight."

It was true. Once I had been a strong girl, muscles as long and tight as a dancer's, my belly flat as a washboard. Now my legs were sickly, the muscle tissue eaten away, the flesh loose on my arms like those pictures you see of starving children. My hair had started to fall out, and the white of my eyes had gone yellow. I wore sunglasses so I wouldn't have to look at them when I stood before the mirror over the bathroom sink, vomiting, blood mixed with it now. Deep in my right side I had a pain that burned hot like a handful of coals. Eddie had quit hitting me by then, afraid, I thought, he might kill me.

I dreamt crazy stuff, wild visions of wind moving in the shapes of monsters across the bedroom wall, howling, talking gibberish. I would be inside them, swallowed up whole, pushing against thick folds of tissue, smothering. I dreamt I lived in an iron box with nothing but the cold touch of metal against my skin, metal fragments scraping off beneath my fingernails as I clawed to get out.

And I dreamt of death, its mouth stretched into a scream, opening into a gulf where sound, motion, sensation stopped, and my body, pulled by its vacuum, felt as it did when I'd quit breathing on the shock table, the weight so heavy around me I was pressed into submission, lying in emptiness so absolute my eyes felt as if they were made of glass, and everything I saw was clear and made of nothing. I woke from the dream knowing I would die, and welcomed it, courted it with one drink, then ten, then twenty. However many it took. And I knew now what Freda would not tell me.

TWENTY-FOUR

In the dream Freda was wearing a red dress, cut low in front and tight around her full breasts, her hair raven, reaching to the floor, spilling down the front of the dress so pretty and sexy. She was in the attic of the house on Poplar Street, her grown son Michael Paul sitting beside her in a high chair, black bats wheeling above their heads in a circle as Freda lifted a spoon to Michael Paul's mouth. His head flopped back and forth as she tried to feed him, the food dribbling out of his mouth. I walked into the attic room and stood watching as Freda pushed the spoon at me.

"It's your turn now, Eva," she said.

And she lay down on the floor, covering herself with her long hair, wrapping it tight about her as if it were the warmest Indian blanket.

The calls started coming all the time that last year I was in Seattle, during the day when I was home alone, flat out on the couch with a bottle beside me. It was Verna who called, Freda's friend who had come to live with her after Freda had finally kicked Owen out. I remember asking why Freda herself hadn't called, and Verna said she wasn't talking to anyone for a while, and besides, it was no emergency. Freda had said to tell me so because she knew I'd ask.

The first news was of my cousin's death—Michael Paul crushed in his car out on the speedway when he ran head-on into a truck, blind drunk, hopped up on pills, with his boyfriend in the passenger seat beside him. The boyfriend had died immediately. Decapitated, Verna said. But Michael Paul had lived for a few days after, his brain swelling through the break in his skull. They were going to cover the hole with a metal plate if he had lived. I heard Freda took him boxes of candy and knelt beside his bed, saying, "Baby, don't you want some? You wake up now and Mama will give you some. Wake up now, baby."

I asked Verna if Freda had cried. It seemed important as I lay there with the phone cradled on my neck, trying to get a shot of vodka down. I needed it, I told myself. With this bad news, I surely needed it. Verna said Freda hadn't cried so you could tell, at least her eyes hadn't puffed up, and I was sure she hadn't cried around Verna, this woman with a strong voice as deep as any man's. I liked listening to her on the other end of the line. It was a hypnotic voice, almost as calming as a drink. Too bad I'd never meet her, I told myself. Too bad I'd die and never shake her hand.

She called again in no more that a month's time to tell me about Rita. I began to think of her as the angel of death, this Verna with no face and body, just a voice that said, "Hello there, Eva," nice and slow and rich like molasses, as if she'd practiced all her life to bring bad news in an easy way. She said Freda told her to tell me bad things came in threes, if I was lucky. I listened, too deep in the calm of the booze to ask what she meant. Rita was in Hickory, Tennessee, she said, in a coma, her skull bashed in, nearly as bad as Michael Paul's had been. She'd run a red light, drunk, and a jeep had hit her, wham, right on the driver's side, and bent the Lincoln in half. I tried to imagine what that would look like, the car a two-ton V with my mother pinned inside.

"We're going down fast, aren't we?" I told Verna.

"You don't sound good," Verna said. "How do you feel, honey?"

"I don't," I said to her before hanging up. "The good thing is I don't feel at all."

I drank harder, amazed I did not die, thinking my brain should go, or my liver, something, anything, to do the trick. How long did I have to stand in front of the door before it opened and I fell through, out into that wild wind that played across the cotton fields and spun with the mad fury of a tornado?

She called next in the middle of the night, this woman with the magic voice who dealt out news like tarot cards. I was on the couch still. Eddie and Olivia had walked by me for two weeks straight, shaking their heads. I paid them no mind. They were ghosts, left-overs of people I had known long ago.

"Come home," Verna was whispering. "She needs you. She's dying."

"So am I," I said. "So am I."

"Come home, child." I heard Verna's voice getting louder. "You hear me? I said come home. Now."

I thought about it as clearly as I could and figured it was better to die there with Freda, away from Eddie and Olivia, who acted as if I were already gone. I didn't blame them, but I wondered why Eddie had never said, after I'd gotten so bad, "Eva, let's take you to a doctor."

Olivia had asked me to get help, but she had grown tired of it, seeing it did no good. I knew how she felt, and I guessed Eddie knew what my answer would be. Or maybe he was waiting until I lay on that couch for a year straight, certain he could carry me out without a fight. I like to think that was it. Being left to die like a dog in the road is an ugly notion.

Verna sent the ticket in the overnight mail, and Eddie drove me to the airport in my dirty clothes, unbathed, my hair a mass of tangles. I drank from a flask, grateful for it, as I looked out the window at the last I would ever see of Seattle. I'd told Olivia I loved her before I left, holding on to the doorway where Rita had stood shaking fifteen years before. She was sitting in the rocker where I had held her as a baby, resting her hands on the chair arms, and I could see that her nails were bitten to the quick. She wouldn't look at me, but she spoke, her voice choking, and I could see tears falling into her lap.

"I love you, too, Mama," she said. "Just get well and I'll come see you. I promise."

"That stuff's going to kill you," I heard Eddie say as he pulled the car up to the drop-off.

"I know," I told him, laughing high and wild, the way I'd heard a man laugh once in an old movie when someone held a gun to his head and he didn't know what else to do.

T W E N T Y - F I V E

I remember how she looked in that high-backed brass bed in her room that was always immaculate, her face floating there in the folds of linen like an angel's. The solid mahogany floors were slick and polished to a deep shine. I used to run across them in my socks and skid halfway to the big oval doors that opened into the kitchen. On the walls were her paintings, a lifetime of dreams, perceptions, and longings, roughed out in thick oils, the mood of them dark and thoughtful. On the wall above her bed hung a painting of her mother as a young woman. In the painting is an old baby buggy tucked inside a lean-to shed that is open on one side. The young woman's back is to the viewer, her hips full and sensual in a clingy cotton dress that is tattered. She is barefoot. Her posture is loose, careless, and you cannot tell if she is moving toward the baby carriage or away from it. Freda had captured the doubt of her own mother in that painting, the girl inside the woman, wondering should she stay or should she go.

On another wall was a portrait of two lovers in a river holding tight to each other, nude to where their bodies disappeared into the black water. The woman was Freda, her eyes glowing, her hair thick down her back in heavy brushstrokes of black. The man's hair was the same, as long as her own, and you could not see his face because his head was pressed against her breasts.

I saw the picture of her mother first as I walked into the room, and then Freda's face beneath it, her head propped up high on fresh white pillows, covered in a lace veil that hung past her shoulders, her skin translucent, as if it had been polished up with paraffin, and her eyes, that shiny obsidian black, staring out at me, searching, trying to make sense of what she saw. She couldn't have weighed more than seventy pounds. I weighed eighty.

I went to her bed, took her hand in my own shaking one, and kissed her on the forehead. She was cool as the bottom of the ravine.

She looked no different to me, just thin. And weary. The beauty was still there, her face free of lines, as smooth as any clay sculpture I had ever done. I knew I could have cast her face from memory, seeing it now, so absolutely perfect. I have never in my life known a woman as beautiful as my aunt, not in fairy tales, paintings, or imagination. When I was a child I had studied her face intently, memorizing every angle and curve, trying to figure how those features came together so miraculously that men drew in their breath when they saw her. She still had her eyebrows drawn out in a long arc, her lips painted blood red.

"What's wrong with you?" she asked, sitting up a bit. "You're skinny and old and yellow, Eva. Come here. Let me see your eyes."

I sat on the edge of the bed and leaned down over her face, obeying. She pulled the bottom lids of my eyes down and studied them.

"Jaundice," she said. "Same thing BQ died of. I'll die from it, too, bloat up black like an old cow. But I didn't get this way from drinking, Eva. This is natural circumstances."

"BQ's dead?" I asked, hoping I could change the subject.

"Dead out on the railroad tracks," Freda was saying. "Skinny as a skunk."

Freda had had him cremated, she told me, and buried him out in the backyard with Michael Paul.

"That's where I'm going, too," she said. "Right out under that pecan tree. I'll show you so you know. And you. You want to join me? I didn't think you'd be this bad. I really didn't, Eva. I just thought you'd get a taste of it, have some trouble, and come to your senses. Verna!" she yelled now. "You show Eva where we keep the beer? Bring her one. And bring that picture I did with the butter knife. The one in back. So how you been, Eva?"

"Fine," I said, looking down at my hands, wishing they would be still. It had been four hours since I'd had a drink. It was time. If I didn't get one soon, my skin would crawl right off me.

She was watching me, the way I swallowed hard every few seconds, how I knotted and unknotted my fingers, trying by sheer force of will to keep them steady. The way I licked my lips. It was no use. She saw what I was and I felt ashamed.

"Fool!" she said, sitting up straight in bed now, her skinny fingers grabbing at the sheets as if she'd rip them loose in one motion, get up out of bed, and put her hands to my neck. "Goddamn you, Eva, you're fine all right. You think I don't know?" she said. "You think I ain't seen this enough in my life so that it's the last thing I want to see before I die, you all crumpled up here like a brown-paper sack somebody just stepped on, looking like somebody's dried-up insides? Look at you. As bad as BQ, your hands shaking like you got palsy. Worse than your mama. Worse, Eva, you hear me? Worse."

I wanted that beer. Now. I was thinking how it was going to feel going down, as sure and as freeing as the religion I had made it. With a drink in me, or two, or four, or maybe six, what Freda had to say wouldn't be hard to hear. I could float off and listen from a distance, where it was safe.

I turned away from her as Verna walked in. She was tall, nearly six feet, and kind-faced, a mannish quality to her, but it was her eyes you noticed first, blue as sapphires and keen. The way they had watched me after she picked me up at the airport was unsettling. She watched me as if she *knew*. She spoke to me as if she *knew*, saying, "Freda won't be pleased by the shape you're in. Just let me take care of you. I know what to do."

Verna had been an army nurse and had worked in the VA hospital in Little Rock in the detox ward until she'd retired and moved in with Freda.

"When she goes," Verna had said, as we pulled into the driveway, seeing the look of panic on my face, "we can do what needs to be done. You know what needs to be done, child. But right now she needs you. Are you listening?"

I nodded my head.

"She needs you. You're all she has."

Verna held a glass of beer out to me, smiling, showing she was no judge of my weakness.

"Drink it," Freda snapped. "You need it. I've seen the DTs. I've seen the fits. Two days sober and you'd be right in the middle of it. That's all it took for BQ, two lousy days, and he was tearing at his face, jerking on the floor like a fish tossed up on the bank. Drink it, Eva."

I wanted to, God how I wanted to, but every time I tried to get the glass to my lips, my hand shook so bad I couldn't even catch hold of the rim with my teeth. I couldn't let her see me like this. I got up to move away from the bed.

"Come back here!" she said. "You come back right now and don't go skulking off like some dark creature, hiding to do your business. Stay here now. You know how to do it, Eva. Go ahead. I've seen it before. It's nothing new to me."

"Please," I said, coming back to the bed. "Please, Freda."

She turned her head, allowing me that last bit of dignity.

I held tight to the wet glass with both hands and could feel my whole body shake with the effort of keeping them still. I set the glass down on the bedside table, hard, got down on my knees, and tipped it toward my mouth, drinking fast, all of it, and when Freda heard me stop, she told Verna to get another.

"I remember when you were just a little girl," I heard Freda saying. "Back from Africa. So dark and quiet, always staring at things like you thought you could make them move or something. Is that what was going through your head?"

"I don't remember," I told her, taking hold of the bottle of beer Verna had just brought in. The bottle was easier to grasp. She knew what she was doing when she brought in that glass, I thought. She set an unopened one on the nightstand. I reached for it and slipped it under the bed.

"Stop that!" Freda said. "Why do you do that?"

"I don't know," I said. "I just didn't want you to have to look at it."

"I'm watching you *drink* it," she said. "You think I care if it sits there? I don't want any of that crap. Put it back up here. You don't go hiding it around here. You drink here, you drink in the wide open."

I did as she said.

"Jesus, Eva," she said. "I have a hard enough time thinking without you distracting me. I'm dying, girl. You think I need to fuss about you hiding beers under my deathbed? You think I need that nonsense?"

She laughed a little.

"Jesus Christ Almighty. I want a picture taken of this. I want a picture to give you to put in that old box so ten years from now you can dig it out and look at it and say, Look at me with that crazy old woman dying there in bed, trying to hide beers underneath her so she won't see. I want a picture. Verna! Come take a picture."

I remembered what it was like to be Freda's handmaiden. Verna had the job now. She appeared at the bedroom door with an Instamatic.

"Ya'll smile," she said, and clicked the camera.

"There," Freda said, sitting back in bed, satisfied. "Posterity. We got posterity wrapped up. Now what?"

I'd pulled up a chair beside the bed and sat there drinking my beer. I was thinking I loved her. It was nice to feel it coming back.

"Are you afraid?" I asked, knowing what the answer would be but just wanting to offer her something, anything. It sounded like a thing you'd say to someone you didn't know well.

"'Course not," she said. "What's to be afraid of? What you *fear* is losing people you care about *before* you die. That's already happened. Michael Paul. BQ. Mama. Leta. Rita, almost. You, just about. Daddy. Even Owen. All gone. What's to be afraid? Can't do anything about it this time. They can't cut part of me away. They tried that. I know what's out there, probably better than I think I know. I won't die. Just move on. You won't believe that though. You never did. Wait and see, Eva. Just wait and see."

I'd finished the second beer and opened a third. I wanted to talk now.

"Not me," I said. "I'm not dead. Not yet."

"You sound proud of it," she said. "What do you call it then, what you are right now? It ain't living."

Her face was suddenly full of pain, and she rolled onto her right side.

"Can I do anything?" I asked, reaching over to help her.

"Sure," she said, her voice strained. "Sure you can do something all right. You can stop drinking before it kills you. That would be a nice going-away present."

"Okay," I said, checking the level of my beer. "Is that what you want me to say? I will."

"No you won't," she said, sounding tired of it all. "NO YOU WON'T. None of you ever did. Why should it be any different with you?"

I felt like a traitor, wishing I were a kid again and could do whatever she asked, presto, quick as lightning, to please her. But this. How could I? It was my ticket out. I knew the feeling, though, when my hands would stop shaking and I'd start feeling warm and steady—then I'd think about quitting and what it would be like not to have to do it, dose myself all day long so I could stay on top of the fear. But not having another drink, ever? No. That seemed wrong. Like trying to walk with one leg. Impossible.

"You used to tag around me all the time," Freda was saying, "when you were little, grabbing on to my legs. I loved you like you were my own little girl. I liked you, too. You were smart."

"Still am," I said, resenting her reference in the past tense.

She laughed sarcastically.

"No you're not, Eva," she said. "Smart people don't kill themselves. Smart people don't waste their lives and fall down in a puddle of self-pity, or think they're doomed because somebody did them wrong. *Strong* people don't make excuses, feel sorry for themselves. What's the matter with that boy I got for you? Couldn't he take good enough care of you? What's the matter, Eva? You had to rely on yourself and couldn't do it? Is that it?"

"Guess so," I said, opening another beer. Verna had set a six-pack on the dresser when my back was turned.

"Look here," Freda said. "Come look at this picture. I want to show you."

She was holding a small, framed painting Verna had brought from the back room. I'd never seen it before.

"I did it with a butter knife," she said. "It happened so quickly I couldn't find my paintbrush."

I looked at her face and saw the delight this gave her.

It was a picture of a man sitting across Poplar Street on the curb, in front of the old house with the octagonal front porch, the pillars of the porch peeled free of paint, bare gray wood now. When I was young it had been pristinely whitewashed, the brightest house on the block. The man was dressed shabbily, his shoulders hunched over, and at his feet was a broken wine bottle, its contents flowing into the sewer drain.

"I watched him come out of the liquor store that day," Freda said, "and sit down on the curb to drink his bottle. His hands were shaking so bad he dropped it, and I could hear him start to cry, right over all that noise on Poplar Street. That's when I went to get the paints. What do you think of that?"

"What?" I asked.

"Him starting to cry, just because his bottle broke. You know how that feels, Eva, to cry about some liquor spilt in the gutter?"

I told her I did, ashamed to say it.

"I went and bought him another bottle," she said. "And he thanked me like I'd given him a holy wafer on the day of judgment."

"Why'd you do it?"

"Because I've seen enough of you to know how bad it hurts. Look at me here, Eva. Look at me. I'm dying. Look at what they've done to me."

She pulled the bottoms of her pajamas down and showed me the crudely stitched wound low on her right side.

"Dr. Cherry knew it was so bad he just stitched me up like I was some old dog. All through me, in the liver, too. I'm eaten up with it, Eva, just like you're eaten up with that poison. You don't want this, to die this way."

She sat up and grabbed at my hair to pull me closer. Matted strands of it came free in her hands, and that's when she started to cry. I'd never heard her cry, not in thirty years, and I couldn't stand the sound, like boards being wrenched free from their moorings, the hollow coo of mourning doves in the still night air, lonesome, agonized, and betrayed. She held the handful of hair up to her mouth, trying to stop the cries, but they came harder until Verna ran to her, fearful she would choke. She patted her back and rubbed, and I could see the loyalty on her face.

I left the room for a while, too terrified to watch her, this woman who had never broken in her life. When I came back she had stopped crying and Verna was gone. She sat perfectly still in the bed, twisting my hair in her fingers.

"It's time you ate something," she said quietly. "But I want to ask you something before I forget. I want you to tell me why you're in this sad condition. I want your words about it, you understand?"

"I had a hard life," I said, not even stopping to think about it.

"I suspected you'd say that. You used to think that made me smart, knowing what you were going to say before you said it. Not true. It just takes watching people year after year to know what they're like. That's what I want to tell you about, that I been watching you, Eva, and you had no more of a hard life than anybody else, just like I always told you, so don't give me any more of that crap. I won't take it now. I won't hear your whining. You live in the past, that's where you're going to die."

"So why?" I said, stung by her words. "Why *am* I this way? Tell me."

"It's a path, Eva," she said. "A path right to the center. Don't you know that by now?"

"You always talk in puzzles."

"How's your baby, Eva? And Eddie?"

"Change the subject," I said. "Like always. When it suits you. When I want to know something *really* important, you just change the subject."

"Damn you, Eva. Tell me how they are."

"Fine," I said. "Better without me, I suspect. I curse the day you brought him here. I curse the day I left. Maybe if I hadn't gone, things would be different. I honestly can't remember anything but misery, Freda. I can't. I tell myself it can't have been all bad. I remember how it felt when I broke out of the hospital, like I could finally do something. I felt so good walking that river. Why didn't I do something, instead of marrying Eddie? I don't even know what I would have done if I'd had a choice."

"What's choice got to do with it, Eva?" she said. "What do you want to do? That's the choice."

"I don't want to be a mother. I never did. I'm lousy at it, just like Rita. I . . . I don't know what to say to her anymore, what to teach her. She hates me, my own girl. I tried being like you for a while . . . all tough and sweet . . . I don't know. I don't know anything. Nothing. Not a goddamn thing. Inside me feels like ground meat. It hurts all the time and I know I'm going to die. It's why I came here, to be with you so I wouldn't have to do it alone. I tell myself that I tried to quit drinking, but I know I didn't. Just words to make myself feel better. What if I did quit? What then? I'd be empty all over again. Sometimes I remember how I used to feel a long time ago when things interested me, and I get a feeling, real quick, like it could be that way again, and then it's gone. I remember how it felt when I went to the river, and how the cotton fields look in the middle of summer, and I do think it's all a circle, but here I am back again, and even if I think I know what's going to happen, maybe I don't, and you can tell me before you die. I don't want you to die, Freda. You're all I ever had. All I ever believed in. It's the truth. I love you. I'm sorry. I'm sorry that I'm like this and that it hurts you. If I weren't drinking, I wouldn't say any of it. I'd just be thinking about getting a drink, like BQ. I shut down without it. You know what it feels like to shut down? I need it so I can ease into the evening, and more so I can sleep, and more when I get up so I won't shake. It drives me crazy, like my skin's going to crawl off me, or my eyeballs are coming loose. I panic. I can't do it. I don't know anyone who's like this. I don't know anyone anymore. I don't have a friend. Not one. And I don't know if Eddie's a good man or bad, or if I ever loved him. I tell myself he's the father of my girl, but how could I have had a daughter? How could I? Look at me."

I turned to stare into the mirror over the nightstand, saw the yellow skin, crusted patches of it beginning to flake off. What was left of my hair was thin and brittle. I bared my teeth at the mirror and saw the blood-filled gums. All I had to do was touch them with my fingertips and the capillaries burst, setting loose a taste of iron in my mouth, strong as the taste from the rocks I used to pull from the ravine.

Freda had pulled the blankets up to her chest and was watching me, her face serious.

"Say some more," she said. "Keep talking. I want to hear."

"I think about her a lot," I said. "Rita. Like I should have gotten her out of my head a long time ago, but nothing I do makes her go away. I understand a little better what it was like for her, but now she's all crunched up and what am I going to do?"

I started crying. It was an empty feeling, sitting there watching the tears roll off my chin into the beer bottle. They made a funny, hollow sound when they hit.

"Make peace with her," I heard Freda saying.

"How?" I asked, looking up. "How can I do that?"

"Go to see her. She's out of the coma. She's damaged, but she's still your mama."

"Like this?" I yelled. "Like this? You think I want her to see me like this, all scabbed up and drunk and ugly?"

"Like you ain't seen *her* that way? She won't know the difference, Eva. She'll just know it's you, that's all.

"No," I said. "Not like this."

"She could die first."

"Christ," I said. "She hasn't yet. I used to think you could mow that woman down with a truck and she'd still crawl to the side of the road, get up, and come back to haunt you."

"Suppose she does?"

"Well goddamn her then," I said. "Goddamn her."

"You ought to do those faces."

"What?" I said, baffled.

"Those faces. Like you did by the river when you were little. Sculptures. Out of clay. It's art. People buy things like that."

She smiled, and I looked at her, bewildered.

"With these hands," I said, "I could make holes for gophers. Dig ditches. Just set me loose with these hands, that's what I could do. Make milkshakes. Stir paint."

"You'll do what you want," she said. "I just wish I could be around to see what it is. Maybe not. Come on now. Help me out of this bed, Eva. It's time you ate."

That first night I lay in my old bed in the back room, staring at the picture of the wino Freda had hung at the foot of the bed. I got up and took it down, drank a bottle of beer, and hung it up again. I got back in bed, crossed my arms up against my chest, and looked at it some more. It must have been a Saturday night because the voices in the church by the alley started up, and I remembered how they used to make me feel electric all over, the hair standing up on my arms, all that sweet hollering about Jesus. Freda had always said people tried to make it home before they died. Here I was, like that lion in Africa, waiting for death to come on like the sunset. In the other room lay Freda, surrounded by her paintings. I thought about her and how she had looked those mornings when I was young, fixing her face in the mirror, studying those looks that made men weak. What had she wanted with men anyway? She didn't need them. Not like I did. I thought about Ronnie and how badly she had wanted me to have him, and how she'd covered her breast that morning she'd asked what we'd done out there in the snow. It seemed so long ago, someone else's memory locked in my head. I looked up at the wino again. That bottle in the gutter was my life, broken by my own hand, smashed, and what was leaking out was all the bitterness of all those years, and I didn't want to die that way, bitter, used-up, broken, with all the rage inside me turned to poison.

I heard the train whistle coming, louder, low and sweet, and I remembered the gospel singers down by the river, baptized in their white robes in that water so muddy you could see the silt stir up in it in little whirlpools where their bodies went down. I had wanted to walk in with them and take the cure, turn my life over to the thing that made their voices rise so strong and pretty. What was it they believed in that they would trust their souls to it, walk into that dark water wearing virgin white and be redeemed? It didn't matter, I figured, as long as it was something. I'd believed in Freda, but she told me once no one person could change your life. At the time she was talking about men, but I remembered what she'd said, only differently now: It had to be a passion, something greater than you. It could have been the stars, I thought, when I was younger, or the way I felt when I heard a bird call to another, or the way the river clay felt in my hands when I worked it, as if I held the flesh and tissue of a living thing, its heart beginning to beat as the shape took form. Or it could be the way I felt when I saw the boy in the back row at school, wearing his sister's shoes—compassion was what that was, not pity. Compassion for the hurt he felt, and I had wanted to feel it for him. There could be a living made of that alone.

Through the house I heard Freda's breathing, a death rattle, like the wings of doves beating in the eaves. I got up to check on her and found Verna sitting on the edge of the bed. A single candle burned on the nightstand. I remembered when this house had been filled with candles.

"She's like this at night," Verna said. Her short silver hair glowed pink in the candlelight, ghostly. "It won't be much longer. A few days maybe. Go back to bed now."

I walked down the hall toward the butler's kitchen, carrying a candle Verna had lit for me. I ran my hands along the wall to steady myself and felt an impression in the wallpaper. I held the candle to it and saw the bullet hole, powder burns around it, and remembered that night long ago when Freda had pointed the gun at John Earl and fired. I always wondered how his dying might have changed my life. I knew now it wouldn't have. My life had been a mess then. It still was, and it didn't matter that Freda had missed. We all came to the same end no matter who fell from the path.

I went back to bed, sipping from the cup of beer I kept beside me. In the evenings I could sip, not guzzle like common folk. I listened to my aunt struggle for each breath in the room down the hall, and it felt like a sacrilege for me to be here, drinking the beer she had bought, sleeping in the bed she made for me whenever I came home. I covered my head and tried to keep the sound out, tried hard to listen for the voices of the gospel singers, for the whistle of another train that might be coming, for the river Freda said would tell me things if I only listened. I couldn't hear any of it. Her breathing was all I heard, louder and louder until I thought the whole house was shaking with it, the walls stretching in and out like brittle drums, old splintery boards cracking with each breath, plaster breaking open on the ceiling and smashing to the floor.

"It won't be easy," I heard a voice say, loud and clear as if it were right inside my head. I burrowed deep beneath the covers and felt a hand on my head, stroking. "But I'll help you if you want. I know how. All you have to do is ask."

It was Verna, I knew now, and I pulled the covers back to look up at her standing beside my bed with a candle. She was big as any man, her shoulders broad, and I could see that her shadow filled an entire wall, rising and falling with the movement of the flame.

"Okay," I said, and the shadow seemed to spread its arms wide above.

"As soon as she's gone. She doesn't need to see it, but tell her. Tell her you said yes."

TWENTY-SIX

The last week she was alive I ate more than I had in a year's time. Freda would make her way to the kitchen, ignoring Verna's protests and mine, hissing at us when we came near her, telling me to go sit and wait for my food. She fixed little portions arranged on a little plate because I had trouble keeping it down at first. She'd bring the plate to the table saying, "Just think how proud you'll be when you can eat off a big plate like the grown-ups."

Her sarcasm was not lost on me. In fact, it was as if she had just discovered it, not the teasing way she'd had when I was young, but a nastiness that came straight out of her anger toward me. I'd told her I wanted to quit drinking, meaning it just a little more than the last time I'd said it.

"You lie," she said. "You say that to make me feel better before I go. You think a lie will make it any easier, Eva?"

"It's the truth," I told her. "Verna said she'd help me."

Freda looked at Verna, skeptical.

"That so?" she said, her eyebrows arched high.

Verna nodded, looking powerful and wise. She scared me a little, so quiet and sure, moving about the house as if she knew exactly why she was there. I'd never seen such rein given to anyone in Freda's house.

"Why not now?" Freda said. "What's wrong with *today*, for instance?"

"You know what it's like," Verna told her. "You want to see it, like BQ was? That what you want these final days?"

"Guess not," Freda said. "Though I don't think it much matters. At least I'd go out knowing she meant it."

They spoke to each other as if I weren't there, and I started to feel panic about it, like I was going in to give blood but they'd take it all—forget to pull the needle out. After she died I could always leave, I told myself. But where? Back to Eddie? To the drunk tank at the local jail? It had been the question of my life, where to go, what to do when I got there. And her death. Was I really convinced it would happen? It was like waiting for a holiday to pass, one that would never come again. We were preparing for it, just as we would for Christmas or Easter or Halloween. Verna had helped to ready her. I could see that. It was Verna's quiet strength Freda needed, not me rattling through the house, teeth chattering, hands shaking until I got myself dosed. The day she died I asked her why she had wanted me to come. What use was I to her? What use had I ever been?

"Because I love you, baby," she said. "And it was time for you to come home."

She brought my supper to the old oilcloth-covered table in the kitchen, slammed it down so hard the fried okra bounced off in all directions. I looked up, startled by what I saw, disbelieving.

Her face that first day I had come home had still been beautiful, not wrinkled at all, but her hair was white, and I had to tell myself, yes, she had aged. But now as I looked at her she was younger than I had ever known, her face smooth as a young girl's, her eyes liquid black, and her hair nearly electric with a pure light of its own. I closed my eyes, opened them, and looked again. She smiled at me, a beatific expression I had seen in portraits of the saints. I remembered the way she had looked that Sunday by the river, holding her face up to the sun as the congregation moved off into the cotton-woods, and it was the same smile she'd had then.

I stood up and put my hands on her shoulders, guiding her toward the bedroom. She felt warm beneath the cotton cloth, her skin smooth as river clay.

Verna had lit dozens of candles in the room, and I helped Freda into bed by the light of them, pulling the covers up close to her neck because she said she was cold. I pulled the lace veil from the top drawer in the nightstand and watched her place it over her head, carefully. I remembered the Kleenex she used to wear pinned to her hair when we went to mass, and how the stuffy ladies of the church used to frown at her.

"And she was a nun," I heard one of them say once, indignant. She had been one before I was born, and it was not something she would ever talk about. It was enough to have told me about the orphanage. I imagined her though, shut away in a convent, her head shaved, never looking in a mirror. Maybe it was why, for the rest of her life, that mirror sat on the kitchen table, year after year, reaffirming her timeless beauty—because she had not discovered it until she was a full-grown woman, had not gazed once at her own reflection from the time she was eighteen years old until she left the church. Later they had taken her breast and told her she could never bear children.

"Eva," I heard her say now, the sweet, childish quality of her voice come back. "Do you know how much I love being alive? Oh God, I love it. Every minute of it, and I'm mad I have to give it up."

I sat there beside her, silent, and looked up as Verna set a beer down on the nightstand.

"Look at her," I said, whispering. "Look at her face."

Verna smiled and took my hand. I could feel the calluses on her palms. She held tightly for a moment and let go.

"I never knew," she said quietly, as she left the room, "whether she willed that or it just happened."

"Come back," I called to Verna. "Please."

I didn't want to be with her alone, watch her fade out, that light in her eyes gone forever. I could feel it happening, even through the alcohol, I could feel her pulling away. I remembered how I had called out to her that time at the hospital. And she had heard me, sat straight up at the kitchen table and looked back over her shoulder. Now she was calling to me.

"It's your turn now, Eva," she had said in the dream.

"The way the land smells after it rains, Eva. Do you remember that?" I heard her saying. "Sweet and dusty. I like that smell. And the pecan tree in the fall when a hard wind comes and the nuts blow up against the kitchen window like buckshot. I like to watch that. Those cardinals that come to the bird feeder, red as a tube of cherry lipstick. Red. What a color. So clean and perfect. You like red, Eva?"

"I love red," I said, not wanting to take my eyes from her. I could feel her now, those simple passions drifting in, and I remembered how it had been to see through her eyes. Was she the one who gave the magic to me, a love of nature so keen it kept me hypnotized all those years, my mouth open, my head tilted up toward the stars? Where had it gone? Why hadn't I remembered until now how priceless it had been?

"What red, Eva? What red you like?" Her voice sounded now as if she were dreaming, sweet and lazy.

I had to think about it, reach through the haze and pick a memory. A leaf I had taken from the ground in Virginia, back at the hospital.

"Strawberry," I said. "Strawberry red, like leaves in autumn. Maple leaves when they turn."

"You like leaves, Eva. I remember how you like leaves, you and Ronnie. Bleeding on the leaves. You still read books, Eva? I've been around the world with all those books. You read them, you hear me? Walls and walls of books here. I say Carl Jung is a prophet. You remember I said that. Don't forget."

"I won't forget," I told her. "I promise."

"The pain's not so bad now," she said. "Come sit closer to me, Eva."

She patted the bed.

I curled up next to her, my head on her chest. She held me close, and I could feel the concave part of her chest where the breast had been. Beneath it I could hear her heart beat, so slow it sounded like a paper drum struck at counts of ten. I didn't want to hear it stop, that final beat stranded, nowhere to go.

"My daddy used to sit out on the front porch of our house," I could hear the words echoing through her body as she spoke them, "and play his guitar and sing. One day the floodwaters came up so high they spilled over the front porch, and Daddy just sat there with his guitar, making up a song about drowning in the flood, and I laughed because our whole yard was like the river, and I knew we wouldn't drown because we were laughing. I used to think nothing bad would ever happen if I just laughed, like it was magic. I laughed when I went to the orphanage. Laughed my silly head off. Daddy wasn't so bad. All that drinking. All over us like dirt. Seeing him kept me from it, I think. I loved him. I was *his* girl. He always said so. But not your mama. Poor Rita. She was so smart. And pretty. Go see her, Eva. Go see your mama before she dies."

"You're my mama," I said, feeling the tears soaking her pajama top, warm and wet beneath my cheek. I never wanted to leave this place next to her, never wanted to lift my head again.

"That picture," she said, trying to lift her arm to point to the woman and the baby carriage. "It's Mama. She was just a baby when she had me. Just a girl. She didn't know whether to push that carriage down the street or into the river, drown me like a sack of puppies."

I held on to her tight.

"Eva," she said, "I'm dying. You know that, don't you? Tell me you know."

I shook my head against her chest. I was sobbing out loud now and she did nothing to quiet me.

Her voice was weak and I could barely hear it, a whisper deep in her lungs, pushing up.

"I'm asking if you really know, Eva, because it's nice. I want you to understand. And all I see are people and what they mean to me. My boy. My baby. You. Such a serious little girl. I thought you'd be a fortune-teller like Mama, cards and crystal balls and candles all around you."

I lay there against her, waiting, listening. I heard my own heart strong in my ears and pulled away, wiping my eyes, looking to her face to see the light of it grow dim beneath the veil. I called out to Verna to come quick, and she stood and watched beside me.

"Like a candle going out," she said, admiration in her voice.

I couldn't bear it.

"Freda," I said, leaning over her, my voice afraid. "Freda. Freda. Wake up. I'm hungry. Time for supper. I didn't finish my supper. Wake up now." I said it over and over again, a whimpering child. "No. Oh God, no," I cried out, and fell to my knees beside the bed, reaching to pull her next to me, her little body curled like a frail child asleep in that huge bed piled high with white linen.

We buried her ashes in the backyard, beneath the pecan tree, right next to Michael Paul and BQ. Owen had died that year, too, but Freda had said she didn't want him out back, not anywhere near her, so his family stuck him in the Watson Chapel Cemetery, way out off Highway 79. I took a ruby agate I'd had for years and dropped it in with the ashes before Verna covered them over. In the center it had a spiral of red like a candle flame.

TWENTY-SEVEN

The first few days I don't remember. I had convulsions, Verna told me later, my blood pressure went out of control, and the capillaries in my eyes ruptured. When I came around I couldn't walk right. I could feel the pain in my liver then, sick and heavy. Verna kept me in the back room, on my old bed, and pumped me full of Serax to stop the shakes.

"I don't wanna do it," I kept telling her. "I've changed my mind. Give me a drink. Now!"

"You asked," she'd say.

It was true. After Freda died and we'd put her to rest, what was left, anyway—that gritty mix of bone and teeth that isn't ashes at all, but fertilizer so rich the pecan tree was heavy with the fruit of it next fall—Verna had come to me and said, "Well," standing over me big and bony as a workhorse too long in the field, her face as lined as an untreated piece of hide.

"Well what?" I said, drunk, finally, after five days of working at it. It was hard to do anymore. It took all day, and then I was out as if someone had put a hammer to my head.

"I said I'd help you if you asked. But you have to ask. That's the trick."

I knew what the fork in the road looked like, split and wicked like a serpent's tongue. I knew the jagged lip of the canyon where I stood, sharp rocks gouging my feet as I tipped forward. I knew. The Road Not Taken. A silly poem. Simple. I remembered it. Who's to say there is a road at all? I pondered, my brain wet, garbage floating in it. You can't think when it's liquefied, not in one long rope of thought anyway. I dangled at the end of that rope, fibers fraying, snap it goes.

The thing takes hold of you and won't let go, like a leech, a fifty-foot wave, a bolt of lightning when you've got your hand wrapped around a flagpole. I don't know what made me this way, and I don't care. All I want is for someone to take it out of me, blast it out with a grenade, do anything that needs to be done, but get it out. I can feel it living in me cold and deadly as sin. The sun rises for it, the moon spins in crazy circles if it says to. I can't make sense of anything anymore. But if you take it away, what will I do, how will I live? I know nothing as familiar as this, nothing that smoothes away the pain so it's just a low buzz, pleasant almost. I could be in pain and live this way, *but not for long*. My insides are eaten up. I see the bruises on my arms and legs, skin going yellow, hair falling out, teeth gray. But I'll kill to have it. Step a little closer. See these hands, steady as a rock.

"Will you help me?" I asked, meaning it, while in that deep, anesthetic comfort, never remembering how bad it got after just four hours. Try four days, honey.

"Give me one. NOW!"

My voice thundered from the back room where Verna had me strapped down in four-point restraints she'd brought from the hospital, part of her detox collection: B vitamins, phenobarb, Serax, Valium, Lithium, potassium for muscle cramps, vitamin C, therol. But no booze. Not one drop, clear as amber, warm, perfect, and holy. Oh, I knew how it felt going down. There was nothing like it in this world, what it did to me. No drug came close, and sex was a child's diversion.

"Verna! You bitch you bitch you bitch. I'm gonna die. You're killing me. Give me a goddamned drink. I swear to God I'll kill you when I get loose. Please. Please. Come on. Please. Just ONE. One! That's all. Freda left you to kill me, I swear to God. Bitch!"

She'd slide into the room so calm the muscles in her face were slack, take a washcloth in her big hands, and put it to my face and neck, cool water on it I wouldn't foul a drop of bourbon with. I'd take mine straight, right in my veins. I thought about drinking gasoline, lying in a tub of it, swimming in it. Nail polish remover. I could remember the smell, sharp and deadly. Anything that had that smell. My mouth watered. Air to a drowning man. Precious. Sweet.

"I need it," I'd say, conniving, trying not to scream at her, losing the battle every time.

"I know."

"You can't! How can you know? I want it. I'm a fucking *alcoholic*. Do you hear me? I *need* it. You didn't say it would be like this."

"I said it wouldn't be easy, Eva. I said that. If you don't do it, you'll die."

"This is worse."

"This is the hardest part. It gets better."

"Promise?" I asked, remembering the treachery of that word.

"I promise."

"How the hell do you know?"

"I've done it."

"Liar!"

"It's nice to see some life in you. Scream away."

I was like the lion, in enough pain from the hunger to kill. I'd often wondered if I would kill to get what I needed. I knew the answer now. It wouldn't bother me, not when all I dreamed about, all I wanted, was a way to get where I had to go—where I could lie limp and careless, my nerves soaked to the sheath, my body primed like a machine. Anger put to death. Fear castrated. It was what I wanted then when my body was haywire and my brain popped like a hundred firecrackers.

I understand need. I have compassion for it. Let me feel your pain, I tell people now, because I have felt it already, and I can help you understand that you will live. And that you will move not toward bitterness and blind agony, but in the vague direction of something better.

• • •

I was propped up in my bed, a poached egg on a tray in front of me. Some dry toast. A glass of apple juice. A week had passed and the cold sweats had stopped. I could make it to the bathroom with Verna's help.

I stuck the end of a spoon into the egg yolk and tried to lift it to my mouth. The yolk jumped off the spoon and splattered down the front of my gown. I started to cry.

"Buck up," Verna said, pulling a chair next to the bed and settling there as if she expected to stay for a while. I didn't want any company. I didn't want a drink either. I just wanted to puke.

"I can't eat this," I said. "I can't even get it to my mouth."

I held my hands out so she could see them tremble.

"It'll go away," she said.

"When?"

"It takes time. A month. Two months. A year. It all depends."

"What do you think?"

"I think you're sober."

"Sounds like a disease."

She laughed. "I thought so, too. A fifth a day, maybe more. Probably more. Definitely more. I'm still lying about it."

Verna had a slow, easy way of talking that could have put me right to sleep if I hadn't been so jumped up. She was the kind of woman you expected to find sitting on the front porch of some Ozark cabin whittling a piece of wood with a pocketknife. The demeanor belied her sharpness. Freda had known what she was doing when she found Verna.

"Why'd you quit?" I asked.

"Same reason you did."

And Verna was tricky. I was learning that.

"I'm supposed to know what that is, is that it?" I said. I shot my hand out at a piece of toast and grabbed it in my fist, quick, before I lost control. I jerked it to my mouth and took a bite. It tasted like sawdust. Verna stuck a straw in the apple juice and pushed it toward me. I leaned forward and sucked at it.

"Yep," she said.

I sat there thinking about it for a minute, sucking at the straw, my lips quivering around it. It was the kind of straw they give you in hospitals, with the little crinkly tip that bends, and I thought how lucky I was she hadn't put me there, sick as I was. It was something I'd made clear to Verna right away when she'd asked how I wanted to get sober. I'd said the easiest way possible, and she'd said nope, no chance. There was her way, and then there was the hospital detox ward, and the two weren't really that much different, except here I'd get the one-on-one care she'd provide, which was a lot like having my own personal pit bull when I looked back on it. But the hospital—no—I hadn't wanted that, never believing they wouldn't find some way to hook me up to a current, keep me there for good.

I'd gotten so tired of it, sick to death of waking up with my skin crawling, my gut heaving, and everything around me looking dirty and wrong. It was worse than all the bad dreams and all the bad times combined, a hell specially ordered in which I stayed, looking out, watching the world get crazier and crazier, thinking one more shot would put a stop to it and it never did.

I was tired of holding up a mirror to my life and saying, This is what you are, this ghost, this shadow, this replica of pain. If it was, then I was doomed, and in my heart I did not believe it. The things Freda had taught me had stuck somehow, deep inside where I thought it was all slash-burned. The way she had taught me by her example that only fools give up meant something now—the notion stirred in me like a low flame quickening to a full blaze and then spreading wild like the gully fires. And if the fire met with the river, then there was life there, too. I hadn't forgotten how it felt to be alive. It had just lain dormant, hardened as the casing on a seed by all that hate.

"Same reason, huh?" I said to Verna, looking past her to the picture of the wino Freda had painted, the one Verna left hanging the whole goddamned time I was in withdrawal, even when I hollered at her to take it down so I could burn it. Even when I said the guy in the painting, that poor old drunk, had no dick. I lit a cigarette, thinking how odd it tasted without a drink.

"I quit because I wanted to quit," I said. "Because I'd had enough. That's why."

"Hey," she said, her voice deep and cheerful the way it was when she got excited about something, which wasn't very often. "Whaddya know. *What do you know.*"

"Not much," I said.

"That's a start," she told me, smiling, looking proud of herself.

TWENTY-EIGHT

I stayed on in Watson Chapel, sending money to Eddie for Olivia's schooling. Freda had left me plenty, all those years of saving and scraping heaped up in a bank now with my name on the account, something I would have liked to have said I'd earned but knew I hadn't. Eddie sent back divorce papers and I obliged him, telling him to give away everything I owned in that house in Seattle—all the empty bottles, the bottle caps, the cardboard cartons that held the bottles—every bit of it. I made a promise to myself that I'd care for my girl when she came east for school. I wrote to her, apologizing for all the wasted years, telling her I understood how it had been, and if she gave me a chance I would make it up to her. I knew she would write back when it felt right. I understood, too, how it takes time to forgive.

It took months for the shakes to stop, and I roamed through that big old house with Verna, tending to it the way Freda had, polishing the floors, burning trash out in the alley next to the church, listening to the service on Sunday morning from a lawn chair in the backyard, my face held toward the sun, a cure for the sickness in my liver Verna said would take time to heal.

I took it slow, knowing that if I went too fast I'd turn brittle and forget how simple it all had to be. When I'd feel the old fears pushing up I'd lie there in the sun and let them wash over me, learning that after a time they would subside, and the next time they came, be weaker still.

"What do I do now that I don't drink?" I asked Verna, petulant, irritated by the length of a single day.

"The next indicated thing," she told me.

"You talk in puzzles, too," I said to her, cranky about it, thinking the next half of my life would be spent deciphering Verna.

At first it was getting out of bed without her help, one side of my body weak from a mild stroke I'd had in withdrawal when the blood pressure had popped the veins in my eyes. Brushing my teeth took time. Dressing myself. Eating. I did that well, eventually, forgoing the average portions of fried okra she put on my plate for whole boxes of the stuff sold down the street at Homer's.

I was no Pollyanna about it. I bitched and moaned and said Freda had never made me work so hard, but it wasn't true. I caught on to it after a while, how it felt to get through the day without a drink. I started remembering how it felt to finish a task and look at the results of what I had done, vaguely proud, wanting to turn to Freda like I did when I was young and say, "See what I did?"

I began to move with the rhythm of that household, understanding what Freda had told me long ago about the importance of ritual and discipline, how it kept the mind from being idle.

I thought about Olivia, how if I could mend myself she might forgive those years when I had sat silent on the couch, watching her pass by me year after year, damned by my ignorance of her life, her passions. I told Verna I wanted to know my girl and that it killed me to know what I had done.

"It takes time," Verna had said, so certain in her belief. "You know damned well it takes time."

I read long into the night now, sitting in Freda's chair in the living room, Jesus and the Manson family to my back, starting with the A section of her vast library, remembering how I had read beneath the covers when I was young, enchanted by each new piece of information.

I started going to the river again, bringing home pails of red clay and shaping figures from it in the middle of the kitchen table. It made a perfect work surface, slick and smooth, and I worked a deep, red stain into the oilcloth that Verna could not scrub out. She said Freda would kill me if she were alive. I'd thumb my nose in the direction of the backyard, never believing that she was truly dead.

How could she be when Verna and I moved through the house, matching the rhythm of her days, remembering her, talking to her, each of us certain she was listening?

I'd sit some nights with the candles lit and listen for the tappings in the wall, but she never came that way, too shrewd, I guessed, to be conventional about it. Instead I'd feel her close, warm as the sunlight that nurtured me now, and I would talk about what it was like and the things I was learning. Freda always loved to hear what people had learned.

One night Verna brought out the old picture box and sat beside me while I looked through it, watching me closely until it made me nervous.

"What's up?" I said.

"I was just thinking."

"About what?"

"Something Freda said."

"And . . . ?"

"About your mother."

I reached into the box and shuffled the photos around until I found the picture of my mother with her head resting on the lap of the old black woman, that vulnerable smile on her face it always hurt to see, and I thought about her now, for the first time since I'd taken that last drink.

"You're shaking, Eva," Verna said.

"Unusual, isn't it?" I said, shooting her a look.

"Freda said go see her. It's time."

"I can't," I said. "I still can't. What good would it do?"

"You won't know until after you go."

T W E N T Y - N I N E

The Mississippi River passes the western edge of Hickory with a pace as slow and somber as a drumbeat, the bridge that spans it from shore to shore painted shiny silver, an arc of light connecting Arkansas and Tennessee. The town looks old, its buildings dark brick, its streets run-down and rutted. From the joints on Main Street you can hear the throaty rattle of gospel blues, and if the streets of heaven are paved with gold, the way they sing about it, then heaven looks like Main Street, barbecue sauce splattered here and there on the inlay.

My grandmother used to live in Hickory, a full-blooded Choctaw woman I called Big Mama. Freda would take me there some summers to visit, across that high bridge and out into the countryside where she lived in a tiny frame house on one hundred acres of land. She died out there under a plum tree, alone, when she was sixty-six years old. A black widow had bitten her, setting off the stroke that killed her. I was nine years old at the time and went to the funeral with Freda, seeing Big Mama's strange family together for the first and last time. There was the cousin named Emma, a beauty with dark skin and eyes like Freda's, so stunning I kept my eyes on her throughout the service. She talked to Jesus, Freda told me. There was Aunt Beanie, who bled from her eyes, a form of rapture, Freda said. BQ shaking on the edge of a pew, his eyes wild as an old dog's. Leta with her quiet Christianity, hands folded in her lap over a lace handkerchief. Great Aunt Bootsie, the aging Hollywood starlet who had dated Joe E. Lewis, bleached her hair platinum, and come home to Tennessee to marry and give birth to eight boys, all of whom died before the age of five.

There was Freda, dressed in white that day while all around her wore black, holding my hand, whispering in my ear, "You feel the electricity in this room, Eva? Circuits buzzing like a high wire? This is your family, child."

And my mother, the baby of them all, the youngest, born a mistake, always a mistake, sitting on Freda's other side, her hands trembling and her face flushed with tears. I ignored her that day, turning my back when she came to hug me, the one time I remember her trying. And when she said, "Eva, I'm sorry Big Mama is dead," I was cruel in my silence.

Freda always said Rita would go back to Big Mama and die right there in Hickory.

Two years ago I went to see my mother in that place outside Hickory where they kept her. It's a county home, old men with no legs lined up along the walls, faces in their food. I didn't think it could be that bad, but it is. Freda had told me about the old days and the institutions they'd had then. No better than cesspools, she'd said. Just the way it is now; people babbling, wetting their pants, nurses walking by as if they have a date to keep. Oblivious. I wish John Earl hadn't put her there. I couldn't get her out. I tried. But he was her official guardian. The courts said so, until the day he dies. He hasn't yet. But it will come.

It had been close to fifteen years since I had seen her. My memory was of that day in Seattle when I had sent her on her way with a curse, her face swollen from drinking and crying, the guilt on her as insistent as the rain that fell that day and into the night.

When she'd come out of the coma her emotional register had peaked at ten years, close to the age she had been when that picture was taken of her in the swing, her head on her mammy's lap.

I walked into the dayroom where she passed time in front of a television set, a glass of iced tea on a card table in front of her. I knew it was Rita by the stooped posture, the round curve of her shoulders that had taken hold years ago when her defeat had gone past reckoning. I stood and watched her for a moment, my hands trembling. It was an unfamiliar feeling now. My mouth was dry, my heart beating thin and quick as if it wasn't really there at all, just on the surface, exposed, and I almost turned to leave, but for a gesture she made. She held the glass of tea in her right hand, started to put it to her lips, but caught herself and raised it instead in a toast, a little dip of the glass that suggested she saw someone sitting there with her. A friend, I hoped.

She had gained weight. I noticed it when she turned to look at me as I walked to her chair. I reached my hand out and touched the armrest lightly, afraid to put my hand on hers, not knowing if she'd want me to, not knowing if I could.

Her eyes weren't the same. One looked smaller than the other, the pupil wide and vacant. Under her right eye ran a scar that reached to her throat, thick and purple, and I thought of the scar beneath my eye, faded now, almost nothing. Her hair was gray, thin, and her mouth lined by deep wrinkles. Her beauty had been ravaged years before.

"Eva," she said. "Eva," her voice disbelieving. She stood up awkwardly, upsetting the chair, her hands all over me now, touching my face, holding my hair out at the tips, looking pleased by the length and texture of it.

"Such pretty hair," she said, and raised a hand to her own, looking embarrassed.

"Mine's gray now," she said, her voice that of a self-conscious little girl, the southern accent thick.

She placed her hands on my shoulders and turned me around as she would a dress doll.

"So pretty," she said. "Look at you. Look at *you*." She turned me back to face her, rubbing her hand up on my cheek the way she would pet a kitten.

"Honey," she said. "Don't cry. Why you cryin'? Have some ice tea. Sit down now. Have some tea."

I dragged a chair up to the card table, tears blinding me, and stumbled against it, upsetting the iced tea. I thought how wretched it looked, that cheap gray table with the cheap glass set on it—the kind that's bubbled out all over the surface, gold-colored, a set for two bucks. I wanted something pretty for her, anything, not the faded housedress she wore, the elastic gone from the waist. She had no jewelry. I clasped the heavy silver bracelets on my right arm, pulled them off as I sank into a chair, sobbing, and cast them on the table.

"Eva," my mother said. "That's all right. It's no reason to cry."

She called out to a nurse. "Betty," she said, "you bring my girl and me some more ice tea. She's come to visit. You bring us some tea now. Please," she added, remembering her manners. "Pretty bracelets," she said, looking as if she wanted to touch them.

I pushed them at her.

"Where you been, Eva?" she asked, sitting down, taking the bracelets into her hands, twirling them.

Where had I been? Oh Mama, I been here and there. Where you been? How's life been to you, Mama? Tell Eva. Eva might understand how it goes.

I dabbed at my face violently with a Kleenex from my purse, unable to shut the tears off. The more I tried, the faster I blotted the tears away, the harder they came, soaking the tissue until it shredded in my hands. My nose was running and I wiped my arm across my face, feeling helpless.

I looked at her, an old woman, her eyes innocent of all those years, as if they had been smashed to bits the day that jeep hit her—off into the air they'd gone, fine as dust, settling so far and wide she'd never find them. There was no hate in me now. I searched for it the way you do in the dark for something familiar, the cold part of my heart I had found so useful. Instead, in that darkness lay compassion, forgiveness, things old and unused, but I grabbed hold. How could I hate her, this woman nearer in age to me now than she had ever been; a woman who had hurt as I had, been raped, beaten, and left for dead, who had punished herself for sins she did not commit, carrying all her life a legacy of guilt, and who had not known, as I had not, the dimensions of her own strength until it was nearly too late?

"Jesus!" I shouted, standing up, the first words I had spoken. I clenched my hands at my sides. "Jesus H. Christ!"

I looked around wildly, saw the wheelchairs filled with staring, white-haired women, some of them smiling shyly, delighted by my outburst.

"I had an accident, Eva," I heard my mother say. "A bad accident. Come talk to me."

Had I ever, in nearly forty years, heard her say those words? Come talk to me.

"I love you," I shouted at the poor woman. "I love you, Rita. I do."

I kept saying it over and over, moving toward her, holding on to her now, down on my knees beside her chair, my head resting on her shoulder. She patted my head, smoothing down my hair.

"I'm sorry," I said. "I'm sorry I took so long to see you."

"I don't drink anymore, Eva," she said. "Since the accident. Years. Do you believe that?"

"I do," I said. "I know. I know you don't. I'm so proud of you. And I love you. I want you to know that. I don't know if I ever told you."

"Of course you did, Eva. I'm your mama. Every girl loves her mama."

It's true, no matter what you do, no matter how it goes, it's true.

"You love me?" I said.

"I do," she said. "I always have. What a silly question."

I spent the afternoon there, drinking iced tea with my mother, so much of it I started feeling clean inside. She was simple now and couldn't follow all I said too well, her mind shattered and reconstructed in another time and place, but she had become something I had never seen her be. Peaceful. She sat at the card table playing with the bracelets I had given her, delighted by their weight and shine and how they looked when she put all ten of them together on her arm. I imagined she would like watching the stars with me now, gazing at that play of light soft as the luster of the bracelets. I told her Freda had died and saw something in her eyes then, the way memories look when they take hold of someone.

"Freda," she said. "Freda's gone? I loved Freda. I'm gonna cry tonight about her. I sure am."

She smiled.

I liked the way she'd said that, as if grief had a place and she would tend to it later.

"What are you thinking?" I asked her.

"How Freda used to boss me around."

I laughed, remembering, too.

Something happens when people are made simple. They become what they truly are, fear and jealousy no longer part of a life that had been destined for pain, disappointment, heartache. It was that way with my mother. I saw now, as I had seen that night she sat on the floor in Yazoo City and cried about the kitten, her true heart, the one that had beat in her when she was a child, a sweet girl who ought never to have been hurt. And I forgave her for being nothing more than human, a woman frightened into emptiness and left in its vacuum with no one on the other side waiting to pull her free. I cannot speak the words telling of that freedom, how loving her finally brought me home, back to the South where I hear the river most every day now, and think not only of Freda but of Rita, who walked its banks when she was a girl, knowing, maybe, as I had, the life that was to come.

My mother died last spring, in her sleep, too young for death, but ready. I could tell the day I saw her she no longer courted it, having known its dimensions while on this earth, but that when it came it would be easy for her, like slipping into a robe of fine, white silk, the smooth feel of the garment like a second soul. I know she is with Freda. I see them in my dreams, one tall and golden as the sun, the other dark and mysterious as the far side of the moon, two shafts of light from the same fractured spectrum, moving as shadow and dawn across a deep-green cotton field.

I wrote to my father at the last address I'd had for him, telling of my mother's death. I had to pretend when I wrote it that I had some notion of who he had been in my life, when the truth was I could barely remember his face. The letter was returned, unopened, and I will never be sure if it was he who cast it back to me or a postman just doing his job. It doesn't seem that important now. Fathers are a different breed, never feeling life quicken in their bellies, never lifting their heads in the still of some cold night to hear the lament of their creation. They go about their business, like Freda said, and if you catch up with them, fine. And if you don't, it is something you can live with.

T H I R T Y

I have placed my bed beneath a wide window in my house. It looks out over the land onto a grove of hickory, sycamore, and maple that fronts the yard where albino catfish swim, iridescent beneath the dark pond water, growing fatter as the seasons pass. I poke them with a long switch taken from the hickory tree and watch their fins flutter and their big flat heads nose down toward the muddy bottom.

It has been four years since my last drink.

At night there are stars out here so thick I can't tell them from the fireflies sometimes. I kneel at the head of my bed each night, press my face against the glass, and study the rising arc of Perseus, the squared-off field of Ursa Major, and the bright globe of Venus low on the horizon. It is communion, that secret dialect taken with me from childhood, and I speak it to the sky now.

I went back to Yazoo City last summer and stood on the edge of the ravine. It is grown over now, thick with grass six feet high, wild brambles, and tea roses. I could smell the water beneath the thickness of the leaves as I sat on the bank until nightfall, listening to the frogs and cicadas, their choruses distinct, resonant in the hot, damp air. As I sat there I thought of how long it takes to come back to what you first knew, an elemental truth that survives even as you move outside its sphere, and how when you return you finally understand why it was necessary to leave. Because if you never understand that pain exists to make you stronger, then what is there to know?

I feed the animals out here. Stray cats come each day. I take the lids from their food tins and string them high up in the trees with fishing line, and in the light of a full moon they have the dull luster of platinum. Crows come, cardinals, bluejays, finches, hawks, and bobwhites, attracted by the shine. I gather their feathers when they are shed, placing them on a low shelf I have built in the kitchen.

Freda's '56 Chevy sits in the gravel driveway. I take it into town sometimes to pick up Ronnie, who still has no car of his own. He works out at the paper mill, feeding boards into a pulper. He hasn't changed. At forty he is still a boy, and when he makes love to me, I know exactly what I am doing when I close my eyes and remember how it felt in the snow that New Year's Eve. I ask myself how many people get to relive it again and again, holding on to something so sweet it breaks your heart to think of letting go.

"I love you, Eva," he says the minute I roll down the car window, watching him there in the lumberyard, covered in sawdust, smelling like new furniture. He says it again and again, sometimes all the way out to the land, not stopping even when I get him into bed, pulling the clothes off his brown body, pressing my mouth to his so he'll be quiet and stop reminding me I cannot say the same words as often, afraid of what they would really mean to him, that I belong to him when I do not, cannot, and won't. He says to marry him. It will never happen, not this day, I tell him, so he asks when I see him next, and I say no again, and he smiles as if it has become a game.

But I do love him. My God how I love him.

Two miles from the land the Arkansas River spreads out wide as a plain, cotton fields growing nearly to its edge. I walk the distance with an empty bucket, filling it with red clay when I reach the banks, digging my bare hands deep so I can feel the weight of it when I lift them up. It is the finest clay on earth, so rich with iron I suck what's left from my fingers on the way home. I shape faces from it on an old table in the kitchen, covered in oilcloth. Verna gave me the cloth, saying I had ruined it and might as well have it.

Today I have finished Freda's head and face, and it is drying by the window on the kitchen shelf, the dark red changing to a warm pink. It is not a bad piece of work, I tell myself. I walk around the kitchen, looking at it from different angles, and see she is beautiful no matter how I turn. I sit at the table with it behind me and study it in the reflection of the round mirror with the porcelain base, then I look back over my shoulder and give it a haughty look, smiling as if I know I am beautiful. I see her smiling back. I have done her mouth just right.

Tomorrow I will start on my mother, and when that is done, the face of my daughter, who has come to visit, and in time, my own. I may marry Ronnie if he is not too tired of asking. He says that day won't come, and I tell him I might die first, there is so much work to be done.

On Sundays I walk to the river and sit beneath the cottonwoods, waiting. Sometimes I bring a sack of meatball sandwiches on Sunbeam bread. Ritual.

In time, I hear their voices strong like a shock wave, smooth and deep as drumbeats carried down the river to where I wait, the hair on my arms standing straight up, my neck feeling prickly and cold with excitement. Through the trees the white robes billow out ahead of them in the wind, and I can see their black hands clapping high above their heads, keeping the beat, their bodies writhing, dipping down, moving toward the water.

I stand up now and join the file, a crazy white woman, my shoulders covered in an old bedsheet, a cape I have made. I clap my hands and they do not even look around, used to me by now. I hear the preacher shout. "Bless you children. Bless you all."

And I walk into the river, singing.

ABOUT THE AUTHOR

Lorian Hemingway was raised in a number of places throughout the Deep South: Arkansas, Tennessee, North Carolina, and Mississippi. On her mother's side, she is part Cherokee. Her paternal grandfather is Ernest Hemingway. She is a free-lance journalist and has published her pieces widely, most notably in *Rolling Stone* and *The New York Times.* She lives in Seattle, Washington.